MY
HUSBAND'S
HOUSE

BOOKS BY SHERYL BROWNE

MY HUSBAND'S HOUSE

SHERYL BROWNE

Bookouture

Published by Bookouture in 2023

An imprint of Storyfire Ltd.
Carmelite House
50 Victoria Embankment
London EC4Y 0DZ

www.bookouture.com

ISBN: 978-1-83790-443-3
eBook ISBN: 978-1-83790-442-6

To book bloggers and readers for their fabulous support and faith in me.
Thank you.

One lie is enough to question all truths.

Unknown

PROLOGUE

Tugging the flimsy jacket I'd grabbed as I raced from the house more tightly around me, I try to ignore the hushed whispers of the clique of mothers from the school my children attend. I'd once been invited into their circle. Now, standing outside it, I feel it acutely, the loneliness of being alone. A woman I'd thought was my friend is with them. In my peripheral vision I catch her glancing furtively towards me. I keep my gaze fixed forward, concentrating on the activity beyond the police cordon, and try to block out the speculation of those drawn by flashing blue lights and morbid curiosity.

'Any idea what they're looking for?' another woman who lives just a few doors away from me asks fearfully.

'Body, I reckon,' a neighbour from the opposite side of the road surmises with a short 'tsk'. 'Has to be, doesn't it?' He nods towards the police divers negotiating the curved wall of the dam to access the water where the reservoir is at its deepest. Other officers, dressed from top to toe in white suits, examine the brickwork, where blood spatters have been found. Under the harsh spotlights, the scene looks surreal, like something from a futuristic film set.

Truth, though, I've come to realise, is far stranger than fiction. It hasn't been announced officially, but I've heard the rumour rippling through the crowd. They're searching for more than one body. My stomach twists painfully as I watch and wait for my nightmare to unfold.

Two officers have been tasked with keeping the public and hungry journalists straining at the cordon at bay, I notice. I'm grateful for that much. Once this hit the headlines, the whole world will know my husband is a suspect, that he's missing, probably running, and then there will be no escape from the hostility. I feel as if I have a physical thing pressing down on me. The smell, putrid, dank and earthy, fills my nostrils and I gulp back the nausea rising like bile in my throat. Rain, heavy and unrelenting, pitter-patters on the surface of the water in time with the rapid thud, thud, thud of my heart. *It wasn't my husband.* I breathe in sharply. He snapped once, with provocation, but he's not capable of these atrocities. He's not! The flash from a journalist's camera blinds me, and I want to run, go back to my house, bolt the doors and shut the world out, but I stay where I am, dry-eyed with shock, my emotions frozen solid inside me.

Is my son capable of violence? Out of some desperate attempt to keep his world safe, might he have been the one who'd attacked a frail, defenceless woman? Fear crackles like ice through my veins as I try to stop my mind replaying the scenario that petrifies me. My daughter weeps on the landing, her hands balled into tight fists at her side, her eyes wide and horrified. 'He's drowning her. He's drowning her!' She gulps back huge, hiccupping sobs.

My gaze shoots to the bathroom. My son doesn't move as I push the door open, doesn't acknowledge me. It's as if he doesn't even know I'm there. Kneeling at the side of the filled bath, my nine-year-old boy is intent on his task. My daughter's Baby Born doll lies in the water, her long, soft hair fanned out around her face. She looks so lifelike my heart jars. My boy is holding her down. His hand around her neck, he's holding her at the bottom of the bath.

I seize his shoulders, haul him up and whirl him around to face me, roughly. Too roughly. 'What in God's name are you doing?'

He looks at me, his eyes unfocused for a second. Then, 'M-making her go away,' he stammers, confusion in his eyes as he searches mine.

It wasn't him. As I turn away from the water, I feel the foundations of my world rocking dangerously and I fight to hold on to the last vestiges of my sanity.

EVENING NEWS

20 YEARS AGO

Father of Missing Girl Commits Suicide

Following a second police search at 13 Trowan Crescent, home of missing nine-year-old girl Holly Grant, police made a grisly discovery: the body of her father, Michael Grant, who was found hanged from a tree at the rear of the property. An ambulance arrived and paramedics tried to revive him but were unsuccessful. An autopsy determined that the cause of death was suspension by ligature.

A manhunt for Holly Grant has been underway since the little girl disappeared while playing close to her home on the afternoon of Friday, 13 June. A spokesman for the Metropolitan Police said they are becoming increasingly concerned for her welfare. Local residents joined the initial search and continue to keep the case high profile, posting photographs of Holly throughout the area. Neighbours report that her father seemed racked with guilt and unable to 'forgive himself'. As far as EN have been able to establish, he is not suspected of any involvement in the little girl's disappearance and the assumption is that, unable to live with his unbearable grief, he took his own life.

ONE

Naomi

Goosebumps prickled my skin as my gaze fell on the old rocking chair sitting on its own in one of the bedrooms. 'Problem?' Ben asked, as I surveyed it with apprehension.

'According to my grandad, Irish legend has it that an empty rocking chair is an invitation for evil spirits to take a seat,' I whispered.

'Really?' Ben's gaze travelled from me to the chair and back.

I nodded sombrely. 'Apparently, if it moves on its own, it means a spirit has already taken up residence.'

Ben was quiet for a moment. Then, 'Do you think we should charge it rent?' he asked.

Seeing the amusement dancing in his eyes, I gave him a nudge. 'Haha. Stop taking the pee, Ben Felton.'

He laughed and wrapped an arm around me. 'I wasn't taking the pee. I take your grandad's superstitions very seriously. I'm not sure spitting on a horseshoe and throwing it over your head is going to be very lucky for the poor sod standing behind you, but...'

'We are not amused,' I told him, my hand going to my growing tummy. My grandad was so superstitious that my mum – God rest her – often said it was a wonder he ever left the house. We actually didn't take him too seriously. But still, some of it rubbed off on me. It hadn't escaped my notice that the house number was 13, which was certainly considered unlucky by some. Didn't a lot of house builders avoid it for that very reason?

Ben gave me a squeeze. 'I'll get rid of it, donate it to a charity shop or something. We'll brighten the whole place up. Assuming you like it?' The last was said with a hopeful look in his eyes. I knew he wanted me to. With his position as clinical photographer at our local hospital being lost to budget cuts, we had no choice but to move. The location of this house was perfect, not too far from the City Hospital where Ben had been relocated. It was going for a snip, according to the estate agent friend he'd done some photography on the side for. As I'd had to give up my teaching assistant's job before my planned maternity leave, we couldn't hope to afford anything like this otherwise. We had to make up our minds whether to go for it before it went on the market, but I just wasn't sure. It was so dark and gloomy. The plum-coloured walls in the hall and sponge-painted peacock green in the lounge didn't help.

I reminded myself of the plusses as I went back to the landing. The neighbourhood was good, not far from Edgbaston Reservoir, which was surrounded by trees and woodland and had an excellent jogging route, according to the neighbour who'd popped out when we'd arrived. She'd introduced herself as Sara. I was a bit taken aback at first. With gorgeous auburn highlighted hair, impeccably made up and trendily dressed, she looked like a fashion model. She seemed really nice, though, offering to take the children to play with her children while we viewed the property. I wouldn't be doing much jogging until the little one was born but knowing that there was somewhere I could run close by would certainly give me an incentive. My concern was, how was it that the property had lain empty for almost twenty years?

'Do you mind if I have another mooch around?' Glancing back at Ben as I headed for the main bedroom, I noted a pensive furrow in his brow. He was obviously worried I wouldn't want to go for it, which meant we would have to rent again. We were both desperate for a place of our own.

He arranged his face into a smile. 'I'll leave you to it and go and check on the kids,' he said and headed for the stairs.

Resting my hand on my bump, I went to the main bedroom window and watched him emerge from the front door and walk down the path, where he paused to fetch some litter from the overgrown lawn. He looked as if he already belonged here and I felt that was a good vibe, cancelling out any bad karma I might be feeling. Turning around, I surveyed the room. The wallpaper in here was a damask print, liveable, but still, to me it spoke of a millennium past. It was almost as if the house was stuck in a time warp, which spooked me a little. All of the bedrooms were huge – I went back to the positives. And we could possibly get the loft converted at some point, which would be helpful with another little one on the way.

Going back to the landing, I went back to the smaller of the two other bedrooms. Having discovered 'Bump' was a boy, Liam would have to share for a while, so this room would be Maya's. She would have bags more space than she had now. Walking around the debris, empty boxes mostly, I negotiated my way past the rocking chair, careful not to set it in motion, and headed for the window. This room looked out over the long back garden, at the bottom of which, under what looked like a gnarled old apple tree, was a small shed. It had shutters on the windows, I noticed. It was a bit dilapidated, one of the shutters hanging forlornly from its hinges, but it might be repairable. We might even be able to turn it into a Wendy house, which would delight Maya. Realising I was picturing my children here, I began to feel a little more confident about the move.

It was as I went back across the room that I noticed a child's drawing pinned to the facing wall. Taken aback, I went closer. It was the kind of drawing Maya might make of her family – two children, two adults. What was odd about it was that instead of a bright yellow sun, there were grey clouds and diagonal black slashes raining down. The taller of the children appeared to be scowling, I noted. With a sudden shiver, as if the ghost of the child who'd drawn it had walked right through me, I hurried to the door and caught my foot on one of the boxes. Bending to move it, I blinked in surprise. Sitting in the corner, looking for all the world as if he'd been abandoned there, was a raggedy old teddy bear. *Poor thing.* Guessing he must have belonged to one of the children who'd clearly once lived here, I reached to pick him up. 'Did they miss you when they moved?' I asked him, feeling a deep sense of sadness as I looked into his blue button eyes. 'We'll adopt you, Little Buttons,' I whispered, dusting him off and carrying him out with me.

After a last look around upstairs, I went back down to the lounge where I tried again to focus on the positives. This was a house we could afford, with a garden for the children. Wasn't that what Ben and I wanted? And it really was spacious. The lounge was twice the size of our current tiny lounge, with a chimney breast and alcoves creating a sense of depth and character you just didn't get in a bog-standard four-walled modern house. There was a curved bay window, too, which softened the room and would make a perfect reading nook. It would need redecorating. Soon, I thought, eyeing the sponge-painted, awful muddy green woodchip wallpaper. I was picturing the room in soft pastels when I heard Ben come through the front door.

'All good,' he reported. 'Sara's feeding them Diet Coke and ice cream.'

'They'll be up for the move then?' I gave him a knowing smile.

'Definitely.' Ben walked up behind me and encircled me with his arms. 'And what about you?' he asked, pressing a soft kiss to the side of my neck.

I twisted to face him, noted that intent look he sometimes had in his eyes and knew he was willing me to say yes. He'd been insistent we see the house. It had spoken to him, he'd said, when he'd driven to view the outside on his own. That had surprised me. Ben was never led by his emotions.

'What's that?' he asked, dropping his gaze to Little Buttons – now duly christened – who I was hugging to my chest.

'I found him upstairs. I think he was left behind.' I glanced at the teddy and then back to him. 'He needs someone to adopt him.'

Ben frowned. 'It's a bit moth-eaten, isn't it?' he observed, clearly not as taken as me.

'Nothing a little love and attention won't fix,' I pointed out, feeling quite protective of him.

'And a needle and thread.' Ben's mouth twitched into a smile. 'His ear's dropping off.'

'He can still hear you.' I covered up his other ear.

Ben raised an amused eyebrow. 'I take it he's now part of the family then?'

'Absolutely.' I nodded firmly.

'And will we be moving into his house or...?'

I hesitated. 'I'll just have another peek at the kitchen,' I said, easing away. I was beginning to warm to the idea, but I still couldn't shake off the feeling of gloom. I'd really wanted something more modern, but I supposed it did have huge potential. The cooker was ancient and would need to be replaced, but the cupboard doors, honey oak in colour, were also liveable. We could replace them with white eventually and get some large patio doors installed on the outside wall, which would let lots of light in.

Feeling happier, I headed back to the hall, where I noted the original wooden flooring had been rescued. The previous owners had obviously been into their DIY. With the walls repainted in white, which would considerably brighten it, and keeping the stained glass in the front door and the windows either side of it, we could mix modern and period decoration here. The house lent itself to that.

As I passed the stairs, I noticed the hall cupboard door was ajar. Ben had peered in there, but as it had no light, I'd passed. I could cope with spiders, just about – fetching a glass and card and putting them gingerly out – but cobwebs in a confined dark space was a definite no. Hopefully, the cupboard could eventually come out and we could fill the space with bookshelves. Pushing the door to, I'd taken a step past it when I heard a distinct creak behind me and froze. Fear lodged like a stone in my throat, I turned slowly around and my heart stalled. The door was open. A scream rising inside me, I backed away from it, and the door moved again. I took another stumbling step and faltered as it inched closed. I stepped forward and back – and the door moved with me. *Idiot.* I inhaled a deep breath, attempting to slow my heart before it beat right out of my chest. It was the *floorboards.* The floor was bowing, quite obviously. I did another little seesaw just to check and then hurried to the stairs, where I gathered Ben was from the boards creaking overhead.

Deciding not to mention the ghost that wasn't, I went to the main bedroom, where I found him sitting on the floor. 'This is where the bed goes.' He patted the floor next to him, indicating that I should join him. The house obviously was speaking to him if he'd been sitting up here mentally arranging the furniture. 'So?' He looked hopefully up at me.

'Um?' I glanced at him and then the space next to him.

'Whoops.' Ben obviously saw my dilemma – that joining him might be a little problematic, not to say ungainly. 'Sorry. I wasn't thinking.' Scrambling to his feet, he took my hand. 'Well?'

'Okay.' I smiled, putting him out of his misery. 'I'm not sure it's what I had in mind, but I suppose it does have lots of scope for improvement.'

Clearly relieved, Ben closed his eyes and rested his forehead against mine. 'I love you, Mrs Felton. Always and forever. Did I ever mention that?' he murmured.

'Once or twice.' I pressed a kiss to his lips. He did tell me – often – and I loved him for that. My thoughts went to my mum and I pictured her face, her smile and the pain in her eyes as she'd told me how much she loved me for the last time. 'I always will,' she'd said, her fingers frail as she'd brushed the tears from my cheeks. 'Wherever you are, I will always be with you, right here.' She'd rested a hand over my heart, which I'd been sure would explode with grief. I'd wanted to ask her how I could ever survive without her. I didn't. It wasn't her fault she had to go. It was the cancer that had stolen her away from me, but I missed her *so* much as I'd grown into womanhood without her.

I recalled how Ben had once said I reminded him of his mother – because she was gentle and kind, he'd added quickly, noting my bemusement. I glanced at him now, wondering how much he missed her, wishing he would tell me more about her, about his childhood after he'd lost her. It was clear he struggled to talk about it though, saying no more than it hadn't been great, so I didn't push him, hoping that, in time, he might be able to.

Ben searched my face worriedly as I studied him. 'I know it's a bit gloomy now,' he said, clearly misinterpreting my concerned expression, 'but we'll soon make it bright and cheery.'

Hmm? Since my husband's decorating skills were questionable, I suspected that job might fall to me. But then, I would have time on my hands with three months before bump made an appearance. *Elias.* My thoughts going back to my grandad, who'd lost my nana years before and who'd nursed a broken heart after my mother died, I decided that that would be a fitting name and hoped Ben would agree. I was growing quite excited about the idea of moving here now. It would be a fresh start. With the uncertainty about his job, Ben had been a bit introspective and down lately, no doubt concerned about having another little mouth to feed. I would have to start job-hunting as soon as I could, but meanwhile I would make the house my project, I decided. We could make this work, even on a tight budget.

As I walked back to the stairs, I glanced again at the lonely rocking chair sitting in the third bedroom. When I'd first set eyes on it, I'd felt wary. But with the house being old and uninhabited for so long, wasn't I bound to be? I felt less so now. In reminding me of my grandad's superstitions, the chair had helped me finally decide on a name for our baby. That had to be a good sign. Didn't it?

TWO

Joan

Watching from her armchair in the window, Joan was surprised to see a car drawing up outside the house next door to Sara's. It had lain empty for years. Ever since poor Lily had disappeared. Now, it appeared someone was finally viewing it, which seemed odd. There'd been no 'For Sale' board up. On seeing Sara emerge from her house, Joan removed her reading glasses and glanced around for her other pair so she could have a better look. She despaired of herself when she realised she'd left them in the kitchen. By the time she got creakily to her feet to retrieve them, the couple who'd just arrived were going through the front door into the house. Such a pity. Joan always put a lot of stock on first impressions. Body language, she'd found, often told her a lot more than words. Noticing Sara was walking back to her own house with two little ones that weren't her own, she presumed they belonged to the prospective buyers. She'd obviously offered to keep an eye on them while they looked around. That was kind of her.

Settling back, she waited for the couple to reappear. If there was one advantage to growing old and arthritic, it was being able to sit quietly in her window and people watch. Joan liked to think she was keeping an eye on things rather than being nosy. She liked to watch her neighbours come and go. She probably knew more about their lives than they did. She knew who shopped where. The carrier bags were a giveaway. Who was friends with who. Who might be having affairs. The Browns three doors up from Sara were going through a testing time, unsurprisingly, since the husband had been involved in extra-marital activities with the divorcée two doors further down. He worked from home – and played away, it seemed. Joan would never spread rumours. Men who cheated were always found out eventually anyway. Women simply knew. Hannah Brown had known. Her eyes had shot daggers made of pure venom at the woman he was involved with, Joan had noticed when she'd accepted an invitation to a neighbourhood barbecue. With alcohol flowing, it had all blown up when the Browns had returned home – or rather, when Hannah had returned home. Matthew Brown had found he couldn't gain access. His language had been interesting when he'd found all his worldly goods raining down on him from the bedroom window, including his personal computer, which must have been painful.

Joan did wonder why mothers didn't warn their sons that, when it came to husbands cheating, women's intuition told them way before the proof of their eyes did. But then, her own son hadn't taken too kindly to her informing him that his wife knew of his affair long before she'd confronted him. He'd told Joan to mind her own effing business. He wasn't a good son. She'd thought she'd been a good mother, but that was the way of things. You tried to instil values in your children, but, in the end, they made their own choices, good or bad. She didn't see much of her son now.

The barbecue had been Sara's divorce celebration. Joan liked Sara. Being a single mum now, and with a propensity to dress a little flirtily, the woman tended to invite gossip, which was terribly unfair. Despite appearances, Joan knew she was actually lacking in confidence after her awful marriage, and she had a heart of pure gold. Even when she'd been married to a man who had dictated her every move, she'd made time for Joan, popping across to check on her, washing and styling her hair for her and bringing her the odd meal whenever she could. In return for her kindness, Joan had offered her shelter when the arguments had turned physical. She'd thought they should put the street bunting up when Sara had found the courage to call the police and get her locks changed. The man really had been a monster. She did hope the new man in Sara's life was all that she thought he was. Joan couldn't see behind closed doors, but she prided herself on reading people well. Sometimes, she wished dearly that she couldn't.

She hadn't realised she'd dozed off until voices from across the road jarred her awake. Leaning to nudge her window further open, she eavesdropped. It was difficult not to with someone new possibly about to move into the area. 'They've been fine,' she heard Sara assuring the couple at her door, who were clearly collecting their little ones. 'You've been watching Minions, haven't you, Maya?'

'Uh-huh. *The Rise of Gru,*' the little girl answered excitedly. 'Auntie Sara says we can watch the other Minions films if we come again. Can we, Mummy? *Pleeease.*'

Joan smiled, her gaze travelling down to the child, who was looking pleadingly up at her mummy as she tugged on her sleeve – and her heart faltered. Assailed by an overwhelming sense of déjà vu, she blinked hard and adjusted her glasses. It wasn't her. It couldn't possibly be, Joan knew it couldn't, but this little girl was so like Lily's lost daughter it was heart-breaking.

THREE

Naomi

'We'll see,' I answered my daughter, who was jiggling excitedly at the prospect of visiting Sara again. I was hugely relieved that she and Liam seemed to have got along with Sara's children. Maya was a chatty soul, but Liam was quiet and awkward in company and didn't make friends easily. I'd spoken to Ben about whether we should ask the school about social skills intervention, but Ben thought he was fine, that he was simply more like him than he was me, a bit introverted at times. I wasn't so sure. I'd spoken to his teacher, who'd said she had noticed occasional 'atypical' behaviour. She wasn't sufficiently worried, though, that she would seek a full behavioural evaluation. Sadly, some of the other mothers at their school hadn't made life easy for me. It had been obvious that, because Liam tended to speak his mind and therefore didn't fit in, they would rather not include me in their clique. I shouldn't have cared, but I did sometimes, when I waited on my own outside the school gates.

They would have to attend a different school here. It would be an upheaval but it would mean that Liam would have a fresh start. Deciding that that would be a definite plus, I urged the children to get a move on and leave Sara in peace – much to Maya's disgruntlement. She clearly wanted to stay with her new best friend, Ellie. 'Come on. You'll be able to see lots more of Ellie soon,' I assured her, steering Liam towards Ben, who was standing behind me.

Sara smiled in Ben's direction, then looked hopefully back at me. 'Does that mean you're...?' She gestured to the house next door.

'It does.' I nodded, glad that I also seemed to have made a friend. With her children attending the local school, I would have an ally. I shouldn't have felt so wary at the prospect of being accepted by the other mums, but there it was. I did.

'Ooh, that's *brilliant*.' Obviously delighted, Sara leaned in to give me a hug. 'We need to swap numbers,' she said, stepping back to grab her phone from her hall table.

Smiling, I reeled off my number and heard my phone ping as Sara texted me hers.

'All done,' she said, beaming me a smile back. She really was extremely pretty and had an amazing figure. I couldn't help noticing the red rose tattoo that peeked above her top. I'd fancied the idea of having a tattoo when I was younger, but I wasn't sure I would have dared have one on my breast. 'I can't tell you how pleased I am,' Sara gushed. 'I was dreading someone who didn't have kids moving in.'

'You might change your mind when this little one comes along.' I pointed to my bump and tried not to feel like a pregnant heifer standing next to her. If our new arrival was anything like Liam was as a baby, he would bawl the house down and, as the houses were semi-detached, Sara's along with it.

'He could never make as much noise as my two.' Sara waved a hand, unperturbed. 'Not that they're badly behaved,' she added quickly. 'They're a handful sometimes, but they're not rowdy or anything.'

I noted the worried furrow in her brow and couldn't help but warm to her. 'I know how much of a handful kids can be, trust me,' I assured her. 'Tell you what, we'll make a pact. You don't feel you need to apologise for your children and I'll do the same. How does that sound?'

Sara looked immensely relieved. 'Like you're going to be the perfect neighbour.'

'You too,' I said, meaning it. She was nice. I got a good vibe from her. 'I'd better go.' I indicated towards Ben, who was walking Liam back to the car, his arm slung over his shoulders. 'There's a great running route, I hear,' he was telling him, clearly trying to sell Liam on the idea of moving here. Like his dad, Liam wasn't into team sports. He had shown an interest in running though, going out with Ben once or twice. Even gracing me with his company one time.

'Make sure to shout if you need help with anything when you move in,' Sara offered. 'Paul and I will be glad to give you a hand if we're around. Sorry you've missed him, by the way. He's just shot off to the DIY shop for some bits for the boiler.'

'Sounds like a handy man to have around.'

'Oh, he is. We're still at the honeymoon stage.' She arched her eyebrows suggestively.

I couldn't help but laugh.

'See you soon,' she said. 'Oh, and if I'm not at work when you move and you want to bring the kids round, no problem.'

'Can we, Mummy?' Maya asked, wearing her best beguiling eyes.

'Maybe,' I answered, not wanting to commit Sara to anything.

'Only as long as your mum reports that you've been on your absolute best behaviour,' Sara picked up, giving her an arch look.

'I will, I promise.' Maya jumped eagerly. Her eyes grew wide as she noticed the teddy I was still holding. 'Who's that?' she whispered in awe.

'His name's Little Buttons,' I whispered back. 'He's feeling lonely and needs lots of loving care and attention.'

A concerned frown crossed my five-year-old girl's face. 'I could give him lots of loving care and attention,' she said earnestly.

I pressed him to my ear, making a show of listening intently. 'He says he would like that.' I smiled and handed him carefully to her. 'You'd better catch up with Daddy and get Little Buttons all snug and warm in the car.'

Maya cradled him gently to her. 'Come on, Little Buttons. I'll keep you safe,' she whispered, turning to follow her daddy. 'Bye, Auntie Sara,' she said behind her, her eyes fixed on the teddy.

Watching her go, I felt any reservations I might have had beginning to melt away. I'd been worrying about how the children would feel about the move, but they were obviously as sold on living here as Ben was. 'Thanks for looking after them.' I gave Sara a hug, then turned to follow Maya to the car. 'Oh—' I stopped and turned back. 'Can I ask you something?'

'Ask away.' Sara smiled and waited expectantly.

'The previous owners, do you know what happened to them? It's just with the house having been unoccupied for years, I can't help wondering.' Truthfully, I was questioning whether something awful might have happened there. I hoped Sara would put my mind at rest.

'I'm not really sure.' She frowned thoughtfully. 'Though rumour has it the woman who lived there disappeared one day.'

My stomach tightened. 'You mean *actually* disappeared?'

'Apparently. She just upped and left and hasn't been seen since, according to old Joan over the road.' Sara nodded at a house diagonally opposite. 'Joan was here then, so I suppose she would know.'

'So did she not have any family? There must have been a family living there – children. I found the teddy bear upstairs in one of the bedrooms.'

'She did have children,' Sara confirmed. 'Or so Joan said. I'm guessing there might have been a divorce or something. She was on her own in the end, it seems. And then one day...'

She disappeared. 'But what about the children?' I frowned in confusion. 'Did she lose custody of them or something? And if she left so suddenly, what happened to the furniture?'

Sara thought about it. 'After so long in an abandoned house, I assume it was all binned.'

'I suppose it must have been,' I mused. 'I wonder why no one came forward to make a claim on the property, though. It seems really odd to me. Doesn't it seem odd to you?' Did Ben know about any of this, I wondered?

Sara nodded. 'It does, but obviously no one did.' She looked me over worriedly. 'I hope I haven't gone and put you off.'

'You haven't,' I assured her. Strangely, despite what she'd told me, or possibly because of it, I felt an odd affinity for the house. As if it needed someone to love it. A family who would breathe life back into the heart of it. I felt almost as if the house was calling quietly out to me. 'It's the perfect house for us. I wish I knew more about its mysterious history, though.'

FOUR

Sara

After a gruelling day trying to make her accounts add up in between clients and then spending some time with the children once she was home, Sara left James and Ellie in front of the TV and headed for the hall. Setting up her own hair salon in the current economic climate possibly wasn't the best decision she'd made. She was utterly exhausted. And her own hair was a mess. She fluffed it up in front of the mirror and found a grey hair amongst the auburn. Panicking, she reached to pluck it out, and then caught herself, her ex-husband's constant put-downs floating back. She was fine just as she was, she told herself firmly. Then she sighed in despair. She didn't believe it. She never would.

She couldn't be that bad, though. Other men liked what they saw. That didn't mean they liked her, though, did it? But Paul did. He'd told her he loved her. She had to stop this, stop doubting herself. She would drive herself mad. Turning from the mirror before she found something else to fixate on, she called up the stairs, 'Could you keep an eye on the kids, Paul? I'm just popping across the road to check on Joan.'

He was busy fixing her leaky bath tap, which he definitely scored points for. Having spent years trapped in a marriage with a monster who would never lift a finger in the house – on the back of which she'd had a fling with a married man, which she now realised was far too close to home and which she bitterly regretted – she thought she might have landed on her feet with Paul.

'Will do. Down in a sec,' he called back.

Sara smiled. She'd been reluctant to go out with him at first. She was so glad now that she had. With no other side to him, and more importantly, no wife, he was just the emotional therapy she'd needed. 'Won't be long,' she promised, collecting up the library books she'd fetched for Joan when she'd been able to grab five minutes and setting off across the road. Joan was frail, but she was still able to manage at home with a bit of help. She'd been there for Sara when she'd needed someone. The least Sara could do was be there for her now, since she didn't appear to have anyone else.

'Only me,' she called, letting herself through Joan's front door with the key she'd given her.

'In here,' Joan called back from the lounge.

Sara found her in her favourite armchair, positioned to enjoy a good view through the window. Joan was an independent spirit. Sadly, her arthritis meant she couldn't get around much, so she tended to live her life vicariously through other people, which at least meant you could rely on her to know what was going on.

'How are you doing?' Sara went across to Joan, placing the books on the occasional table next to her.

'Not too bad, lovely,' Joan replied chirpily. 'A bit tired. I think that jog around the reservoir did for me.'

Sara laughed. 'You need to pace yourself, Joan. Fancy a cuppa?' she asked, heading for the kitchen.

'Just the ticket. That should perk me up a bit. You'll find some chocolate digestives in the biscuit tin,' Joan called after her. 'Couldn't do me a favour and pop Lucky some food in his dish while you're in there, Sara, could you?'

'No problem,' Sara assured her. 'Talk of the devil.' She glanced towards the flap in the back door as, obviously aware that food was imminent, the black cat slid sleekly through it. Padding across to her, he wove a figure of eight around her ankles and gave out a plaintive mewl, as if he were starving. Sara knew better. Joan would starve herself before letting her cat go without food. Bending down, she picked him up. She hadn't been that big on cats, but Lucky was such a pretty, pleasant-natured thing – if a little elusive – that she couldn't help but take to him.

Cat fed and tea made, she returned to the lounge. 'Are those okay?' she asked, nodding towards the books as she set the tray down. 'I wasn't sure whether you'd read them.'

'Perfect. I do love a bit of historical fiction, and Kate Hewitt writes it so well,' Joan assured her, placing the book she'd been looking at back on the arm of her chair.

'Someone came to view the house next door to me the other day, did you notice?' Sara asked her.

'Vaguely,' Joan answered, and Sara was surprised. Joan noticed everything and usually couldn't wait to have a good chinwag about the neighbourhood goings-on.

'The woman seems really nice,' Sara chatted on. 'She has children around the same age as mine, which is a huge relief with the houses being semi-detached. Keeping my two quiet for long is nigh on impossible sometimes.'

'That's children for you,' Joan said with a melancholic smile, and Sara felt bad for her that she didn't see much of her own son.

'The husband's quite a dish, isn't he?' Joan commented. 'I noticed as he walked away from your house.'

'I can't say I noticed.' Flustered, because that's exactly what she thought, Sara turned away to pick up the biscuits.

Joan was silent for a second. 'Did you catch his name?'

'Ben, I think. I didn't really talk to him.' Sara passed her a biscuit and changed the subject. 'They'll be taking on a huge project if they do buy it. It's been empty for ages, hasn't it, Joan? Didn't you say twenty years or so?'

'About that,' Joan replied, looking deep in thought.

'That's a hell of a long time.' Sara frowned, her thoughts going to what Naomi had said. 'I know you told me the woman disappeared, but did her children not make a claim on the property?'

Joan placed her biscuit back. Stroking the cat who'd leapt nimbly onto her lap, she took a while to answer. 'She lost them, sadly,' she said eventually, turning to gaze out of the window.

Sara felt her heart jar. 'Lost them how? Do you mean her husband got custody?' Might the woman have lost her entire family? In some terrible accident, possibly? That would have been beyond bearable. 'Joan?' Seeing she looked distracted, she gave her arm a gentle shake. 'How did she lose them?'

Joan turned back to her. 'The roses are beautiful, aren't they?' she said.

Sara studied her, puzzled. She seemed to have lost the thread. 'Gorgeous.' Her gaze flicked to the front garden, where the roses were actually in desperate need of cutting back. 'I'll get Paul to prune them for you, shall I?'

'Paul?' Joan looked at her questioningly.

'My boyfriend,' Sara reminded her, growing worried. Joan knew who Paul was. Sara had introduced him to her.

'Ah yes.' Joan nodded, a faraway look in her eyes. 'He has children, doesn't he?'

'Just one. A daughter,' Sara confirmed. 'She lives in Spain with her mum. Remember, I told you?'

'Oh dear, that's a shame.' Joan knitted her brow. 'He doesn't get to see much of her then?'

'No, sadly.' Sara sighed, feeling for Paul. 'His ex-wife's parents are well-off expats living in the Canary Islands, apparently. Paul said he realised his daughter would have a better life out there, so didn't fight for custody. He misses her, though, terribly. He's hoping to fly out in a couple of months. I'm trying to swing some time off so I can go with him. I can't wait to meet her.'

Joan smiled, but there was a troubled look in her eyes. 'That will be nice,' she said.

Sara had no idea what to say. The conversation was stilted. Awkward. Joan had never been like this before. She was always keen to have a good natter. 'You were telling me about the woman who lived in the house next door to me, what happened to her and her family,' she prompted her.

'Was I?' Joan glanced away again, towards the empty house. 'I can't say I really remember much about it, to be honest.'

Now Sara was definitely worried. Joan was normally as sharp as a tack, and she had a memory like an elephant. 'Joan?' She crouched down beside her. 'Are you all right? You're not feeling unwell, are you?' Might this be early-stage dementia, she wondered?

Joan looked back at her, and what Sara saw in her eyes shook her. She looked scared. But what on earth of? Had she realised her memory was failing? Or was it something about the house?

FIVE

Naomi

The house really was speaking to him. I watched slightly gobsmacked as Ben continued the task of instructing the removal men. I was exhausted from packing endless boxes, and I'd had my patience stretched thin by the children, who were obviously overexcited by the move. The thing that bemused me was that Ben seemed to know where he wanted everything – as in precisely where he wanted every single item. It was as if he had a floor plan. I was surprised when I noticed him getting tetchy outside with one of the men because he'd found some item or other wasn't where he'd specified. I was completely taken aback when I went upstairs minutes later to find him berating one of the men for not placing the bed against the right wall. 'It goes over there,' he said, pointing to the place he'd said it would go when we'd viewed the house. 'I told you quite specifically where we wanted it.'

'Oh right.' The young man, not much more than a teenager,

shifted awkwardly as Ben looked him over, unimpressed. 'I'll go and fetch Gareth then, shall I,' he offered, 'and we'll move it?'

'Good idea.' Ben smiled tightly. 'Since we're not paying you a small fortune to move the furniture around ourselves.'

'Ben?' What was the matter with him? I looked at my husband in astonishment as the young man headed past me, his cheeks flushed with embarrassment. 'Was that necessary?' I asked him. 'We could always move it later if we need to. I'm actually not sure I don't prefer it where it is. We'd have a lovely view of the treetops through the window.'

'You shouldn't be hauling furniture around. You're pregnant,' Ben pointed out, as if he needed to. With the baby alternately practising his kickboxing skills or resting on my bladder, I was fully aware of my condition. 'We hired them to move us,' he went on. 'Are we supposed to just say cheers and give them a tip for dumping the furniture anywhere they please?'

'They're not, Ben. They've been working really hard without even a break. You're being rude.' Ben was agitated as he glanced at me. 'What's this really about, Ben?' I asked, studying him carefully. I couldn't remember a time when I'd seen him short-tempered.

He ran his fingers through his hair. 'Nothing,' he said. 'I just—'

'Mummy!' Maya interrupted, calling urgently from downstairs. 'Liam's taken Little Buttons and he won't give him back.'

'I'll go and deal with more important matters, shall I?' I asked Ben pointedly.

'Naomi.' Ben caught my arm as I turned to the door. 'I'm sorry.' He sighed. 'I'm just a bit het up, what with the move and the new job. I didn't mean to upset you.'

I could see he was genuinely contrite, but still, he'd unnerved me. This wasn't like him. 'It's not just me you're upsetting, though, is it, Ben? Perhaps you should try being less controlling,' I suggested. 'I mean, it's not really a major cata-strophe if the bed ends up against the wrong wall, is it?'

'Controlling?' Ben stared at me incredulously. 'I've never been controlling in my life.'

I quietly cursed myself. I hadn't meant to say that. He was meticulous, sometimes bafflingly so, constantly tidying things up – even the salt and pepper pots had their rightful place on the table. He would laugh at himself if I ribbed him about it, though. He'd never raised his voice, never been aggressive in any way. I felt safe with him, perhaps because he was so predictable, which was why I supposed I felt a bit destabilised now.

'I know,' I conceded. 'I'm sorry. I think we're both too exhausted to think straight.' I gave him a small smile. 'We'll talk later. I should see to the children.' As the weather was fine, I'd left them playing in the back garden, but they were inside now and the front door was open.

Reaching the foot of the stairs, I found Maya in tears. 'What's going on?' I asked, threading an arm around her.

'Liam's stolen Little Buttons,' she sniffled. 'He pulled the plaster off his ear and he said I was stupid because I talk to him, but I said that *he* was stupid because he said Little Buttons was deaf because he only had one good ear. He's not, is he, Mummy?'

'No, he's not,' I reassured her as she paused for breath. 'People with one good ear can usually hear perfectly well.'

'See, he *can* hear. Mummy said so.' Maya nodded triumphantly, her gaze going past me to where Liam appeared from the kitchen.

'No, he can't. He's not real. He's a stuffed toy,' he stated flatly.

'He *is* real.' Maya's tears fell in earnest. 'Give him back.'

'Liam...' I sighed. I did wonder sometimes at my boy's inability to be empathetic.

'What?' Liam's face was a picture of innocence. 'I am going to give him back.'

His hands were behind him, I noticed. 'Now, Liam.' I pointed him towards Maya, and then breathed in relief as I spotted Sara heading down our path.

'Hi, how's it going?' she asked, smiling cheerily as she reached the front door.

'Badly.' I managed a wan smile, my gaze travelling between my two fractious children.

'Oh dear.' Sara stepped inside as I moved away from the door. 'I sense someone might be a little overtired,' she said, crouching down to Maya and easing the hand she was kneading her eyes with away from her face. 'How about you two come around to my house and help me finish off some chocolate cake, hey?'

Maya's eyes lit up at that.

'Liam?' Sara looked towards him.

Liam's mouth twitched into a smile. 'Cool,' he said, finally producing the teddy bear from behind his back. 'I fixed him for you,' he said with an awkward shrug.

I blinked from the bear to my boy in pleasant surprise as he passed him to Maya. He'd taped up his ear. He'd obviously used some of the parcel tape I'd used on the moving boxes and patched him up. He really was so like his father – a complete enigma sometimes. 'Are you sure?' I turned to Sara. I was grateful for her kind offer, but gathering she was not long home from work, I didn't want to impose.

'Positive.' She nodded. 'My two had a slice each with their packed lunch. I don't want them sneaking another slice and ending up on a sugar high, and I can't possibly consume any more calories myself. Why don't you come with us? Take the weight off your feet for five minutes?' Her gaze strayed to my bump. 'You look as if you could use some time out.'

'I could,' I assured her, sighing wearily. 'The children aren't the only ones getting fractious.' I glanced at the ceiling.

Sara rolled her eyes as there was a timely crash followed by a curse above us. 'Best give him some space,' she suggested, heading on out.

Urging Liam and Maya before me, I followed. Sara was right, I decided. With starting his new job tomorrow on top of the move, Ben was bound to be a bit agitated. We were probably best out of each other's way for a while.

As we walked down the path, I noted a woman emerging precariously from the house diagonally opposite. 'Is that the woman you mentioned lived here when the previous owners did?' I asked Sara.

'Joan, yes. And I have no idea what she's thinking, trying to negotiate that step without her walking frame.' Sara took off towards her, and I grabbed the children's hands and followed.

'Why didn't you ring me, or yell across if you needed something, Joan?' she scolded her, though not unkindly.

'I'm fine.' The woman waved a hand. 'I just needed some fresh air.' Glancing at me with the briefest of smiles, she dropped her gaze to Maya, studying her so intently that Maya shied away and scuttled behind me.

'Joan. Are you sure you're all right?' Sara asked her, looking perturbed.

The woman's gaze snapped up again, but she wasn't looking at Sara or at me, rather past me towards our house.

Perplexed, I twisted to follow her gaze and realised it was Ben she was staring at. And Ben, who'd come out of the house, presumably to check where we were, was staring back at her – hard. A chill of apprehension prickled my skin. I might be mistaken, but my husband seemed almost to be glaring at the woman.

SIX

Sara

'She'll be all right now she's settled with a cuppa and her library books,' Sara assured Naomi as she led the way into her kitchen. 'I'll pop over later and check on her.'

'She seems nice,' Naomi commented. Joan had been more like her old self and quite chatty with her once they'd helped her back inside. 'I wonder what all that was about with Ben, though?' She frowned, clearly puzzled about Joan's odd behaviour outside.

As was Sara. Ben had seemed put out by Joan staring at him, heading back into the house with a deep frown on his face. While Naomi had been in Joan's kitchen, having offered to make the tea, Sara had asked Joan why she had been staring at him. Joan had looked perplexed and replied, 'Who, dear?' When Sara had tried to jog her memory, she'd looked blank. She would have to try to persuade her to make a doctor's appointment. Knowing Joan wasn't one to visit the surgery for every 'little ache and pain', she wouldn't be easily persuaded, but Sara was growing extremely concerned about her.

'She probably heard him getting irate with the removal men and wondered what was going on,' she suggested, and then wished she hadn't when Naomi's face fell. 'I can't say I blame him,' she added quickly. 'He was fed up with them putting things in the wrong place, which is understandable.'

'You spoke to him then?' Naomi looked at her in surprise. 'I'm amazed you made him stand still long enough. He's so insistent on overseeing everything I've barely been able to get his attention.'

'Just briefly,' Sara assured her. 'I was on my way in. I think he's concerned about you having to cart things around once they've left.'

Naomi nodded. 'I get that, but it's just so not like him. He's never normally bad-tempered.'

'It's just the stress of the move, I expect.' Sara steered Naomi across to the table. 'Sit,' she instructed, 'before you drop. You two, too.' She gestured to the children and went to fetch the cake from the fridge. 'You can eat your cake before Paul brings my two back from the park, and then you can watch some TV here for a while and give your mum and dad some time to get organised.'

'Yay! More Minions!' Maya scrambled gleefully up onto a chair, Liam following her lead but with a little less enthusiasm.

'Thanks, Sara,' Naomi said appreciatively.

'No problem. It'll get them out of your hair for a while, at least.'

After passing the children their promised large portions of cake, she cut Naomi an extra-large slice. 'For energy. You look as if you could use some,' she said, pushing it towards her. The poor woman looked dead on her feet. Sara didn't wonder why. Moving house with two children running around must be a nightmare, and this was without being pregnant into the bargain.

'I could.' Naomi smiled, took a forkful, then almost spat it out as Maya proclaimed, 'Finished,' and clanged her fork down.

'Maya! You little glutton,' Naomi chastised her, her face a mixture of amusement and disbelief.

'I'm glad someone's a fan of my cooking,' Sara said, arching her eyebrows. 'M&S,' she whispered to Naomi, then cocked an ear as she heard the front door open. 'That will be Paul. Time for Minions, guys.'

'*Yes*,' Maya whooped and climbed hurriedly down.

Liam followed suit as Paul poked his head around the kitchen door.

'Not interrupting anything, am I?' He glanced curiously between Sara and Naomi, then sidestepped quickly as the children charged towards the door. Liam had finally found a spark in his step and was trying to beat Maya in a race to the lounge.

'Just girl-talk,' Sara assured him, getting to her feet. 'Naomi, this is Paul, my boyfriend. Paul, this is Naomi, my new neighbour. Shoes off, kids, and straight into the lounge,' she instructed her own children as she headed to the hall to check muddy shoes were being removed. 'You can watch some TV before dinner, but make sure you behave.'

'She's offered to have my two for a while, thank God,' Naomi said to Paul. 'I was fast reaching the end of my patience.'

'She's a good sort,' Paul answered. 'Always looking out for other people. That's why I love her. As well as the fact that she's gorgeous and intelligent, obviously.' He winked in Naomi's direction as Sara came back to the table.

'Flattery will get him everywhere. He thinks.' Sara rolled her eyes.

'I live in hope.' Paul smirked. 'Tea or coffee?' he offered. 'Or would you prefer I leave you two to it?'

'Do you mind keeping an eye on the kids for five minutes?'

Sara gave him her best winning smile. 'Give us a chance to have a bit of a natter in peace?'

'No problem,' Paul assured her. 'Give me a shout when you're finished. Mind you, you might have to wake me up. James and Ellie gave me a run for my money playing footie. I couldn't keep up with them.'

'I'll give you a massage later,' Sara called after him as he limped theatrically back to the hall.

'Now there's an offer a man can't refuse.' Paul chuckled and headed onwards.

Naomi watched him go then turned to Sara. 'He seems nice,' she said, clearly taken.

'He is.' Sara smiled. 'He came to fix my plumbing and stayed.'

Naomi widened her eyes in surprise.

'Well, he's not too shoddy, is he?' Sara laughed embarrassedly. 'And more importantly, he makes an effort. He's not critical, either. I really needed that after the marriage from hell and then stupidly getting involved—' She stopped, her cheeks heating up as she realised she was giving out too much information. 'Let's put it this way, I made a huge mistake on the rebound. Paul seems up front, you know? He's a breath of fresh air, to be honest.'

Naomi looked at her with a mischievous twinkle in her eye. 'So, is it love or lust?'

Sara thought about it. 'You know, I think I might just be a little bit in love with him,' she admitted.

'Just a bit?' Naomi arched an eyebrow.

Sara glanced coyly down. 'It's early days.'

'The children seem to like him,' Naomi said, seeming to approve.

'They do.' Sara nodded happily. 'He has a daughter of his own so he knows how to be with kids. Your two like him too.

Maya and Paul were so busy chatting the last time they were here, it's a wonder anyone else could get a word in.'

Naomi smiled knowingly. 'She is a bit of a chatterbox, isn't she? Mind you, I'd rather she was confident and outgoing than a little mouse. Liam's more like his father.'

'James is nothing like his father, thank God.' Sara shook off a shudder. 'I was always treading on eggshells when he was around.'

'Oh. No, I didn't mean...' Naomi looked alarmed. 'Ben doesn't normally get so agitated. He's usually quite quiet. He's obviously more stressed than I'd realised, as you said.'

'*Hell.*' Realising she'd opened her mouth and put her foot in it, Sara felt terrible. 'Me and my big mouth. Honestly, I do despair of myself. I wasn't making comparisons, Naomi, honestly.'

Naomi's gaze flicked uncertainly down.

'Liam was actually quite quiet when he was here. Extremely well behaved, I thought,' said Sara, trying to redeem the situation.

Naomi nodded and smiled, though a little tentatively. 'He generally is,' she said. 'Can I tell you something?' she asked, looking back at her.

'Of course.' Sara noted her serious expression worriedly. 'Anything.'

'It's about Ben,' Naomi said, causing a prickle of apprehension to run through Sara. 'He has seizures. Not often,' she added quickly. 'He doesn't like to talk about it much. It's a man thing – his pride, I think. He tends not to discuss anything too emotional.'

Sara felt a stab of relief. She'd thought for an awful minute she was going to say she suspected her husband of having an affair. 'Definitely a man thing.' She sighed and reached for her hand. 'Paul's the same. Trying to get him to open up sometimes is like trying to get blood from a stone.'

Naomi smiled at that, but Sara could see she was troubled. 'He was diagnosed with non-epileptic attack disorder as a child,' she went on. 'He goes off on his own sometimes, because he needs to get as far away as possible from the situation that's causing his stress, he says. I really worry when he does that, though.'

Sara wasn't surprised. Surely Ben must realise his wife would be worried, imagining he might be out in some remote place and unable to get help.

'I worry about Liam, too. That's part of what I meant when I said he's like his father. He tends to be a bit introspective, preferring his own space. Our GP said stress-related seizures are not inherited, but...'

'You worry, nevertheless,' Sara picked up. 'Of course you do. You're his mum. You're bound to.' She gave Naomi's hand a squeeze.

'Ben thinks I worry too much,' Naomi confided with a sigh.

'And *he's* bound to do that.' Sara smiled sympathetically. 'Also a man thing. Just so you know, you can talk to me. Okay? If you want to have a natter or a good moan, I'm your woman.'

Naomi smiled, now looking relieved. 'Thanks, Sara. It really helps having someone to talk to.'

'Anytime.' Sara smiled reassuringly back. 'God knows there were times when I needed an ear, and I'm sure there will be again, now I'm in a new—' She stopped as Paul came back into the kitchen.

'Sorry, I've been sent out to fetch drinks.' He gave the two women a smile as he walked across to the fridge. 'Won't be a sec.'

Naomi returned his smile, but still she looked a little pensive. 'So, is there any more news on the mysterious history of the missing woman?' she asked, and Sara guessed she'd also been worrying about that.

Recalling what Joan had said about the woman losing her

family, she wasn't sure what to say. The last thing she wanted to do was worry Naomi further. 'I'm afraid not. I did ask Joan about it, but as you might have gathered, it seems she's getting a bit forgetful in her old age.' It wasn't quite a lie.

'What, you mean the woman who lived next door before?' Paul asked, pulling a bottle of Diet Coke from the fridge and going to the cupboard. 'Wasn't her young daughter murdered or something?'

'*Paul.*' Sara looked at him stunned. This couldn't be true. She was sure Joan would have mentioned it if it was. But whether it was true or not, judging by Naomi's horrified expression and her hand going protectively to her tummy, that was the absolute last thing she'd wanted to hear.

SEVEN

Sara

'What on earth were you thinking?' Sara asked, struggling to believe that Paul could have been so insensitive. Clearly shaken by his announcement about the little girl, Naomi had mumbled something about Ben thinking he'd been deserted, gathered up her children and promptly left.

'I assumed it was common knowledge.' Paul's tone was a mixture of confused and apologetic as she strode past him. 'It's not exactly a minor incident, is it?'

He followed her as she headed upstairs to grab her iPad. If what he'd said was true then there would be something online, even if it was twenty-odd years ago. What Joan had told Sara about the woman losing her family had left her shocked. This, though, a child who'd lived in the house right next door being murdered, it was too unbearable to contemplate.

Paul trailed after her as she marched to the bedroom. 'I assumed you knew.'

'I didn't.' Sara eyed him despairingly over her shoulder.

'Right. Well, I'm sorry, obviously. I honestly don't get why you're so upset, though.'

Sara turned to look at him in astonishment. 'Because it *is* upsetting. Do you not think Naomi's going to be upset? She's pregnant, for goodness' sake. She has children. She's probably regretting moving into the property. She'll certainly be wondering why I wouldn't have told her something I must know, since my boyfriend, who's only been around for two minutes, obviously does.'

Paul looked wounded at that. 'A bit longer than that, Sara,' he said. 'Long enough for you to know I wouldn't deliberately upset anyone.'

Sara felt bad. She hadn't meant to snap at him, but she couldn't help herself. With all Naomi had on her plate, the last thing she needed was to feel uncomfortable in her own home. 'How did you know?' she asked, trying to establish whether it was just idle gossip or fact.

'Joan told me.' Paul shrugged. 'Which, since you two are so close, is why I thought you would already know.'

'Joan?' Sara looked at him in confusion. 'When? The subject never came up when I introduced you to her and I haven't seen you speaking to her since.'

'She lives diagonally opposite,' he pointed out, his expression now one of exasperation. 'I can hardly avoid speaking to her, can I?'

'And you didn't think to mention it to me?'

Paul tipped his head to one side. 'No, I didn't,' he said, his expression puzzled. 'I didn't realise I was supposed to report back every time I say good morning to someone.'

'That's not what I meant.' Realising how petty she sounded, Sara tried to backtrack.

Paul surveyed her carefully. 'Is my talking to the neighbours a problem, Sara?' he asked, a wary edge to his voice. 'It clearly bothers you.'

'Of course it's not. It's just that I can't understand why Joan would mention something so awful having happened – in the house right next door – to you and not to me.'

'I see.' Paul nodded. 'Maybe she didn't think I was going to be around for more than two minutes either,' he suggested with a sad shrug.

'Paul?' Feeling awful, Sara went after him as he headed back to the landing. She'd hurt his feelings. Clearly, she had. But even if he'd thought what Joan had told him was common knowledge, he really should have thought to check with her before blurting it out in front of Naomi.

EIGHT

Naomi

'You're back then?' Ben asked, coming into the kitchen.

'I am.' I took a deep breath and concentrated my efforts on finding bits and pieces from one of the boxes.

'The kids seem a bit subdued,' he commented.

They were definitely that. Maya had been upset at being dragged away from her new friend and the Minions film she'd been looking forward to. Now sitting in our drab lounge, surrounded by boxes, with only their tablets to entertain them, both of the children were sulking.

'Where did you go?' Ben came across to help.

'Just next door. Sara invited us round for cake. I was glad of the break, to be honest.'

'Oh right.' He nodded pensively.

I debated whether to ask him about what Paul had said. I couldn't understand why we wouldn't have known about something so tragic happening here. Surely Ben's estate agent friend would have known about it? But then I supposed it wasn't exactly a selling point. It had shocked me, finding out like that, and I was also confused. If Paul knew about it, wouldn't Sara have known too? In which case, why wouldn't she have mentioned it? I could only think that she'd thought it would upset me and was waiting for the right moment, hence her obvious annoyance when Paul had blurted it out. I would have a word with her, I decided. After rushing off, I should do that anyway. I didn't want to lose her friendship, particularly with Liam and Maya due to start at the local school.

'Who's the bloke?' Ben asked, cutting through my thoughts.

I glanced at him, confused. 'What bloke?'

'The guy next door. I heard Sara was divorced and gathered he was fairly new to the scene. I just wondered about him. I felt he was a bit odd, didn't you?'

I squinted at him. 'No. Why?'

'Not sure.' Ben furrowed his brow. 'He was there when I went round to check on the kids when we were viewing the house. Sara said he was upstairs doing some job or other, which was fair enough. But I would've thought he would have come down when we collected the kids.'

I thought about it and recalled what Sara had said. 'He'd gone out to the DIY shop. Sara mentioned it.'

'Ah. That might explain it. Still, I'd be a bit wary of him if I were you. Around the kids, I mean.'

I stared at him, astonished. 'Don't be ridiculous, Ben. You've never even met him. You can't go around telling people to be wary of someone around their children without good reason.'

The furrow in Ben's brow deepened. He didn't answer.

'Ben?' I looked *him* over warily. 'Is there something you're not telling me?' I wasn't sure I could take any more shocks in one day.

'No.' Ben shook his head. 'Nothing. I got a feeling the man was keeping a low profile, that was all.'

'So you're imagining he might have some kind of a history? Judging him without even having set eyes on him?' I searched his face, incredulous.

My mind went back to the child whose life had been cruelly snatched away. *Did* Ben already know about her? Had he also decided not to tell me because he'd thought it would put me off living here? 'Is something bothering you?' I asked him carefully. 'Something you've heard?'

Ben eyed me curiously. 'About?'

'The house. Do you know anything about the family who lived here?'

'No.' Ben turned his attention to emptying one of the boxes. 'Why?'

I hesitated. 'I just wondered why you would suddenly feel so protective of the children. Whether one of the neighbours might have said something.' Joan possibly, which might explain the odd look that had passed between them.

'No, no one's said anything.' He turned back to me. 'It's nothing, just me being neurotic. You're right, I shouldn't be judging people without having met them. I guess with us moving into a new area my mind went into overdrive. Ignore me.'

He smiled, but his eyes burned with that intensity I sometimes had to work to interpret. I wasn't impressed with him being so judgemental, although I understood his concern, to a degree. Sometimes, you couldn't help imagining awful scenarios. It was part of parenting – making you extra-vigilant, reminding you that you would kill before letting any harm come to your children. My hand strayed to my tummy. How could I condemn him for that?

'I'm going to be at home, Ben,' I reminded him. 'I won't be working for ages yet. The children will be safe, I promise. You worry too much.'

'I do a bit, don't I?' he admitted, now looking despairing of himself.

'A lot,' I assured him with a chastising smile.

He walked across to me, encircling me with his arms. 'Have I ever mentioned how much I love you, Mrs Felton?' he asked, finally looking more relaxed.

'Now and then.' I smiled.

'No, really,' he added, the intensity back in his eyes, a flicker of the insecurity I noticed occasionally. 'I would be lost without you – you know that, don't you? You taught me how to love and I...' He faltered, glancing down and awkwardly back at me. 'I know I can be moody sometimes, but don't give up on me, will you?'

I searched his face in shock and surprise. Pleasant surprise. Ben wasn't good at showing his vulnerability, and it meant a lot to me just then. 'Never,' I assured him, threading my arms around his neck. 'You don't get off that easily.' My lips were a breath away from his when Maya burst through the door. '*Mummy*, we're hungry,' she whined. 'Little Buttons says his tummy's rumbling.'

'He's not real,' Liam pointed out, rolling his eyes as he came in behind her.

'Yes, he is.' Maya scrunched her face into a scowl. 'Listen, you can *hear* his rumbly tummy.'

'Sad.' Shaking his head, Liam skirted around the outstretched teddy bear with a world-weary sigh.

'No, I'm not! *You* are.' Maya's bottom lip quivered, her eyes filling up as she clutched Little Buttons close to her chest.

'Enough, you two.' Ben clapped his hands together. 'Or no pizza.'

'Yay! Cheese Feast.' Tears forgotten, Maya jiggled excitedly.

'Pepperoni Feast with extra pepperoni.' Liam had a different choice, unsurprisingly.

'Half and half. And no arguments or else.' Ben looked sternly between them.

'Cool,' Liam said, considerably brightened up at the prospect of pizza. 'Can I go up to my room yet?'

'Yep. I'm pretty much organised up there now. Enough for us all to get some decent sleep anyway.' Eyeing the ceiling, Ben kissed my cheek, then walked across to sling his arm over Liam's shoulders. 'Coming, munchkin?' He extended a hand for Maya, who planted hers happily in his.

I smiled as I watched him lead his children to the hall. Yes, he could be moody, but he was who he was: a man who couldn't easily let go emotionally, but also a man who realised it and tried. And every time he did, I loved him more for it.

Following them up a minute later, I smiled as I passed by Maya's room to see them all gazing out of her window.

'Are we going to have a treehouse, Dad?' Liam asked, looking hopefully up at him.

'Absolutely,' Ben assured him. 'We only moved here because there was great scope for a treehouse.'

'But you're going to fix up the shed into a Wendy house first, aren't you, Daddy?' Maya asked uncertainly.

'No, he's not. He's building the treehouse first,' Liam said confidently.

'He is *not*,' Maya argued. 'Daddy said the shed didn't need much fixing up when he moved the rocking chair in there so he's going to do that first.'

He'd moved the chair in there? I hadn't realised he'd done that, though it was as good a place as any until we could take it to the charity shop. I carried on, leaving Ben to sort that little argument out.

He certainly was organised. Going into the main bedroom I noted he'd emptied a fair few of the boxes. And that the bed had been put where he'd said it should go. I felt a new worry niggle away at me. What was it, I wondered, this new obsession with the furniture being exactly where he wanted it to be? He'd never been like this before. We'd always made decisions about what went where together. Why had he changed so suddenly? It seemed to me that since crossing the threshold of this house, he was making decisions without me.

NINE

Naomi

Hearing Ben in the shower and realising I must have slept through the alarm, I hurried out of bed. I'd lain awake half the night, images of what might have happened to the little girl who'd lived here clicking graphically through my mind. I'd imagined her to be Maya's age, so small, so vulnerable. I could almost see her – her face pale and petrified, her eyes recoiling in fear. Eventually drifting somewhere between sleeping and waking, I'd heard her, a small, tremulous voice calling for her mummy, and then she'd screamed, a scream filled with such abject terror, it pierced my heart like a knife.

Scrambling out of bed, I'd blundered to the landing, echoes of her pitiful cries following me as I'd hurried fearfully to Maya's room. Finding her sleeping, her eyelids softly fluttering, one small arm wrapped protectively around Little Buttons, my heart started beating again. My little girl had sworn she would love the raggedy bear forever. She hardly ever let go of him.

Love for my daughter crashing ferociously through me, I reached to smooth her hair gently from her forehead. He was real. To her he was real. *Please God*, I prayed silently as I tucked up her duvet, *help me keep my little girl safe.*

I'd found Liam fast asleep too, his iPad, which he'd obviously snuck up with him, poking out from the top of his duvet. Easing it gently away from him, I pressed a soft kiss to his cheek. Liam wasn't into shows of emotion. I missed him, the little boy who used to cling to me, desperate for me not to leave him at nursery. He was growing up. Too quickly.

I was making coffee, my thoughts back on the little girl who'd once lived here, when I noticed something on the worktop. But that shouldn't be here. *Couldn't* be here. I'd wiped the tops down with antibacterial spray last night – perfunctorily, as I was rushing, but I would have noticed this. A sense of foreboding settling in the pit of my belly, I placed the flat of my own hand alongside the perfectly formed, sticky handprint, so small it had to be that of a child. Maya's? Or Liam's? But how? When?

My gaze flew to the food cupboard as a thought occurred. I yanked it open, and my palpitating heart slowed to somewhere near normal. I couldn't recall having bought strawberry jam, yet there it was, sitting on the bottom shelf. Still, I couldn't quite believe that either of the children would have crept down the stairs and made a strawberry jam sandwich in the middle of the night.

Looking in the sink for signs of an unwashed spoon or knife, I almost jumped out of my skin when Ben spoke behind me. 'Morning. Did you manage to get some sleep?'

'Some,' I answered distractedly. 'You didn't come downstairs in the night, did you?' I asked him, though I wasn't sure why. It obviously wasn't his handprint.

'No. Why?' He walked across to slide his arms around me.

'No reason.' I tried to dismiss it. Sleep deprivation was obviously addling my thinking. Plus, Ben would think I'd gone mad if I started wittering on about mysteriously appearing hand-prints. 'You didn't sleep too badly,' I said, turning my cheek to his kiss.

'Surprisingly,' he said, yawning widely.

'Can I ask you something?' I ventured, my mind now on another mystery.

'Ask away.' He smiled appreciatively as I passed him his coffee. 'Though I can't promise a sensible answer until my brain kicks in.'

I hesitated. 'Did Joan upset you in some way yesterday?'

Ben looked puzzled. 'Joan?'

'The old woman across the road.'

'Ah, right.' He nodded.

'You were staring at her.'

'Was I?' He took a sip of his coffee. 'I hadn't realised.'

'You actually seemed quite angry,' I pushed on. It might have been nothing, but it was playing on my mind.

'Did I?' Ben widened his eyes in surprise. 'I wasn't. She'd had a go at me earlier but I wasn't too bothered. I was distracted, that was all. Plus, I hadn't got my contacts in.'

Ah. I felt a smidgen of relief, but still, I was curious. 'It seems a bit odd that she jumped on you, though. What did she have a go at you about?'

'She said the removal men were making too much noise, but to be honest, I thought she looked a bit batty, so I just ignored it.' Ben glugged his coffee back and headed for the sink with his mug. 'So are you okay with the bedroom arrangement?' he asked, grabbing a slice of the toast I'd made in the absence of anything else to hand.

Had he registered what I'd said then? 'It's fine, although I still think the bed would be better against the window-facing wall,' I said, reminding him anyway.

'Oh right.' Ben placed his toast down without taking a bite. 'Well, I'll move it then, if you're determined it should go there.'

I looked at him, taken aback. 'I'm not *determined*. It doesn't bother me that much. I would have liked the view but it's not that important.'

Ben's forehead creased into a frown. 'So why mention it?'

I took a breath. I didn't want to go on about it but I felt I had to say something. 'Honestly? Because the fact that you ignored what I wanted did bother me.'

'I didn't *ignore* you.' He laughed in bemusement. 'I just didn't think it was that important.'

'It's not.' Feeling upset, ridiculously, I turned away. 'I've said it's fine. Just forget it.'

'Right,' Ben said again, a despairing edge to his voice. 'Are you sure this isn't all something to do with some silly superstition, Naomi?'

'What?' Bewildered, I turned back to him. He was annoyed. I could see it in his eyes.

'To do with which way the bed's facing bringing bad luck, or something equally crackers?' he went on, now discernibly agitated.

'It's nothing to do with superstition,' I retaliated, feeling defensive, but with no idea why I should be. I might throw salt over my shoulder occasionally or walk around a ladder to avoid having paint or scaffolding drop on my head, but I wasn't obsessive. Was I? My eyes going to the handprint, I wondered if I actually might be. 'It's to do with you being in a strop about where the bed went and then taking no notice of what my views were.'

'A strop?' Ben stared at me incredulously. 'I don't believe this.' He sighed and kneaded his forehead. 'What are we arguing about here exactly, Naomi?'

'I am *not* arguing.' I felt my throat tightening. 'I simply—'

'Look, can we just drop it?' He tugged in a breath. 'I've said

I'll move it. I'll do it tonight. Right now, I have to go to work or I'll end up being late. Debating about where a bed goes, for Christ's sake.'

I watched, shocked, as he spun around and strode into the hall. 'Ben?' Tears dangerously close to the surface, I followed him.

'I'll see you later,' he said, disappearing through the front door.

I was about to go after him, even though I was still in my dressing gown, but I stopped myself. He wouldn't thank me for making him even later. What had just happened? I stood in the dark, gloomy hall, feeling scared and disorientated, and suddenly deeply lonely. I couldn't understand it. Ben wasn't like this, argumentative and petty. He wasn't an open book – I'd married him knowing there were things I didn't know about him, things he didn't feel able to share about his past – but the Ben I'd just seen... I didn't know him at all. Was I overreacting? Had *I* been the argumentative one? I cursed myself for being so reactive when I knew he was due to start his first day at work, then cursed out loud as I eyed the depressing plum-coloured walls. I was tempted to paint them bright yellow, paint the whole house yellow. Tears wetting my cheeks, I turned around – and then froze, icy fear trickling down the length of my spine as the understairs cupboard gaped open in front of me.

TEN

Sara

Sara counted silently to five, then stepped smartly between her two warring children. 'What in God's name are you arguing about?' she yelled, all attempts to hold on to her patience out of the window. It possibly wasn't the best parenting approach, but it worked. The kids were shocked into silence.

'Well?' she asked, guiltily moderating her tone, one eye on the clock. After oversleeping, they were all going to be late at this rate.

'It's *him*,' Ellie blubbered, pointing at her brother. 'He knows the fuzzy green one is mine.'

Fuzzy green...? Sara scrunched her forehead, confused. *Ah.* Noting James tucking something hastily behind his back, she gathered it was the novelty pens with the flashing heads, their latest fad and about which they argued continually. 'James?' Folding her arms, she eyeballed him meaningfully.

James got the message and reluctantly revealed what he was

hiding. 'She's got my bobble blue one and she won't give it back,' he muttered grumpily.

'You stole mine first.' Ellie glowered at him.

'Did not.'

'Did. You snuck it off my dressing table while I was—'

'*Enough.*' Sara intervened, took a deep breath to calm herself, then crouched down to their level. 'So, she said, how can we resolve this issue, do you think?'

'James?' She looked to him when neither of them spoke.

James shrugged, partly in embarrassment, partly because he didn't want to give in, Sara guessed. 'We could swap pens,' he mumbled begrudgingly.

'Excellent plan.' Sara nodded, impressed. 'Ellie?'

'Only if he gives mine back at the same time.' Ellie squinted at her brother mistrustfully.

'Sounds good,' Sara agreed. 'Right, on my count of three, you swap. Okay?'

Both kids nodded, albeit unenthusiastically.

'And you say sorry to each other, yes, because that's what mature children do.'

Two minutes later and miracle accomplished, to Sara's amazement, Ellie and James were scrambling happily to the front door to grab up their school bags.

'I'll take them, if you like,' Paul offered, coming down the stairs as Sara turned to go after them. 'It will give you a breather. Grab an extra coffee, why don't you?'

'Thank you,' she said, wondering at another miracle – that she hadn't scared him off, jumping down his throat the way she had. It had been obvious he hadn't meant to be insensitive when he'd dropped the bombshell about the little girl next door.

'No problem.' He kissed her cheek and went to grab his car keys from the hall table. 'Thanks for an enjoyable night.' He turned at the door to give her a wink as he ushered her two darlings out before him.

Sara smiled, her cheeks heating up as she recalled their passionate 'making up'. After stupidly getting involved with a man who was very much married, she'd been running scared. She hadn't envisaged anything long term when she'd gone out with Paul, but now she was nurturing a hope that it might be. She still couldn't believe her luck at finding his card in her postbox. With her loft tank leaking and an overflow pipe pouring water all over the garden, she'd needed a plumber fast – and he'd come straight away. It had obviously been meant to be.

Deciding she would take the opportunity to get to the salon early and grab a coffee before her first client arrived, she collected her coat and car keys and headed out. As she came out of her front door, she noticed Ben climbing into his car and hurried down her path to catch him before he left. 'Ben,' she called, 'can I have a quick word?'

He frowned as he looked her over. 'Sorry, late for work,' he said, and closed his car door.

Good morning to you, too. Sara watched him drive off, gobsmacked. She hadn't wanted an in-depth conversation. She'd just wanted to invite him and Naomi around for a meal. It would be an opportunity to smooth things over, she'd thought. Checking her watch, she decided she would speak to Naomi instead. She didn't want Paul's thoughtless comment playing on her mind.

Reaching her door, she knocked and waited. Naomi was probably busy with her children, who wouldn't be in school until the start of the new week. Thinking she would text her instead, she was about to leave when Naomi pulled her front door open.

'Hi.' Sara smiled warmly. Her smile slipped, though, as she saw Naomi's forlorn expression. 'Naomi? What is it, sweetheart?'

Apprehension swept through her as Naomi promptly burst into tears, and she stepped quickly inside. 'What's happened, lovely?' she urged her, wrapping her into a gentle hug. 'It's not the baby, is it?'

Breathing in sharply, Naomi shook her head.

'Is it something to do with Ben? Have you had an argument?' Trepidation crept through her at the thought that they might have.

'No, not really.' Easing away, Naomi pressed a hand under her nose. 'Sort of. But it's not him, it's me. Hormones, probably. It's nothing, honestly.'

'If I might point out, it's definitely not nothing if it has you in floods of tears. Come on, let's get you a nice cuppa and you can tell me all about it.' Sara steered her around towards the kitchen. She would text the salon and get one of the girls to stand in for her. She couldn't leave Naomi like this.

'Mummy, what's wrong?' came a worried little voice from halfway up the stairs.

Seeing Maya sitting there, hugging the teddy bear she took everywhere and with a worried look on her face, Sara attempted to reassure her. 'Mummy has a bit of a headache, that's all. Do you think you could be a good girl and be extra quiet for a while?'

Maya glanced uncertainly between Sara and her mummy. 'Uh-huh.' She nodded.

'She can watch CBeebies on my iPlayer,' Liam offered from where he stood on the landing, a perturbed frown on his face. 'Come on, Maya.' He gestured her up. 'Mum needs some space.'

Well, that was very mature of him. Sara was impressed. From what she'd seen of Liam, she'd thought Naomi was right and that the boy did take after his father. He was clearly also caring, though.

'Thanks, Liam.' Naomi managed a smile. 'That's really thoughtful of you.'

Hearing the catch in her voice, Sara urged her on. 'We

won't be long,' she called as the kids disappeared along the landing.

Once in the kitchen, she made sure Naomi sat at the table, then she found the kettle and switched it on. 'So, are you going to share what it is that's upset you so much?' she asked. 'Something obviously has, and I'm guessing it's not just hormones.'

'It is, partly, I think.' Naomi wiped a hand over her face. Sara passed her some kitchen towelling. 'Ben and I did have a few words,' she confided. 'It was silly. An argument about nothing. He's obviously stressed, what with the house move and starting his new job today. I wish I hadn't said anything now. He has to negotiate the city centre traffic and he's not going to be concentrating.'

She was feeling guilty, and probably shouldn't be. Sara knew all about that. She'd been there – in the beginning, putting up with her husband's gaslighting and passive aggression, and blaming herself. It had soon spiralled. The more he found he could bully her, the more he did. He'd almost broken her. And then she'd fallen into that idiotic affair and realised she was in danger of falling for another bastard. 'Has he got far to go?' she asked, realising why Naomi would be worried, because of the seizures.

'The City Hospital.' Naomi gave her nose a blow. 'On the other side of town.'

'I'm sure he'll be fine. He seemed to be when he drove off,' Sara assured her. 'Right now, you need to worry about you and that little bump of yours.'

Going across to Naomi, she parked a mug of tea in front of her, then found the sugar on the table and pushed that towards her. 'So, these few words you had were about...?'

'That's just it.' Naomi glanced at her, her huge green eyes still awash with tears. 'I'm not sure what it was about really.' She had another blow. 'You remember Ben got annoyed with the removal men?'

Sara nodded. 'I do.' She'd told Naomi she didn't blame him. And she didn't. He had obviously wanted to get the place straight and not leave Naomi with loads of stuff to lug about.

'I understood, to a degree.' Naomi sighed. 'But he seemed so agitated when they put the bed in the wrong place – as in, not where he wanted it – I was taken aback, to be honest. I said at the time that it didn't matter and that I would actually prefer it where it was. The thing is, the bed ended up where he wanted it anyway, and that's okay, but I felt... Oh, I don't know. It was all a stupid misunderstanding. What made it worse was that Ben guessed why I hadn't wanted it there. It's bad luck to have a bed facing the door.' She smiled wanly. 'I'm superstitious. I can't help myself, especially moving into a new house, which is actually a gloomy old house with creaking floors and doors. I didn't dare admit that was the reason, though.'

Didn't dare? Sara felt her hackles rising. The woman was vulnerable, whether or not she thought she was. He had no right to make her feel too scared to speak.

'He said he'd move it later,' she went on. 'I said it wasn't important, but he seemed so agitated, hence the ridiculous tears. I clearly am emotional right now.'

'Which you're likely to be, which he really should be aware of.' Sara folded her arms, feeling not very impressed with Naomi's husband.

'He's stressed,' Naomi said again, making excuses for him.

Sara felt anger squirm inside her. It could have been her sitting there in floods of tears. 'Naomi.' She crouched down and took hold of her hands. '*You've* moved house too. You're pregnant. You have two demanding children to look after. You don't need his moodiness to deal with on top of everything else.'

'He doesn't mean to be.' Again, Naomi defended him.

Sara had done that, too, pretended to people that everything in her life was roses, smiled through her heartbreak. How could she put Naomi on her guard, though, without intimating she knew Naomi's husband better than she did?

She took a breath. If Naomi told her to mind her own business, so be it. At least she would have warned her. 'That's what I told myself,' she said. 'You're making excuses for him, Naomi, and you shouldn't be.'

'I'm not making excuses.' Naomi looked at her, taken aback. 'He got a bit annoyed, that was all.'

'And left you sobbing your heart out?' Sara raised her eyebrows.

Naomi dropped her gaze. 'He didn't realise how upset I was.'

'Look, Naomi' – Sara gave her hands a squeeze – 'all I'm saying is don't give in to his moods.' She took another breath. 'My ex was volatile,' she said, praying that she wasn't risking Naomi falling out with her. 'He used his moods to control me – subtly at first, and always in a way that would leave me questioning myself. I always felt as if I was walking on eggshells around him. It took years to see it wasn't me, that no matter how hard I tried to appease him, nothing changed. When I finally stood up for myself, he exploded, hence his rapid departure, assisted by the police.'

'But Ben's not controlling,' Naomi refuted with a nervous laugh. 'He would never be violent. Not ever.'

She wasn't going to acknowledge it. Sara wasn't surprised. 'Probably not.' She forced a smile. 'I just want you to be aware of how easy it is to fall into the trap. The good-looking ones are the worst, blinding you at first with their charm. I only wish someone had opened my eyes. I suppose they might have done if he hadn't isolated me from my friends, growing so jealous if I went out that I simply stopped going out in the end. I couldn't even invite anyone in for—' *Damn.* She stopped as her phone rang. It would be the salon. She'd forgotten to text them and her client had obviously arrived.

As she stood to answer it, Naomi got abruptly to her feet. 'I need to get on,' she said brusquely. 'I have to see to the children.'

'Naomi...' Telling the salon receptionist she would call back, Sara hurried after her to the hall.

'I know you mean well, Sara,' Naomi said as she headed to the front door, 'but I honestly have no idea what you're talking about. The fact is, you don't know Ben. *I* do. The idea of him being violent is absolutely ludicrous.' Pulling the front door open, she stood aside. 'I'd like you to go now please.'

ELEVEN

Sara

Sara cursed herself as she drove towards the high street. She shouldn't have said that to Naomi. It had been completely insensitive. She'd undoubtedly left her confused and probably more upset than when she'd arrived. She'd felt she'd had to say something, though. She would never forgive herself if anything happened and she hadn't alerted her to the signs. At least she would be wary now. She tried to console herself with that thought, but still she felt bad. Why had she not just paused for thought? She would have to call round again, assuming Naomi would even open the door to her. Tell her that her own experiences had coloured her thinking and that she was only worried for her because she'd been so obviously upset. Whatever her own feelings about the man, she owed Naomi an apology. She just hoped she would accept it.

Reaching the salon, she parked up behind the building and debated. She might do better to send her a quick text. If Naomi didn't reply then she would order her some flowers or a cake or something. She wanted her to know that, even if she did stop talking to her, she would be there if she should need her. She just wished she'd been able to find more online about the fate of the missing little girl. She'd hoped she might be able to put Naomi's mind at rest, but with it having happened so long ago, details were scant. With Naomi learning what she had, though, it was no wonder she felt emotionally fragile.

Sighing, Sara typed out a text.

Hi Naomi, I just wanted to say I'm sorry. I was so worried when I saw how upset you were and after what you told me, I'm afraid my own anger at being hurt at the hands of a manipulative man kicked in. I felt I had to say something, but it was wrong of me. I don't know Ben that well. I had no business interfering. Please accept my apologies and ignore me. I wouldn't blame you if you did. Take care and remember I'm here if you need anything. Anytime. Sorry. Sara. X

Hoping Naomi wouldn't ignore her, because she really was concerned for her, she hit send, then climbed out of her car and headed for the salon. Her first client this morning was probably an ex-client by now. Overall, it hadn't been a good start to the day.

'She said she'd call to reschedule,' Milly, the receptionist, said as she walked through the door. 'I told her you had a family emergency. I hope that was okay?'

Sara's heart sank. She hoped the woman would call. She was a regular, a good client. Plus, she was one of the mums who regularly chatted at the school gates. She would hate to be the topic of conversation. 'Thanks, Milly.' Sara smiled and sighed and tugged off her coat. She was hanging it up on the coat rack when she paused, surprised to see Ben passing by, heading towards the shopping centre. Hadn't he said he was late for work when she'd tried to have a word with him this morning. So what was he doing here?

Was he sending her some kind of message, she wondered? As in, I don't particularly want to speak to you and I don't want you involved in my wife's life? Well, that was just tough, wasn't it? He should know that if he chose for whatever reason not to speak to her then he'd look like an idiot. He should also know that, knowing what she did, she would be keeping a very careful eye on him.

Pulling the salon door open, she hurried out and went after him. 'Ben?' she called, stopping him in his tracks.

He took a second before turning to face her. Getting his story straight, Sara thought cynically. 'I thought you were running late for work,' she said, strolling towards him.

'I was.' He smiled – amiably, Sara noticed. What was he up to? 'I had a call. My first appointment was cancelled, so I thought I would come and order some flowers for my wife.'

Sara was about to say, 'Because you feel guilty?' but managed to stop herself. Naomi wouldn't want him knowing she'd confided in her. 'Your first appointment at your new job?' she said instead.

'That's right.' Ben nodded, his smile still affable.

'I'm surprised you managed to get another position so quickly,' Sara commented. Then she folded her arms and waited.

He narrowed his eyes, searching hers quizzically, then dropped his gaze. 'I had a seizure,' he said, his voice tight.

Sara looked him over. 'It's not a crime being ill, Ben,' she said. 'It is a crime not to inform your employees of an illness that might put a patient's future at risk, though, don't you think?'

Ben squeezed his eyes closed, and seeing he'd got her message, Sara turned away.

'Sara—' He caught her arm. 'Please don't tell Naomi,' he begged, his eyes quietly pleading as she looked back at him.

TWELVE

Naomi

Glancing at the first line of Sara's text, I was tempted to delete it. She hadn't meant to upset me, I was sure. I *had* been upset, though – considerably. I'd been flabbergasted when she'd suggested that Ben was controlling. I'd used that actual word, but did I really believe it? I knew some people were so insecure in their relationships that they tried to control the person they professed to love in some misguided attempt to keep them. But weren't people who were guilty of coercive behaviour also critical, constantly putting you down, making you doubt yourself? That wasn't Ben. He just wasn't like that. The thought of him being violent was preposterous. He was moody sometimes, but never aggressively so. I supposed I did find myself giving in to him a lot, though, as I had about what went where in the house.

It was Ben who'd insisted we move here. Had I given in to him because I was afraid of upsetting him? No, that was nonsense. I had seen that Ben wanted me to say yes, but he hadn't pressured me. He'd stood back and allowed me to make up my own mind. I was microanalysing everything now because of what Sara had said, and I didn't need to. I sympathised with her – her marriage must have been hell – but I was also angry with her. If she'd decided she didn't like Ben for whatever reason, then I doubted we could be friends, and I'd so hoped we could be.

Even so, I couldn't bring myself to ignore her text. *Might be difficult to ignore you as we're neighbours.* I hesitated, then added, *Apology accepted. No harm done. x* and pressed send. That was the adult thing to do, I felt. I truly believed Sara had meant well. She was wary, as she was bound to be, because of her own history, but she was wrong.

Determined to talk to Ben later, once the kids were in bed, to ask him outright whether there was more bothering him than he was telling me, I went upstairs to check on the children. They were still in Liam's room, as quiet as little mice, amazingly. 'Liam?' I pushed his door open to find him and Maya sitting on the bed, glued to his iPad. Smiling, I went across to them. 'Watching anything interesting?'

'*Despicable Me 3.*' Liam rolled his eyes indulgently. 'She's obsessed with Minions.'

Maya dragged her gaze away from the tablet. 'Little Buttons is getting a bit bored now though, Mummy,' she ventured, her gaze hopeful as she looked up at me.

I squeezed my eyes closed. I'd forgotten I'd promised them a trip to the park, and we were all still in our jimjams. 'Tell you what, you finish watching your film and then get dressed and we'll head off. We'll grab something to eat at McDonalds, and then we have to call at the school and have a look around. We'll go to the park afterwards. Okay?'

'Yay! Bagsy we go on the seesaw first.' Maya clutched Little Buttons excitedly.

'Roundabout,' Liam said.

'We'll toss a coin,' I suggested, before the argument got started. 'And make sure to wear the clothes I've put out for you.' I eyed Maya meaningfully, who was fond of wearing her sequin and lace party dress whenever she could get away with it, then headed off to my own room. Realising I had some time while the children were engrossed, I settled down to have a quick browse online and see if I could find anything about the missing little girl.

I soon realised that, with the internet in its infancy back then, the information available was meagre, and I searched instead for a newspaper archive site. Two articles confirmed that the little girl, aged just nine, had gone missing after cycling off on her bike. She'd disappeared on Friday, 13 June 2003. My heart folded up inside me. If she'd never ventured out that day, the unluckiest day of the year, she would still be here. *Not* silly superstition. I swallowed angrily. Would her parents have thought it was?

A hard lump clogging my throat, I looked at the photograph of the bike. A Girl Power Spice Girls bike, blue in colour with purple tassels hanging from the handlebars, at the time it had been every little girl's dream. It had been my dream, but my grandad hadn't been well off and, though I'd wished, I hadn't imagined my wishes would come true. He'd sold the pocket watch that had belonged to his father and bought me a second hand one. It had been more special to me than if it were brand new. Tears welled in my eyes as my gaze fell on a photograph of the little girl. Petite and delicate-featured, with an impish smile and mischievous chestnut-brown eyes peering through a wild tangle of dark curls, she was beautiful, so like my own innocent little girl that I felt something tear inside me. There was no mention of her being murdered. What happened to her? Ben would no doubt think I was being oversensitive – I possibly was – but I could almost feel this child's fear. Her mother's pain. Where had the woman gone when she'd left this house never to return? What had been going through her mind? Had she given up hope? Is that why she'd walked out of her life, because she simply couldn't bear the weight of her grief? Two of them missing, mother and daughter. A cold chill shuddered through me as I gazed around our bedroom, which had once belonged to the woman. Her presence seemed to permeate its walls.

Rubbing the goose pimples popping out on my arms, I looked at the bed, which was almost taunting me with its bad aura. I was halfway across to it, ready to heave it across to the other wall myself when a timely kick from Elias reminded me that it wouldn't be wise. I needed to look after myself in order to look after our children, this child growing inside me.

Closing the search, I was about to go and shower when my phone alerted me to a message. I didn't recognise the name: Nicole Jackson. The profile picture was a photograph of a baby. I didn't use Facebook or Messenger much generally, but I had posted on a group for pregnant mums recently, reassuring a woman who was worrying about her pregnancy. Thinking it might be her, I checked it. *Found this about your house. Thought you would want to see it.*

I hovered warily over the attachment, wondering whether it was safe. But it quite clearly wasn't random, or from someone who knew nothing about me. The sender knew where I lived. My skin prickling icily, I opened it, and my heart skidded to a stop. It was a newspaper article. *Father of Missing Girl Commits Suicide*, the headline blared. My breath stalling, I scanned the article.

Following a second police search at 13 Trowan Crescent, home of missing nine-year-old girl Holly Grant, police made a grisly discovery: the body of her father, Michael Grant, who was found hanged from a tree at the rear of the property. An ambulance arrived and paramedics tried to revive him but were unsuccessful. An autopsy determined that the cause of death was suspension by ligature.

My throat ran dry. He'd hung himself. Suspended himself from the heavy bough of the tree that overhung the garden shed. The same shed we'd been going to give to our little girl as a Wendy house, and which now housed the rocking chair that had once sat in what was now my little girl's bedroom.

THIRTEEN

Naomi

Keen to get off from the school before the pupils started spilling out, I checked the children had buckled up properly and climbed tiredly into the driver's side. I was so distracted by that article, and the woman who had sent it, that I wasn't being very good company, and Maya and Liam were both restless. She had to be someone who knew me, I reasoned, but there'd been nothing on her profile to tell me who she was – no photographs, no personal details. Assuming it wasn't a fake account, and I'd no way of knowing whether it was, I'd initially wondered whether she was trying to be helpful. Now I wondered whether she was spitefully trying to upset me. But why? Apart from Sara, I didn't know anyone in the area. I was glad now that I hadn't been off with Sara when she'd apologised. What she'd said about Ben had unsettled me majorly, but I was sure she wasn't the sort who would be vindictive just for kicks.

My jittery nerves hadn't been helped by the attitude of one

of the mothers in the playground as we'd left the school. I was aware it might well be me – that after my previous experience feeling isolated at my children's school, I might be a little over-sensitive – but I didn't think I'd misread the look that one woman shot me when I asked her to move her car. It had been ten minutes until school finishing time and a group of women had clearly arrived early. As I'd been crossing the playground, I saw her block me in, probably on the assumption that my car belonged to someone who was also waiting for the children to come out. 'They're keen to get to the park,' I'd explained with a smile, thinking she would understand I wanted to beat the rush. But she'd glanced between her friends, rolled her eyes and then headed off across the playground without a word.

'I think there's plenty of room for you to reverse,' I'd said, as I hurried to catch up with her.

'No problem,' she'd replied airily. 'I think you'll find the park will still be there, though,' she'd added, smiling acerbically back at me. I'd had no idea how to respond to that, so I'd just smiled faintly again and waited patiently while she'd moved it. God, sometimes I wish I could toughen up.

Burying a sigh, I started the engine, my heart heavy as I guessed I might already have blotted my copybook. 'So, do you like your new school?' I asked the children, glancing in the rear-view mirror.

'Yes,' Maya answered excitedly. I guessed she would be keen now she knew she would be in Ellie's class. 'Liam?' I looked hopefully at him.

'It's okay.' He shrugged, showing as much enthusiasm as he normally did. I supposed that would have to do. He wasn't looking sullen at the prospect of starting there, which was a huge relief. As long as the children were happy, I could deal with the odd catty mother. The thing I was struggling with most, after learning what I had about the house, was how I would ever let them out of my sight.

For goodness' sake, just stop, I willed myself. I couldn't think like this. The tragedy that had befallen that poor family had happened years ago. This was supposed to be a new chapter in our lives, a good chapter. I would make that house into a home filled with love and laughter if it killed me. I had to. We were there. We'd only just moved in. We couldn't sell up and move again. There was no way our finances would stretch to that. No way Ben would agree to it. He would think I'd gone stark raving mad if I suggested it. I had to talk to him, though. Tell him how I was feeling. I probably would go mad if I kept it all to myself. I wasn't looking forward to his reaction – he would no doubt cite my superstition as the reason I was so upset by what I'd learned – but I had to be able to talk to him about all of this, didn't I?

'Are we going to the park now, Mummy?' Maya asked as we drove off.

'We are,' I assured her. It was a lovely day, warm and bright. Some sunshine and fresh air would help chase the shadows away.

The children's play area was packed when we arrived. A chill crept through me as I gazed at the little ones running excitedly around. How easy would it be to lose sight of your child, for him or her to slip off and be taken, never to be seen again? I was growing neurotic, I knew I was, but I just couldn't seem to shake the feeling that something bad was going to happen. It was because of what Paul had said, Sara's comments about Ben and that awful article, the logical part of my brain tried to reassure me. But it wasn't, my instinct argued. I'd felt uneasy when I'd first laid eyes on that rocking chair, which had somehow ended up in the garden shed. I wasn't sure I would dare tell Ben how apprehensive I felt about it being there. I pondered that, and why it was I wouldn't dare, as I held the swing for Maya to climb onto.

'Mummy,' she said, distracting me from my troubling thoughts, 'have you thought of a name for our new baby yet?'

Shaking myself, I smiled down at her. Even on the swing, she was clutching Little Buttons close, looking up at me so earnestly I could just eat her. 'I have,' I said. 'Elias, after your great-grandad.'

Maya knitted her little forehead and whispered something to the teddy bear. Then, 'Little Buttons likes that,' she said with an assured nod.

'Good.' I laughed. She'd grown so fond of the bear, she was practically glued to it. 'Would you like me to hold him for you so you can hold on to the swing?' I asked her.

'Yes,' she decided after a second's thought. 'It's time for his nap now anyway.'

'In which case, I'll tuck him safely in my shoulder bag where he'll be nice and snug.'

She watched as I placed him carefully inside. 'Make sure he can breathe,' she said, a flash of alarm in her eyes as she strained her neck to check on him.

'Oops.' I uncovered his snout. 'Okay?' I glanced at her for approval.

'Uh-huh.' Satisfied, she settled back down. 'Can you push me, Mummy?' she asked, kicking her legs out, though she hadn't quite got the hang of pumping them yet.

'Absolutely,' I said, going behind her.

'I want to go as high as Liam,' she declared.

I watched my boy next to her, soaring high into the air. 'Possibly not quite that high, Maya. Little Buttons will worry and he won't get a wink of sleep.'

I pushed her in silent contemplation for a while, then, 'Mummy, was great-grandad really old when he died?' she asked out of the blue, causing me to catch my breath. It was a perfectly normal question for an inquisitive five-year-old to ask. Still, with my emotions on edge, it took me aback.

'Quite old,' I answered. He hadn't been, though. Sixty-nine was no age. I'd missed him terribly when he'd gone, feeling bereaved all over again after losing my mum. It was fifteen years ago now, seven years after my mum died, but I still missed him, his quiet wisdom and his twinkly-eyed smile. I was glad that Maya had asked about him. She was asking a lot about life and death lately – as in, where do people go when they die? What does heaven look like? I guessed it was something to do with me being pregnant, and the life-and-death cycle. I could only hope that she and Liam would never know about the little girl who'd lived in their house. Who'd disappeared from their house, never to be found.

'As old as that lady?' I followed Maya's gaze to see a frail-looking woman sitting on one of the benches. She wasn't young, but it was hard to determine what age she might be. She looked a little lost somehow, sitting there all alone, watching parents watching over their children. She was wearing a thick coat, I noted, despite the warm weather. It was too big for her, as if it didn't belong to her, and a bit scruffy. She had a carrier bag next her on the bench. Judging by the cardigan hanging out of it, it looked to be bulging with clothes. Did she have a family, I wondered? Anyone to watch over her?

Feeling sorry for her, I was debating whether to go across and talk to her when Liam caught my attention, leaping off his swing and setting off across the play area at a run. 'Going on the roundabout, Mum,' he shouted behind him.

Slowing Maya's swing, along with my palpitating heart, I helped her down and went after him. 'You wait for me next time, Liam,' I chastised him as I caught up. 'You know you shouldn't run off like that without asking first.'

'Sorry,' Liam said, but his expression told me he wasn't really taking me seriously, despite how many times I'd drummed the risks of stranger danger into him.

Sighing, I set Maya on the roundabout as he slowed it. I was being overprotective – I knew I was – but with anxiety churning away inside me since receiving that message, I couldn't seem to help it. 'Not too fast, Liam,' I warned him, and seeing he had got that message, I tried to relax.

A loud shout behind me soon put paid to that. 'James, hold on!' a man yelled, his voice filled with panic. It was Paul, I realised. He must have approached the swings as we'd left them. My heart thumped as I watched him race towards where Sara's boy was hanging precariously from the top of the climbing frame.

FOURTEEN

Lily

Lily sat on her usual bench, watching the activity in the playground. 'Poor Lily', some people called her, mothers catching hold of the hands of their children as they walked past her. Some seemed to know her. Some would smile tentatively. Some would scowl. She wasn't sure why. She didn't know them. Or perhaps she did and had just forgotten their faces. Lily sighed. She watched so many people come and go as she sat there, day after day, waiting for the one person she would never forget. She would come. Lily nodded to herself and buttoned up her coat. She would wait. Here on the park bench. She would know she was here. She would come.

With the warm sun on her face, she closed her eyes, lulled by the melodic sound of children at play – their chatter, laughter, sometimes tears. Her eyes drifted open as the sobs of a young boy who'd fallen from the climbing frame reached her. His father, she assumed – someone Lily was certain she'd seen before – was soon with him, assessing the damage before gathering the boy to him.

He'd left his daughter to go to him. Lily's gaze went to the little girl sitting on the swing, which had slowed with a creak, her legs dangling. Poor little mite. She watched as her thumb went to her mouth. She couldn't be much more than five years old.

Her gaze travelled back to the father. The boy had grazed his knees, and his father was inspecting his wounds – rightly so, as he might have grit in them, but he really shouldn't have left a girl so young all on her own. Seeing the girl looking tearful as she gazed after her daddy, Lily's heart went out to her, and she picked up her carrier bag and hurried across to her. 'Are you all right, little one?' she asked her.

The girl looked up, making wide eyes at Lily over her thumb.

'Oh dear.' Lily watched a tear spill down her cheek and reached a hand out to her. 'Let's take you to your daddy, shall we?'

With the little girl's hand in hers, she'd barely turned around when there was a loud shout behind her. 'Oi! What the bloody hell do you think you're doing?'

Lily was alarmed for a second, and then bewildered, as the girl's father hurtled menacingly towards her. 'Keep away from the kids, you barmy old bat,' he seethed, grasping hold of the girl's other hand and hauling her away.

He was furious, all but snarling at her, and Lily really couldn't understand why. 'She was frightened,' she tried to explain. 'I was just trying to—'

'Clear off.' The man gestured her away. 'Your sort shouldn't be allowed to hang around here. We've all seen you, ogling our kids.'

'She doesn't mean any harm.' A woman across the play area came to her defence. 'She's just sitting there.'

'But *why* is she?' the man called back, hitching his little girl up into his arms. She was crying in earnest now; so was his boy. He was upsetting them both. Couldn't he see that? 'If it were a bloke sitting there, they'd soon shift him on, wouldn't they, hey?'

Lily felt herself go hot and clammy under her coat as all eyes seemed to swivel in her direction. Her own eyes filling up, she dropped her gaze and turned around, thinking it might be best to just slip quietly off. She'd obviously done something wrong, but she wasn't sure what. She really didn't want to cause any trouble.

'And don't come back!' he shouted after her as she headed off along the path that led to the exit.

Lily kept walking, though one of her shoes was too big, flopping up and down on her foot and impeding her progress. She wasn't even sure the shoes were hers. She didn't recognise them. Had someone stolen hers in the night? People were always taking things away from her. She searched endlessly for them, but she never found them.

She'd just crossed the bridge when she heard a woman calling her name. She snapped her head up to see a lady police officer coming towards her. 'Hello, Lily,' she said. 'How are we doing?'

Someone must have called them. Lily couldn't understand why. They often turned up to move her along when she was doing no harm. She looked the woman over. She always referred to her in the plural, but she seemed nice. She had sympathetic eyes. There weren't many people Lily met who looked at her kindly.

'Come on, my lovely. Let's give you a lift in our car and get you a nice cup of tea, shall we?'

Lily brightened at that. She couldn't remember when she'd last had one.

'Shall we sort that coat out for you while we're at it?' the woman offered. 'You've got it buttoned up all wrong.'

'Bit warm for a coat, isn't it, Lily?' the male officer who'd joined her asked.

Was it? Lily glanced down as the woman set about rebuttoning it. She didn't feel warm. She hadn't felt warm in a long time.

FIFTEEN

Naomi

'Paul? What on earth...?' Reaching him across the play area, I stared at him aghast. 'She wasn't hurting anyone. She was just trying to help,' I pointed out.

When he realised it was me and that I'd obviously witnessed the whole shocking incident, Paul's face flushed with embarrassment. 'We can't know that, though, can we?' He shrugged awkwardly.

I looked him warily over, then turned my attention to James, who was probably more shocked by Paul's outburst than by the fall from the climbing frame. 'Are you okay?' I asked, crouching down to him.

'Uh-huh.' Nodding, James scrubbed away his tears with the sleeve of his sweater. 'It's only a scratch,' he said bravely. In actual fact, he'd grazed both of his knees and they looked extremely sore.

'Nothing an ice cream on the way home and a cuddle from

his mum won't fix, hey, James?' Paul lowered Ellie to her feet and draped an arm around James's shoulders.

'Can Maya come with us for ice cream?' Ellie asked tentatively.

Paul reached to take hold of her hand. 'I don't see why not.' He smiled down at her. 'As long as her mum doesn't mind?' He looked expectantly back at me.

'Can she come home and play after, Uncle Paul?' Ellie asked hopefully. 'I promised to show her my new Baby Born Magic Boy.'

Maya's eyes widened in excitement. 'Can I, Mummy?' she asked eagerly.

I hesitated. It was clear that Paul was aware he'd overreacted, but with so many things coming at me, I was feeling more emotionally jittery than ever. I wasn't sure I was ready yet to pick up any conversation about Ben and his behaviour, especially after seeing Paul being every bit as temperamental as Ben could ever be.

'*Pleeease*,' Maya wheedled. 'I promise I'll be good.'

Finding myself wavering, I glanced at my son, who was watching the goings-on with quiet interest. 'Liam?'

'Okay.' He shrugged. He didn't seem overly keen, I noticed. He and James weren't yet best buddies. My heart sank. I so wished he would make a best friend. He'd never really got close to anyone his own age.

'We could play *Candy Crush Saga*,' James suggested, looking hopeful.

Bearing in mind his injuries, I didn't have the heart to say no. 'Just for an hour or so then.' I glanced pointedly at my two. 'It's your dad's first day at his new job, and I want you all scrubbed up and ready for dinner when he comes home.'

'That's settled then.' Paul clapped his hands together. 'Can you walk okay?' he asked, looking James over in concern.

James answered with a determined nod, took a step and winced.

'Ouch.' Paul empathised. 'Tell you what, how about I give you a piggyback ride? You did take a nasty tumble there, mate. Even the bravest soldiers have to have a bit of respite when they've been injured.'

James's mouth twitched into a small smile. 'Okay.' He nodded.

Giving him a wink, Paul turned around and crouched down so that James could climb onto his back. 'Right, hold tight,' he said, straightening up. 'You guys travelling with us?' He glanced between Maya and Liam.

'No,' I intervened. 'They have to get changed,' I tacked on quickly.

'But, *Mummy*, we're going to get ice cream.' Maya gawped at me in disbelief.

I took hold of her hand. 'We'll grab some from Tesco Express on the way.'

'But it won't be the same,' Maya protested, her bottom lip protruding petulantly. Truthfully, I didn't blame her. I was being overprotective, but I couldn't help it. Ever since we'd crossed the threshold of the new house, things had felt off. I knew that Ben would be despairing of me and my tendency to 'count magpies', as he called my 'crackers' superstitions, but I couldn't help that. I couldn't change who I was and nor did I want to.

'We don't have the washing machine plumbed in yet, Maya. I don't want you making a mess of the clothes you have on,' I told her firmly. In reality, after seeing Paul's outburst just now, I wasn't comfortable letting them go in his car. 'As well as which, I think James should get home and get those injuries bathed as soon as possible. We'll get ice cream on the way, I promise, and once you're both changed, if Sara's agreeable, you can take it round to her house and share it. How does that sound?'

Maya was still wearing a scowl, but guessing there was no wiggle room, she nodded reluctantly. Liam seemed quite happy to go with the flow. He could be moody sometimes, quietly so, like his father – or at least like his father had been up until recently – but he was generally pretty easy-going.

'I could do that for you,' Paul said, hitching James higher on his back. 'Plumb your machine in, I mean. I could do it this evening, if you like.' He smiled good-naturedly, and I began to feel bad for judging him. He might have treated that woman harshly, but his motives were understandable. He'd been protecting Sara's children. 'I, um... Thanks,' I accepted appreciatively. I really did need the washing machine plumbed in, and I had no idea where to start looking for local tradespeople.

'No probs,' Paul said as we turned towards the car park. 'Why don't you come round and have a natter to Sara while the kids are there, and I'll nip around to yours and sort it before your husband gets back?' he suggested. 'It should only take ten minutes. I have all the gear in my van.'

I glanced gratefully at him. 'Are you sure? It would really be a help. Obviously, I'd be happy to pay you.'

'I wouldn't hear of it,' he said, looking offended. 'Sara would give me a load of grief if I accepted payment anyway. She's still peeved with me for putting my size tens in it when we last spoke.'

'It was just a misunderstanding.' I smiled, feeling more comfortable with him than I had moments ago.

'Even so, I should have thought before saying anything. Sorry about that.' He smiled sheepishly back at me. 'And about losing it with that batty woman just now.' He gestured behind him. 'I didn't mean to be quite so aggressive, but... Well, when I heard about what happened with that girl, you know, albeit years ago, I guess my protective gene kicked in.'

He was talking guardedly in front of the children but I got his drift. He clearly felt the same way I did.

'She's not coming back, is she, poor kid?' he went on with a sigh. 'Which means I was right about what did happen to her, but... Anyway, I'm sorry.'

I glanced sideways at him, my feelings seesawing back to flabbergasted. Was that supposed to make me feel better? It didn't. Did he not realise that I lived in that house? That *my* child very probably slept in the same room that little girl had? Holly – that had been her name. I had almost been able to hear the walls whispering it as I'd read that dreadful article. Quite clearly Paul, who certainly *didn't* think before speaking, was oblivious to the fact that insisting she was murdered would make sure I never slept comfortably in that house again.

SIXTEEN

Sara

'Hi.' Sara smiled as she pulled her front door open. 'How are you?' she asked cautiously. After her observations about Ben this morning, she was half-expecting Naomi to drop her children off and run.

'Feeling fat and frumpy.' Naomi smiled back, thank goodness. 'Apart from that, fine.'

'You don't look fat or frumpy,' Sara assured her, stepping back to let her in. 'You look pregnant and gorgeous and radiant, doesn't she, Maya?'

'Uh-huh.' Maya nodded. 'Can we have our ice cream now, Mummy?'

Naomi rolled her eyes in amusement. 'You may,' she said. 'And thank you for the gushing compliment.'

'That's okay.' Maya scooted after Ellie as she led the way to the kitchen, Liam strolling leisurely after them.

Naomi shook her head. 'How's the patient?' she asked.

'Nursing his wounds and lapping up the attention,' Sara answered. 'Thanks for bringing the kids round. That should take his mind off things for a while. I thought you wouldn't want to talk to me ever again. I'm sorry,' she tacked on quickly. 'I wasn't thinking. It was my own insecurities at play. I shouldn't have said what I did about Ben and... Anyway, I'm sorry.'

Naomi laughed as Sara shrugged apologetically. 'If you don't breathe soon, you'll implode,' she said.

Sara exhaled in relief. 'You don't hate me then?'

'Don't be daft.' Naomi looked at her in surprise. 'I didn't react very well. I'm so hypersensitive just now, what with the house move and little bump practising his gymnastics, I almost burst into tears if anyone so much as looks at me the wrong way. As well as which, Ben has been a bit of a pain. As I said, he's not usually so moody. I think we're both feeling a bit stressed out by everything.'

'So are we still friends?' Sara asked, avoiding passing comment on Ben. Her opinions, she'd decided, were best kept to herself.

'Absolutely.' With her hands full of ice cream, Naomi leaned in as Sara reached to give her a hug.

Paul emerged from the kitchen as they turned in that direction. 'They're sitting at the table with spoons at the ready.' He nodded behind him. 'Just off to plumb Naomi in,' he said, leaning to kiss Sara's cheek.

'Thanks, Paul.' Handing him her keys, Naomi smiled appreciatively.

'No problem.' Paul gave her a cheery smile back. 'It's the least I can do for a lady I've distressed. Won't be long.'

'I think he's trying to make amends,' Sara said, as he headed through the front door.

'It's working,' Naomi assured her, following her to the kitchen. 'That's one job off my ever-growing list at least. Right, you lot.' Four deceivingly angelic faces looked expectantly back at her. 'Ice cream. We have chocolate fudge brownie and unicorn vanilla. Small scoops, mind. Your mum's not going to thank me if you don't eat your dinner.'

'Unicorn vanilla!' the girls said in unison. The boys plumped for chocolate fudge brownie, and all of their dishes were cleared in a flash, Maya being keen to make the acquaintance of Ellie's new Baby Born doll and Liam and James to get to Candy Crush Saga.

'Peace at last.' Sara sighed as she cleared the dishes, then she parked a fresh bowl piled high with mixed ice cream in front of Naomi and joined her with two spoons.

'Paul's good with your two, isn't he?' Naomi said after a minute's blissful indulgence.

'He is.' Sara nodded, trailing her tongue up the back of her spoon. 'There would never have been a relationship if the kids hadn't taken to him.'

Naomi nodded. 'So, do you think you might make it official?' She eyed her interestedly.

'Get married, you mean?' Sara widened her eyes. 'I doubt it. Well, not for the foreseeable anyway. I think I'll be running scared of that kind of commitment for a good while yet. I'm not sure Paul would be ready to rush into marriage again yet either.'

Naomi nodded, understanding. 'How long's he been divorced? If you don't mind me asking?'

'I don't.' Sara smiled, gathering why she was fishing. She would be forming opinions about Paul, especially after he'd blurted out that comment about the little girl next door. 'A couple of years,' she supplied. 'Long enough for him to be lonely, he said.'

'What was she like, his ex?' Naomi asked. 'Does he talk about her much?'

'Not a great deal.' It occurred to Sara that Paul didn't often mention his ex, which was no bad thing. 'Their split was amicable, apparently. He says they just grew apart, and he doesn't slag her off or anything, which is reassuring. She lives in Spain with their little girl. Her parents are well-off.'

'Spain?' Naomi looked surprised. 'But doesn't he miss his daughter?'

'Terribly. But he said it was a no brainer when it came to making the decision to let her go. He works long hours, lives in a poky little flat. He knew she would have a much better life out there, so...'

'That's very generous of him.'

Sara noted a flicker of surprise in Naomi's eyes. She understood why there would be. She supposed not many men would be happy with their child being taken to live abroad. 'He's adamant his daughter's happiness is paramount over his,' she added, not wanting Naomi to think he simply didn't care about his daughter. 'He's one of the good guys. I reckon I could have done a lot worse.'

The kitchen door creaking open caused them both to start. 'Caught in the act,' Paul smiled. 'Thought I could hear my ears burning.'

'It was all good,' Sara promised him, getting up and going across to him.

'Glad to hear it.' Threading an arm around her waist, he eased her towards him and kissed her cheek. 'Job's done,' he said, turning to Naomi. 'There was a bit of a leak under the sink. I fixed that, too, while I was there.'

'You're an angel.' Naomi looked considerably relieved.

'If a little thoughtless sometimes.' Paul sighed in despair of himself. 'I think your old man's here, by the way. I saw his car approaching as I came down your path.'

'Didn't you stop to say hello?' Sara asked, as Naomi jumped to her feet, checking her watch.

'Needed the little boy's room.' Paul pointed a thumb towards the hall.

'I'd better get off,' Naomi said. 'Thanks so much again, Paul. Just let us know if we owe you anything.'

'It's on the house,' Paul replied. 'I'm sure your husband would do the same for us.'

Naomi didn't look too sure about that. 'Come to our barbecue then,' she said. 'I haven't actually organised it yet, but as soon as I do, I'll let you know and I'll make sure to get your favourite tipple in.'

'Invite accepted.' Paul nodded appreciatively.

'That was nice of you,' Sara said, as Naomi disappeared into the hall to round up her children.

'I'm that kind of guy.' Paul gave her a wink and Sara turned to demonstrate her own appreciation.

'See you soon, Sara,' Naomi called a second later, causing them to pull apart.

'I'll text you,' Sara called back. Then, 'Damn, she's forgotten her keys,' she said, plucking them up from where she'd left them on the table and heading out after her.

She was halfway up Naomi's path when the sound of Ben's voice from inside the open front door caused her to stop in her tracks.

'What the hell was *he* doing in the house?' he demanded, his tone furious. And this was the man Naomi refused to believe had controlling tendencies? Naomi had said Sara didn't know him, but actually, Sara felt she most definitely did. Were these seizures he claimed to have even genuine? Sara wouldn't be surprised to find they were fabricated to manipulate people's emotions.

SEVENTEEN

Naomi

I looked my husband over, staggered. 'He was plumbing the washing machine in,' I said, answering his ridiculous question with a disbelieving laugh. 'What do you *think* he was doing here?'

Ben said nothing, continuing to stare at me instead, his dark eyes drilling into mine. 'What on earth's going on, Ben?' I demanded.

'I... Nothing. I just...' He sucked in a breath. 'I don't want him here, Naomi.'

My gaze travelled from him to the flowers on the hall table. A beautiful bouquet of yellow roses, clearly chosen with care. Yet his mood was at complete odds with the thought behind that gesture. I looked him over, unnerved and troubled by a side of him I'd never seen before. This wasn't Ben. The man I knew and loved, the man who remembered that yellow roses were special to me because they were my mother's favourite, would be horrified if he realised how I felt right now. 'He's our neighbour, Ben. He was helping us out.'

My throat tight, I turned my attention to the children. 'Go and wash your hands, you two,' I said, ushering them to the stairs. 'And then you can have half an hour of TV before dinner.'

The children did as I asked, but I didn't miss Maya's confused expression as she turned for the stairs, or the reproachful glance that Liam shot his father.

'He was here on his own. You gave him the run of the place,' Ben said, as I walked to the kitchen.

Incredulous, I glanced back at him. 'I was next door,' I pointed out – unnecessarily, as I'd quite obviously just come from there. 'I met Paul in the park earlier. He offered to plumb the machine in while the kids had ice cream and I had a chat with Sara.'

'Getting quite chummy then, is he?' Ben retorted, a suspicious edge to his tone.

Really? 'Ben...' Pressing my fingers to my temples, I turned to face him as he followed me into the kitchen. 'I have no idea what's got into you, but you need to stop. *Now.* I don't need this. I already have two children, for goodness' sake.'

'Stop what?' Ben tipped his head to one side. 'Am I supposed to *not* wonder what a man we hardly know is doing on his own in our house?'

This was *unbelievable.* Anger uncoiled inside me. 'And another child on the way!' I yelled, tears springing to my eyes. 'I can't do this, Ben. I *won't.*' I placed a hand over my tummy as Elias kicked furiously. 'I have no idea what your problem is, but please don't take it out on *me.*'

'My problem is *him.*' Ben growled, waving a hand in the general direction of next door. 'The guy strolled out without even looking—'

'*Ahem.*' Someone coughed loudly from the hall. Sara, I

realised, my heart plummeting. 'The front door was open,' she said, glancing warily between us. 'You left your keys, so I thought I'd, um...'

'Thanks, Sara.' Wiping my cheeks, I walked across to her, making no eye contact with Ben.

She scanned my face worriedly as she handed me the keys. 'No problem. I wouldn't have wanted you panicking about where you'd left them on top of everything else you have to worry about. Too much stress is not good for you – or the baby.' She glanced pointedly past me to Ben. 'Is there something wrong, Ben?' she asked bluntly. 'It's just I couldn't help but overhear.'

'I... er, no,' Ben replied awkwardly.

'Paul fitted your washing machine okay then, did he?'

'Er, yes. He appears to have done. Tell him to let me have an invoice.'

'There's no charge.' Sara scrutinised him carefully. 'We're both happy to do all we can to help Naomi out. She has a lot on her plate, doesn't she?'

Sweeping a final derisory look over him, she turned back to me. 'You know where I am if you need me,' she said, leaning in to give me a hug.

I answered with a small, defeated nod. It was clear she was thinking her first estimation of Ben had been right. And why wouldn't she, when he'd just lived up to that estimation? His tone, his attitude – everything about him – portrayed a man who was controlling and thought he had every right to be. What had happened? Ben was like a different person. Or else I'd been walking around with blinkers on. Had those traits been there all along and I'd just never noticed them? I couldn't believe that.

Feeling emotionally jaded, I closed the front door behind Sara and went back to the kitchen. 'It's cold chicken and salad for dinner,' I said flatly. 'I don't feel up to doing much else, to be honest. Assuming you're not going to do one of your disappearing acts, that is?'

Ben sighed as I walked past him. 'Christ, Naomi, I'm sorry,' he murmured. 'I've had the most bloody awful day at work and... I've been an idiot, haven't I? Please believe I'm sorry.'

I took a breath, kept my back to him. I knew some of the medical imaging he did was upsetting, and I sympathised, but having a bad day was no excuse for upsetting not just me, but the children, the neighbours. I didn't respond. I was so angry I couldn't bring myself to look at him.

'I guess you don't want to hear my apologies. I can't say I blame you.' Ben's voice was despondent. 'I should get changed,' he said.

'What happened?' I stopped him as he walked to the door. 'At work?' I shouldn't care, but despite Ben's mood seeming to swing like a pendulum, I couldn't help myself.

Running a hand over his neck, Ben turned back. 'I was working with a craniofacial surgeon. The patient was a young boy with craniosynostosis,' he answered tiredly. 'The bones in his skull fused together too early,' he added, 'meaning his brain can't expand properly.'

My breath stalled. 'How old?' I twisted to face him, my mind shooting to my own children, my baby.

'Twelve months,' Ben provided, clearly upset. 'They're looking at surgery to revise the contours of his face and skull to make room for his brain to grow. The thing is, he may already have neurological problems, and he's such a plucky little thing... It broke my heart, to be honest.'

I squeezed my eyes closed, my own heart breaking for the poor child. What must he be going through? His parents. They must be utterly broken. 'I'm sorry,' I said, knowing how difficult he found it to deal with situations that involved children disfigured through injury or abnormal development.

'Me too.' He ran his fingers through his hair. 'But however

bad a day I've had, I should never have taken my frustrations out on you. When I saw that bloke coming out of the house, though...' He paused.

I studied him hard. 'There's more to this, isn't there? Something you're not telling me?'

He nodded, drew in a long breath. Exhaled slowly. Noting the reticence in his eyes as he searched mine, I felt a chill of apprehension run through me.

'Ben, tell me,' I urged him.

'A friend of mine, someone I used to work with...' He faltered. 'His wife was attacked. Some bastard assaulted her in her own home.'

My stomach lurched. 'Oh God, no. Is she all right?'

'Bruised, traumatised.' Ben looked sick to his stomach. 'Turns out it was someone they knew – a neighbour – which is why I might be a bit paranoid. I don't mean to be. I didn't know you were at Sara's. I thought you were inside and... it jolted me.'

'Oh, Ben.' My throat closed. I felt awful, petty and horribly judgemental. 'Why didn't you say something before?' I moved towards him.

'I didn't want to upset you.' He smiled disconsolately. 'But I ended up acting like a jerk instead and I upset you anyway. I really am sorry. You're right. You don't need this on top of everything else.'

I didn't, but at least I felt better for knowing what had been eating away at him. 'Paul's all right, Ben,' I said, attempting to reassure him. 'He was just helping us out.'

'I know.' Ben nodded guiltily. 'I suppose I should buy him a bottle or something, if he's not going to accept payment?'

Unable to stay angry with him, I mustered a smile. 'You can make it up by cooking for him. And the rest of the neighbours.'

Ben raised his eyebrows in surprise. 'You're thinking of holding a dinner party already?'

'A barbecue,' I said, realising I'd backed him into a corner.

He might think it was a bad idea so soon after moving in. I needed to do this, though – relax a little and shake off my own paranoia. The house had an awfully sad history, it seemed to be steeped into its walls, but it was up to us to shoo away the ghosts. 'I want to make this into a happy home, Ben. I'm determined to. Being on good terms with our neighbours is important to me. I've already mentioned it to Sara. What do you think?'

Ben eyed the ceiling. 'Looks like it's already happening.' He smiled indulgently. 'We might need an actual barbecue, though. The old one was rusty. We dumped it when we moved, remember?'

'Oh.' I frowned. 'I'd forgotten about that.'

'I'll pick one up from the DIY store tomorrow,' he offered. 'And I'll tackle the jungle out back at the weekend, assuming you're not actually thinking of this weekend?' He looked dubious. The garden needed an awful lot of work, as did the house, but if we waited for everything to be perfect it would be years before we could invite anyone round.

'Next weekend possibly, while the weather's good?' I suggested.

He nodded. 'I suppose it's as good as any.'

'Thank you.' I felt the knot of tension slacken inside me. 'Can I ask you something?' I searched his face hesitantly. 'About the house?' I'd been going to leave it, but I knew it would only eat away at me. 'Did you know about its history? How long it had been standing empty?'

He thought about it. 'I gathered it had been empty a while. The guy at the estate agency wasn't sure how long.'

I frowned, puzzled. He sounded as if he didn't know him. 'Your friend?' I checked.

'David.' Ben nodded.

'Which estate agency was it again?' I asked. In actual fact, I couldn't remember whether he'd told me in the first place.

'Dunnells.' Ben strolled to the window to look out at the garden. 'He said the details were sketchy.'

'So he didn't know about what had happened here then? The family tragedy?'

'What tragedy?' Ben turned back to me, his expression mystified.

'The little girl disappearing,' I said, then realised I hadn't actually said anything before because we'd been sidetracked arguing about nothing. 'Her mother also disappeared; apparently after her husband committed suicide,' I went on now I'd mentioned it. I needed him to see why I would be concerned about events that had happened under this very roof.

Ben didn't answer immediately, glancing down instead. His eyes were narrowed when he looked back at me, which took me by surprise. 'I take it the neighbours have been gossiping?' he said.

'No, not really,' I answered uncertainly. 'Sara mentioned something about the little girl, but only because I asked after finding the teddy bear.'

'So she thought she would share second-hand gossip with a pregnant woman who's going to be spending a lot of time here on her own and is bound to be upset by it?' Ben's look was now somewhere between incredulous and annoyed. 'That was thoughtful of her. Are you sure these are people you want to reach out to, Naomi? It strikes me that they really don't have your best interests at heart.'

EIGHTEEN

Naomi

'Got anything interesting planned for today?' Ben asked, coming into the kitchen as I prepared the children's breakfast.

I glanced at him. 'Apart from listening to neighbourhood gossip like a gullible idiot, you mean?' Aware of the children at the table behind us, I spoke quietly. Inside I was fuming. After giving Ben short shrift, I'd stewed on what he'd said about the neighbours all night, rather than get into an argument about my supposed suggestibility. That in itself had made me angry. I shouldn't be tiptoeing around Ben's feelings on subjects that were important to me, to us as a family. *Walking on eggshells.* Sara's comment about her ex came jarringly to mind.

Ben sighed apologetically. 'I'm only concerned for you, Naomi. For the kids. I'm sorry, okay? I don't know what else I can say.'

I scanned his eyes, not sure I was convinced. Did he realise I'd hardly slept, wondering what was happening to my life? To us? The howling wind hadn't helped. I'd drifted off eventually, only to be jerked awake with my heart pounding. A shiver ran through me as I heard it again, a little girl calling mournfully, *Help me. Help me.* It had been the wind whispering through the leaves on the trees, but my fevered imagination, caught between sleeping and waking, had convinced me it was the lost little girl trying to find her way home.

'I worry about you being here on your own,' he said with another despairing sigh. 'Irrationally, probably, but I know you tend to take things to heart and I don't want thoughtless gossip upsetting you, that's all.'

I blinked in astonishment. Did he honestly not realise what it was that was upsetting me? It was *him*. Precisely because he was acting irrationally.

I didn't answer, turning to busy myself with the coffee instead.

'So, do you have any plans?' Ben asked after an awkward pause.

'I thought I would have a look in the DIY store for some decorating ideas. Keep myself busy, you know, stop my mind wandering.'

He obviously missed the facetiousness in my voice. 'You're not actually thinking of decorating in your condition, are you?' he asked, surprised.

'Condition?' I looked back at him in bemusement. 'I'm not ill, Ben. A few simple jobs are not beyond me because I'm pregnant. I know my limitations, don't worry.' *I'm not stupid as well as gullible*, I didn't add, although I was sorely tempted. 'I'll have a look at some barbecues while I'm there,' I said, making sure that he knew I was going ahead with the barbecue anyway.

'I know you do. I don't mean to be so overprotective,' Ben answered sheepishly. 'Just promise me you won't try to carry anything heavy to the car. Or unload it. I'm concerned you might strain yourself. I take it I am *allowed* to concern myself about that?'

I found myself backtracking. He obviously was worrying and I was possibly overreacting. 'I won't,' I promised. 'And, yes, you are allowed to concern yourself about that. I know you worry, Ben.' I took a breath. 'However, I would just like to point out that my mind's not impaired by my "condition" either. I'm perfectly capable of doing a few things around the house *and* of realising that speculation about what happened here is not necessarily fact. I actually consider myself to be quite intelligent.'

'Right.' Ben nodded sombrely. 'I'll consider myself suitably reprimanded.'

He was trying not to smile, I noticed, eyeing him in despair. 'You're not taking me seriously, are you?'

'You better had, Dad,' Liam warned him. 'Or she'll give you the look.'

'Oh God, no, not the look.' Ben's eyes widened in feigned horror.

I twizzled to face Liam. 'What look?'

'The one that says you're in big trouble.' Liam scrunched his forehead into a scowl.

'I don't look like that. Do I?' I glanced back at Ben to find him scowling too.

'Nope,' he said. 'Not often.'

'Ignore them, Mummy,' Maya said with a world-weary sigh. 'They're just being immature.'

Ben's amused eyes swivelled to his daughter. 'You're right, we are being immature.' Laughing, he swept her up as she extended her arms to him. 'Mummy's quite capable of making her own decisions, and I'm acting like an idiot. She's also got a gorgeous face, just like you.'

Maya giggled as he planted a kiss on her nose. 'We're going to the park after Mummy goes shopping, aren't we, Mummy?'

she said excitedly as Ben lowered her back to her chair. 'Liam's going to teach me how to pump on the swings, aren't you, Liam?'

'I suppose.' Liam replied grudgingly. 'As long as you don't act like a little kid and start sulking.'

'I *don't* sulk.' Maya outmatched the boys' scowls by a mile. '*You* do.'

'Don't,' Liam retorted. 'Only girls sulk.'

'They do *not*. Boys do.'

'Don't.'

'Enough, you two,' Ben intervened. 'Finish your breakfast and then go and get dressed, or you'll be going nowhere.'

'Are you coming to the park, Daddy?' Maya asked.

'Daddy has to go to work, sweetheart,' I reminded her.

'That's right.' Ben kissed the top of her head, and then went around to give Liam's hair a ruffle. 'I'll see you two later. Be good for your mum.' He gave them his no-nonsense eyes then walked across to me. Then he hesitated. 'Am I still in the doghouse?' he asked, his expression contrite.

'I'm considering it.' I gave him my best stern look.

It clearly wasn't working. 'Don't take too long. It's getting a bit draughty in here.' His mouth twitched into a smile as he leaned in to kiss my cheek.

I couldn't help but smile back.

'Bye,' he said softly and headed for the hall. 'Oh, by the way' – he glanced back – 'did anyone ever tell you you're beautiful when your angry?'

'Be gone, Ben Felton.' I laughed.

'More so when you're not.' Ben gave Maya a wink and dodged out.

This was more the Ben I knew. The gentle, amusing man that I loved. Following him to the hall, I gave him a wave as he drove off. He was right, I decided, I was possibly taking things too much to heart. The house being so gloomy and dark didn't help. Sighing, I shoved the perpetually creaking understairs door closed. I would try to be more positive. Making a start on the decorating would help.

Still, though, I felt I needed to find out as much as I could about the history of the house. Maybe then I could put things into perspective and put my worries to rest. Picking up my phone from the hall table I googled Dunnells Estate Agents and rang them.

Maya poked her head around the kitchen door as I waited for them to pick up. 'Are we going soon, Mummy?' she asked.

'Half an hour,' I mouthed as someone answered. 'Hi,' I said into my phone. 'It's Naomi Felton here. We purchased 13 Trowan Crescent a short while back and I just wondered if you had anything on file about the history of the house, since it was empty for so long before we bought it.'

There was a brief silence, then, 'Trowan Crescent,' the woman answered, sounding mystified. 'I don't recall us having a property in that location up for sale.'

I frowned, an immediate sense of panic rising inside me. 'Are you sure?' I asked. 'I mean, could you double-check? I think David was the agent.'

More silence.

My panic quadrupled. 'You do have a David working there, don't you?'

'David Hemmings, yes,' she said. 'I would usually have the information on file, though.' She sounded more puzzled by the second. 'He's not here at the moment, but I'll check with him when he comes in. Would you like me to get him to call you back?'

I took a breath. 'Please,' I said, leaving my number and ending the call. She was obviously confused, or else not doing her job properly. Nodding to myself, I dismissed the sense of unease that had crept through me.

NINETEEN

Naomi

After mooching around the DIY store and then Dunelm, where I spotted some gorgeous white floral-print wallpaper, we finally arrived at the park. The kids scrambled out of the back of the car almost before I'd released the locks. 'Wait!' I called as they both bolted off across the car park, too focused on getting to the play area to check for moving cars.

Clearly hearing the urgency in my voice, they ground to a halt, thank God. Another fraction of a second and it might have been too late.

My chest hammering, I hurried to the reversing car, full of apologies. My heart dropped like a stone as I recognised the driver. It was the woman from the school who'd made the catty comment when I'd asked her to move her car.

'What were you thinking, letting them charge across the car park like that?' she fumed, her face puce with anger.

'I'm sorry,' I stammered. 'They ran off before I could grab

hold of them.'

'You might do well to instil some basic road sense into them,' she muttered.

I felt my hackles rise. It was me in the wrong, my children – who knew better – but was there any need for her to be so absolutely horrible? 'They were just...' *Excited*, I'd been about to say, when she tore her gaze away from me and raised her window.

Cow. I stared after her as she completed her manoeuvre, swinging the car around and driving off.

'Sorry,' Liam said as I turned to him, his gaze sinking to the ground.

'Sorry, Mummy.' Maya blinked sheepishly up at me. 'We forgot to look.'

I took a breath and tried for some level of calmness. 'Okay.' I nodded. They'd learned their lesson, I was pretty sure of that. It was a pity someone didn't teach that woman a lesson in manners. 'Just make sure you *do* stop and look next time you're anywhere near a road *or* a car park. Even cars travelling slowly can hurt you if the driver doesn't see you in time.'

'We will,' the kids said in unison, both of them now looking at me guiltily, which made me feel guilty.

'Come on,' I said, taking hold of Maya's hand and draping an arm around my boy's shoulders. 'You can help me get your bikes out of the back of the car, and once we're in the park you can run off as much steam as you like.'

I had no doubt that the woman would 'share' with her friends. I wasn't sure how I would cope with *that* inevitable gossip. By ignoring it, I supposed. Though I guessed that I would be the one who was pointedly ignored by that particular group. I would just have to live with it. Again. My heart dropped another inch.

Deciding I would do better to face that bridge when I got to it on Monday, rather than dwell on it, I checked my phone as I followed the children towards the play area. There was no missed call from the estate agent. I felt a flicker of irritation, mostly with myself. Ben had said Dunnells, hadn't he? There was a Connells on the High Street. Might I have misheard? Despairing of myself for being so perpetually distracted, I was about to ring again, and then try Connells if I got no sense, when I noticed the woman Paul had been awful to. She was sitting on a bench next to the one where the children had skidded to a halt. Did she come here every day? I guessed she might, that this was her way of passing the time. My heart broke for her. She looked so sad and lonely sitting there. Did she have no family to look out for her?

My mind went to my mum, who would have been a similar age. I would give anything to have her here – someone who would understand that the tragedy surrounding the house had brought home how vulnerable my own children were. I was superstitious, Ben was right about that, but could he really blame me for worrying and wanting to know more? Despite his apologies, I felt he did blame me, and that he'd shut me down by concerning himself with my welfare and what gossip I might be influenced by.

'Hold Maya's hand, Liam,' I called, reaching the bench as the children parked their bikes and raced off. 'And be careful approaching the swings.'

'We will.' Liam waved behind him. I held my breath as I watched them, but forced myself to give them some space. Seeing him help his sister onto a swing, grab the one next to her and show her how to pump her legs without going too fast, I felt proud of him. He wasn't always easy, but I could see he was really trying.

'They're full of energy.' I smiled towards the woman. 'I'm hoping they'll wear themselves out before teatime.'

She was looking at me, but she didn't answer. It was almost as if she were looking right through me. She didn't seem quite with it, poor thing.

'I'm Naomi,' I said, going to sit next to her. 'Pleased to meet you.'

The woman studied me intently, then gazed towards the children. 'How old is she?' she asked. 'The little one?'

'Maya?' I followed her gaze. 'Five,' I replied. 'Liam's nine. I love them to bits but they can be a real handful sometimes.'

She glanced at me again, her eyes filled with confusion. 'But that's too young,' she said.

Unsure of what she meant, I didn't know how to answer. 'To be on the swings, do you mean? She's quite sensible.'

'Her bicycle's the wrong colour.' The woman's gaze travelled to the bikes.

Confounded, I watched as she leaned forward, a hand fluttering to her chest and her expression almost bewildered. I was upsetting her. She was clearly distressed. I got to my feet. 'Do you have anyone I can call for you?' I asked, growing worried for her. 'Someone who could come and collect you?'

The woman said nothing, but she fixed her gaze back on Maya. Might Paul have been right? Might she be a danger – to herself or inadvertently to the children? Reluctant though I was to leave her, I turned away, going across to Maya and Liam.

'I can do it, Mummy. Look!' Maya cried, delighted, as she kicked her little legs out.

'Brilliant.' I smiled distractedly and went around behind her where I could keep an eye on the woman.

She didn't move. Sitting transfixed, she continued to watch Maya the whole time we were there. She watched her on the roundabout, her eyes flicking intermittently to Liam. She watched her on the seesaw and the climbing frame.

Her gaze was still locked on her as we walked back to collect the bikes.

Liam mounted up and cycled off ahead of us. Maya was cycling after him when the woman reached a frail hand out after her. 'My baby,' she whispered. 'I knew she would come.'

TWENTY

Sara

'You're a bit keen, aren't you?' Sara called, spotting Naomi as she approached the school gates. As her last client this afternoon had cancelled, Sara had come early to bag a parking spot. She hadn't expected to find many other mums here yet. She was pleased to find Naomi here though. She hadn't had chance to say more than a passing hello since last week.

Naomi had obviously been miles away, and she almost jumped out of her skin. 'Sorry, I didn't mean to startle you.' Sara leaned in to give her a quick hug. 'Paul said I frightened him to death the other day. He was going through some paperwork and didn't see me come into the kitchen. I'm obviously quite scary.'

'You're not,' Naomi assured her. 'I was deep in thought about the lounge. The colour scheme in there is hideous, and I'm keen to start decorating. You know, make the house our own.'

Sara couldn't blame her for that. She would feel the same

knowing what Naomi now did. 'I get it,' she said. 'Just don't overdo it. Give me a shout if you need a hand with anything. Paul's at home, too, in between jobs. You can always borrow him. As long as you promise to give him back.'

Naomi smiled, though she still looked distracted, Sara thought, and more than a little troubled. 'Can I ask you something?' she said, her eyes flicking to Sara and away again. 'That woman...'

Sara followed her gaze across the road to see a woman standing there, a carrier bag clutched in front of her and a fretful look on her face.

'Do you know her?' Naomi asked.

Sara looked back at her. 'No,' she said, concerned as she noted Naomi's worried expression. 'Why?'

'No reason,' Naomi said. 'I've seen her around a couple of times and I just wondered. She seems a bit confused. I can't help but feel for her.'

'She might be suffering from early onset dementia,' Sara suggested, sighing sympathetically. 'I worry about Joan lately. Dementia is so awful – memories slipping away from you like sand through a timer. My grandad had it. I wouldn't wish it on anyone.'

'I think she must be.' Naomi looked back at the woman. 'She sits on a bench in the park. It's almost as if she's waiting for someone. Did Paul mention it? He had a bit of a run-in with her.'

'Paul?' Sara frowned. 'No.' She glanced towards the school as the bell rang. 'I can't imagine Paul having a run-in with anyone, let alone a defenceless woman. What on earth was it all about?'

'She approached Ellie when Paul dashed off to help James after he fell from the climbing frame,' Naomi supplied. 'I think he was a bit fraught, that was all, worrying that he'd turned his back on Ellie,' she added quickly.

Sara was dumbfounded. 'Had she done anything? Other than approach her, I mean?'

'She took hold of her hand.' Naomi glanced at her worriedly. 'I think she was only trying to help. She looked as if she was going to take her across to Paul, but I can see why he would have lost it. You can never be too careful, can—'

'Lost it?' Sara interrupted, stunned. 'I've never known Paul lose his temper. Not once.'

Naomi glanced awkwardly down. 'I probably shouldn't have mentioned it, but seeing her here, I wondered if there might be more to it. I'm obviously reading too much into things. Ignore me.'

It was pretty hard to ignore. Sara studied her for a second. She was about to ask her to explain how he was supposed to have lost it, exactly, when she was distracted by a tug on her arm.

'Can Maya come to tea, Mummy?' Ellie asked breathlessly, having run across the playground, Maya close behind her. 'We want to teach my new Baby Born doll to pump on the swing, don't we, Maya?'

Still trying to get her head around what Naomi had just said, Sara took a second to answer. Then, 'Not tonight, darling,' she said, her emotions churning.

'*Please.*' Ellie clearly wasn't going to take no for an answer. 'Maya said she wanted to, if her mummy said it was okay.' She looked pleadingly at Naomi.

Naomi shifted awkwardly, as if she didn't quite know where to look, as Sara answered sharply, '*No*, Ellie. We're going to see Auntie Jenny tonight, remember? Maya can come another day.'

She shouldn't have been snappy, but she was shocked by what Naomi had told her. Paul had mentioned nothing of this. She needed to speak to him. 'See you soon,' she said, not quite meeting Naomi's gaze as she walked away.

Scanning the playground for James, she spotted him with

two of his friends and went across to fetch him. Liam was also there, she noticed, standing off from the other boys.

She didn't like herself much for thinking it, but Sara wondered whether Naomi might have been exaggerating things. Because of her comments about Ben, possibly? But Naomi wasn't like that – bitter and spiteful. She was sure she wasn't. It just didn't make sense.

She glanced in Naomi's direction as she headed for the gates, and felt awful as she watched her trail across the playground, her children's hands in hers, her head bowed and looking utterly alone. She would have to go round and talk to her, once Paul had given his side of the story. She couldn't leave things like this.

Sighing, she walked to the gates after her, then stopped as one of the other mums called out. 'Sara, hi.' She waved and hurried across to her. 'Is that your new neighbour?' she asked, nodding towards Naomi, who was disappearing through the gates.

'That's right.' Sara girded herself for the inevitable grilling. Katie was always desperate for any gossip, which she would then take great pleasure in sharing with the clique of mothers she'd been standing with.

'Is she all there, do you think?' the woman asked, causing Sara's mouth to drop open.

She looked at her askance. 'What do you mean, *all there*?' she asked irritably.

Katie shrugged. 'She seems distracted. You know, not very with it. I almost reversed over her children charging through the park car park last week. You'd think she would keep a closer eye on them, wouldn't you?'

Sara seriously felt like poking her spiteful eyes out. 'She's probably exhausted – being pregnant with two little ones and a house to sort out,' she suggested.

'Of course. She would be.' Katie's face creased sympathetically. 'So, what's she like?' she asked, changing tack – clearly eager for any snippet Sara might provide.

'Nice,' Sara said simply.

Katie actually looked disappointed. 'She's a bit standoffish, though, isn't she?' she said, her brow furrowing, her eyes fishing. 'We thought she might come across and introduce herself.'

'She's a bit shy.' Sara smiled through gritted teeth. 'Plus, she wasn't feeling very well today. She's obviously keen to get back home.'

'Oh.' Katie pondered that. 'Poor thing.'

'I'd better go,' Sara said. 'I'm due at my aunt's. She's making tea. Better not keep her waiting. See you tomorrow.'

'Will do.' Katie seemed happy with that, and Sara exhaled in relief as the woman about-faced back to her friends.

Hurrying on, she paused outside the playground. The odd woman was still standing there – staring after Naomi, she realised. There was something not right, Sara could feel it. Why *was* she hanging about outside the school? At the park? Might there be some truth in what Naomi had said. It was possible that Paul might have reacted, possibly overreacted, if he suspected her of waiting around for an opportunity to approach children.

TWENTY-ONE

Sara

Seeing Paul's van parked outside the house, Sara was hugely relieved. 'Hi,' she called, coming through the front door. 'Go and get changed, you two,' she urged Ellie and Liam, shooing them towards the stairs. 'I'm just going to grab us all a drink and a snack and then we'll get off.'

'Hey, how's things?' Paul looked up from his phone as she came into the kitchen.

'Good. How's your day been?' Tugging off her jacket, Sara draped it over a chair and went to put the kettle on.

'Busy,' Paul answered. 'Not that I'm complaining. I've got another job to go to, but I thought I'd drop by and see how my favourite girlfriend was doing.'

Sara smiled as he came across to her. See, this was what Paul was like, good-humoured and laid-back. If he had 'lost it', as Naomi claimed he had, there had to be a good reason.

'She's doing fine, thank you,' she said, turning her cheek to his kiss. 'My last client cancelled, and I thought I'd pop over to see my aunt.'

'Good idea.' Paul nodded. 'Do you want me to get dinner? I should only be an hour or so, just got to replace a leaky radiator valve for a customer. Unless you're eating at your aunt's? In which case I will console myself with takeaway and try not to feel abandoned.'

There he went again with the jokes. Sara suspected he would actually relish being abandoned, so he could settle down for an indulgent evening watching the rugby he'd recorded. Smiling, she glanced over her shoulder to tell him so and was surprised to see him gazing pensively down.

'You don't really think I'm abandoning you, do you?' she asked, a prickle of alarm running through her. Her ex had started out like this, making her feel guilty about going out, so subtly at first that she hardly noticed, and then little by little turning the screw, growing so insanely jealous towards the end that she was sure he would have done anything to stop her going. He'd locked all the doors and taken her keys once. A shudder ran through her as she recalled the steely hostility in his eyes. She hadn't realised how terrified she'd been until he'd gone and she'd learned how to breathe again.

'What?' Paul looked quickly up.

'You look a bit fed up.' She looked over at him worriedly. 'You don't have a problem with me going off at short notice, do you?'

'No. God, no.' He laughed. 'Don't be daft. You don't have to ask my permission to go out. I was distracted, that's all. I just remembered I forgot to call someone back.'

Sara felt the tension leave her body. She had to stop this. Naomi's edginess – which was understandable, since she lived with a man who clearly liked things his own way – was making *her* feel edgy. She'd never felt that around Paul before. 'Jenny said she'll make the kids' tea,' she said, answering his question about dinner. 'I rang her on the way, but if you fancy Indian you could get me a chicken korma. I'll eat with you later, if that's okay with you?'

'Perfect.' Paul smiled, looking pleased. 'I'll grab us a nice wine while I'm out.'

He was perfect. She marvelled at his readiness to fit in with her. He'd done nothing to make her doubt him. She needed to remind herself of that and stop looking for reasons to. 'I saw Naomi at the school,' she said, going to the hall to hurry Ellie and Liam up.

'She okay?' Paul asked, handing Sara her tea as she came back in. 'It was Maya and Liam's first day, wasn't it? I'm guessing she was nervous about leaving them.'

'She told me about the incident in the park,' she went on, opening the way for him to share his version of events. 'Something to do with a woman approaching Ellie,' she reminded him when he looked blank.

'Oh right.' Paul nodded and turned away to top up his tea with milk. 'It was something and nothing. How come she mentioned it?' He glanced curiously back at her.

'The woman was at the school for some reason. Well, standing across the road from it.' Sara went back to the hall. 'Come on, you two. Auntie Jenny's cooking tea for you, remember?'

'Are you talking about the same woman?' Paul asked as she came back, his forehead creased in confusion. 'In her late sixties? Looks like a bag lady?'

'Yes, so Naomi said. I think she was a bit spooked, wondering what she was doing there. So was I, to be honest.'

Paul studied her intently, his expression one of disbelief, and then something behind his eyes shifted, growing disconcertingly dark. 'What the *fuck* was she doing outside the school?' he spat, taking her completely aback. 'Silly, stupid old—'

'Paul!' Her stomach lurching, Sara stopped him as the children came charging into the kitchen.

TWENTY-TWO

Naomi

'Mummy, I can't find Little Buttons.' Maya came dejectedly into the kitchen as I was gazing into the fridge, looking for inspiration for tea.

'Did you take him to school?' I eyed my little girl suspiciously, suspecting she might have snuck him in in her bag.

'No.' Maya shook her head. 'He was tired so I tucked him in bed, and now he's not there.'

Oh no. Seeing tears spill down her cheeks, my heart squeezed. She loved that bear. She carried him practically everywhere. 'Have you checked deep down in the bed,' I asked, hurrying across to her.

'Yes.' Maya said tremulously. 'And under it and down the side of it. I even looked in the wardrobe and the drawers and the bathroom and the lounge. He's not *there*.' She gulped back a breath and rubbed her eyes with her fingers. 'He's not anywhere, Mummy.'

'Oh, sweetheart.' Crouching down, I hugged her close as a sob shook through her little body. 'Come on. I'll come up with you and we'll look together, shall we?'

Maya hesitated. Then, 'Liam's taken him,' she said, her voice small, her bottom lip quivering. 'Tell him to give him back, Mummy.'

I hugged her closer. 'I don't think he has, Maya, but I'll ask him. Okay?' Liam could be insensitive, not because he meant to be, but simply because he didn't quite get things sometimes, but he wouldn't see his sister so upset.

After wiping her tears and helping her blow her nose, I led her upstairs to her bedroom and was bemused to find my son belly down on the floor, his legs protruding from under Maya's bed. Assuming he was hunting for Little Buttons, I went across to him. 'Any signs?' I asked.

'Nah,' was Liam's muffled response as he shuffled out. 'I thought she might have been scared of meeting a spider and not looked properly, but he's not there.'

Noting his reference to Little Buttons as 'he', I couldn't resist an urge to give him a hug too as he got to his feet. 'Thank you for checking.' I smiled.

'It's okay.' Liam shrugged embarrassedly. 'I just wanted to stop her crying.' The last was said with a despairing eye roll, but I guessed it was Liam working on his macho image. 'I'll go and have another look downstairs,' he offered, turning towards the door.

He paused as he reached Maya and I gazed in surprise as he threaded an arm awkwardly around her shoulders. 'Don't worry, we'll find him,' he said, his voice gruff.

Maya glanced at him, her eyes flecked with a mixture of uncertainty and wonder. She didn't entirely trust her brother, who did tend to endlessly taunt her, but I could see she was giving him the benefit of the doubt. I eyed them both in wonder.

After going through the entire house with a fine-tooth comb

and trying to cheer Maya up with her favourite unicorn vanilla ice cream after tea, I finally persuaded her to bed, tucking her up with Alex the Donkey, her favourite snuggle toy before Little Buttons had come along. Where on earth was he? We'd searched everywhere I could think of.

Taking my time over her bedtime story, I stayed with Maya until she'd drifted off, then tiptoed to the door and went to check on Liam.

'Is she okay?' he asked, still wide awake and reading on his Kindle. I decided to leave him be. After all the excitement, he obviously wasn't tired and it wouldn't hurt him to have an extra five minutes.

'Sleeping,' I said. 'Still upset.'

Liam nodded, his forehead creased in concern. 'I was thinking we should maybe buy her a new teddy, but it won't be the same, will it?'

I smiled in pleasant surprise. I'd been worried about what I perceived to be my boy's inability to connect emotionally. I'd been judging him, I realised. He wasn't insensitive; he just had difficulty showing his feelings sometimes. 'You're right, it won't be.' I went across and kissed the top of his head – whether he liked it or not. 'But we will go shopping and buy her something to cheer her up. You too, for being such a caring young man. Well done. I'm proud of you.'

With little Elias kicking energetically under my ribs, I went wearily downstairs to meet Ben coming through the front door. 'Sorry I'm a bit late,' he said, parking his briefcase and coming across to me with a huge carrier bag in his hands. 'I detoured to the shopping centre to pick up something I'd ordered for the kids.'

Kissing my cheek, he handed me the bag with a huge smile on his face. 'They've had a lot to deal with – moving house, starting a new school – and I thought they deserved a reward for being so good.'

Pulling the handles open, I peered into the bag and then looked back at him in astonishment. I couldn't quite believe it as I fetched out the most beautiful reborn baby doll, underneath which was the Marvel Avengers Lego set Liam had coveted when we'd last visited the shopping centre. Either this was a miraculous coincidence or my husband was psychic. 'How did you know?' I asked, staring at him now in wonder.

Ben frowned, confused. 'Know what?'

'Maya lost Little Buttons. I almost rang you to ask if you'd seen him. We've turned the whole house upside down looking for him. I'd already decided to take the children to the shops and buy them something straight after school tomorrow.'

'Oh hell.' Ben sighed and rubbed his forehead. 'Should I go up and see her?' His gaze travelled worriedly to the stairs.

I shook my head. 'No, she's asleep. She's been really upset, though.'

'She's bound to be,' Ben conceded. 'But she'll get over it now she has something else to pour her love into.' He smiled reassuringly. 'It was a bit of a moth-eaten, bedraggled old thing, after all.'

I resisted saying anything. He clearly didn't understand that she loved Little Buttons precisely because he was moth-eaten and bedraggled and needed someone to love him. I was sure she would love the doll, too, but I wasn't so sure she would easily get over the loss of Little Buttons.

'So how did school go?' Ben asked.

'Okay,' I said, following him as he headed for the kitchen. 'They both like their teachers, and Maya's made friends with some of Ellie's little friends.' I decided not to say that Liam hadn't mentioned any friends, or that I seemed to have already made an enemy. I had at least one friend in Sara, though. At least I hoped I did. She'd been a bit off with me when I'd mentioned Paul's run-in with the woman from the park. Thinking of whom... 'That strange woman was there,' I said, heading for the cooker to fetch out the casserole I'd been keeping warm. 'Standing opposite the school.'

Ben stopped in his tracks halfway across the kitchen. 'What woman?'

I hadn't told him about her, I realised, immediately remembering why: because Ben being so disproportionally angry about Paul being in our house had thrown me. 'I saw her in the park. A couple of times, actually. Paul saw her, too,' I went on, keeping my voice casual, since he seemed to have a problem with Paul. 'He was wary of her for some reason.'

Ben looked away. 'Was he?' he said, heading for the red wine on the work surface. 'Did he say why?' He poured himself a large glass, drank it back, then waggled a glass in my direction.

'No, thanks.' I shook my head and indicated my bump, reminding him I was abstaining. 'She sits on a bench, watching the children playing,' I continued as I went to fetch the cutlery from the drawer. 'I must admit I was a bit spooked when I saw her outside the school.'

Ben poured himself more wine, taking another large swig, which surprised me. He never normally drank much before dinner. 'Sorry, long day,' he said, finishing off that glass too. 'She's probably harmless.'

'That's what I thought.' I nodded in agreement. 'I still found it a bit disturbing, though. She seemed so lost and lonely.'

'You can't adopt her, Naomi,' Ben said, walking across to the cooker. 'You take these things too much to— *Damn!*' He stopped, cursing sharply, and dropped the casserole lid with a clang.

Oh no. Surely he must have realised it was red-hot. 'Are you all right?' I hurried across to him as he headed for the sink to run cold water over his hand.

'It's not too bad. I'll live,' he said, glancing in my direction.

I tried to leave it, I really did, but the spilled salt from the cellar Ben had knocked over was too much of a bad omen to ignore. Taking a quick step towards it, I pinched some up and threw it over my left shoulder.

'Naomi, Naomi,' Ben sighed, 'you really are jumpy, aren't you? Is meeting strange ladies bad luck or something?'

'I'm not jumpy,' I protested. 'It's nothing to do with that. It is bad luck to—'

'Spill salt,' Ben cut in. 'I know.' He smiled indulgently. 'I also realise why you don't want the bed where it is, so if it makes you feel better about all these supposedly bad things happening, I'll move it. Okay?'

Reassured that he cared, even though I knew I must seem neurotic sometimes, I felt a surge of relief. 'Thank you.'

'No problem,' he assured me, tugging off his tie as he headed back towards the hall. 'Thanks for keeping dinner for me. I'll just get out of my work clothes. Won't be a sec.'

Ten minutes later, wondering what was keeping him, I followed him up, hoping he hadn't got it into his head to move the bed now. I was taken aback when I found him standing at the side of the bed, hands in pockets, head down and seemingly lost in his thoughts. 'Ben?'

He didn't seem to hear me. 'Ben? Are you okay?' I asked, causing him to jolt.

Drawing in a breath, he nodded and glanced at me. 'Ben, what is it?' Shaken, as I noticed a faraway, almost haunted look in his eyes, I placed a hand on his arm.

'Nothing.' He shrugged and glanced away again. 'I was just thinking about my childhood.' Hearing the tightness in his voice, I felt my stomach twist with apprehension. He rarely talked about his childhood. *It's in the past. I prefer to look forward, not back*, he'd once said.

'And?' I prompted him.

'That's where I was. Under the bed.' He nodded towards it. 'Not here, not this bed, obviously, but that's where the police found me. They took me into care. I never felt safe anywhere after that.'

'Oh, Ben.' My heart fractured for him. He'd only ever said that he'd grown up in care, that it wasn't the greatest experience but that it was okay. When pressed, he would never say more. 'What happened to your parents?' I asked carefully, wondering what awful thing might have caused him to be taken from them.

'My parents are dead,' he said, and turned abruptly away.

TWENTY-THREE

Sara

'I checked your tyre pressure while I was doing mine,' Paul said, poking his head around the kitchen door. 'The driver's side was down so I pumped it up.'

'Thanks.' Sara glanced up from the culinary masterpiece she was attempting to create, smiling gratefully. She'd been meaning to check them but hadn't managed to find the time. Paul was definitely handy to have around.

'No probs,' he assured her. 'I'll go out and grab some wine and a few beers, shall I? Assuming the barbecue's still on this afternoon?'

'It is.' Thank goodness, Sara thought. After establishing that Paul had indeed 'lost it' with the odd woman who hung about around children, she'd gone straight next door to apologise to Naomi for being so off with her. Paul hadn't told her because he hadn't wanted to worry her, apparently, which Sara could understand. Still, though, she wished he'd said something. He'd been furious when she'd mentioned the woman had been outside the school. It was obvious he felt she might be a threat.

'I'll get off then. I won't be long,' Paul said, and headed for the front door.

'Could you get some Diet Coke for the kids?' she called after him. 'Naomi will probably have some, but just in case.'

'Will do,' Paul answered cheerily.

Once he'd gone, she turned her attention back to her recipe. Not being a master chef, or indeed having any aspirations to be, she'd chosen to make a poached salmon as her contribution to the barbecue because she'd thought it would be easy. Big mistake. There'd been lemons to grate and slice, fresh herbs to prepare. It was supposed to be topped with a salsa verde. She'd had no idea what to do with the capers so had left those out. The sauce looked okay, though. Ish. Eyeing it thoughtfully, she arranged a few slices of lemon artistically around the salmon and stood back to survey it. It wasn't too bad, even if she did say so herself. She might as well pop it next door now, she decided, guessing Naomi would want to organise her buffet table before the guests arrived.

Neatly avoiding Joan's cat as it mewled hungrily and zigzagged between her feet, she headed up Naomi's path and found the front door ajar. 'Hello?' she called. 'Only me.'

She was about to give it a nudge when it was yanked open from inside, almost giving her heart failure and the cat an early supper. 'Hi.' Ben wiped an arm across his brow and smiled affably, which threw her. 'Excuse my appearance. I'm trying to put the new garden furniture together. I think it might have been easier to build it from scratch.'

Sara eyed him curiously. 'You'll get full marks for effort,' she said.

Ben took a breath. 'I hope so. I need all the points I can get.'

Sara nodded. He was acknowledging how badly he was treating his wife then? Had he told Naomi about the situation he'd had at work, she wondered? As Naomi hadn't mentioned it, she thought not.

'Can we make an effort to get on, do you think?' Ben asked, glancing over his shoulder. 'For Naomi's sake.'

Sara shook her head cynically. So that was what the sudden friendliness was all about. 'I always make an effort to get on with people,' she assured him. 'And I wouldn't dream of doing anything to upset Naomi. Unlike some.'

Ben didn't say anything, though she could see from the flicker of frustration in his eyes that he wanted to. 'I'll take this through, shall I?' she offered. 'It's my contribution to the buffet table.'

She could feel his eyes on her as she walked past him towards the kitchen. 'Sara...' he said behind her, his voice edged with despair. 'Look, we clearly need to—' He stopped as Naomi came down the stairs.

Hoping she hadn't heard their exchange, Sara arranged her face into a smile. 'Wow,' she said, looking Naomi over as she reached the hall. 'Love the outfit.'

She was wearing a gorgeous boho-print dress and she looked fabulous, definitely radiant. 'Really?' Naomi glanced down, smoothing a hand self-consciously over her bump. She clearly didn't realise how good she looked. 'I wasn't sure. What do you think, Ben?'

'It's nice,' he said, joining them. Sara noticed, though, that his smile wasn't overly effusive.

Naomi obviously also noted his lack of enthusiasm. 'You don't like it, do you?' she asked, disappointment flitting across her face.

'I do,' Ben insisted. 'You look terrific. You always look terrific. It's just...'

'What?' Naomi now looked extremely self-conscious and Sara had to force herself not to comment. *Don't ask for his validation*, she felt like yelling. *Wear what you feel comfortable in.*

'I thought you might wear the dress I bought you for your birthday, that's all,' Ben said with a shrug. 'It doesn't matter, though. That dress looks great.'

Oh, nice move. That was the way to do it. Guilt her into wearing what you want her to wear. Sara wasn't wrong about him. She had no way to communicate that to Naomi without ruining her day and possibly her life, but she *knew* from experience she wasn't.

TWENTY-FOUR

Sara

Arriving at the barbecue with Paul and the children to find Naomi had changed her outfit, Sara was positive her estimation of Ben Felton was spot on. He looked like butter wouldn't melt, but under the surface – behind the congenial smile he flashed as he walked around the garden topping up glasses – he wasn't who he appeared to be, and her stomach knotted with apprehension for Naomi. She was vulnerable, not because she was female or because she was pregnant, but because she couldn't see what he was like. Sara was watching him, though. There was nothing she could do unless Naomi asked for her help, but she would be there for her if his façade slipped, and it would. In Sara's experience, it always did.

Naomi waved as she saw them and hurried across.

'I see you got changed.' Sara feigned surprise. She was intrigued to hear Naomi's explanation.

Naomi looked slightly embarrassed. 'I felt guilty,' she said outright – and Sara's mouth almost dropped open. 'My birthday was the week before the move and with everything going on I forgot Ben had bought me this dress. He made a special effort because I was pregnant and I didn't want him thinking I didn't appreciate it.' She smiled in Ben's direction and he smiled back. 'What do you think?'

Sara ran her gaze over the dress. It was okay, a simple loose black midi, but truthfully it was more evening than daywear. 'It's nice,' she said, 'but isn't it a bit...' She searched for the right word.

'Black,' Naomi finished, rolling her eyes amusedly. 'I know. He thought it would be more slimming.'

Sara was now utterly gobsmacked. Did she not realise what she was saying? Did she actually think she should be body-conscious – at all, let alone when she was *pregnant*?

'You look gorgeous. Like the hair,' Paul intervened, leaning in to kiss Naomi's cheek as Sara attempted to compose the emotions that were churning like a washing machine inside her.

'Ben says he likes it up.' Naomi smiled, and Sara thought if she didn't say something soon, she might self-combust.

'I do,' Ben confirmed, appearing next to Naomi and threading an arm around her. Sara couldn't help but feel he was staking his territory. 'But I love your hair however you wear it.'

There he went, reinforcing his desires as to how his wife should look – and no doubt how she should think and feel – and then making her believe that it was her choice. The man was a smooth operator. Sara's blood boiled.

'Hi, Sara.' Ben turned to her with a smile and gave her a quick kiss on the cheek. Sara felt like moving away but she could hardly do that without making it obvious.

'Paul.' Nodding in his direction, he extended a hand. 'Pleased to make your acquaintance,' he said. 'Finally.'

The 'finally' was a bit loaded, Sara noted.

Paul obviously did too. He gave him a tight smile back. 'I

hadn't realised you were that keen,' he said, holding Ben's gaze as he shook his hand. 'We should go for a pint one night. Get to know each other better, since we're living next door.'

Ben's gaze travelled between Paul and Sara and something behind his eyes shifted. His look was now one of almost cynical amusement. 'Pubs aren't really my thing,' he said, and looked away.

'Right.' A scornful smile now tugging at his mouth, Paul shook his head.

'Did you bring the children?' Ben asked, glancing around, seemingly oblivious to the awkwardness he'd created.

'Over there. With Maya and Liam.' Sara nodded across to where the four children were seated around a table, looking like little angels. Ellie and Maya were playing with Maya's new doll, and James and Liam seemed to be engrossed in Lego-building together.

Ben followed her gaze. 'I'd better get the food on before they complain of starvation. See you shortly.' He gave Naomi's shoulders a squeeze and headed off to the barbecue.

'We've left some wine and beers on the drinks table,' Paul called after him.

Ben didn't respond. Unless he had a hearing problem, which as far as Sara knew, he didn't, he was either ignoring him or being completely rude. She was really struggling not to say something now. But she held her tongue. Naomi had worked hard to organise this, getting the garden in some sort of order, inviting the neighbours. Sara would try to talk to her again, but not now. 'I'd better go and fetch Joan,' she said with a smile.

'Is she coming?' Naomi looked surprised. 'She's welcome, of course. I did send her an invite but I wasn't sure she would be up to it.'

'Oh, she's coming,' Sara assured her. 'She's determined to. God forbid she should miss out on the neighbourhood gossip.'

'I'll come with you, lend a hand,' Paul offered, as she turned for the gate.

'No need.' Sara smiled back at him. 'She rang me just before we came out to say she was almost ready. And she has her walking frame. You keep an eye on the kids, I won't be long.'

Joan was ready and waiting when Sara let herself in with her key, standing in the hall with her frame and looking more like her old self. 'On your starting blocks, hey, Joan?' Sara smiled, relieved to see her looking perkier. Joan had been so confused lately, as if she'd lost some of her spark. She was a bit nosy sometimes, making everyone's business her own, but she had a good heart. Sara knew she genuinely cared for people. 'How are we doing?' she asked, hooking an arm through one of hers.

'Better.' Joan smiled. 'I've had a bit of a go at my hair. What do you think?'

'Not bad.' Sara looked her over and felt guilty that she hadn't had time to give her a wash and set today. Joan had obviously had a bash with the curling tongs she'd brought her back from the salon. 'You'll have all the men chasing after you.'

Joan chuckled. 'They should be so lucky.'

Sara squeezed her arm. She was fond of the old woman. Too fond, probably. She would miss her terribly if anything were to happen to her. Her thoughts went back to the comment Paul had blurted out in front of Naomi. 'Can I ask you something, Joan?' she ventured as they made their way to the front door. It was an emotive subject. She'd been reluctant to mention it before now, but since Joan seemed sharper...

'Anything, my lovely.' Joan nodded. 'I'll answer if I can.'

'The little girl who disappeared from Naomi's house,' Sara said hesitantly, 'Paul mentioned you said she'd been murdered and I—' She stopped as Joan ground to a halt at her side.

'I said *what*?' She looked at her in astonishment. 'I said no such thing, Sara,' she refuted, now looking indignant. 'Why would I? They never discovered what happened to her. I'm sure I would have known if they had.'

That wasn't what Paul had said. Sara felt her stomach tighten. Had Joan said it? And then forgotten that she had?

'I'm sure many people, including the police, might have reached the conclusion she had been murdered,' Joan went on with a sad shake of her head, 'but the poor little mite's body was never found and it was never officially confirmed.'

'Are you sure?' Sara asked, and then felt bad as Joan's face dropped. She was as good as telling her she thought she was muddled.

'I'm absolutely positive,' Joan said with a determined nod. 'I've lived in hope all these years that that little girl might turn up. I would certainly never repeat something that was no more than idle gossip and speculation. I have no idea why this boyfriend of yours would say I did when I've hardly spoken to the man.'

TWENTY-FIVE

Naomi

He was a good host. I watched as Ben circulated, smiling and filling glasses, making sure everyone was fed. He looked relaxed, finally. After working long hours this week, learning the ropes and attending meetings about safe patient photo-taking and storage, he'd been so exhausted I'd begun to regret insisting on having the barbecue so soon. He'd also been called out to an emergency yesterday, which he'd found majorly upsetting. It was a child abuse case where it was essential to depict what the health professionals saw before the patient – a little girl our own daughter's age – underwent the necessary emergency treatment. His photographs meant that crucial evidence could be preserved should the case the police were trying to build reach court. I hoped to God that it did. Ben hadn't revealed too many details, but the fact that he'd gone straight out to run off his visible anger had told me how devastated he was by the injuries he'd seen.

Overhearing the animated conversation of the group he was standing with, mostly men heavily into football, I walked across to him, placing a hand on his back. 'Okay?' I checked, smiling as he glanced at me.

'Fine.' He smiled back, but as he wasn't into football, I guessed he was finding the conversation a bit tedious. 'Couldn't be an angel and uncover the puddings, could you?' I asked, thinking he might be in need of rescuing. 'I'm dead on my feet.'

'No problem.' He kissed my cheek, then, after pulling out a chair at the garden table and making sure I sat in it, went happily off to the kitchen.

'He looked a bit bored,' commented Sara, who was sitting at the table with Joan.

'Football's not really his thing,' I explained. 'He's more into jogging and going to the gym – when he can find time.'

'Ah.' Sara nodded. 'He should talk to Paul about the gym he goes to in Harborne. He says he rates it.'

'Oh right. I'll tell him to swing by and have a look.' I smiled. 'He has a lot going on at work so he's a bit pushed for time but I'm sure he'll appreciate the recommendation.' I doubted Ben would actually take a look. I still had no idea why, but he simply didn't rate Paul. The atmosphere between the two men was cool, to say the least. I doubted very much they would become gym buddies.

'How are you, Joan?' I turned my attention to her. I hadn't had a chance to talk to her since our first meeting at her house, when Joan had stared so strangely at Ben, which still mystified me.

Joan looked me over searchingly. 'I'm well, thank you. Concerned about you,' she said, a deep furrow creasing her brow.

'Me?' I raised my eyebrows in surprise. 'I'm fine. This little one is making his presence felt' – I placed a hand over my tummy – 'but other than that everything's perfect.'

'Really?' Narrowing her eyes, Joan studied me intently, making me feel quite uncomfortable. 'He's treating you well then, is he?'

'Who, Ben?' I looked at her, confused. 'Yes. Why?'

Joan took a second to answer. 'Just curious,' she said eventually, which was no explanation at all. Her question had been pointed, I was certain of it. Why would she ask if Ben was treating me well, unless she imagined he wasn't? She didn't know him or anything about him. Unless...? Had Sara been discussing Ben with her? My gaze shot in her direction.

Sara shrugged, looking as bemused as I felt.

'Ben's always treated me well,' I said, wondering what on earth he was supposed to have done for everyone to have formed such a negative opinion of him. Getting irate with the removal men surely wasn't it. 'He's a caring man,' I added. 'And a good father.'

'Talk of the devil.' Sara nodded towards the back door. 'He certainly seems caring of Lucky.'

I followed her gaze to see Ben emerging from the house, cradling Joan's cat in his arms. 'He snuck in to sample the salmon,' he said, rolling his eyes good-naturedly as he approached. 'I think he approves.' He smiled at Sara and I felt a little sense of triumph. There, didn't that show how caring he was?

'Oh dear.' Joan pushed herself up from her chair. 'Lucky, come here, baby,' she said, her voice tremulous. 'Come to Mummy. We need to get you home to your nice warm bed, don't we?'

'I'll take him,' Sara offered, getting to her feet, Joan not being very stable on hers.

'That would be helpful, Sara.' Joan smiled appreciatively. 'Thank you.'

Ben held on to the cat as the girls chose that moment to come rushing across the garden. 'Can we have some ice cream, Mummy, can we?' Ellie asked, flinging herself at Sara's waist.

'Unicorn vanilla,' Maya said excitedly, her arms outstretched to me. 'It's our favourite, isn't it, Mummy?'

'Hold your horses, girls.' Sara caught their hands in hers. 'I just have to take Lucky home and then we'll all have ice cream. Okay?'

'I'll take him,' Ben offered. 'Let me have the key and I'll— Ouch!' He winced as Lucky, clearly startled by the children's clamouring, decided to take flight, scratching his hand in the process.

'Looks like cats hate you as much as you hate cats, mate.' Paul laughed from where he was still standing with the other men.

Ben breathed in hard and examined his hand. It was an interminably long minute before he breathed out. 'I don't hate cats, *mate*.' Looking up, he shot Paul a blistering glance. 'I'm allergic to them.'

What in God's name was *that* all about? Bewildered, I looked at Sara.

She was staring confounded at Ben as he spun around and stalked off. 'Ignore them,' she said, smiling tightly. 'It sounds to me like men locking horns.'

Yes, but why? They seemed to despise each other. Seeing Paul's thunderous expression as he glowered after Ben, my stomach turned over.

TWENTY-SIX

Naomi

Ben was nowhere to be seen when I hurried into the house. 'Ben?' I called out to him as I searched downstairs, then went upstairs. Going into our bedroom, I noticed the clothes he'd been wearing were on the chair. My heart missed a beat as I checked the wardrobe. His trainers weren't there. He'd gone out running? While we were hosting a barbecue? A mixture of confusion and anger bloomed inside me. What was going on? What had gone on between Ben and Paul that I didn't know about? And what about Ben and Sara? I'd seen them deep in conversation when she'd brought the fish round. A conversation that had stopped suddenly when I'd appeared. Why had she labelled him manipulative and aggressive when she'd barely even spoken to him before now? But she had, hadn't she? Outside, when we'd moved in. And before that, when he'd collected the children from her house, the first time we'd met her. Had it been the first time Ben had met her?

'Naomi?' She'd obviously decided to come in search of me, calling from the kitchen as I descended the stairs. 'There you are,' she said, looking relieved as she reached the hall. 'Is Ben all right? I have no idea what's happening between those two. If you ask me, they could do with their heads banging together for acting like teenagers after all your hard work.'

That inflamed me. Ben had worked hard too, despite being exhausted. He'd tackled the heavy jobs in the garden at the crack of dawn this morning. He'd shopped for the barbecue and the garden furniture, otherwise there would have been no barbecue. And now he'd disappeared, undoubtedly because he was feeling stressed. 'Do you really not know, Sara?' I asked, stepping down the of the stairs and facing her.

'No.' From her surprised expression, I guessed she was taken aback by my accusatory tone. 'They've obviously clashed in some way, but—'

'What did Joan mean?' I stopped her. 'Asking me whether he was treating me well? Why would she say she was concerned for me?' I could hear the anger in my voice and I felt bad about it, but I couldn't help it.

Sara furrowed her brow. 'I'm not sure. I suppose because she is concerned about you. You are pregnant, after all.'

I wasn't convinced. The woman's eyes had been slits of pure suspicion. 'Why did Paul say that about the cat?' I went on. Thinking about it, why had Ben told him he was allergic? He was, but not majorly. They made him wheeze, that was all, but why had he felt the need to tell Paul that?

Sara looked uncomfortable. 'I honestly have no idea, Naomi.'

'Ben doesn't hate cats,' I snapped. 'He was cradling it in his arms, for goodness' sake. He offered to take the bloody thing home!'

'Naomi...' Looking me over sympathetically, Sara moved towards me.

I stepped back. I didn't want her sympathy. Despite the assumptions people were making, there was *nothing* wrong with my husband. Nothing wrong with my marriage. 'Have you been sharing information regarding your badly skewed opinion of Ben with the entire neighbourhood?' I eyed her reprovingly. 'Is that what this is all about?'

'No, I have not, Naomi,' Sara refuted categorically. 'I spoke out of turn, for which I'm truly sorry, but I'm not a gossip. I've been on the receiving end of it. Trust me, I would never do that to you.'

'But you don't like him,' I challenged her. 'Joan doesn't. Paul clearly doesn't. I just don't understand why. Have you met him before? Is there something going on that I don't know about?'

'No.' Sara shook her head in bewilderment. 'Of course I haven't. I would have told you if I had.'

'Then why all this animosity towards him?' I felt the tears rising.

'Oh, Naomi.' Sara moved again towards me. 'Come here,' she said, wrapping her arms around me. 'Joan is confused. You saw that for yourself. As for Paul, that was just his bad idea of a joke. And I... I formed an opinion too soon because of my own experiences, but also because you seemed so upset. I said some things I shouldn't have, things I bitterly regret. Please believe I'm sorry.'

She looked into my eyes, her own brimming with tears. 'Forgive me? I couldn't bear it if I thought you were unhappy here because of my thoughtlessness.'

She really did look distraught. And I must sound paranoid. I felt paranoid. 'I'm sorry, too,' I said, taking a breath and attempting to compose myself. 'I'm confused, hot and tired. Worried about Ben. I didn't mean to snap at you.'

'I know. And I know you must be worried.' Sara wiped a tear from her cheek as I wiped one from mine. 'God, what a pair.' She sighed and rolled her eyes. 'Come on, come back outside. We'll see your guests off and then I'll give you a hand clearing up. Okay?'

I nodded. I didn't have a lot of choice. I could hardly stay inside hiding. I was grateful for Sara's support, but still unsure how she felt about Ben. She hadn't actually admitted her opinion of him had been wrong. Where was he? He'd been upset, and this was his way of dealing with it, going off to give himself space. I understood, but it didn't stop me worrying. *Come back, Ben*, I willed him as I followed Sara out to the garden.

Maya was chatting to Joan, I noticed – probably because Paul seemed to have made a quick exit with Sara's two and Joan was a captive audience. 'She is gorgeous,' Joan was saying as she admired Maya's new doll. 'And so lifelike. But what happened to your lovely little teddy bear?'

She'd obviously noticed Maya carrying Little Buttons everywhere then. She really did pay rapt attention to everyone else's business, didn't she?

'I don't know.' Maya glanced sadly down and then back to the woman. 'He's gone missing. We've looked and looked, but we can't find him anywhere.'

Joan glanced up and fixed her gaze on me, and what she said next caused my heart to jolt. 'Keep a close eye on her.'

TWENTY-SEVEN

Naomi

Snuggled up with Ben on the sofa, my mind was only half on the late-night drama we were watching. I'd forgiven him for going off from the barbecue last weekend, though I was still annoyed that he'd left without telling me. Also, I was still trying to fathom out what Joan had meant and what was going on between Ben and Paul. I hadn't had chance to speak to Joan since. I was debating whether to call on her after dropping the children off at school tomorrow when my phone alerted me to a text. 'Sorry. I should have muted it.' I grabbed it from the arm of the sofa. 'Oh no.' Reading the content, I unfurled myself and sat sharply up.

'What is it?' Ben pulled himself up next to me.

'Joan's cat.' I glanced worriedly at him. 'It's gone missing. The night of the barbecue, apparently.' Which meant it had been missing for three whole days A kernel of panic took root inside me as I recalled Paul's comment, the cat scratching Ben and the general animosity there appeared to be towards him. 'Sara wants us to check the shed,' I said, getting to my feet.

'Oh right.' Ben nodded, ran his hands over his face and pushed himself up. 'I'll go. There's no light down that garden path.'

Once he'd collected the keys for the padlock and a torch from the utility cupboard, he headed down the garden. 'Make sure to close the shed door once you've looked,' I called after him, imagining the cat slinking in and getting trapped anyway.

Ben waved behind him, indicating he'd heard me. I watched him go as far as the bottom of the path, where his torchlight disappeared. I waited a minute for it to reappear. And then another minute. Where was he? Growing concerned, I squinted, peering into the almost pitch black before me. The only thing visible by the thin light of the moon was the apex of the shed, the rest of its outline shrouded by foliage. Above it hung the broad bough of the gnarled apple tree. An icy shiver ran through me as it creaked ominously. 'Ben?' Finding my torch on my phone, I clutched it tight and stepped out.

There was no answer, no sound at all but scuffles in the foliage. It's just foraging nightlife, I told myself firmly, shining my torch hastily around. It might even be the cat. There was no cat, nothing visible moving. 'Ben?' I called shakily again. Why wasn't he answering? My palpitating heart slowing to a dull drumbeat at the base of my neck, I trod carefully down the path, lighting my way over the rickety railway sleepers that formed the long steps.

'Shit.' My insides turned over as I almost lost my footing. Cursing my ridiculous flip-flops, and with a hand pressed protectively over my baby, I pushed on. As I reached the shed, there was no sound at all, nothing but the creaking bough. But how was it creaking when there was no wind? I snapped my eyes upwards as I passed under it, my fevered imagination conjuring up the swinging ghost of a man suspended from it by a rope. The shed door was open, swaying slightly, as if also caught by an invisible breeze.

'Ben, where are you?' My voice a frightened whisper, I shone my torch into the shed and my heart stopped beating. It wasn't the bough of the tree that was creaking. My husband was there. His head dripping with blood, he was sitting in the cobweb-festooned rocking chair.

TWENTY-EIGHT

Naomi

Once Ben was comfortable, propped up on several pillows, I climbed under the duvet and nestled into him. 'Does it hurt?' I asked, glancing up at him.

He eased me closer. 'I'd be lying if I said I didn't have the mother of all headaches.' He sighed. 'I'm just bloody glad it was me who went down that path and not you.'

'You should really go to the hospital.' I frowned as I scanned his face. His complexion was pale against the white sheet and he'd lost an awful lot of blood.

'I'm okay,' he assured me again. 'It's not that deep.'

'Are you sure it's all right to sleep, though?' I studied him worriedly.

'I'm fine, honestly.' He smiled weakly. 'As long as I can talk and walk without difficulty and my pupils aren't dilated, there's nothing to worry about, I promise you.'

I wasn't convinced. The cut looked deep to me. 'Do you still not remember what happened?' I pressed a hand to his chest, never more grateful to feel the reassuring beat of his heart.

'Not a clue.' He breathed in, blew it out slowly. 'One minute I was looking up at the tree, thinking I'd heard the cat up there, the next I was counting stars. I guess I must have slipped and fallen backwards.'

But that didn't make sense. The cut was on the back of his head, but it was towards the top. He'd felt groggy afterwards, he'd said, and had needed to sit down. And the rocking chair had been right there, silently beckoning him. It was a bad omen if ever I saw one. I felt like setting fire to the shed with that damned chair inside it. If not for the children in bed, I might have done it.

Ben gave me a squeeze. 'You should rest,' he said. 'Sleep deprivation's not good for Bump.'

I hadn't told him the name I was thinking of, I realised. I would tell him tomorrow. He would like it, I was sure he would. Snuggling further into him, I pressed my hand softly over my tummy. *Night-night, Elias.* I smiled as I felt my baby answer with a small kick. I'd very nearly fallen on that path, but my baby was safe. I couldn't help but think of the irony of all that had happened tonight while we'd been searching for an elusive black cat called Lucky.

After hours trying to free my mind of disturbing images of limp bodies swinging from trees, wondering what might have happened to that poor missing child and now the missing cat, I felt myself drifting. I was barefoot in the garden, the weather warm and balmy, a soft breeze whispering through the leaves on the trees and birds singing high up in the branches. Wings flapping. Twigs snapping.

I'm not alone.

My gaze shoots towards a rustle in the foliage. He's here. I can sense him. He treads silently, stealthily, his movements fluid and sinuous, pausing occasionally, as if beckoning me to follow. I do as he bids, ignoring the rapidly darkening sky and the abrupt deluge of rain that soaks through me, plastering my nightdress to my skin. The garden stretches out before me, elongated suddenly. Endless miles of overgrown grass and shrubbery.

I push on, ignore the sharp stones on the path that bite into the soles of my feet, the debilitating stitch in my side. I can't lose sight of him. Breathless with exertion, my baby kicking frantically, I force myself on. He stops suddenly. Bathed in a soft glimmer of light as the clouds part to reveal the impassive face of the moon, he turns to face me. It's not him. The silhouette growing and swaying and undulating before me isn't that of a cat. The eyes that look back at me, blue-green orbs with vertical irises, look like cat's eyes. But they're not. My breath catches as the pupils grow round and I realise I'm looking into Sara's eyes. Narrowed eyes, judgemental eyes.

'You don't know him. You should leave him. You know you should leave him,' she hisses. 'Poor fool. Poor fool, you.' She spits. And her talons shoot out, razor sharp, a whisker away from my belly. Elias! I hear the mewl of a cat. The screech of a cat.

No, not a cat.

A baby. Distressed.

It's a dream.

I was dreaming. Wasn't I? My heart jolted, jerking me to sitting. Sweat wetting my body, panic twisting inside me, I rested the flat of my hand on my tummy. His movements were normal, gentle, like soft butterflies. He was fine. Not distressed. Relief flooding every cell in my body, I tried to shake away the cloying remnants of my dream.

Meow. It came again. I could hear it distinctly. My gaze snapped to the open window, where the curtains billowed softly in the breeze. Reaching for Ben, a new panic unfurled inside me as I found his side of the bed empty. Throwing back the duvet, I scrambled up, found my flip-flops with my feet, and went across to the window to peer out. The cat *was* there. Lucky. I could see him under the pale glow of the streetlights.

Quickly, I went to the bedroom door, plucked my dressing gown from the hook and hurried down the stairs. The front door was on the latch. Had Ben heard it too? He shouldn't be out there. I pulled the door open and stepped out. 'Lucky,' I whispered, catching sight of him as he padded along the pavement on the opposite side of the road.

'Lucky,' I called quietly again as he glanced back at me, the amber flash of his eyes reigniting the fear I'd felt in my dream.

'*Lucky*. Here, boy.' As he padded aloofly on, I tried again, pursing my lips and making a 'ps-ps-ps' sound in the hope of enticing him.

He stopped and turned to look at me, mewling plaintively.

'Come here, Lucky. Come and say hello.' I started towards him. Then stopped, frozen for a single petrified heartbeat as another sound reached me – tyres screeching inches away.

I heard the impact before I felt it – dull, sickening. Fear sliced through me for a split second, and then I was flying, tossed like a rag doll in the air. White-hot pain jarred every bone in my body as I landed heavily on the unforgiving wet tarmac.

No. Please, no. I could hear him. He was crying. Bewildered, pitiful sobs, deep in my belly. Distressed. He was *distressed*. Squeezing my eyes closed, my heart frozen inside me, I crawled a hand towards the slow trickle of lifeblood flowering beneath me. My blood, my baby's blood, staining the drab, grey road crimson. *Elias! Save him. Someone, please save my baby.*

Bright white light sliced through my vision. I could hear someone screaming. It took a second for me to realise that someone was me.

Ben? Where was he? *Please help me. Please! Help! Me!* 'Ben!'

He couldn't hear me. Through the cacophony of noise, my own pitiful sobbing, doors slamming, people shouting, how could he? 'Ben!'

'I'm here. I'm *here*, Naomi. Right here.' I felt his hand in mine, heard his deep, guttural moan as he dropped to his knees beside me. 'I'm here,' he said hoarsely again. 'Stay awake, sweetheart. Please try... *Naomi!*' He squeezed my hand tight. 'For fuck's sake,' he yelled, 'someone call an ambulance!'

Don't be angry. Please don't be angry. I wanted to tell him, to reassure him, but I couldn't make my mouth shape the words.

'Dear God, please don't,' he murmured, a sob catching in his throat as he looked heavenwards. 'Please don't do this.' Tears streaming down his face, he moved closer, brushed my hair from my face and pressed a soft kiss to my forehead. His eyes were filled with confusion and pain as he looked pleadingly into mine.

'Our baby,' I whispered.

'Don't try to speak, sweetheart,' he said, his voice agonised. 'Save your strength.'

He turned away and panic rose white-hot inside me. 'Don't leave me.' I tried to squeeze his hand but someone was stealing my strength away. *My baby.*

'I'm here, Naomi. I'm not going anywhere.' He promised me softly. 'It's going to be okay.'

He was lying. It wasn't going to be okay. I could see in his eyes he didn't believe it. 'Lucky,' I managed. *Not lucky. Not for me.*

'The cat? *Jesus.*' Ben closed his eyes.

'Elias.' Swallowing back the salty, metallic taste in my mouth, I whispered our baby's name.

Ben looked back at me, his eyes dark, intense, tortured. 'It's a good name. Strong.' He nodded, understanding. 'I love you, Mrs Felton,' he choked. 'Always and forever. Do you know that?'

I knew he did, felt safe in that knowledge as I watched the stars above me go out one by one.

TWENTY-NINE

Ben

Forgive me. Ben squeezed his eyes closed. *Please bring her back to me.* His heart frozen inside him, he prayed silently as he sat by Naomi's side, not letting go of her hand for even a second lest she wake.

He wished with every fibre of his being that he'd never set eyes on that woman. She was going to ruin his life. Why had he done it?

He breathed deeply, tried to stop the tears falling. Failed. 'Dammit.' He'd ruined his wife's life. His children's lives. He was responsible for this. *All* of it.

'Are you okay, Mr Felton?' a nurse asked kindly, placing a hand on his shoulder as she came to do Naomi's observations.

Nodding stiffly, Ben swiped the tears from his face. He wasn't okay. He didn't deserve to be. Didn't deserve her sympathy.

'Would you like a drink? Tea? Coffee?' she asked him.

'No. Thanks. I'm good,' he assured her.

She looked doubtful. 'You should try to get some rest,' she said, glancing worriedly back at him as she went to check the monitor. 'You look exhausted. The family room is empty. Why don't you stretch out in there? I'll call you straight away if she comes round.'

He shook his head hard. He wasn't going anywhere. He needed to be here when she woke up. And then what? Would he hold her, cry with her? Lie to her? *Keep* lying to her? Or would he tell her? Confess to what a complete bastard he was? That he'd been desperately hoping she would never find out the truth? It would break her heart. Blow them apart. It was what he deserved, but how could he do that to her now?

'I'm on until morning,' the nurse said, walking to the door after checking the IV drip. 'Give me a shout if you need anything.'

Ben nodded his thanks as she left. The silence was too loud, giving him too much room in his head. No matter how hard he tried to shut them down, the thoughts kept coming, the memories creeping back to haunt him. He was an eleven-year-old kid again, hiding like a five-year-old under the bed, terrified of coming out, terrified of the dust balls and creatures that lurked in the dark. But the thing that terrified him most of all was himself, the thing he'd done, the things he'd been complicit in doing to cover it up. His father had been right. There was something wrong with him. He should have stopped what was happening. That day had turned into a nightmare he would live with for the rest of his life. He was weak. He always had been.

Bile rose in his throat as he recalled the taunts of the boy who'd constantly reminded him how pathetic he was. The boy who'd made it his mission to fuck up his life, because he'd apparently 'stolen' his life. He'd conceded, as time had gone on, that he himself had struggled to relate to people. He lacked empathy, the psychologists said. The evil shit who'd made his life a living hell, though, he simply wasn't capable of human emotion. Affable and caring on the outside, he was a master of concealment. He empathised with no one. Cared for no one. He simply couldn't. And now... Still, he was too weak to stand up to him.

His phone vibrating yanked him from his thoughts. Ben shook himself. He couldn't believe he was thinking about himself, feeling sorry for *himself*, when his wife was lying there unconscious, her whole world ripped apart. He should never have become involved with her. His past was his present; he'd known he could never escape it. He was who he was: someone who was incapable of being all that Naomi deserved. He would hurt her, he'd known that, too. He had hurt her. His thoughts only for himself, his actions – it was all beyond forgivable. Emotionally, she might never recover. That was down to him. There was no way to fix it.

He drew in another sharp breath, held it and pulled his phone from his pocket. Seeing that the text was from Sara, he cursed silently.

How is she? I was going to pop in and see her, but I wasn't sure whether you would want me to?

No, he sent succinctly back. Sara was the last person in the world he wanted here now. After all that had gone on between them, there was nothing he felt inclined to say to her, especially after their meeting on the high street when she'd made it obvious she could reveal things to Naomi that would blow his marriage apart in an instant. And he certainly didn't want her leaving his kids with Paul. He had no idea what she was doing with him. Did she? *Probably not a good idea under the circumstances*, he added, hoping she would get the message.

He stuffed the phone back in his pocket and focused on his wife. Even after all she'd been through, and with her face badly bruised, she was beautiful: eyes which were every conceivable colour of the forest and rarely judgemental, sensual lips which curved so easily into a smile – he'd wanted to taste them the first time he'd met her. Yet she seemed not to be aware of her attractiveness. And she was kind. Genuinely kind, deep down at the core of her. What the hell was *she* doing with *him*?

Swallowing back the jagged stone in his throat, he bowed his head. *Please wake up, Naomi.* He prayed hard again, even knowing his prayers would never be answered. He'd prayed when she'd been brought in, shut himself in one of the toilets and prayed with all of his might. God hadn't heard him.

Grazing his thumb gently over her slender fingers, he paused at the pale band where her wedding ring should be. They'd taken it off when she'd gone into surgery. She should never have married him. She should never have gone anywhere near him.

His heart stalled as he sensed a movement, almost imperceptible, just the tiniest flicker of her fingers. And his heart fractured inside him when she snatched her hand away from his and placed it on her stomach.

THIRTY

Naomi

I knew. The second I laid my hand on the flat of my belly, I knew.

I'd tried to hold on to him. I couldn't reach him. He was floating away from me, his heart, which had beaten so strong inside me, growing fainter as his small body drifted further away, softly, softly, ebbing and rolling like a fragile foetal anemone in a hostile sea.

'Elias,' I whispered, as his cries, weak and bewildered, cut through me like an accusation. I'd failed him. Failed in my most fundamental obligation as a mother. I hadn't kept my baby safe.

He's stopped crying. I stopped breathing. I couldn't hear him. There was nothing. Complete silence. White lights. Too bright. They would hurt his eyes. *Oh God. Elias, come back to me. Please come back to me.* Where was he? What had they done with him? Where had they taken him? My chest exploded. Where *was* he? My baby?

'Elias!' I flailed, tried to tear my arms from the hands that were holding me. 'I have to go to him. I have to find him. *Elias*. I have to...' I fought the man who was restraining me, the tears that were choking me. I had to *go*. '*Please*. I have to...'

'Naomi, it's me,' he said gutturally. 'You're safe.' He held on to me, drawing me to him as the sterile stench and beeps and alarms reached me. Urgent voices. They couldn't save him. My baby wasn't safe.

'Where is he?' I whimpered, disorientated and so very frightened.

He breathed in sharply. 'I'm sorry, Naomi. *So* sorry.' His voice cracked. I felt him draw breath into his body. He didn't breathe out.

Lifting my head from his shoulder, I rested my gaze on the tortured face of my husband, whose tears confirmed what I didn't want to believe. I'd lost him. The child I'd carried inside me for six months had been stolen away from me.

'I'm sorry,' he repeated, the pain in his eyes palpable. 'We can get through this,' he whispered. 'We have to try. Be there for each other. For Liam and Maya. We won't forget him, Naomi. Not ever.'

He squeezed me gently as I rested my head back on his shoulder.

'Elias,' I murmured.

'Elias.' He caught a sob in his throat and I made myself hold him. I wasn't sure I was ready to, but I knew he was hurting. It was his loss too. He would feel it as painfully as I did. I knew he was right, that my children, who would grieve the loss of their baby brother as keenly as I did, needed me. I wasn't sure how I would get through this though. How I would ever say goodbye to my baby. Whether I was strong enough to stop the tears falling.

THIRTY-ONE

Sara

Sara debated after reading Ben's response, and then sent a short, pointed reply: *Your children are fine, btw. I'll give them your love.* Drawing in a tight breath, she placed the phone down before she was tempted to send another asking him what the hell was wrong with him. His children weren't fine. What child would be after seeing their mummy lying broken in the road, hearing screaming sirens as the ambulance whisked her away from them? He might have at least asked about them. What a totally self-centred man, she thought angrily, and then pulled herself up. She needed to put her own feelings aside. Naomi would be devastated. When Sara had rung the hospital pretending to be her sister, they'd told her that she should make a full recovery physically. Sara knew, though, that she wouldn't recover so easily emotionally. She needed to think of her now. Any issues she had with Ben would have to wait.

Unsurprised when he didn't reply, she headed to the lounge

to check on the children. Ellie was being a little angel, taking Maya – who was constantly tearful – under her wing. Liam seemed to have gone into himself, uninterested in anything but staring at his iPad. 'Okay, guys?' she asked, trying to keep her tone light.

'Uh-huh.' Ellie pulled her attention away from the TV screen. 'We're playing the *Waffle and Friends* game to take Maya's mind off her mummy,' she said maturely. 'I've told her she'll be home soon, like you said, but she's a little bit worried. Aren't you, Maya?'

Watching Ellie thread her arm around Maya's shoulders, Sara felt her heart swell with pride for her daughter. 'She will be, sweetheart.' Smiling reassuringly, she went across to Maya, crouching down and taking her hands in hers. 'And she'll be so pleased you've been such a good girl, I bet she'll give you the biggest hug ever.'

Maya nodded, but it was such a sad little nod, it was heart-breaking.

'Fancy some ice cream?' Sara asked her. Maya looked uncertain. 'We have unicorn vanilla,' she added, hoping to tempt her. Maya managed a small smile, and Sara gave her a squeeze.

'Boys?' She straightened up and turned expectantly towards them.

James glanced up from his tablet, which he was also glued to. 'I'll have some later,' he said with a listless shrug.

'Liam?' she asked, in answer to which Liam shook his head but didn't look up.

Sara sighed. 'Haven't you two got a game you could play together?' She looked between them.

James shrugged again. 'Liam doesn't fancy it.'

Sara buried another sigh. The boy was too quiet. He needed to not be so inside himself, especially now. But she guessed having a word with his father about it wouldn't do much good. She would talk to Naomi, but not yet.

Deciding to leave them be, she went back to the hall to find Paul coming through the front door. 'Hi.' He smiled apprehensively. 'Everything all right?'

Sara carried on to the kitchen. 'I wouldn't say that, exactly.'

'Did you find out what happened?' Paul asked, following her.

'A hit-and-run,' Sara replied shortly. She'd been off with him since it had happened. Sure that his thoughtless comment at the barbecue had somehow set off the chain of events that had followed, she couldn't help herself.

'I gathered that,' Paul replied warily, obviously catching the edge in her tone. 'I meant do we have any idea why Naomi was out there in the middle of the night?'

'You didn't gather that bit then?' Sara couldn't keep the sarcasm from her voice.

Paul glanced at her quizzically.

Sara headed to the freezer. 'She was out there looking for the cat,' she said flatly.

'I see.' Paul nodded. 'And you're angry with me for what reason, exactly?'

Sara gave him a look as she walked across to the work surface with the ice cream.

Paul sighed in exasperation. 'Sara, I have absolutely no idea what I'm supposed to have done. Would you like to enlighten me?'

She looked at him in despair. He really didn't get it, did he? 'Has it not occurred to you that if you hadn't come out with that silly remark about Ben hating cats, Naomi wouldn't have been out there looking for it?'

Paul looked at her in astonishment. 'It was a *joke*.'

'Not a very funny one,' Sara pointed out. 'Naomi thinks people don't like Ben.'

'*You* don't like him,' Paul reminded her.

'That's beside the point,' Sara replied tersely. 'If Naomi was out there in the dead of night looking for the cat, then it was obviously because she was trying to redeem Ben in some way. She's clearly been worrying about it, what with him going off at the barbecue and—'

'Hang on.' Holding up his hands, Paul stopped her. 'You're actually saying that Naomi being hit by a car was *my* fault?' He searched her face in disbelief.

'No, I...' Realising that she had implied that, Sara tried to backtrack. 'I'm not saying that. You have to admit it was thoughtless, though.'

'Right.' Paul smiled sardonically. 'I'm obviously that kind of guy.' His expression a combination of hurt and disillusionment, he turned away and walked back to the hall.

'Paul...' Sara went after him. 'I didn't *say* that. I just think it wouldn't have happened if—'

Paul swung around to face her. 'I think you did, Sara,' he said, furious. 'Why don't you go the whole hog, hey? Tell me you think it was me at the wheel of the sodding car? I wasn't here when it happened, after all, was I?'

Looking her over scathingly, he shook his head, pulled the key she'd given him from his pocket and placed it on the hall table. 'Thanks for making me feel great about myself,' he muttered, and yanked the front door open. Then he paused. 'You know, I have to wonder why she was out there on her own. Did it occur to you to wonder where her husband was? He's clearly a complete nutjob. Was *he* in the house when it happened? Or had he taken off again? Just a thought.'

Sara's heart missed a beat. She had no idea where Ben had been at the time of the accident. A hard lump in her chest, she flew to the front door and down the front path. 'Paul! Come back,' she shouted, as he climbed into his van.

He slammed his door. She watched, shocked and confused

as he drove off. Might Ben have been involved? No. The idea was preposterous. But she only had his word that Naomi had been looking for the cat. She'd accepted his explanation, but there'd been no sign of Lucky.

She had wondered, though, whether Naomi had been fleeing the house. Where had Ben been? He hadn't appeared immediately. If he'd been in the house, surely he would have? The police had been satisfied it was a hit-and-run by some random stranger, but what if it wasn't?

THIRTY-TWO

Sara

After checking on the children, who thankfully hadn't overheard Paul and her arguing, Sara got them all the promised ice cream. James changed his mind and decided to have some, which encouraged Liam to have some too. She found the boys playing *Super Mario 3D World* together when she took the ice cream through to them. It was a relief to see Liam do something other than stare at his tablet.

Leaving the boys to it, she went upstairs to Ellie's room where the girls were playing. Nudging her way through the door with their ice cream bowls, she turned around with a smile and her breath caught in her chest. The two girls were kneeling on the floor, bathing their dolls in the baby bath Sara had given to Ellie. Her daughter's little Baby Born doll looked so lifelike it could almost be mistaken for a real baby. Poor Naomi. Sara's heart bled for her. How would she cope seeing the girls playing like this?

'Ice cream, girls,' she said, working to keep her tone light. 'Eat it up before it melts.'

'We will.' Fishing her doll out of the water and plonking it on a hand towel, not quite as carefully as one should a real baby, Ellie jumped to her feet. 'Maya says her mummy's going to let her help bath their new baby,' she exclaimed, her eyes filled with excitement. 'Can I help if we have a new baby, Mummy?'

Floored for a second, Sara wasn't sure what to say. 'We'll see,' she said, swallowing back a hard lump of emotion. She felt she ought to be preparing Maya and Liam, but she wasn't sure how. Placing the bowls on Ellie's dressing table, she glanced at Maya to see her cradling her doll gently in her arms, and her heart broke for her.

'Mummy's going to let me hold him too,' the little girl said, her eyes wide with the innocence of childhood, and it was all Sara could do to hold back her tears. She was immensely relieved when the doorbell rang and saved her from having to pursue the subject.

'Back soon,' she said, and headed quickly to the landing. This was all so unfair. Naomi had done nothing to deserve this. If Ben was responsible in any way for what happened to her, she would... She wasn't sure what she would do, but she would find a way to make sure he paid.

Composing herself as she reached the front door, she pulled it open and was surprised to find Joan standing there, leaning heavily on her walking frame. 'Joan, what on earth? You shouldn't be crossing that road on your own.'

'I'm not a child, Sara,' Joan reminded her, but Sara could tell from the only slightly admonishing look in her eyes that she hadn't taken umbrage. 'Do we know how Naomi is?' she asked, her face flooded with concern.

'Badly bruised,' Sara answered, sighing sadly. 'She also has a broken wrist and there was some internal bleeding.'

'The baby?' Joan asked cautiously.

Sara shook her head. 'She'll be allowed to come home tomorrow or the day after, if she's well enough. I can't bear to imagine how she'll feel leaving the hospital empty-handed.'

'Oh no.' Joan closed her eyes, tears squeezing from under the lids. 'That poor girl. I *knew* something like this would happen.'

Sara frowned in confusion. 'Something like what, Joan?' she asked, apprehension prickling the length of her spine.

Joan scanned her face hesitantly, then glanced away. 'It was too much for her, moving house, all that stress,' she said angrily. 'I have no idea what that husband of hers was thinking, moving her here.'

Sara was in total agreement. A house move with two small children would be stressful for anyone, let alone someone six months pregnant. She had a distinct feeling, though, that Joan was being evasive. And what did she mean 'moving her *here*'?

'Do you mind if I come in?' Joan nodded past her.

Realising she'd left her standing on the doorstep, Sara shook herself. 'No, of course not. I was forgetting my manners, sorry.' She stepped out to help her.

'Thank you.' Joan smiled once she and her walking frame were inside. 'I was wondering whether you might do me a huge favour,' she asked tentatively, as she followed Sara to the kitchen.

'Of course,' Sara assured her, eyeing her curiously as she helped her into a chair.

'It might seem a bit insensitive, given the awful thing that's happened. And you might well think I'm imagining things, but...' Joan faltered.

Sara was alarmed when another tear rolled down her cheek. 'What is it, Joan?'

'Lucky,' she said, with a tremulous breath. 'I can hear him meowing. It's such a plaintive meow. I'm sure he's shut in and he'll end up starving to death.'

'Shut in where?' Sara was surprised. She was sure everyone in the vicinity had replied to her message asking them to check outbuildings and garages.

Joan searched her sleeve for a tissue, found one and dabbed at her nose. 'Next door.' Her gaze travelled that way.

Sara looked at her doubtfully. There was no way the cat could be in Naomi's house. Unless he'd slipped in while all the commotion was going on in the road, of course. 'Are you sure?' she asked, worried that Joan might be becoming muddled again.

The old woman nodded determinedly. 'I looked for him after that husband of Naomi's said that was why she was chasing about in her nightie. I went down their path at the side of the house and I could hear him as plain as day. He's locked in their shed. I'm absolutely positive he is.'

But Naomi had texted her back to say they'd checked the shed and there was no sign of Lucky. Unless…? Uneasiness crept through her as she recalled Paul saying that Ben hated cats. He wouldn't have locked the cat in, though. Would he? No, no one could be that cruel. 'I'll go and look,' she said. 'Could you stay here while I do? The kids are all busy playing, but just in case.'

'I won't budge, and I'll shout through the back door if there's a problem,' Joan promised.

Sara nodded and headed for her own back garden. There was a section of the fence between the two houses that was more scalable than Naomi's back gate, which was likely to be locked.

Minutes later, she was standing outside the shed, where she found the door padlocked. *Damn.* She should have thought of that. She pressed her ear to it. 'Lucky?' she called. Hearing nothing, she was thinking that Joan had imagined it when there was a scuffling from inside. 'Lucky?' she called again.

There was no further sound. Lucky knew her well enough and Sara was sure he would meow if he was in there. She shouldn't be here. Ben could come home at any minute. She would have to ask him to take another look when he did. She wasn't happy, but it was the best she could do without breaking the door down.

Sighing, she turned away. She'd taken a couple of steps when she heard another scuffle. There *was* something in there.

She turned swiftly back. If it was Lucky, he must have got in after they'd checked. But *when* after they'd checked? Naomi had replied to her message late, saying they were going to bed and that they would talk more in the morning. But she hadn't stayed in bed. She'd run out of her house in the dead of the night and blindly in front of a car. Sara breathed in sharply. She'd heard it. Something had woken her; she hadn't been sure what. She would never forget the squeal of those brakes, the sickening thud of the impact.

There was something wrong here, she could feel it in her bones. If the cat was in there, then in Sara's mind, the question was why, rather than how. Grabbing hold of the padlock, she rattled it. It was definitely locked and it was solid steel. She could never cut through it, even with bolt cutters, which she didn't have lying handily around. The clasp holding the lock might be breakable, if she could just find something to force it with. Dragging her hair from her face, she glanced around the garden in frustration, then stood stock-still as she heard it again, scratching and scuffling coming from inside the shed. She doubted a mouse would make that much noise. She *had* to get in there.

Spotting a garden fork thrust into a mound of freshly turned soil, she hurried across to grab it and went back to the shed. Lifting the fork, she managed to force one of the prongs into the U-shaped metal that housed the lock, then she hesitated, a shudder running through her as she considered it might be her worst nightmare – a rat, or several. In which case, she would just have to run, fast. Steeling herself, she pushed down hard on the fork handle. *Urgh.* Bloody stubborn thing, it wasn't budging. Gritting her teeth, she forced her weight down on it. The sound of wood splintering was incentive enough to force her on, and she mustered every ounce of strength she possessed.

It gave with a groan, cracking so suddenly she fell backwards, landing clumsily on her haunches. She was scrambling for purchase in the damp soil when something flew from the shed like a bat out of hell, landing heavily on her chest. Her stomach lurched, her mind picturing plump, hairy rodents with long, scaly tails. The scream of terror that was half out of her mouth died in her throat as she focused. It wasn't a rat, she realised, as the creature, definitely furry, took flight over her shoulder, but a cat.

Sara's heart settled clunkily back into its moorings. 'Lucky, come here, sweetheart,' she called, manoeuvring herself carefully onto all fours. Keeping her movements slow, her voice low, she pushed herself to standing and walked towards him. Lucky arched his back as she approached. He was scared, wary, but he didn't run.

'It's okay, Lucky. I've got you. It's okay.' Talking encouragingly to him, she picked him up, cuddling him to her and stroking him softly as she walked back to peer into the musty interior of the shed. The hairs rose on her skin as her gaze fell on the rocking chair. Sitting in it was Maya's beloved old teddy bear.

THIRTY-THREE

Naomi

Keeping an eye out for Sara, who was due back from a two week trip to her mother's in Cornwall, I was walking back to the gates after seeing the children into school when someone called to me across the playground. Katie, I realised, the woman who'd almost reversed over my children and accused me of being an incompetent mother. She'd apologised since, made overtures of friendship, but I couldn't warm to her. 'Hi.' She smiled as she reached me. 'Could I have a quick word?'

Noting the look in her eyes, part apologetic, part sympathetic, trepidation tightened inside me. Individually, some of the women seemed nice enough, but as a clique I found them intimidating. With Sara having gone away shortly after I came out of hospital, I'd accepted an invitation to join them for coffee on a particularly low day emotionally, although I didn't yet feel up to talking much, not even to Sara. Listening to them once we were in the café, I couldn't help noticing how they'd relished gossiping about other parents, psychoanalysing their kids in between mouthfuls of chocolate cake, identifying behavioural problems that they'd clearly decided reflected family circumstances. I'd felt a knot forming in the pit of my belly as they'd nattered on, faces animated, voices disapproving, the conversation punctuated with tsks and sighs, and gasps of, 'She *didn't?*' or 'You're *joking*. Well, it's no wonder her child is so disruptive. And what about Ryan Jenkins? Now there's a child with special needs if ever I saw...' Sweat had broken out over my body as I'd listened, disbelieving. What was I doing with these people?

'Liam's very quiet, isn't he?' someone had said suddenly, causing all faces to angle expectantly towards me. Noting the gleams of anticipation in their eyes, badly masked with sweet smiles, nausea rose hotly inside me.

Leave. Make an excuse and go. Glued to my chair, the cake I hadn't been able to swallow lodged like a brick in my throat, I'd struggled for a suitable response. 'He's sensitive,' I mumbled eventually. 'They've both had a lot to deal with, the children. I, um... Actually, I don't feel too well. I think I should...'

Cursing the tears that had sprung to my eyes, the rattling crockery as I'd risen abruptly from the table, I headed unsteadily to the door, a chorus of sympathetic noises behind me. 'The baby,' someone had whispered too loudly. 'Poor thing,' another had sighed in exaggerated sympathy.

I'd made my escape. Katie, who the others in the group appeared to suck up to, had told me since that the girls had understood completely. Had they? Did they realise I'd gone home that day and cried until I'd almost wept my heart out? That I'd crawled into my bed, a pillow clutched to my tummy, as if that could take the place of my baby? That I'd wanted to stay there – simply go to sleep and not wake up again? If not for my children, I might have.

I was stronger now, trying to be. In a way, that enlightening coffee morning had reminded me I had to be. However low I felt, however painfully empty inside, I had to get up in the morning, put one foot in front of the other and keep functioning – for Maya and Liam. For Ben, too, who was as broken as I was, yet was trying so hard to be there for me.

Looking at Katie now, hovering uncertainly, apprehension prickled through me as I wondered what this 'quick word' might be about. Deep down in my gut though, I knew. Katie confirmed it. 'I just thought I would give you the heads-up,' she said, 'about Liam.'

My heart stalled. 'What about Liam?' I stuffed my hands in my pockets and braced myself. I wanted to shake her.

'He hit one of the other children.' She delivered her bombshell – and I felt myself reel as another fault line ripped through my life.

'There was no serious harm done, though I think the other boy's mum will want to have a word with you,' she went on, while I tried to do the simplest thing in life and just breathe. 'I was just wondering... Have you considered asking his teacher about social skills intervention?'

THIRTY-FOUR

Naomi

Realising I might be pushing myself too soon, I wiped an arm over my forehead and debated whether to cut my run short. I didn't want to. Outside I was coping, appearing to, going through the motions. Inside I was fighting, trying hard not to sink into the dark abyss that beckoned me. Before my pregnancy, running was what I did to keep not just my body healthy, but my mind. The house was too gloomy. Claustrophobic. I had to get out. Focus my energies on moving forward.

Since Katie had thoughtfully given me the 'heads-up' about my son's behaviour, I had a new impetus. I'd spoken to Liam's teacher, who apparently knew nothing about the incident. Making sure to keep it low-key, I'd asked how he was fitting in generally. She'd been understanding, agreeing that he struggled. She'd also agreed that a behavioural evaluation might be a good idea, but said we would need to push for it. I intended to. I would be there for my children. I would do battle with whomever I needed to.

Anger swirling inside me, I forced myself on, my eyes fixed forward, concentrating my efforts through the balls of my feet. Passing a mother pushing a buggy, I clamped my eyes closed. Then snapped them open as a car shaved past, inches from the kerb. A stark image, blinding headlights slicing through my vision. I felt it over again, my bones jarring throughout my entire body as I landed. I saw Ben leaning over me, his eyes dark, intense, his tears wetting my cheeks. I don't recall much after that – until I woke up in the hospital bed with a hard knot of dread tightening inside me.

That's when the real pain had hit, raw and unrelenting, ripping right through me. I'd known immediately, with ice-cold certainty, that I'd lost my baby. *Why?* Acrid grief crashed through me, causing my step to falter. I saw him so vividly I could almost reach out and touch him. *Elias.* I whispered my baby's name. *Why?* My throat closed, tears rising so fast I had no hope of holding them back. His small body had been perfect – limbs, hands, feet, fingers, toes. All accounted for. All perfect. Yet it was impossible for him to survive. His little lungs weren't fully formed, his heart not strong enough to beat independently of mine.

Swiping away my tears, I swallowed back the stone lodged like grit in my throat and pushed harder, increasing my pace, trying to outrun my nightmare.

Lucky had been found, apparently – not in the street, Sara had told me when she'd phoned, but in someone's garden. I hadn't really been listening, I didn't feel capable of taking things in. I was certain, though, that he had been there that night. A black cat, unmistakably that cat, had crossed my path. Not lucky, I reminded myself, not for me. I could feel the burn through my thigh muscles. I kept running.

Cracks in the pavement, not unlucky. I planted one foot

determinedly in front of the other, careless of where they landed. Ben was right. My superstitions were ridiculous. In convincing myself bad things would happen because of rocking chairs and wrong-facing beds, I felt I'd tempted fate. In my head, I knew I hadn't. My heart, though, was still so heavy with guilt.

Run. Don't think, I commanded myself, trying to quash the dark thoughts that had dogged me as I lay in the hospital – wishing I was dead, that it could have been me instead of my baby. Thoughts that were still with me as I'd walked empty-handed and broken-hearted from the hospital. It was seeing my little girl's face, her eyes awash with frightened tears, my boy's eyes, uncertain, filled with trepidation, that woke me to the fact that, however desolate I felt, I had to go on. I was their mummy. My children needed me. I would always be Elias's mummy too, and I would tell them about him, explain what had happened, but not now, not yet. We had to heal. I had to grow stronger. For Liam's sake, I had to be fearless in the face of those who would bring him down because they considered him different.

My adrenaline pumping, I forced myself on, focused on my breathing – in, out, in, out – and the pounding of my feet until I reached the reservoir, quad and calf muscles screaming. I bent my head, clasped my thighs and gasped to draw breath.

Finally, my energy spent, I sank to the ground. It was a perfect early autumn day, a damp, earthy smell clinging to the air, crisp sunlight breaking through the clouds. The grass would soon be a rich carpet of golds and reds. I watched a spectacular murmuration of starlings soar across the sky, other joggers running by, workers commuting, teachers shepherding excited children along the circular walking trail. How many bones lay under the ground I sat on? How many memories were buried beneath this earth?

Running my fingers through the dewy grass, I didn't realise someone had approached me until she spoke. 'Naomi?'

I looked up to see Sara, her face creased with concern. 'Small world,' she said with a tentative smile. 'It's my day off, so I thought I would take a walk. Actually, that's a lie. I saw you go out and thought you might come here. Are you all right, sweetheart? I left you a couple of messages. I was a bit worried when you didn't call me.'

'Sorry. I should have done. I just...' I trailed off and dropped my gaze. Sara was trying to be there for me. I didn't want to push her away, but I didn't know how to say I couldn't bring myself to talk about things. Not yet.

'You need some space, I get it.' Sara hesitated and then sat down beside me. She glanced worriedly at me and then fell silent.

After a quiet moment, I felt her slip an arm around my shoulders. 'You know where I am if you need me,' she said softly, giving me a squeeze. 'I don't have a way to fix this, sweetheart, God knows I wish I did, but it might help to talk.'

I answered with another small nod, but I wasn't sure I would take up her offer. I hadn't been able to bring myself to speak to anyone in depth apart from Ben. After our first heartrending conversation, the choking sobs as we'd held each other after we'd buried our baby, I'd found it difficult to talk even to him. We'd decided on a white coffin. It was so impossibly tiny. Ben had carried it in his arms, and it had almost broken him. What had broken me was realising after the event that I hadn't wanted Elias cremated. I'd sprinkled his ashes on my Mum's grave, who lay with her mother and now with my grandad, but afterwards I'd felt as if he'd been stolen twice over and that I had nothing tangible left of him. I'd wished dearly that day that my mum was still here, that I could talk with her as I so easily had as a child, that I could have known my father, the man who'd abandoned her. It was never to be. That was part, I think, of why my own small family was so important to me.

I'd asked Ben about his parents, wondering whether he

might feel a need to visit their graves. He'd said he couldn't, and gathering from his dark expression that it would bring him no solace, I hadn't probed. Perhaps I should have. It was so obvious he was hurting – much more than people who didn't know him could see.

Since then I'd avoided talking to the neighbours – largely because of the antagonism towards Ben, which would only hurt us more and which I would never understand. Plus, there was the cat, Lucky. It wasn't his fault, he was just an innocent animal, and I didn't like myself for it, but seeing him strolling around, lying stretched out and carefree on the pavement, I couldn't help but feel bitter. I still didn't know where he'd disappeared to, how he'd come to reappear on what had turned out to be the worst night of my life.

'It's beautiful, isn't it? Tranquil.' Sara nodded towards the vast expanse of water.

I had to agree. It was the kind of view that didn't demand anything of you. I thought that's why I'd headed here, albeit unconsciously: in search of tranquillity. As I stared out at the water, I couldn't help wondering what secrets it held, what lay beneath its murky depths. 'Where was he?' I asked, after a pause. 'Lucky, was he very far away?'

Sara hesitated, as if reluctant to answer. 'You know, we didn't actually see him that night, after your...' She stopped, obviously struggling to find the word to describe the tragedy that had robbed us of our baby. I didn't blame her. She wouldn't have wanted to say 'accident'. It was more than that, so much more. I hadn't hallucinated the cat, though. Lucky had been there. I'd seen him clearly under the light of the streetlamps. I'd heard him.

'He turned up, that's the main thing,' I said. 'I bet Joan's relieved.'

'Immensely.' Sara smiled. 'He's her only company.'

Again, I nodded, and tried to bury any resentment I felt. He was Joan's baby, in a way. I knew how much he meant to her. 'Do you think he might have been in someone's garage?' I asked, preferring to keep the conversation on safe ground. Even talking about our children would expose my emotions. I didn't want to give in to them here.

'Not exactly.' Sara's gaze flicked to mine and then away again. 'We actually found him in your shed. That is, I did. He was locked in. I had to force the door. The wood splintered, I'm afraid. I offered to pay Ben for the damage but—'

'Hold on.' I stared at her, incredulous. 'Lucky was in our shed?'

'We heard him crying.' She glanced evasively again towards the water.

'Who? When?' This couldn't be right. There were gaps in my memory, but unless I was going mad, which I wasn't, then that cat had most definitely *not* been in our shed.

'Joan, at first,' Sara said tentatively. 'And then I heard him, so I—'

'But we checked it,' I spoke over her. 'I texted you to say we had.'

'I know.' Sara's expression was both sympathetic and awkward. 'I was thinking that maybe you'd missed him. It was dark, after all.'

My heart boomed, my mind racing as I recalled the events before we'd gone to bed. Ben hadn't just gazed into the shed. I'd found him sitting in there *bleeding*. 'We looked thoroughly,' I assured her. 'Ben almost knocked himself unconscious while he was looking. The cat wasn't there.'

'I'm sorry. I didn't realise.' Sara's gaze drifted away, yet again. 'There was something else,' she said. 'Inside the shed.' I noted the reticence in her eyes as she looked back at me, and the knot of apprehension I seemed to carry permanently around inside me tied itself tighter.

'What, for goodness' sake?' I squinted hard at her. It hadn't stopped, had it? Even now, she was still determined to hate my husband. *Why?*

Sara drew in a breath. 'Maya's teddy bear. It was in there, on the rocking chair.'

'Little Buttons? What utter rubbish.' I laughed in absolute astonishment. 'What are you implying exactly, Sara?' I studied the woman who claimed to be my friend with deep suspicion. 'That Ben found the cat and deliberately locked it in as some act of revenge? That he hid the teddy bear away from his own daughter?'

'No.' Sara shook her head, flustered. 'I just don't understand—'

'It's ridiculous. All of it. It's like a bloody witch hunt,' I seethed, scrambling to my feet. 'You'll stop at nothing to turn me against my husband, won't you?'

'Naomi, wait! I'll walk with you,' Sara called after me as I turned away.

'I'm running,' I growled back, and took off. Why was she doing this? A hard fist of anger tightened in my chest. Was she jealous? So bitter she didn't care that she was breaking what was left of my heart? She'd split up with Paul, according to Ben. Did she resent my happiness? Did she blame Ben for the breakdown of her relationship? It had clearly deteriorated after the comment Paul made at the damned barbecue. I had no idea what was going on, but as soon as Ben came home, I aimed to find out.

THIRTY-FIVE

Naomi

Fumbling my key into the lock, I shoved the front door open and banged it behind me, desperate to shut the judgemental, tongue-wagging neighbours out. I'd noticed Joan sitting at her window, no doubt ready to report back to Sara. Were they all in collusion? The holier-than-thou mothers' clique too? If it wasn't so cruel, after what both Ben and I had been through, it would be laughable. Why were they doing this? Why was Sara? Was it Ben she had something against or was it me?

And where was the teddy bear? If it had been found, surely it would have been given back to Maya? Anger driving me, I searched the house, checking every nook and cranny. I went to the shed, my heart somersaulting as I noticed the splintered wood on the door. She really had been determined to get in there, hadn't she? The cat must have been inside. Why else would she have broken in? Had she been trying to set Ben up? To split us up? But if she'd really wanted to do that, she would have done something to the poor thing – starved it, or... I pulled myself up, realising I was travelling down a very dark road. I was becoming obsessed. I would drive myself out of my mind at this rate. Still, though, I couldn't escape the feeling that someone wished Ben harm. Wished my family harm.

Tentatively, I pulled the shed door open and peered inside. There was no teddy bear. Nothing but tools, dust motes and cobwebs – and that damned rocking chair. Closing the door, I about-faced, then froze as I heard a creak behind me. It had seemed to come from inside the shed. *Go away!* Ignoring it, I strode on. As far as I was concerned, the evil spirit was already in residence. It lived right next door.

Frustrated, I went back inside and rang Ben on his mobile. His voicemail picked up, meaning he was busy at work. Checking the clock, I realised it would be hours before he was home with the children. Ben had some time owed and had offered to pick them up when he could. Today, I was relieved. It meant I could avoid another run-in with Katie and her gang. I'd been devastated by what she'd told me, and then bloody angry. Liam did struggle emotionally. With all that had gone on in his life recently, though, could they not have allowed him a little slack? He'd denied hitting the boy. I wasn't one hundred per cent sure I believed him, but did they have to take it to the clique committee, where they would undoubtedly vote on whether to ostracise me and my son? Well, they needn't bother. I would make sure to avoid those women in future. With no idea what I might say to her, I would be making sure to avoid Sara too.

Feeling defeated and drained, I went back upstairs to shower, aiming to go out again to the shops. I couldn't keep still – hadn't been able to since I'd left the hospital. I needed to be doing something, anything but thinking, hopelessly trying to make sense of the nonsense after we'd moved in and the nightmare that followed.

I'd intended to start job-hunting, but I hadn't been able to bring myself to. I hadn't yet come to terms with the fact that I would be going back to work much earlier than I'd anticipated. I'd poured my energies into physical activity instead, cleaning the house like a woman possessed. Walking, aimlessly. Running as soon as I'd felt able to. Anything that might exhaust me enough to stop my mind whirring, to stop the images of that godforsaken night crashing into my head. Nothing worked. I still felt empty and desolate inside.

THIRTY-SIX

Naomi

An hour later, after a trip to Dunelm for the white floral wallpaper I'd seen there, some gloss paint and a new wallpaper scraper, along with a steamer that was on sale, I made myself a strong cup of coffee and went to the lounge, determined to remove the awful green sponged woodchip from the walls. Starting with the chimney breast wall, I set to work, soon realising that the paper wasn't going to come off in nice easy strips. It seemed to be stuck on with superglue. After placing newspaper down to catch the mess, I employed the use of the steamer, working on the window end of the wall. The sponging was a shade lighter here, I noticed. Painted with a different batch of paint possibly? Thinking about it, shouldn't there be an alcove this side of the chimney breast? I stood back to survey the whole of the wall. There was one on the other side. The previous owners had obviously filled this one in making the wall flat, possibly to house a corner television table. That was a shame. Alcoves provided focal points in a room, housing pretty ornaments, plants and books. Testing the wallpaper, I found this section came away more easily. The plaster underneath was quite soft, which would make the job of recovering the alcove a darn sight easier. I would have my work cut out, but right now I relished that. It would tire me out, hopefully affording me some much-needed dreamless sleep.

Focused on my work, my thoughts on Sara, who might well be just on the other side of this wall, I jumped a mile when Ben spoke behind me. 'What on earth are you doing?' he asked, sounding wary.

Since I had the wallpaper scraper in my hand, I thought it was pretty obvious. 'I thought the room needed lightening up.' I glanced to where he stood in the doorway. 'Plus, I needed something to keep me busy.'

Ben sighed and nodded. I guessed he understood why. 'Upstairs and get changed, guys,' he called back to the children, who were scrambling out of their coats in the hall. 'Looks like it's pizza for dinner tonight, but only if you're on your best behaviour.'

'Yay!' Maya and Liam chorused, and they thundered up the stairs, squabbling as they went about whether they were going to have Pepperoni or Cheese Feast.

'And don't forget to wash your hands,' Ben called after them.

I smiled, feeling better for the normalcy around me, even though my world still felt bewilderingly off-kilter. 'I bought that paper I saw,' I said, nodding towards the rolls I'd stacked against the wall in the bay window. 'I think it will be perfect.'

Pulling off his tie as he came into the room, Ben glanced in that direction. He looked tired. I felt a pang of guilt. He was hurting inside as much as I was. He'd cried quiet tears of heart-wrenching grief as he'd held me when I came round after the anaesthetic. Since then, apart from when we'd both broken down at the funeral, he'd been stoic, making sure to be there for me. I needed to remind him I was there for him too. Placing the scraper down, I went to him. 'Thank you,' I said, keeping my dirty hands away from him as I leaned in to kiss his cheek.

Ben looked at me uncertainly. 'For?'

'Looking after me. Putting up with me being so manic lately.'

'It's fine. I get it.' He smiled. Still, though, his eyes were filled with dark shadows. 'This is a bit keen, though, isn't it?'

'You have to admit it needs doing, and I have some time on my hands, so...' I shrugged and turned back to the walls.

I heard his deep intake of breath as he walked across to me. 'It will get easier,' he said, encircling me with his arms and pressing his lips softly to my neck. 'It won't go away, but it will get easier to deal with, I promise.'

Leaning into him, I swallowed back the painful lump in my throat. He'd been here before, bereaved and bewildered. I could only imagine what he must have gone through, being orphaned as a child, brought up in care and starved of his mother's love, his father's guidance. I so wished he would talk more to me. I would try to encourage him to, I decided, but perhaps right now it would all feel too raw.

'Need a hand?' he asked.

I shook my head. 'No. I just wanted to make a start. I think I've done all I can for today.'

'I'll go make us a cuppa then.' He gave me a squeeze and eased away.

'Thanks,' I said appreciatively. 'Ben...' I stopped him as he walked to the door.

He turned back.

'I was wondering about this wall. Does it look unbalanced to you?'

He tipped his head to one side and surveyed it. 'Not really.'

I knitted my brow. 'But shouldn't there be an alcove the

other side of the chimney breast? There usually is, isn't there?' The one time I'd been in Sara's lounge I hadn't really been looking at the walls, but I was sure her chimney had an alcove on each side.

Ben considered. 'Possibly,' he said. 'I like it the way it is, though. It gives the room character.'

I looked at him, puzzled. 'I would have thought two alcoves would lend the room more character.'

Ben frowned thoughtfully. 'Maybe,' he said. 'I'll get that tea.'

Quickly shoving the decorating paraphernalia against a side wall, I followed him through to the kitchen. 'Did everything go okay at work?' I asked him.

'It's been a long day.' He smiled disconsolately. 'I'm shattered to be honest.'

Of course he was. He'd barely had a whole night's sleep since we'd lost Elias. I only had to look at the bruises under his eyes to realise that. And then he had to come home to this mess. It was no wonder he wasn't in the mood to discuss alterations to the house.

'I've decided to start looking for a job,' I said, making my decision. Our finances were stretched, which would be adding to his worry. 'Teaching assistant jobs are few and far between,' I chatted on, trying to ignore the tightness in my chest as I considered the prospect of going back to work knowing I wouldn't come home to my baby. 'I doubt they'll be looking for anyone at the children's school, but they might know of something at one of the other local schools.'

'Hey, slow down.' He turned to me with a mixture of alarm and surprise. 'We're not that strapped for cash yet.'

I eyed him uncertainly. I wasn't convinced. I thought it was more likely he was just trying to reassure me.

'You're wearing your worried face,' he said, his mouth curving into a knowing smile as he came across to me. 'You don't need to worry.' Wrapping his arms around me, he pulled me to him. 'You go back to work when you're ready, not before.'

Locking his gaze on mine, he gave me his best stern look, but his eyes, mesmerizingly intense, were filled with concern. How was it possible that people didn't seem to like him? Why did Sara not like him? He'd never done anything to her. Yet she was like a dog with a bone, trying to find reasons to justify her obvious antipathy towards him.

I nodded and rested my head on his shoulder. They were all unfounded, the things she said about him. I knew him. 'Can I ask you something?' I said, glancing up at him.

He smiled. 'As long as it's nothing too complicated.'

'Little Buttons... Sara said she found him. Did she give him to you?'

'Maya's teddy bear?' Ben frowned. 'That's news to me,' he said, stepping away with a shake of his head. 'And no, she didn't. I would have told you if she had.'

I knew it. She hadn't found him. She was clearly trying to stir up trouble. Or else she was holding on to the bear, and I couldn't imagine what reason she would have for doing that.

'Where did she find him? Did she say?' Ben asked, going back to the work surface to make the tea.

'In the shed.' I hesitated. 'She also said she found Lucky locked in there.' Knowing that would sound to him exactly as it had to me, like an accusation, I looked guardedly across to him.

His shoulders visibly tensing, he placed the kettle he'd just picked up carefully back down. 'Also news to me,' he said. 'Jesus, she really doesn't like me, does she?'

Sure that my confirming it wouldn't help matters, I refrained from commenting.

'I have no idea why she would have said that.' Emitting an agitated sigh, Ben faced me. 'I suppose I'm going to have to tell you now. I didn't want to, but...'

'Tell me what?' My heart faltered.

He eyed me reluctantly. 'We had a break-in,' he said, taking a tight breath. 'I came back from the hospital one day to find the kitchen window smashed.'

A break-in. I stared at him, poleaxed. 'As in, there was someone here, in our house?'

'There was nothing much taken,' he assured me quickly. 'Just some cash I'd left in the fruit bowl. When I discovered the lock on the shed had been forced, I assumed it was kids looking for bikes or something. I reported it to the police, but it didn't do a fat lot of good.'

I was struggling, really struggling, my emotions colliding, confused thoughts whirling around in my head. 'But why didn't you say anything?'

Ben kneaded his forehead. 'I don't know. I should have before now, probably, but... How could I, with all that you were already trying to deal with? I fixed the window and decided not to say anything until I thought you were strong enough. What I can't fathom is why the bloody hell Sara, who also knows damn well what you've been through, would tell you a complete pack of lies.'

THIRTY-SEVEN

Naomi

I knew it was Sara at the front door. I'd seen her approaching through the lounge window. She'd texted me a couple of times asking how I was, which I found astonishing considering she clearly didn't care. She would know I was home – my car was on the drive. Plus, I'd made no effort to be quiet while scraping the rest of the paper off the lounge walls. I wasn't going to answer the door, though, nor was I going to reply to her texts. After being on the point of storming round there, my anger at tipping point, I'd decided to take Ben's advice and have nothing to do with her. I couldn't believe she'd actually had the gall to come here.

After a minute, she rang the bell a second time, then rapped on the door. Then lifted the letter flap. 'Naomi? Are you all right?' she shouted through it.

I ignored her, continuing to pour my energy into removing the layers of yellowing paint from the doorframe.

There followed a brief silence, then another rattle of the letter flap. 'I'm worried about you, Naomi,' she called. 'Could you at least text me and let me know you're okay?'

I ignored that too. Did she honestly think I wanted to talk to her in any form?

When she finally left, I decided I would text her – a short, succinct text, from which she would hopefully get the message. Downing tools, I grabbed my phone from the coffee table. *I'm fine. Busy. If you have Maya's teddy bear, could you leave it in the porch. Thanks.*

I'd barely placed the phone down again when she shot a text back: *I left it in the shed. Really worried about you. Are you sure you're all right?*

Was the woman mad? A pathological liar? Why would she not just leave me *alone*? Anger churning my insides, I plonked the phone down. I was tempted to go and bang on her door, ask her outright what her problem was, but I couldn't see how a blazing argument would help. I just didn't feel strong enough.

Sighing with hurt and confusion, I went back to my task, which I had been finding quite therapeutic. Eventually I got down to the bare wood of the doorframe and realised it was quite beautiful. Thinking I might leave the woodwork natural, I traced my fingers down the rest of the frame, pausing as I came across what appeared to be notches carved into it. That was a shame. Would filler fix it? Examining the damage more closely, I was surprised to find it was a height chart.

Realising I'd uncovered a little bit of history, sadness engulfed me – for the family who had lived here, the lost little girl. Might this have been her height chart? My heart pitter-pattering, I squinted at the lettering above the notches, trying to read the name. Crudely carved, it looked like Alan. Or Adam, possibly? I couldn't quite make it out. The age looked to be eight. Another below it charted his height at seven, and then lower at six years old. There'd clearly been a boy living here.

When? I hadn't heard or seen mention of one in the family of the lost little girl, but might he have been her brother?

Empathising profoundly with the pain the girl's poor mother must have endured, I was deep in thought when the slam of Ben's car door jarred my attention. Going to the lounge window, I couldn't quite believe it when I saw that Sara had accosted him on the drive, even though the children were with him. I was about to fly to the front door when Ben headed towards it. I heard him open it and usher the children inside.

'Hi, you two. Won't be a sec,' I called, continuing to watch as he walked back towards Sara. I wasn't sure what words were exchanged, but from the livid look on Ben's face as he turned abruptly away from her seconds later, I guessed they'd been short and sharp.

'Mummy, why can't I play with Ellie?' Maya asked, trailing tearfully across the lounge towards me.

With no clue what to say to her, I bent down and wrapped her into a hug. 'You can, sweetheart,' I tried to reassure her, thinking there had to be a way to let the children play together. 'I think her mummy's really busy at the moment, though, so perhaps not for a few days.'

Maya looked at me from under her eyelashes. 'She could come here,' she said. 'I could go round and ask her.'

'What, with this mess?' I glanced around the room. 'Anyway, it's late now, isn't it? We'll be eating soon.'

'Tomorrow then?' Maya bargained.

'We'll see.' I smiled, but my heart broke for her. I would have to talk to Sara, I realised. Somehow, we had to reach a compromise for the children's sake, although I would definitely want Ellie around here. I wasn't sure what the situation was between Sara and Paul, but since he'd appeared to be part of the we-hate-Ben brigade, I didn't want Maya or Liam around there being influenced by either of them.

'Where's Liam?' I glanced past her to the hall.

'Gone upstairs,' Maya answered glumly. 'He wanted to finish his game with James but Daddy said he couldn't and now he's having a moody.'

That did it. I *had* to talk to Sara. That Liam had made a new friend was a major breakthrough. What message would it send if he was suddenly banned from seeing James? Straightening up, I took Maya by the hand. 'Come on,' I said, injecting some enthusiasm into my voice. 'You slip upstairs and wash your hands, and then you can help me choose what we're having for pudding after our casserole.'

I would go round to Sara's once the children were in bed, I decided. Whatever Ben's views were, I felt it was crucial we let Liam and James's relationship continue.

He'd gone straight through to the kitchen, I gathered, hearing sounds of crockery being extracted from the cupboard. Urging Maya up the stairs, I went in and was surprised to find him pouring himself a large glass of wine. At this time in the evening? The children had had an after-school club, which is why Ben had been able to collect them, but still – it was too early to be drinking. I glanced from the clock back to him as he half-emptied his glass and then topped it up again. 'Want one?' he asked, glancing at me and then taking another swig.

I shook my head. 'It's a bit too early for me,' I said, hoping he would take the hint. He didn't, glugging back the rest of the glass. 'What was all that about with Sara?' I asked carefully. Liam clearly wasn't the only one in a mood.

'She said she hadn't seen you and asked me what was wrong.' He laughed disparagingly. 'I told her she was the problem and suggested she stay out of our lives.'

I looked him over with a mixture of shock and apprehension. He was angry, palpably so. 'And what about the children?' I asked. It was becoming clear that no one was thinking how all of this would affect them, Sara included.

Ben furrowed his brow, clearly not getting my meaning.

'Maya and Ellie are friends,' I pointed out. 'Liam is forging a friendship with James. We can't stop them seeing each other, Ben.'

Ben sighed and kneaded his forehead. 'Her two can come here,' he said after a pause. 'There's no way we're having anything to do with her, though, or that prat she was shacked up with. No fucking way. Do you hear?'

THIRTY-EIGHT

Naomi

Dinner was turning out to be fraught. Ben had been in one of his silent moods since I'd angrily accused him of issuing orders, which he hadn't needed to do. I was in full agreement with him about Sara's children coming here. Liam had taken his time to come to the table and was sullen when he did. 'Don't you like the casserole, Liam?' I asked him as he poked disinterestedly at it.

Liam shrugged. 'It's okay.'

'He's sulking,' Maya piped up. 'Because he hasn't got many friends.'

Worry surged inside me. His teacher had agreed we should put him forward for a behavioural evaluation, which was a huge step, but I was desperate for him to be more socially engaged in the meantime. I'd planned to talk to Ben about it this evening, but that hadn't happened.

'I'm not bothered about making friends,' Liam mumbled, stabbing at a carrot. 'The kids at school are immature.'

'Everybody needs friends, Liam,' I said gently. 'Why don't you have a think about joining some of the sporting activities at school?'

Liam shrugged. 'Don't fancy it.'

'But you could give it a try.' I glanced at Ben, hoping he would back me up.

Ben looked Liam over thoughtfully, but he didn't say anything.

Sighing in despair, I pushed my chair back as Liam climbed down from the table without finishing his food, probably to glue himself to some game or other on his tablet. 'Could you clear up?' I asked Ben, feeling peeved.

'What?' Ben was still distracted, clearly. 'Sorry, yes, no problem.' Seeming to shake himself, he got to his feet. 'Finished, Maya?' he asked, managing to muster a smile for her.

'Uh-huh,' Maya nodded. 'Can I have my ice cream in the lounge, Daddy?' She made her best beguiling eyes at him. '*In the Night Garden* is on soon.'

Ben made a great show of thinking about it. 'Okay,' he agreed, helping her down from the table. 'Only for half an hour, though.'

'But, Daddy' – Maya was aghast – '*Bedtime Stories* is on after. We *always* watch *Bedtime Stories*.'

'You drive a hard bargain.' Ben smiled. 'Right, *Bedtime Stories* it is, and then straight to bed, no arguments. Deal?'

'Deal.' Maya giggled gleefully as he swept her up into his arms. Obviously, he was making an effort to lighten the mood. I was grateful for that much.

Once he'd settled Maya down, he came back to the kitchen. 'Don't worry about Liam,' he said. 'He's just acting out. I'll go up and have a word with him. See if I can get him to open up a little.'

He was right, Liam was acting out, but it was no surprise. Neither of the children had really understood when I'd told them the baby brother they were expecting had been poorly and that God had taken him for an angel. They'd both been devastated. And now we had Sara's ridiculous behaviour to contend with, which was only upsetting them further.

I buried a sigh and was about to fetch the ice cream when I heard a scratching sound, followed by a tap on the front door. Frowning, I went to the hall, wondering who could be calling this late in the evening. *Sara.* Who else would it be? I wanted to talk to her, and I would, but not with Ben here. Steeling myself, I hurried towards the door and pulled it open – then froze.

What on earth was *she* doing here? *How* was she here? Had she been following me? She'd been at the park. At the school. And now she was here, on my doorstep. Unease crept through me. 'Can I help you?' I asked warily.

'I'm not sure.' The woman looked at me in bewilderment and then back down to the key she still held in her hand. 'I was trying to let myself in but my key doesn't seem to fit.'

A lurch of fear shot through me. Why in God's name was she trying to let herself into our house? Had it been her who'd broken in?

'I'm sorry, but I think you've made a mistake,' I said curtly. 'This is actually our...' Seeing her obvious confusion, how terribly pale and frail she was, I stopped myself. Her coat was buttoned incorrectly, I noticed, and she was wearing odd shoes. She looked so lonely standing there, so lost and fragile, that my heart went out to her.

'The lock must be broken,' she said, her eyes shiny with tears as she looked back at me.

I didn't comment. She'd obviously come to the wrong house and plainly needed help. 'Why don't you come in and let me make you a cup of tea,' I suggested, offering her a reassuring smile as I moved back from the door.

'I can't think what else could have happened.' The woman glanced at the door and down to the key again as she stepped in. 'The lock's never stuck—'

'What the hell are you doing here?' Ben yelled behind us.

The woman snapped her gaze towards him. 'I know who you are.' She frowned, her eyes flooding with shock and anger as they drilled into his. 'Get out of my house!'

'You need to leave,' Ben growled, moving so swiftly to take hold of the woman's arm that I stumbled backwards into the wall.

'Ben!' I recovered myself, grabbing hold of his other arm as he almost manhandled her through the front door. 'Stop!'

Skirting around in front of him, I placed myself physically between them, and my insides turned over. His face was blanched of all colour, his eyes filled with palpable terror.

THIRTY-NINE

Naomi

'What in God's name are you *doing*?' I demanded, attempting to wrestle him away from the woman, who was half his size.

'She needs to go,' he seethed, his chest heaving.

As he made again to push past me, I stood my ground – with difficulty. Ben was much taller and stronger than me. For the first time in his presence, I felt true fear. 'Let go of her, Ben,' I warned him. 'If you don't, I'll call the police.'

'But he's not Ben.' The woman's expression went back to confused. 'Adam? Why are you doing this?' She looked at him imploringly.

Ben sucked in a breath, his thunderous gaze fixed hard on the woman. Seconds ticked by, heavy with tangible tension, and then he breathed out and, finally, stepped away.

'It's okay,' I tried to reassure her, my gaze flicking cautiously to Ben as I shepherded her back inside. 'I've got you. You're safe.'

She looked at me with fear in her eyes and then back to him. 'I don't know what I've done to upset him,' she murmured, clutching her coat tight to her chest. 'He's not normally like this.'

Who did she think he was? Icy apprehension prickled the entire surface of my skin as I looked my husband over.

He glanced from me to the woman, and what I saw in his eyes shocked me to the core. They were filled with something I had never seen in him, nor thought I ever would. He was looking at this fragile woman, who could surely pose no threat, as if he despised her. 'She needs to go,' he repeated, his voice hoarse.

'Why?' I scanned his face, willing him to explain, to look at me. 'Who is she? For pity's sake, tell—' I stopped, my gaze shooting to where Maya stood uncertainly in the lounge doorway.

'Is that the lady from the park, Mummy?' she asked, her eyes travelling apprehensively from me to her father.

'Go upstairs, sweetheart.' I nodded her up. 'I'll come up in a minute.'

Forcing a smile, I attempted to steer the woman into the kitchen, but for all her frailty, I couldn't budge her. She seemed transfixed, her gaze focused on my daughter. 'Holly,' she whispered, stretching a hand out towards her.

Cold foreboding travelled the length of my spine. Holly? The lost little girl?

'Jesus Christ,' Ben uttered. 'Maya, go upstairs.'

Maya scowled petulantly. 'But, Daddy, I want to watch—'

'Now!' Ben shouted, causing Maya to jump.

What was *wrong* with him? As tears sprang from Maya's eyes, I went quickly to her, taking hold of her hand and manoeuvring her past me to the foot of the stairs. 'Go on up, sweetheart.' I urged her. My breath stalled as I realised Liam was standing at the top of the stairs, a glower on his face as he stared down at us.

'I knew I would find her,' the woman murmured tremulously, her gaze still fixed to Maya as I tried to encourage my little girl up the stairs. 'I knew she would wait for me.'

'That's enough!' Ben's voice was desperate. 'Get out! Now!'

My blood ran cold. 'Liam, you need to you look after Maya,' I instructed him urgently.

Liam glared at the woman, then equally angrily at his father. 'Come on, Maya,' he said, dragging his mutinous gaze away and extending his hand to her.

Once the children had reached the landing, I whirled around.

The woman was staring after them. 'I need to speak to her,' she said, her eyes feverish as she edged towards the stairs.

I stayed put at the foot of them. I wasn't about to let her anywhere near my children.

'I have to go to her. She needs me,' the woman cried. 'I heard her, calling out to me. She—'

'It's not Holly!' Ben yelled, moving quickly towards her.

'I heard her.' The woman attempted to pull away from him as he grasped her arm.

Ben yanked her back hard. 'It's not fucking Holly. You need to leave.' He pulled her, almost dragging her to the front door.

'But I live here.' The woman's her eyes pivoted pleadingly towards me. 'This is my home.'

'Not anymore.' Ben pulled the front door open.

'For pity's sake, you'll hurt her.' I flew towards him as he all but shoved her out onto the doorstep.

'Go! And do *not* come back,' he seethed, slamming the door shut behind her.

My heart banging against my ribcage, I stared at him in absolute horror. Then, as furious as I was frightened, I attempted to move around him. I couldn't let her go like this. I wouldn't. I had to know what was going on.

Ben blocked me. 'Leave it,' he said.

Leave it? Staggered, I stepped back from him. His eyes were flint-edged, his expression as hard as granite. 'I'm going after her.' I snatched my gaze away from him and tried again to get past.

Ben stopped me, taking hold of my forearms, which only fanned the fury burning inside me. 'Why are you doing this?' I yelled, pushing him away. 'Who is she?'

'No one,' he answered tightly.

'You know her.' I ran furious eyes over him. 'She knows you. What the bloody hell is going on?'

'Nothing.' He wouldn't look at me. 'She was mistaken.' He made to walk past me.

I sidestepped. 'You're lying! Do you think I can't see that?'

He kneaded his temples. He didn't answer.

Bitter disillusionment swept through me. 'You obviously think very little of me, don't you, Ben?' I said, my tone flat. 'Of the children?'

That hit home – the latter, at least. He snapped his gaze back to me. 'That's not true, Naomi,' he said shakily.

I held his gaze. 'Then why lie to me?'

His eyes flicked away again. 'I'm not. I...'

I waited for him to finish, to say something. Anything that would make any kind of sense of this madness.

He said nothing, and my heart folded up inside me. My husband was lying to me. My life was unravelling around me, our family fracturing, and he didn't seem to care. I studied him for a long, silent moment, then moved to the lounge door.

'And this, Ben?' He looked at me with a mixture of unease and confusion as I pointed to the height chart on the doorframe. 'Is this nothing? A coincidence? Is that what you would have me believe?' I indicated the name I'd found carved into the wood-work. Not Alan, but *Adam*. Was this the man standing in front of me?

Who was he?

FORTY

Naomi

'Don't you dare.' I watched in disbelief as Ben picked up his car keys from the hall table and walked to the front door. 'Ben!' I yelled, fury spiralling inside me. Was that even who he was? 'If you leave, you don't come back, do you hear?'

He faltered, but he didn't turn around. Was he going to say nothing? Go into one of his ridiculous bloody silences? Now?

'I've had enough, Ben. I can't take any more,' I begged him, my throat closing, tears rising. And I cursed them. I wanted to weep, break down and sob. But how would that help? There were two children upstairs who would be terrified by all of this. Did he really care nothing for them?

Still standing with his back to me, he didn't utter a word. I was at the point of shaking answers from him when he spoke. 'I'm sorry,' he said quietly.

What did he want me to say to that? It's fine? I'll go and put the kettle on and forget about the woman you've just thrown out on the street? A woman who'd clearly lived here? I took a breath, warned myself not to lose my temper. It would achieve nothing other than to drive him out of the door. Did I want him to go? I felt so desperate, I didn't know. I wanted answers. The truth. Did I not deserve that much?

'What are you sorry for?' I asked him guardedly, praying he didn't lie to me further. I had no idea whether there was any coming back from this – I didn't know what I was dealing with – but I was sure there wouldn't be if one more lie passed his lips.

'Everything.' He drew in a sharp breath. 'It's my fault. All of it. What happened to you. The baby...' He faltered.

I felt myself reel. 'Elias,' I whispered, exhaling hard.

'I'm sorry,' he repeated, his voice thick with emotion.

Every sinew in my body tensed. 'How was it your fault?' I asked, fear tightening like a slipknot inside me.

He turned slowly to face me. Still, he wouldn't meet my gaze. 'I should have told you the truth.' His tone was flat, hopeless. 'I don't know why I didn't. I knew she was suspicious. That she knew. I...' He stopped, exhaling hard.

'What truth?' I shouted. 'Who knew? Suspicious of what? For God's sake, Ben, talk to me!'

He didn't answer and I wanted to fly at him, hit out at him, hurt him as much as I was hurting inside. Conversely, as I watched him press a thumb and forefinger hard to his eyes, I wanted to hold him, have him hold me, soothe me and make the pain go away. Impossible. It was never going to go away. It was only going to get worse and I didn't think I could bear it.

After an agonisingly long moment, he looked at me. His eyes tortured, he studied me for a long, searching moment, and then he bowed his head. 'She's my mother,' he murmured.

Uncomprehending, I stared at him. I felt as if my world was imploding. Yet, I knew. Somewhere inside me, I'd known the second that woman had addressed him as Adam. I didn't respond. I had no words. I couldn't think straight, couldn't breathe.

His gaze flicked back towards me. 'I had no idea she would turn up here,' he said, as if that could explain or excuse anything. 'I should have—'

'You told me she was dead!' I hurled my truth at him. I was married to a liar, a manipulator, someone my heart had bled for because I'd believed he'd suffered such a tragic loss as a child. Sara had been right, I realised. I'd been living with a man I didn't know at all. How was that possible?

'I thought she was. She walked out. Disappeared. I never heard from her. Not a single word, Naomi.' He stopped and dragged a hand over his face. 'I guess telling myself she was dead was my way of coping, Maybe I wanted her to be. I don't know.'

His voice was strained, his body language that of a defeated man. A man who'd been found out? I bit down hard on my anger. 'What's her name?' I asked. There were a million questions tumbling around in my head. Had he cared about her? That was my overriding question. Ever? Did he now? It certainly didn't appear that way.

'Lily,' he answered quietly.

Lily. I silently repeated it. 'And you had no idea she was alive until she walked through that door?' I was sceptical.

He pinched the bridge of his nose. Contemplating his answer? Wondering whether to add another lie to his pack? 'I made some enquiries,' he said eventually. 'Contacted the care home about six months ago. They said they'd tried to trace her. She'd had some kind of breakdown. The details were sketchy. They didn't tell me at the time. Maybe because they didn't want to get my hopes up. I don't know.'

He paused, scanning my eyes cautiously. Was he wondering how much I was likely to believe? 'I saw her,' he went on awkwardly. 'On the street. Sitting on the pavement, outside a shop. I wasn't sure it was her. I was in the car, driving through Harborne. By the time I'd found somewhere to park and walked back, she'd gone.'

He'd never said a word. 'So is that why we moved here?' I asked, recalling how keen he'd been to put an offer on the house. 'Because you thought she might turn up?' Had it been anything to do with his job at all?

He nodded. 'Partly. Seeing her brought it all back. I suppose I was looking for answers.'

'About what happened to your sister?' I asked, my mind whirring as I tried to make sense of it.

Blinking hard, he glanced at the ceiling. 'That,' he admitted. 'And about my father. He committed suicide,' he said, his voice cracking, 'not long after Holly went missing.'

Nausea swirled inside me as I recalled the headline I'd found: *Father of Missing Girl Commits Suicide.* I'd been shocked – devastated – as I'd imagined the impact on his wife. Never in a million years could I have imagined that the man who'd hung himself from a bough of the tree just yards from our back door had been my husband's father. A part of my heart broke for Ben. Now it made sense – the way he was, the long silences, the lone runs. He had been running from his past.

'The house was never up for sale, was it?' I asked, though I didn't need to. I'd convinced myself that the woman at the estate agent was incompetent rather than believe what had been staring me in the face. The house didn't belong to us. The ghosts that haunted it wanted the cursed thing back!

He shook his head. 'It was mine,' he said. 'It passed to my mother from my father, and then, eventually, I was able to make a claim on it.' He stopped. I saw the slow swallow slide down his throat and guessed he was struggling. Not half as much as I was. 'I didn't want to come here.' He met my gaze, finally. 'Bring you here, our children. It was the last place on earth I wanted you to be, but...'

Sensing another bombshell, I braced myself.

'I didn't have a choice.' He drew in a breath. 'The hospital trust didn't relocate me.'

'They sacked you?' I felt the foundations shift violently beneath me.

Ben glanced away. He looked like he wanted to disappear inside himself. 'I hadn't told them about the seizures.' Another lie. 'I ended up making a mistake, meaning evidence wasn't catalogued properly for use in court,' he went on falteringly. 'It was an abuse case. The guy walked. A formal complaint was made and... The hospital couldn't let it slide. You were pregnant and... I panicked. I thought we might not be able to meet the rent, that we might end up homeless, and I didn't know what else to do.'

I studied him, thunderstruck. 'But you had your new job to go to?'

'It wasn't confirmed.' He looked more guilty by the second. 'They took their time getting back to me. I think they only offered it to me because they were desperate. It's also a grade below my pay scale.'

'Why didn't you tell me?' I didn't understand. Surely he must have known that he could have.

'I should have. I'm so, so sorry.' He looked desperately towards me. 'I know you can't forgive me, but please believe I didn't mean to hurt you.'

I looked away, nausea swilling inside me as reality sank in.

'Naomi?' He stepped towards me.

'Who is "she"?' I raised a hand, stopping him. 'You said "she" was suspicious, that "she" knew. Who was suspicious? What did she know?'

'Who I was,' he replied, a fatalistic edge now to his voice.

'Joan?' I recalled how she had studied Maya so intently the first time she'd seen her that she'd sent my little girl scuttling shyly behind me. How she'd stared at Ben, almost as if she'd seen a ghost.

He nodded.

'And Sara?' There was something going on between them. Some reason Sara had seemed to instantly dislike him. There had to be.

He hesitated. 'She knows the woman whose evidence I screwed up.' He shrugged, shamefaced. 'I guess that's why she hated me on sight.'

Sara hadn't told me. She could have. If she'd really wanted to turn me against him, surely she would have?

'Does Paul know?'

He sighed expansively. 'I'm guessing so, yes. He definitely seems to hate me.'

The unpalatable truth hit home. They all knew things I didn't. How could he have done this?

'What do I call you?' I swallowed back the anger burning inside me. 'You're not Ben Felton, are you?'

He didn't answer. He didn't need to. His name was Adam. His family name: Grant. I'd borne his children. Yet I had no idea who he was. Who *I* was.

'I've just buried our baby.' Pain twisted inside me. 'I had to register his death, naming you as his father: Ben Felton. How could you have let me do that?' I swallowed back the knot in my throat, which was growing more excruciatingly painful with each blow. 'How could you do that?'

'I'm sorry.' His voice cracked. 'I didn't mean to. I... didn't know how to stop it.'

'Stop *what*?' The tears came, exploding with confusion and anger.

'Naomi, please... don't.' He moved towards me, tried clumsily to hold me.

I pushed him away. 'Maya and Liam have your name,' I

reminded him, another piece of my heart fracturing. 'The wrong name.'

He moved again towards me. 'Naomi, please believe I didn't plan this. I didn't—'

'Don't!' I stumbled a step back. I couldn't have him near me, not now.

'Please don't cry.' He reached for me. 'Please let me—'

'Leave her alone!' Liam yelled from the top of the stairs. 'Don't you touch her.' He thundered down to the hall, his hands balled into fists at his sides, his small chest heaving as he faced his father.

'Liam.' I flew to my son, wrapped my arms around him and drew him backwards towards me. 'It's okay, darling. I'm fine,' I tried to reassure him. 'Everything's all right, I promise.'

'It's not!' Liam cried, struggling to pull away from me. 'He's ruined everything!'

'Liam, please don't.' Ben's voice was hoarse with shock. 'I'm sorry. Please let me explain.'

'No! You're a liar! You're *not* sorry.' Liam squirmed in my arms. I was sure if I let him go he would hit his father.

'Liam, listen to me, please.' Ben choked. 'I love you. I love all of you more than my life. Please believe I didn't mean for any of this—'

'Liar!' Liam shouted over him. 'You don't care about us. You don't care about anyone! I hate you! I hate that horrible woman, too. I wish she *was* dead! I wish *you* were.'

FORTY-ONE

Sara

Hoping it would be Naomi at the front door, Sara hurried to the hall. She was so worried about her. Hearing a kerfuffle on Naomi's doorstep while she'd been tucking Ellie into bed had ramped up her worry. She'd rushed to the front bedroom window and had been flabbergasted to see the strange woman Paul had 'lost it' with wandering off down the road. That couldn't be a coincidence. Recalling how the woman had been loitering that time outside the school, the thought occurred that she might have been following either her or Naomi. Naomi, most likely, since she'd turned up at her house. But why? Might she really be dangerous? She didn't look like a child abductor, but then what did child abductors look like? There was more to this. Sara had no idea what was going on, but having also heard Naomi and Ben arguing, she couldn't escape the feeling that Naomi might be the one who was in danger.

Bracing herself to apologise to her, she pulled her front door open, then stepped back in surprise.

'Can we talk?' Paul asked, his expression contrite.

Sara hesitated. He'd walked out on her. But then, she had been awful to him. She hadn't meant to blame him for what had happened to Naomi, but it must have sounded that way.

'I wanted to apologise.' Paul glanced awkwardly down and back. 'I shouldn't have stormed off like I did. I was bloody annoyed, to be honest, that we were arguing about that prat next door.'

'You'd better come in.' Sara moved swiftly back lest Naomi should overhear.

Giving her a small smile, Paul stepped inside. 'Are the kids okay?' he asked.

'Fine.' Sara nodded. 'They've not long gone up to bed.'

'Ah, right. That's a shame.' He shrugged disappointedly. 'I was hoping to say hello to them.'

Uncertain what to say to that, whether they were together anymore or not, Sara avoided answering. 'Do you want some tea or coffee?' she asked instead.

Paul shook his head. 'No, thanks. I can't stay. I have a job on.'

Sara arched an eyebrow. 'At this time?'

'Afraid so. Single mum, three kids and her plumbing's backed up. I can't leave her in the lurch.' He sighed good-naturedly, reminding her of why she'd been attracted to him in the first place – because he was a caring person, which was at odds with him flying off the handle the way he had.

There was an uncomfortable moment, then, 'You lost your temper,' Sara said, looking him over guardedly. She was still wondering about what he'd said about Ben not being in the house when Naomi was struck by that car, but as he had a customer waiting, now wasn't the time.

'I know. I shouldn't have.' Paul ran a hand over his neck.

'Look, I didn't want to say anything – the bloke was obviously having a bad day – but...'

'But what?' Sara urged him, a knot of tension tightening inside her as she wondered what he was about to tell her. From the grim expression on his face, she was sure it wasn't anything good.

'Joan's cat was on top of his car,' he went on finally. 'I was coming out of the front door at the time. I thought he was about to shoo it off. He didn't. He picked it up by the scruff of its neck and threw it off.'

Sara stared at him, stunned. 'You're joking.'

'I wish I was.' Paul shook his head in despair. 'All I can say is it's a bloody good job cats have nine lives. It landed in the road. If it hadn't been nifty it might have been curtains. To be honest, I'm wondering whether the man's all there.'

'Oh no.' Sara felt sick. He *had* locked Lucky in the shed. She knew it. 'I'm sorry,' she said, realising why Paul had been annoyed at being labelled the bad guy. 'About launching into you the way I did. I was just so upset for Naomi I wasn't thinking straight.'

Paul smiled understandingly. 'It's okay, I'm thick-skinned. It stung at the time, though, that you thought I would say something just to stir up trouble. It's not me, Sara. I don't believe in interfering in other people's business. I was so amazed to see him cuddling the cat, though... I guess I wasn't thinking either.'

She dropped her gaze guiltily. 'I'm sorry,' she repeated, feeling extremely wrong-footed.

'No harm done,' he assured her, with another easy shrug. 'I'd better go. I have a single mum in need of rescuing.'

Sara stopped him as he turned for the door. 'Will you come back?' she asked. She wouldn't blame him if he said thanks but no thanks, but she wanted him to know she was still interested, even if he wasn't.

Paul turned back. 'Do you want me to?'

'I do.' Sara smiled. His comment had caused trouble, there was no escaping that, but he wasn't malicious or aggressive or any of the things she'd been worried he might be. Ben Felton, on the other hand... Anger welled up inside her. She'd been right about him. Naomi might be in danger and she had to make sure she was there for her.

'Good.' Paul walked back to kiss her cheek. 'I'll try not to be too long.'

Sara caught his hand as he turned for the door. Stepping towards him, she pressed her mouth to his, wanting him to know how much she'd missed him. They were mid-clinch when Ellie called from the landing: 'Mummy, I need the loo.'

Paul rolled his eyes and eased away. 'We'll pick up where we left off later,' he promised, giving her a wink and patting her behind as she headed for the stairs.

Once Sara had sorted Ellie out, she popped her back to bed and then went to her own room. Ellie's interruption had been quite timely. She dreaded to imagine what Paul would have thought of her tatty, comfy underwear.

She was selecting something more provocative when the sound of Paul's key fob beeping drew her to the window. Peering out, she saw him standing at the driver's side of his van. Catching her looking, he shook his head and kicked his tyre, then gave her a wave and climbed inside. His tyre pressure was down, she guessed. He was a real stickler for vehicle safety checks. Mind you, with her tendency to make a mental note to do it later and then forget, she was glad that he was.

FORTY-TWO

Naomi

After calming Liam down and managing to encourage him back to bed, I sat down next to him. 'Okay?' I asked. I could see from his tense body language – arms folded tightly across his chest as he leaned against his headboard – that he was far from okay.

'He's been lying,' he muttered, his face set in a thunderous scowl.

I reached to stroke his hair. 'I know.' I didn't want to defend Ben, condone his lies, yet part of me didn't want to destroy him completely in his son's eyes. 'He was wrong to, but I think he was trying to protect us, Liam. Make sure we had a home.'

He didn't look convinced. 'What was that mad woman doing here?' he asked.

I hesitated, unsure how much he'd heard.

'He said she's his mother. Is she?' My boy scrutinised me carefully.

I breathed deeply. 'I think so.'

Liam's scowl deepened as he attempted to digest this. 'So why did he tell you—?' He stopped, his gaze snapping towards the landing as the front door banged closed downstairs.

Guessing, just as Liam clearly had, that Ben had left, my heart sank, then plummeted as Liam shuffled angrily down in his bed. 'I hate him,' he seethed, his voice both tearful and furious. 'Everything's gone wrong since we came here. I hate this house and I hate *her*! I want her to go away.'

'Liam...' Devastated by his outburst and desperately worried, I tried to console him, but Liam only burrowed deeper.

'She needs to go away,' he repeated. His voice was muffled and tight with the tears he was trying hard not to cry.

I reached to place a hand on the bulge that was him. Liam curled himself tighter. Even through the duvet I could feel the tension emanating from him. Biting back my own fury, I left him to make sure Maya was okay, still tucked safely up in my bed. I found her wide awake and hugging her ancient snuggle toy close in place of Little Buttons. I still had no idea where he was.

'Why is Liam angry?' she whispered, her wide eyes filled with uncertainty as they searched mine.

'Because Daddy and I had a little argument.' I bent the truth. How could I ever tell my children that their world was about to fall apart? But I didn't have to tell Liam, I realised, my heart growing heavier, if that were possible. With the wisdom of a child who was suddenly older than his years, he knew.

'Is that why you're sad?' Maya's small brow creased in sympathy.

Swallowing emotionally, I smiled and smoothed her hair from her forehead. 'I am a bit sad, but we'll sort it all out, darling. Try not to worry.'

A flicker of doubt crossed my little girl's face.

'Close your eyes, sweetheart.' I leaned down to kiss her cheek. 'I'll be back soon and we'll cuddle up, okay?'

Placated by that, Maya nodded, pulled Alex the Donkey closer to her and closed her eyes. A second later they sprang open again. 'Will you give Daddy a good night kiss for me when he comes back?' she asked, her expression now one of alarm.

'I will, sweetheart,' I promised, my voice catching.

After making sure she was tucked up, I went to the landing, where I pressed my back against the wall, took several slow breaths and tried desperately to stem the tears that spilled down my cheeks. Apart from the excruciating pain in my chest, I felt numb, utterly depleted. For the thousandth time, I asked myself, *Why?* There was no answer. No reason. A jumble of thoughts fought for space in my head as I went over what Ben had said, and I couldn't make sense of any of it.

What would I do? Assuming he came back, did I want him to stay? Did I want to be here, in this house, which with his mother reappearing very likely wasn't even mine? I didn't. Liam had been right: things had started to go wrong the second we'd moved here. I'd sensed something, I knew now with certainty that I had – an aura that had been impossible to explain. With no income of my own, though, where else would I go? Yet more unanswerable questions crowding into my mind, I hurried to the stairs, treading almost blindly down them.

Trembling with fear – for my children, my husband, for myself – I sank to my haunches at the foot of them, dropped my head to my knees and quietly sobbed. Where had he gone? Had he taken his car? Would he come back? I shouldn't care where he'd gone, or how, and I shouldn't want him back. But I did care. His stress levels now would be off the scale. He might have a seizure, God forbid at the wheel of his car.

Standing unsteadily, I headed to the hall table to check whether his keys were there. Relieved when I saw they were, I was about to go to the kitchen when I stopped. There on the hall floor, stuffed through the letter flap while I'd been upstairs, was an envelope.

Wiping a hand across my eyes, I blinked hard and stared down at it. It was a plain white envelope. No address, I noted, picking it up.

My heart stalled as I wondered whether Ben had pushed it through. But why would he have done that? Cold foreboding crept through me as I recalled how defeated he'd looked, how bitterly ashamed and lonely. A new fear gripping me, I turned the envelope over and tore at the seal. With trembling fingers, I pulled out the note and unfolded it. Seeing it was typewritten, I frowned in confusion. As I started to read the contents, my stomach tightened, and then turned violently.

Dear Naomi,

I'm writing this because I think you should know that your husband is keeping secrets from you. Are you aware that he's having an affair? If you confront him, I imagine he will deny it. You might believe him, telling yourself he isn't capable of such deceit. But ask yourself, is he? Have you not wondered why he wanted to move here so urgently?

If you don't take heed, I think you may be in grave danger. Love can inspire, but it can also drive people to great acts of despair, madness or even murder. Where was he the moment that car struck? I may be wrong, but I would urge you to leave him immediately.

Yours,

A concerned friend.

Nausea rose hot in my throat. No. Not possible. I felt the floor shift and the walls in the small confines of the hall loom in towards me. No! What Ben had told me was devastating. But this? This was ludicrous. Malicious! Fury unfurled like a viper inside me and I ripped the letter in half, then into quarters. Then I tore ferociously at it, shredding it again and again.

It was a lie. Ben wouldn't. *Adam*. I didn't know who he was. Tears choking me, I sank to my knees, the letter, along with the remnants of my life, my marriage, scattered like confetti around me.

Who? My mind ticked feverishly. Who was he having an affair with? Who would send this? Was it one and the same…? My heart jarred as the blindingly obvious hit me.

Sara. The furtive, sometimes heated conversations they'd had crashed into my mind. I'd wondered at the barbecue whether they'd known each other before we moved here. Why she'd seemed to take such an instant dislike to him, making him out to be some kind of controlling monster. I'd even accused her outright of trying to turn me against him. I'd told myself I was paranoid. But I wasn't. That's exactly what she'd been trying to do. She'd wanted me to leave him. I almost laughed at my naivety. Quite clearly something had happened between them. And Sara had decided she wanted it to keep happening. She wanted him. And Ben – *Adam* – what did he want?

They'd taken my baby from me. Vitriol burned like acid inside me. Were they trying to take my sanity too? I thought of the contents of the letter: *Love can inspire, but it can also drive people to great acts of despair, madness… murder.*

I would fight. While I had breath in my body, I would fight. I would not let them take everything from me.

FORTY-THREE

Naomi

.

I noted heads turning towards me as I walked past the clique of gossiping mothers on the way to the school gates the next morning. As I'd made no effort to speak to them, nor they me, since Liam had purportedly hit out at another child, I guessed the topic of their conversation might be our questionable 'family circumstances'. They were certainly questionable now, and wouldn't they have a field day if they knew my husband was a cheat and a liar. Perhaps they already did. Wasn't that the nature of these things: the wife being the last to know? If Sara and Ben had been seen together, if Sara had let something slip, rumour would travel like wildfire. I didn't care. I cared about my son, though, and the accusations they'd made about him, which were just wrong. He was withdrawn sometimes, but he wasn't violent.

Focusing on putting one foot in front of the other, because it was all I knew how to do, I walked on, scanning the playground as I went. There was no sign of Sara. She must have dropped her children off fast and run. Because of her argument with Ben, I wondered. She would probably guess that I'd seen her accost him on the drive.

She would be at work now. Did I want to confront her there? I thought not, but I drove to her salon anyway, idling the car in the parking bay in front of it. I could see her through the window. Was she the kind of woman my husband would fancy, fall so deeply in love with that he would be driven to an act of despair or murder to rid himself of his wife? Resort to gaslighting to make her question her reality, her sanity?

She was beautiful. Her auburn, highlighted hair bouncy and glossy. Always perfectly made up and dressed trendily – provocatively. A pang of jealousy shot through me. I'd never seen her in anything but tight jeans or leggings and with tops cut low enough to show off the rose tattoo on her breast. Of course she was the kind of woman men would fancy. How could she not be – especially next to me, my face pale and make-up free, my post-pregnancy figure far from desirable? I gulped back a jagged knot in my throat. How long had it been going on? Had it started when I was pregnant? Before? Was that a factor in why Ben had wanted to move here – to have easy access to the woman he was sleeping with? Is that why he'd hated Paul on sight – because he hadn't expected to find Sara had moved another man into her life?

Realising she'd seen me and was walking towards the salon door, I pulled hastily out of the parking bay, the sharp blare of a horn telling me I hadn't checked for traffic. Tears squeezed from my eyes and I blinked hard, trying to force them back. I needed to concentrate. My children needed me.

Arriving at the house to find Ben's car wasn't there, I pulled my phone from my bag, convinced my Bluetooth wasn't working and that he would have called. He hadn't. There were no missed calls, no messages. Should I ring the hospitals? He'd left on foot and been gone the whole night. What if he'd had a seizure? I shouldn't care, but I did.

Feeling frozen inside, I climbed out of the car and glanced around, wondering which of my neighbours might know about my husband's supposed affair. I'd tried to give Sara the benefit of the doubt. Not wanting it to be her, I had tried to imagine who else might have posted that letter. I'd wondered whether it might be someone's idea of a cruel joke. Paul certainly wasn't Ben's number one fan. I'd considered whether it was someone genuinely trying to warn me. But now I was convinced it was someone who wanted me out of the picture. Sara. She'd befriended me, then banged on about Ben being controlling. She'd even tried to convince me that it was him who'd locked the cat in the shed, that he'd taken Little Buttons away from Maya and locked him in there too. She wanted me to leave him. It was obvious.

Joan was in her window, I noticed, as I looked across to her house. Might she have seen who'd delivered it? Might *she* have? She'd disliked Ben from the outset, for reasons I'd then found unfathomable. I knew now that she'd been aware of who he was. Still, though, she'd disliked him. Because she'd known that I didn't know, I wondered? Or was there more? Something to do with his past, which Ben had never been open about? Deciding to speak to her, I went across the road, my stomach clenching painfully as I heard the petrifying screech of brakes all over again, felt the sickening impact that had killed my child. I tried to shake it off, tried hard not to picture my baby's sweet, perfect face, to no avail. I would carry his image for the rest of my life.

Closing my eyes as I reached her gate, I composed myself and walked up her path to ring her bell. It took a while for her to answer; remembering she would struggle to get to the door, I felt a pang of guilt. I was deliberating whether to leave when I heard the sound of her approaching the door.

'Naomi, how are you?' She searched my face sympathetically as she pulled the door open. 'I've been meaning to come across but I wasn't sure whether to. Sara said you were coping, but I've been so worried about you.'

My tears dangerously close to the surface in the face of her seemingly genuine concern, I felt some of my anger dissipate. She might know nothing about the letter. To launch into her would be cruel. 'I'm okay, thanks, Joan.' I managed a smile. 'I was hoping to have a chat, if you have time.'

'I have all the time in the world, dear,' she assured me. 'Come on, come in and get warm. That weather's turning.'

I stepped in, closing the door behind me as she turned her frame and negotiated her way towards the lounge. I helped her into her chair, waited until she was comfortable, then took a breath. 'It's about Lily,' I said.

'Oh.' Something behind the woman's eyes shifted. 'He's finally told you then, has he?' she asked, her expression growing wary.

'He had no choice.' My voice sounded defeated, even to my own ears. 'She came to the house.'

Joan looked surprised. I didn't think it was feigned. She obviously hadn't been in her window last night. I studied her, my heart drumming against my chest as she considered for a moment. Then, 'And has he told you everything?' she asked, her eyes narrowing.

I frowned, unsure what she meant. Was she talking about Lily being Ben's mother? The affair he was supposed to have had or was having. Was he? I felt another part of me die inside as I considered how many lies he'd told me. Had anything he'd ever said meant anything? His marriage vows, his declarations of love? When he'd cradled his children in his arms, had the promises he'd made to protect them been genuine? The heart-broken tears he'd cried for Elias, had they been real?

'About him being the last person to see his sister alive?' Joan clarified, and I felt as if the ground had been ripped from beneath me.

FORTY-FOUR

Joan

Joan berated herself as soon as the words fell from her mouth. Seeing the colour drain from Naomi's face, she prised herself from her chair. 'Sit down,' she said, taking hold of one of her hands. She was so cold it was as if she hadn't got an ounce of blood in her body.

Her face ashen, Naomi stepped shakily back and dropped heavily down on the sofa.

Cursing her arthritic limbs, Joan shuffled across to ease herself down next to her. 'I should have told you. I suspected who he was. Once I was sure, I should have said something, but...' She stopped, sighing in despair of herself. She really hadn't been sure Ben was who she'd thought – until her gaze had fallen on little Maya. She was the image of Holly. She'd handled it all so badly, but her intentions had been good. Hoping that the man had managed to put his past behind him and build a new life, she hadn't wanted to jeopardise it, but she could see now that she'd been wrong to withhold what she knew. 'I take it he didn't tell you about the circumstances surrounding her disappearance?' she asked gently.

Squeezing her eyes closed, Naomi answered with a short shake of her head. Joan noted her sharp intake of breath and reached to massage her back in slow, soothing strokes. As if anything could soothe this poor woman after all she had been through. She gave her a moment.

'He said... He told me Holly had disappeared, that his mother was dead. And then she turned up on our doorstep.'

She'd come home. After all these years. Joan could scarcely believe it. 'I see.' She nodded, confounded. 'That must have been a terrible shock.'

Naomi wiped at the tears on her cheeks. 'It was.' She swallowed. 'She recognised Ben, but she wasn't making much sense.'

That didn't surprise Joan. Lily had always been highly strung. With all that had happened, Joan suspected that grief might have driven her to a very dark place, hence her sudden departure, leaving her son all alone. Searching her cardigan pocket for a tissue, she handed it to Naomi. 'It's clean,' she said, and waited while Naomi attempted to compose herself.

How much should she tell her? Naomi was married to the man. She'd borne his children. She'd just buried a child. Joan's heart bled for her. She had to tell her what she knew now. Hopefully it would help her make some sense of it all. Although Joan didn't know what had truly happened on that dreadful day when Holly had failed to come home, speculation had been rife. Joan hadn't believed it. But the Grants had, judging their son guilty. They'd limped through the days and weeks afterwards, no longer a family, fractured and incomplete. They'd closed themselves off in that house, hiding from bloodthirsty reporters. Afterwards, they'd stayed behind those walls, rarely emerging. And then one day, Michael Grant had simply lost the will to keep living. Lily's house lights had shone day and night after that, until the ghosts that had surely haunted her had driven her away.

Joan braced herself. 'You know about his father?' she asked tentatively.

Naomi seemed to fold in on herself. 'Someone sent me an article,' she said, her voice quavering. 'I hadn't realised it was Ben's father until now.'

Joan stared at her with a creeping sense of dread. She might have wondered who would do such a thing, but she had an awful feeling she knew. If it was who she suspected, then, unlike Adam, this man's appearance had changed. As a youth, he'd been overweight, with a mop of unruly dark hair. Now he was all muscle, his head shaved.

'What did you mean?' Naomi asked, pulling her from her thoughts. 'You said that Ben was the last person to see his sister alive.' There was fear in her eyes as she turned to her: ice-cold, tangible fear.

Joan could see she'd guessed the implication. She really had no choice now but to tell her as it was, or how it had appeared to be. Her mind would only fill in the blanks otherwise. She took a second to get her thoughts in order, then, 'They went out together on their bicycles,' she said, 'Holly and Adam – you've gathered that that's your husband's name?'

Naomi nodded, her face growing paler, if that were possible.

Joan's heart wrenched for her. 'They weren't supposed to go beyond the road, but invariably they would slip off, stretching their boundaries, as children tend to.' A deep sadness washed through her as she recalled the two children, who were often up and down the road on their bikes: Holly sometimes speeding off; Adam, whose job as the older sibling was to look after her, chasing her like mad.

Tears welling in her own eyes, she blinked them back and continued. 'Holly was a bright girl, talented, the apple of her parents' eyes. She could be a little spiteful, though.' Joan frowned, remembering how Holly had once thrown Adam's football into the garden of a miserable neighbour who'd accused Adam of drowning his cat in his pond. It hadn't been Adam – Joan had been as sure as she could be about that. It had been the cruel little wretch Zachary, who loved taunting him and who she now suspected had resurfaced. She'd seen the boy running up the road, laughing and plucking his wet T-shirt from his chest.

'Spiteful how?' Naomi asked, concern in her eyes. For her husband, Joan guessed. She did hope that concern wasn't badly misplaced.

'She wasn't a nasty child,' she clarified, not wanting to talk ill of Holly. 'I would often see her teasing her brother, though. Just because she could, I think. Lily tended not to admonish her, and I remember thinking that perhaps she should. Adam rarely fought back. He was a quiet boy, withdrawn, bullied by other boys sometimes – one in particular, who worked at humiliating him, trying to get him to react.'

'And did he?' Naomi asked. Joan guessed why: because she couldn't imagine him reacting. Her husband clearly hadn't changed. Joan's mind went back to the barbecue. Taunted then, Adam had been angry, but rather than retaliate, he'd walked away.

'Rarely,' she answered honestly. 'Although when I went out once to intervene, I did catch a thunderous look in his eyes. He didn't express his emotions easily. I wondered whether Lily should perhaps approach the school about getting him assessed.'

Seeing a troubled frown cross Naomi's face, Joan guessed she was thinking of her boy, who seemed very much like his father.

'So what happened? On the day Holly went missing?' Naomi pressed her.

Joan hesitated. She wasn't sure Naomi was ready to hear it. But now Lily had reappeared, she guessed she would know sooner or later. 'They cycled off to the reservoir,' she revealed. 'Adam, Holly and one or two other children. Several witnesses saw them there. Adam had a puncture, and Holly refused to wait and cycled off. According to the other children, Adam was furious when he caught up with her. One child said they saw him push her. I'm not sure I believe that was true. After that, no one knows. There were no eyewitness accounts of what might have happened to her, but much later, as it was growing dark, Adam came home alone.'

Naomi scanned Joan's eyes, bewilderment in her own. 'They blamed him,' she whispered, clearly horrified.

Joan drew in a breath. 'Nothing was proven – the police couldn't be certain – but yes, I think people did. Sadly, I suspect his parents did too.'

Naomi stared at her, stunned.

'They took him back to the reservoir that night. He didn't want to go. I watched his father almost drag him to the car.' Joan closed her eyes, reliving memories of a terrified boy being hauled down the path, his father clutching his arm so tightly he'd had no hope of escaping, no matter how hard he'd squirmed. *I don't want to. I didn't do anything!* She heard his cries again, desperate, pitiful. Adam had dug his heels in, terrified of getting into that car, until eventually Michael had carried him.

She shook off a shudder. 'I'd hoped to catch them when they came back, to offer them whatever support I could. It got so late, though, I couldn't keep my eyes open. I didn't see much of them after that. I never saw Adam again – not until the police arrived, a while after his father's suicide. Lily had left him, I gathered. I saw them bring Adam out to the police car. I've never seen a more lonely, frightened child in my life.'

'I have to go. I have to try to find out where Ben is.' Naomi shot so suddenly to her feet, Joan had no hope of keeping up with her as she flew to the door.

By the time she reached the hall, Naomi was across the road and disappearing through her own front door. She would have to ring her, once she'd figured out where she'd left her phone. Or go across to her. The woman was going to need a shoulder.

Turning back to the lounge, she stopped, hesitating for a second before pulling the second drawer of the hall cabinet open. Carefully she extracted what she'd found in the gutter on the dreadful night Adam had been dragged screaming to his father's car. Seeing them come home, she'd gone across to their house, intending to offer whatever help she could. She'd stopped short when she'd seen it: one little patent red shoe. Holly had been wearing the shoes when they'd cycled off. She was sure she had been. She couldn't fathom how it had come to be lying in the gutter. She'd realised, though, that if Adam had found it while searching for Holly – and she believed in her heart that he had searched for her, that he hadn't hurt her – then the fact that it had been in his possession might be incriminating, unfairly so.

She shouldn't have kept it. At the time, though, she'd also believed that the boy had suffered enough.

FORTY-FIVE

Lily

The evenings were drawing in. It would be dark soon. It was also growing colder, but not intolerably so, a mild southerly breeze sending soft ripples across the water. Sitting on a bench on the path that ran around the reservoir, Lily tugged the blanket she wore over her coat more tightly around her and settled down for the night. Sometimes, as her mind drifted, she could see her baby, riding her bicycle where she shouldn't be. But she wouldn't be here tonight. She was at home, playing hide-and-seek, waiting for Lily to find her. Lulled by the lapping of the water, she closed her eyes, counting silently to one hundred. 'Coming, ready or not,' she whispered.

The Christmas *Radio Times* was still on the coffee table when she went into the lounge, *Harry Christmas! Have a wizard time!* splayed across the front of it. The lady police officer was there, but Lily hadn't been able to find Holly anywhere. Lily felt frightened suddenly. She didn't want this woman here. She wanted her to go away. Wanted everyone to go away – the reporters that persistently knocked the door, the telephone that rang off its hook – she wanted it all to stop.

'I'm here to support the family, Lily.' The woman spoke kindly, as she had so many times over in her head. 'To make sure information is conveyed to you in a timely fashion.' But there had been no information, no sighting of her daughter since she'd cycled off on her Girl Power Spice Girls bike. There wouldn't be any sighting of her. Lily knew this. The woman didn't need to be here.

'It's blue,' she said, her gaze drifting to the muted television where *Buffy the Vampire Slayer* was playing. Holly would have mithered to watch it. Lily wished she'd allowed her to now.

'What's blue, Lily?' the woman asked her.

'Her bicycle.' Lily's throat tightened as her mind shifted.

It was Holly's birthday. The weather was bitterly cold, rain sleeting down, but still Holly insisted on testing out her brand-new bike. Lily shivered as she stood outside, watching her ride the length of the road and back.

'Blue with pink flowers on the chain guard and purple tassels on the handlebars,' she added.

But the woman knew that. She'd already told her. 'Her helmet was pink.' Had she told her that? Lily couldn't remember. Her thoughts were disjointed, random memories tripping over each other. Holly giggling, singing the lyrics to 'Wannabe'. Lily found herself humming it. Holly crying with frustration whenever she couldn't get her own way. Holly taunting her brother.

Adam scowling. 'He never retaliates,' she said, her gaze going to Michael, who'd appeared in the police officer's place. Her heart ached as she took in her husband's appearance. He'd aged, quite literally overnight, his face haggard, wisps of grey at his temples, purple half-moons under his eyes. In his eyes, fear and incomprehension.

Lily looked away, her gaze drifting again to the TV magazine. The boy on the front reminded her of Adam, the same tousled dark hair, the glasses, which other children goaded him about – that little brute Zachary the worst of all. Lily knew it wasn't just his glasses that set Adam apart from the others. It was his long silences, the way he quietly observed things. The seizures, which had begun since his sister had gone, had provided rich fodder for those who wanted to torture him. Lily dearly wanted to help him, but how could she when he didn't want her anywhere near him? He hated her. She'd felt the fury emanating from him when she'd finally found her way home. She did tend to lose track of time, things changing around her yet staying the same. The house hadn't changed. Holly, she was still the same beautiful little girl she'd lost and found. She hadn't meant to leave Adam for so long. She shouldn't have abandoned him.

'*If you wanna be my lover,*' she sang softly, settling her mind back on Holly, who gyrated along to the song like a girl much older than her age.

'Barmy old bat,' a male voice muttered.

Lily snapped her eyes open to see the snarling face of a teenager up close to hers. 'You need locking up in a loony bin, you do, luv,' he snarled, his foul breath smelling of beer. 'Got any money?'

Before Lily could tell him no, he'd snatched up her precious bag and was rifling through it, tugging out her belongings and tossing them aside.

'Christ, what a load of old crap,' he said to the teenage boy he was with, who was standing back, puffing on an odd looking cigarette.

'Give it her back, Jakey.' The youth sighed. 'She's not hurting anyone.'

'Yeah, right. She's offending my delicate sensibilities, ain't she? You can smell her a mile off.' Clearly not finding what he was looking for, the yob swept a derisory glance over her, then lobbed the bag as far as he could into the water. 'Nightie-night.' He smirked over his shoulder as he strolled off.

Lily jumped to her feet, a tear freezing on her cheek as she watched the bag sink, inside it the 'Posh' Spice Girls necklace she'd taken from Holly when she'd said goodbye to her. Why did he have to do that? She'd wanted to give it back to her. 'Bastard!' she shouted after him.

The yob stopped and spun around.

'Leave it, Jake.' His mate caught his arm as he lurched towards her. 'Unless you want to spend the night in the nick.'

The yob stopped and wiped an arm across his mouth. 'Your card's marked, missus,' he warned her, jabbing a finger at her. 'You'd better make yourself scarce.'

Feeling hurt and confused, Lily hurried away. Why were people so awful to her? She'd done something terrible, but they didn't know that. And she'd only done what any mother would do, following her instinct to protect her child. She shouldn't have left Adam. When she'd finally found him again, her heart had sung, and then he'd glowered at her in that terrifying way, and it had sunk like a stone.

He was doing it now. A cold chill seeping through her, Lily stopped in her tracks as she saw him standing just yards ahead, staring, making no move towards her. Even from this distance, she could feel the seething heat from his eyes. How was it possible for such a young boy to be filled with such palpable anger?

FORTY-SIX

Sara

Paul came into the kitchen as Sara was shoving the breakfast bowls she hadn't had time to clear away that morning into the dishwasher. 'Fancy a stroll by the reservoir?' he asked her. 'The weather's quite mild. I thought we could all go to the pub after and grab a bar snack.'

'Nice idea...' She glanced apologetically at him as she closed the dishwasher.

'But?' He obviously noted her lack of enthusiasm.

'To be honest, I'm dead on my feet. We had a couple of walk-ins at the salon and I've barely had time to breathe.'

'You work too hard.' He went across to her, sliding a hand around her waist and giving her a squeeze.

'Needs must.' She sighed.

'Tell you what – I'll take the kids, shall I?' he offered. 'Give you some time to chill.'

'That would be great, thanks.' Sara smiled appreciatively. It would give her a chance to try again to contact Naomi, who wasn't returning her messages or texts. After the way she'd pulled away from the shop, an oncoming car just millimetres away from ploughing into her, Sara was growing extremely worried. She couldn't understand what Naomi had been doing there. If she'd wanted to speak face to face, why hadn't she just come in?

'No probs.' Paul smiled amiably. 'I'll grab some pizza on the way back. It'll save us having to cook.'

'Brilliant.' Sara was grateful. Because of her previous experience at the hands of a bullying man, she'd been too ready to judge him. She wouldn't do that again in a hurry.

'Back soon,' Paul said, leaning in to kiss her cheek as she swept a cloth agitatedly over the work surfaces. 'Kids,' he called, heading for the hall. 'You, me and footie at the reservoir? Pizza after, what do you think?'

'Yes!' was the unanimous answer, followed by the thundering of feet along the landing.

Smiling as they headed out, Sara went upstairs, desperate to kick off her shoes. She was pushing her feet into her slippers when she noticed Naomi heading up her front path. Relief sweeping through her, Sara hurried back down the stairs, opening the front door as Naomi knocked. 'Hi.' Noting the pensive frown creasing Naomi's brow, she smiled hesitantly.

Naomi didn't smile back. 'Do you mind if I come in?' she asked, nodding past her to the hall.

Perplexed, Sara stood back. 'You're welcome anytime, Naomi. You know that.'

'And Ben?' Naomi said as she stepped in. 'Was he welcome anytime, Sara?' Turning to face her, she fixed her gaze on hers, and Sara stepped back in shock. Her eyes were icy and filled with accusation.

'Naomi?' Sara shook her head, confused. 'I have no idea

what you're talking about. Are you okay?' she asked, her concern escalating.

Naomi avoided the question. 'I think you know very well what I'm talking about, Sara.'

Staring at her, stupefied, Sara noted the angry flush to her cheeks and realised she was serious. 'Come through to the kitchen,' she said, turning to close the front door. 'We clearly need to talk.'

Naomi didn't move, preventing Sara walking past her. 'Why did you pretend not to like Ben?' she asked, studying her carefully.

Sara laughed, flabbergasted. 'I wasn't pretending.'

'Really?' Naomi's mouth curved into a cynical smile.

'I haven't the first clue what you're talking about, Naomi.' Sara felt herself growing flustered. Worse, defensive.

'You said you didn't know him.'

'I don't.' Sara laughed, astonished. 'You were upset. I—'

Naomi spoke across her. 'Yet from your character assassination of him when you came round to my house, it seemed to me that you knew him very well.'

'I was worried about you.' Sara stared at her, utterly confused. 'I was trying to warn you about him.'

Naomi scoffed. 'Can you not hear yourself, Sara? Do you not realise that in trying to dig yourself out of one hole, you're digging yourself into another? Of course you know him. Even without Ben telling me you do, it's bloody obvious. Do you think I'm a complete idiot?'

Sara had no idea what to say to that. The woman's insinuation was obvious. Where was this coming from? Naomi clearly suspected that Ben was cheating on her. Had someone said something implicating Sara? 'You're upset,' she said. 'After all that's happened, obviously you would be. Please come into the kitchen and—'

'After all that's happened?' Naomi laughed scornfully. 'You

mean Ben locking cats in sheds on purpose? Deliberately running me over when I'm pregnant with his baby?' Naomi's eyes were burning with anger. 'Him being a manipulator and a monster?'

'He *has* been manipulating you!' Sara retaliated, her own temper rising. 'He's been lying to you, Naomi. Whether you can see it or—'

'I gathered that!' Naomi shouted. 'Did you send that letter?'

Sara studied her hard. 'What letter?' she asked shakily. The woman was talking in riddles.

'I think you know very well what letter.' Naomi eyed her steadily. 'The one that was posted through my door last night. Why would you think he was a manipulator?' she went on, before Sara could answer. 'Something you felt duty-bound to inform me of?'

'This is ridiculous.' Sara's throat tightened. 'I think you should go, Naomi.'

'Was it because he took what was obviously on offer and then walked away? Did you expect more? That he would fall hopelessly in love with you, wouldn't be able to live without you? Did you decide that he was just like your abusive ex? If he even existed; we don't see much of him visiting his children, do we? That Ben had also used and abused you when he didn't come back for more? Is that it?'

'Naomi, please just stop,' Sara begged her.

'It was you who started this, Sara,' Naomi replied stonily. 'With your ridiculous accusations. You were the cheerleader for the we-hate-Ben brigade, after all, weren't you? I don't see you hanging around with that clique of superior bitches at the school, but I'm betting you're one of the we-hate-Liam brigade, too.'

'That's enough, Naomi.' Trembling, Sara reached to open the door.

'Did you get a kick out of it, Sara? Fucking my husband? Seeing me crumble?'

'Just *go*, will you?' Tears spilling from her eyes, Sara held the door wide.

'I'm going, don't worry.' Naomi strode past her. 'By the way, did it occur to you to wonder who else might be responsible for the run of shitty things that have been happening? The missing cat saga? Me being enticed into the street and then mown down by some callous bastard who didn't care that I was pregnant? If you didn't send that letter, then ask yourself who else might have. Someone who clearly hated Ben on sight, that's who – because you'd been cheating on him. You need to look closer to home for manipulative liars, Sara.' She glanced at her as she walked past her, her eyes furious and full of bitter disappointment.

FORTY-SEVEN

Sara

Sara was still shaking when she heard Paul and the children clatter through the front door. 'We're back, Mummy,' Ellie shouted.

'In here,' Sara called, pushing her wine glass aside as Ellie charged into the kitchen.

'I scored two goals,' she exclaimed gleefully.

'Did you indeed?' Sara bent to give her a hug. 'Well done you!'

'Only because Paul let you.' James rolled his eyes as he followed her in.

'No, he did *not*.' Ellie gave her brother a scowl. 'He couldn't get to the ball, could you, Paul?'

'Not a chance.' Coming in behind them, Paul shook his head. 'You sent me completely the wrong way. You're definitely England squad material.'

'See.' Ellie nodded triumphantly. 'Told you.'

'Yeah, right. Whatever.' James smirked. 'Can we have our pizza now? I'm starving.'

'Upstairs and wash up first,' Paul instructed them, placing the pizza on the work surface. 'Did you manage to grab some rest?' he asked Sara, giving her a peck on the cheek as the kids scooted out.

'Not really. I pottered around and got a few jobs done.' Should she tell him about the dreadful argument with Naomi? She was worrying now that Naomi might approach him, having also accused him of sending hate mail. She was riddled with guilt as well, suspecting that Naomi might be teetering on the edge of a breakdown. Where was Ben in all of this?

'Bit early, isn't it?' Paul nodded at the wine glass Sara had left on the work surface.

'You said I should chill,' she pointed out, picking it up and taking a swig.

'Fair enough.' Paul set about unboxing the pizza.

'So it went okay at the reservoir then?' she asked, careful to keep her voice casual. 'No tears or tantrums?'

'No. They were as good as gold.' He grabbed the plates and carried them to the table. 'I reckon they'll sleep well tonight.'

'Great.' Sara smiled. 'Thanks for that.'

'Like I say, no problem. It's good they're so at ease with me – if we're going to make things between us more permanent, I mean.'

Were they? He was talking about living together officially, presumably. They hadn't actually discussed that, but she supposed it was the next natural step. They were as good as doing that anyway.

'Oh, that prat from next door was there, by the way,' Paul said, as Sara fetched the cutlery.

'Who? Ben?' She frowned. Had he and Naomi had a major falling out? From what Naomi had said, she guessed they must have. The fact that he was at the reservoir on his own when he should be at work seemed to confirm it. Sara wasn't sure how she felt about that.

'Yep.' Paul fetched the Coke from the fridge and grabbed the red wine.

'What was he doing?' Sara asked, wishing she could go and see Naomi, even after all the awful things she'd said to her. It was clear she was devastated, indicating they had argued badly, and that was partly her fault.

'Nothing much.' Paul shrugged. 'He was sitting on one of the benches, staring out at the water.'

'Did he see you?' Sara felt a flutter of nerves in her tummy as she wondered whether they'd spoken.

'Can't fail to have done.' Paul sat at the table and poured himself some wine. 'James kicked the ball right at him. The bloke didn't even acknowledge him, ignorant git.'

Sara felt a surge of relief. She didn't want Paul dragged into something that would only cause more friction between them. 'You really don't like him, do you?' She knitted her brow thoughtfully.

Paul took a sip of his wine. 'There's not a lot to like, is there?' He glanced at her. 'With a bit of luck his wife's dumped him and he was sitting there contemplating his future.'

'Why would you say that?' Sara asked, alarm bells ringing.

'Just wishful thinking. We'd be shot of him then, wouldn't we?' he answered, taking another mouthful of wine. 'Are you staying on white or do you want some red?' He picked up the bottle and waggled it in her direction.

'White's fine, thanks.' She studied him cautiously. 'Can I ask you something?'

'As long as it's nothing too complicated,' Paul replied with an easy smile.

Sara paused, unsure how to ask. 'Naomi received a letter,' she started hesitantly. 'You don't know anything about it, do you?'

Paul's expression was quizzical. 'What kind of letter?'

'I'm not sure precisely.' Sara glanced down and back. She didn't want to sound like she was accusing him. 'It's obviously a poison-pen letter, though. It's caused terrible trouble between Ben and her. She's really upset about it.'

'Ah, right, so he's cheating on her then.' Paul's mouth twitched into a scornful smile. 'Well, I'm sorry Naomi's upset, but considering the trouble he's caused between us, forgive me if I don't shed any tears over the tosser she's married to.'

'I don't know what the content was,' Sara said, growing more wary.

'When did she receive it?' Paul asked.

'Yesterday. You didn't see anyone approaching her house when you were checking your tyres, did you?'

'Nope.' He shook his head. 'There was no one around, as far as I could see.'

Sara nodded and tried to banish the suspicion blooming inside her. 'I suppose we'll never find out.' She sighed and joined him at the table. 'There are some strange people about.'

'That there are,' Paul agreed with a tsk.

'There's something else I wanted to ask you about,' Sara said tentatively.

Paul arched an eyebrow. 'Are we doing twenty questions?'

Sara smiled. 'Last one, I promise.'

'Shoot,' he said amiably.

'About the trip to Spain you mentioned. Any idea when it might be? It's just I have to organise cover at work and the kids are really looking forward to it.'

'Not sure.' Paul took another drink, studied the bottom of his glass and then reached for the wine. 'The ex is playing silly buggers. I let you know as soon as I can, though.'

Smiling shortly, he glanced past her as Ellie and James came in, arguing about who was going to eat the most pizza.

'I reckon that will be me.' Paul reached to serve it up. 'Come on, hurry up before it's cold. I thought you two were starving.'

Sara smiled at the children as they scrambled to sit down, then glanced back at Paul. She couldn't help noticing the lack of eye contact when she'd asked him about the trip, or that he'd given her the same answer he had before. Thinking about it, although she had heard him talking to his daughter on the phone, he didn't talk to her often. He didn't talk that much about her either, strangely.

FORTY-EIGHT

Sara

'Won't be a sec,' Paul said, heading for the hall once the children were in bed. 'Just going to do a quick recce of the supplies in the van and make sure it's locked up.'

'I'll check whether there's anything worth watching on TV.' Sara followed him with a smile. She took a step into the lounge as he went through the front door, then stepped smartly back, her gaze straying to his wallet on the hall table. She hesitated, then picked it up. Taking a breath, she opened it, found his driving licence, then grabbed the pen and pad she kept on the table and made a note of his address.

After slipping the wallet back onto the table, she darted to the lounge window to check he was still busy and then went back to the kitchen, where she hoped he might have left his phone. It was there, sitting on the table. Hurrying across to it, she picked it up and keyed in the code she'd made a mental note of when he'd entered it earlier. Her heart palpitated as she scrolled through it, checking his photos, phone contacts and texts, then almost stopped dead as Paul came through the front door. *Shit.* Placing the phone quickly back down, she flew across the kitchen and busied herself filling the kettle.

'Haven't seen my phone, have you?' he asked, his brow furrowed.

'On the table, I think.' Sara nodded towards it and quietly prayed that he didn't notice she'd placed it face down. 'So will you give up your flat?' she asked, hoping to distract him until the phone went back to sleep. 'If we decide to take the plunge and live together, I mean.'

Paul looked at her in surprise. 'My dingy shoebox of a room in a shared house, you mean? It'll be a wrench but...' A broad smile on his face, he came across to her. 'I think I could be persuaded.'

Threading an arm around her waist, he pulled her towards him. His lips were a breath away from hers when his phone rang. 'Damn.' He sighed and went to answer it. After listening for a while, he nodded. 'Sounds like the cold water tank. I could come now, if you like?' he said into the phone, then mouthed, 'Sorry,' in Sara's direction.

Sara smiled indulgently.

'Right. I know where that is,' he said. 'I should be there in about fifteen minutes, give or take a few.'

'Plumbing disaster, I take it?' she asked as he finished the call.

'Afraid so. They've got water dripping through the ceilings. I can't really say no.' He shrugged apologetically.

'You're a saviour.' Sara assured him, turning her cheek to his kiss. 'Do you think you'll be long?' she asked, as he headed for the door.

'Not sure. It's an old house. Sounds like the whole system's dodgy, so it might take a while.'

'I'll keep the bed warm,' she promised.

'Do that,' he said, sailing off with a wink.

Once the front door closed, Sara headed for the lounge to make sure he'd driven off. She needed to ring Joan, who she was sure wouldn't mind helping her out. It was at times like this she dearly wished her parents weren't miles away in Cornwall. She would have to cite some emergency of her own for leaving the kids with Joan. She would think of something. After finding not even a whisper of anything to do with Spain on Paul's phone, no texts exchanged, no phone numbers listed, no photographs of his daughter, she felt it *was* an emergency. She hadn't seen where he lived. As Paul seemed to prefer coming here, she hadn't given it much thought. It might be that he was embarrassed about the accommodation, of course. She desperately wanted to give him the benefit of the doubt. She couldn't do that, though, until she'd found some evidence that his daughter existed. She'd thought she would be safe with a man who had a child of his own – that her children would be safe. Now, she didn't know what to think.

Going back to the hall to dig her own phone from her bag and ring Joan, she prayed she would find something that would prove her wrong. Because if she didn't, it would mean her judgement of men was seriously skewed. *Did it occur to you to wonder who else might be responsible for the run of shitty things that have been happening? You need to look closer to home for manipulative liars, Sara.* Naomi's parting words came jarringly to mind. But why would Paul have sent that letter? He would have absolutely nothing to gain by it. Still, though, she couldn't dismiss her suspicions. She did have trust issues, but there was something awry about the picture Paul had painted of his life. She could feel it.

Minutes later, she headed across the road with the kids bundled up in their PJs and dressing gowns with coats over.

Joan opened her door as she approached. 'Well, this is a nice surprise.' She smiled welcomingly down at the children. 'Come on, come in,' she said, manoeuvring herself back from the door. 'It's getting chilly out there.'

'Thanks, Joan.' Sara ushered Ellie and James in. 'Are you sure you don't mind?' she asked, stepping in behind them. 'I should only be an hour or so.'

'Not at all. You and the children are welcome anytime,' Joan assured her. 'They can snuggle up with me and watch one of those DVDs you left here last time.'

'*Toy Story 4*!' Ellie cried.

'Nuh-uh. *Fantastic Beasts*,' James decided, racing to the lounge ahead of his sister.

'Behave you two. Sit on the sofa until Joan comes in,' Sara called after them. 'I'm sorry it's such short notice,' she said to Joan. 'It's just that my friend is on her own and she has to stay there until the police arrive.'

'What an awful thing to have happened.' Joan tsked and shook her head. 'Is she all right?'

'She's okay. Shaken, obviously, as you would be when someone breaks in while you're in the bath.' Sara felt bad about lying, but if Paul came back and spoke to Joan, at least she would have her story straight. She also felt like the world's worst mother, dragging her children out of bed. She couldn't leave it, though. Paul would be back at some point tonight, and she didn't feel she could be natural with him until she put her mind to rest. The thought that he might only have been after what he could get depressed her. The thought that she might have exposed Ellie and James to someone who might be suspect terrified her.

'Did they take very much?' Joan asked, her brow creased sympathetically.

'No, not much, just some bits of jewellery. It's just that she's scared being there alone.'

'You get off. The children will be fine,' Joan said. 'I thought at first it was something to do with Naomi,' she added as Sara turned to open the door, freezing for a second as she saw Ben heading for his front door.

'Naomi? What about her?' Sara turned back, apprehension tightening her stomach as she wondered whether Naomi had told Joan about the letter, or that she'd thought it was Sara who'd sent it.

'Her husband not being who he says he is,' Joan went on.

What? Sara looked at her askance.

'She knew his name was Adam,' Joan went on, oblivious, 'but when I confirmed he was the brother of the little girl who went missing, I'm sure the blood drained from her body. Poor thing. After all she's already gone through as well.'

Sara felt her own blood run cold. She knew it. The man was a liar. But why pretend he was someone else? Was he trying to drive the woman insane? If that were his aim, judging how Naomi had been acting when she'd stormed around to her house, he was bloody well succeeding.

FORTY-NINE

Naomi

Sitting listlessly on the sofa, I stared at the walls, which weren't likely to ever see the wallpaper I'd bought. In throwing myself into the decorating, I'd been trying to distract myself from the pain, from the guilt every time I realised that in blundering out in the dead of night still half-asleep I'd endangered not only myself but my baby. I'd killed him. Nothing could distract me from that fact. Now, apart from the panic that spiralled inside me every time I considered what the future might hold, I felt numb. Where was he, the man I was beginning to believe was some kind of unfeeling monster?

'Mummy...' Maya said timidly from the lounge door. 'Why are you crying?'

I snatched my gaze towards her. 'I'm not, sweetheart. I have a cold, that's all. It's making me sniffle.' Swiping away my tears, I smiled and got quickly to my feet.

Neither of the children had been asleep when I'd checked

on them half-an-hour after they'd gone to bed, yet they'd been as quiet as mice, probably wondering why it was so quiet down here. Hurrying towards Maya, I drew her into a firm hug. Feeling her small body close to mine, a physical pain ripped through me as I pictured Elias, his features so perfect, his fingers and toes so tiny. I could almost smell him, the sweet, unique smell that binds mother and child together forever. Had his father forgotten him already? Did he not feel the same debilitating grief I did? Even faced with the soul-crushing evidence he didn't care for me, I couldn't make myself believe that.

Squeezing my little girl close, I kissed the top of her head, then eased away. 'Are you not sleepy?' I asked her.

Maya shook her head. 'I'm too worried,' she said, sounding so grown up suddenly that my heart wrenched for her. He was taking away their innocence. How could their own father do that to them? They'd lost their little brother and now their father appeared to have gone away too. How were they supposed to process any of this?

'Do you think you could be an extra special good girl for me and read your *Where's Bluey?* book for a while?' I asked her. 'I'll tuck you in, but then I have some phone calls to make. As soon as I've done that, you can tell me about all of the things you've managed to find.'

Maya considered. 'How many minutes will you be?' she asked.

'Not many,' I promised. 'I'll be as quick as I can.'

'Okay.' She nodded. There was a flicker of uncertainty in her eyes, though, as she searched mine. 'Is Daddy coming home soon?' she asked tremulously.

My heart plummeted. 'I'm not sure, sweetheart. He's really busy at the moment,' I lied, my throat tightening as I realised I would have to continue to lie to them to try to keep their world safe. 'He might be very late.'

Maya frowned. 'Will you ask him to come up and give me a kiss good night when he does?'

'Of course I will,' I assured her, forcing another smile. Straightening up, I took hold of her hand and led her back upstairs. After making sure she was snuggled up with Alex the Donkey and her favourite storybook, I pressed a kiss to her forehead and went to check on Liam.

He wasn't sleeping. I hadn't thought he would be. 'Are you not tired?' I said, going across to him.

His eyes glued to his Kindle, Liam shrugged then shook his head.

'Ten more minutes.' I gave his hair a ruffle. 'And then lights out. Okay?'

Liam answered with another shrug of his shoulders. I was torn. Would he shrug me off if I hugged him? Considering the mood he was in, I guessed he might and decided to leave him be – selfishly, because I knew I would feel his rejection. 'I just have to ring someone.' I waited, wishing he would make eye contact with me. 'I'll be back up soon.'

Liam nodded this time, an indifferent nod, but I knew he wasn't indifferent. I knew my son. He was confused and hurting.

Silently cursing Ben, I went back down, grabbed my phone from the lounge and went to the kitchen. I'd tried to tell myself I didn't care, but how does one just stop caring for someone? I had to ring around the hospitals, try to find out if he was all right. And if he was? Then his lack of contact had sent a clear message. He didn't want to face me. In light of the contents of that vile letter, though, I guessed it was more likely he didn't want to be with me.

Holding for the Accident and Emergency Department at the City Hospital, I felt a hollow emptiness inside me. I was sick to my soul that I had been so completely taken in by him. I must have been blind not to have realised that the antipathy between him and Sara had been manufactured. It had been lies. All of it, lies.

Ben wasn't there. He wasn't in his department either. I was about to hang up when I heard a key in the front door. My heart lurching, I jabbed the end call button.

'Daddy!' Maya exclaimed excitedly from the landing. Her antennae had obviously been on red alert, waiting for her dad to come home. Did Ben care that he was about to shatter all her illusions about him?

'Hey, munchkin,' he said emotionally. 'Have you missed me?'

My chest constricted. How could he ask her that when he was destroying his family?

'Uh-huh,' Maya answered. 'Where have you been, Daddy? We've been worried about you.'

Ben hesitated before answering. Was his guilt eating away at him? I hoped it was, that it would haunt him for the rest of his life. 'There's nothing to worry about, baby,' he said eventually. 'I've just been working really hard.'

Liar. My blood pumped so fast my head swam.

'How about I come up and tuck you back into bed?' he suggested. 'It's really late now. You'll be tired in the morning.'

'Okay,' Maya said, sounding much brighter.

I heard her little feet pitter-patter along the landing, Ben's heavy tread on the stairs as he went up after her. It was all I could do not to fly into the hall and scream after him that he had no right to tuck her in, to pretend to care for her, to play at being a daddy to her. How could he think that he had?

Folding my arms tightly across my chest, I stayed where I was and waited. I felt something break inside me as I heard my little girl chatting animatedly to him, giggling as Ben warned Alex the Donkey not to snore.

I fixed my eyes hard on the ceiling to stop the tears falling as he walked to the landing, calling softly back, 'Night-night, munchkin. Love you to the moon and back.'

I followed his progress to Liam's room. 'Okay, Liam?' he asked him. Hearing no reply from Liam, I guessed he'd answered with a shrug.

Ben waited a second, then, 'Night, son. Sleep tight,' he said throatily.

I wanted to weep, to beg him to stop all this. But I couldn't. Because he couldn't. Even without the cheating, whether it was true or just some malicious attempt to malign him, he couldn't unsay the lies he'd told. The past he'd kept buried – he couldn't explain that away. My insides turned over as I recalled what Joan had said: *They cycled off to the reservoir... Adam came home alone.*

I swallowed back the fear and anger burning my throat as he came down the stairs and finally into the kitchen, closing the door behind him. 'The wanderer returns,' I said, my expression, I guessed, conveying the bitter disillusionment I felt.

He at least had the courtesy to look at me, rather than evasively away as I'd expected him to. 'I'm sorry,' he said, his voice hollow.

Anger swelled in my chest and I bit back the expletive that flew into my head. 'Such a shallow little word, isn't it, Ben?' I said instead. 'Or should I say, Adam?'

'Adam,' he whispered, after a heavy pause.

Adam. The man I'd married, never guessing he wasn't who he said he was. 'I need you to tell me what happened with your sister.' I eyed him steadily. 'Everything!'

He closed his eyes. 'Whatever you've heard about me, it's not true,' he murmured, breathing out slowly. 'I didn't harm my sister.'

His eyes were filled with guilt as he looked back at me, and a knot of dread tightened like a hard fist inside me. How was I supposed to believe him?

FIFTY

Naomi

'What happened?' I asked, a confusion of raw emotion churning inside me.

Ben – Adam – whoever he was, said nothing, standing mutely instead, his thumb and forefinger pressed hard to his forehead.

'For God's sake, talk to me,' I begged him. 'You owe me that much.'

Still he said nothing. Moving to drop heavily into a chair, he buried his head in his hands, a strangled sob escaping him, and my blood ran cold.

'If you did hurt her, you have to tell me. This can't go on. I won't let this go on, do you hear me?'

'I didn't!' He snapped his gaze towards me.

I searched his face. His eyes pleaded with me to believe him.

'I didn't,' he repeated, his throat thick with emotion. 'I swear I left her by the water.'

Seeing his tears, I wanted to go to him. I couldn't. My world had been turned upside down and had its insides ripped from it; I simply didn't have the capacity for sympathy. 'So, what happened?'

He dragged his hands over his face. 'I don't know,' he said gruffly. 'There were some other kids there, at the reservoir, taunting us – me more than Holly, because I didn't fit in, I guess. There was one in particular, a relative. He took the piss regularly.'

My thoughts shot to Liam and I felt another piece of my heart fracture inside me. 'What relative?' I asked, trying to keep up with him. To picture the scene. Sadly, I could. 'Did your parents not do something about it?'

'No one close.' Ben drew in a breath. 'And no, they didn't. He denied it, so...'

Seeing his expression, a mixture of hurt and embarrassment, I didn't pursue it.

'I had a puncture,' he went on falteringly. 'I told Holly to wait while I fixed it or to walk with me. She took off. She was always damn well ignoring me.' He paused, glanced at the ceiling, swallowed hard. 'I caught up with her eventually but she refused point-blank to come home with me.'

Recalling his recent bouts of uncharacteristic anger, his incandescent fury when his mother had turned up, my breath stalled as the thought crashed into my head that this might be a lie. He would have been stressed by his sister's behaviour – he was bound to have been. Hadn't he said himself that when that happened, he needed to get as far away as possible from the situation that was causing the stress? That if he couldn't get away, his stress increased and he couldn't control his behaviour, his thoughts, what was going on in his head? 'So you went home alone,' I said guardedly.

He nodded, his gaze now fixed firmly down. 'I walked off at first, thinking she would follow me. She didn't. When I went back to where I'd left her, she was nowhere in sight. I searched for her. I looked for hours. It was pouring with rain, getting dark. I...' He stopped, sucked air into his lungs. 'I tried but... I couldn't find her.'

My stomach roiled. Was this the truth? How could I tell? Had they blamed him, even his own parents, because he was 'different', prone to unpredictable outbursts? Had he been judged, just as people seemed determined to judge Liam?

'What happened to her bike?' I asked past the constriction in my throat.

'They never found it.' Ben looked back at me. 'They searched the reservoir and the surrounding area. She was never found.'

Tears climbed my throat as I pictured the delicate-featured little girl with the impish smile, her small body lying lonely and broken in some godforsaken place.

'Do you believe me?' he asked, jolting my thoughts back to him.

I wrapped my arms around myself, glanced away. I wanted to. He was the father of my children, the man I'd loved with all of myself, despite his 'differences'.

'You don't, do you?' His voice was tinged with fear.

Silence pervaded the room. How could I tell him I did, when I didn't know?

Ben got to his feet. 'I need some air,' he said simply.

I watched him walk back to the kitchen door, his body stiff, as if he were holding his breath in. I took a tremulous breath of my own, then said, 'I received a letter.'

He stopped where he was. 'From?' he said, at length.

'I'm not sure. A neighbour.'

He said nothing.

'It said you're having an affair. Are you?'

He ran his hand over the back of his neck. 'If I said no, are you likely to believe that either?'

I didn't respond. I had no way to. I didn't even know why I'd asked if I wasn't going to accept his answer. Perhaps because I wanted him to know how deep my hurt ran.

'Thought not,' he said tightly. 'I have to go.'

FIFTY-ONE

Sara

Sara looked at Joan, appalled. And she'd thought *she'd* been married to a monster. This Adam character took manipulative behaviour to a whole new level. He was obviously a complete sociopath with no regard for other people. Why he had moved back to the house that must have been a childhood nightmare was unfathomable. For financial reasons, presumably. Whatever his reasons, in lying so profoundly to the mother of his children – a woman who'd just lost a child, for God's sake – he was obviously a very selfish, sick individual.

'Will you be all right?' Sara glanced worriedly at Joan, who would undoubtedly have been shaken to the core by all of this. It was no wonder she appeared to be so confused.

'I'll be fine.' Joan waved her towards the door. 'And I'm always glad of a bit of company. Go on, you get off to your friend. I'll have the kettle on when you get back.'

Sara nodded. 'I'll only be an hour or so,' she promised,

heading off, though she was in two minds now whether to go. But then, after learning what she had, she felt compelled to get to the bottom of what was going on with Paul. He'd seemed to hate Ben – or rather, Adam – from the outset. None of it made any sense. Much less why Paul might have lied about having a daughter. To get her to drop her guard around her own children was the obvious reason, but she desperately didn't want to think that of him.

Once in her car, she dug her phone from her bag and browsed again for information on the house next door. Finding the scant article she'd read before, she scrolled to a photograph of Holly Grant and her breath caught in her chest. She'd been a beautiful child, with huge, deer-like eyes and a smile that could melt hearts. There was definitely a likeness to Maya. Sara wouldn't have noticed unless Joan had mentioned it. But then she'd had no reason to look for it. The little girl was sitting astride her bike in one photo, blue with sparkly purple tassels hanging from the handlebars, and looking mightily proud of herself, as if she might have just learned to ride it.

Trying desperately not to imagine what might have happened to her, how frightened and lonely she might have been in her last moments, Sara scrolled further and found a photograph of Holly's brother, Adam Grant, apparently the last person to have seen her alive. It was Ben. There was no mistaking that dark, broody look in his eyes. He obviously had plenty to brood about, she thought angrily.

He was in the house now. What was going on behind that closed door, she wondered? Fear for Naomi spiralled inside her. She would have to try to talk to her, convince her that she was genuinely concerned. Sighing, she reached to start the engine, then stopped as Ben emerged from the house. He was off on one of his solitary walks, Sara deduced, as he bypassed his car. Her anger spiking, she shoved her car door open and headed him off as he turned to walk past her house.

'Sara.' He nodded. 'Going to see Naomi?' he asked, a scornful smile on his face. 'Or delivering a letter, possibly?'

Sara's mouth dropped open. She couldn't believe the absolute arrogance of the man. Did he think for one second that she could be remotely as despicable as him? 'You're a complete bastard, do you know that?' she fumed, making no effort to hide her contempt.

He dropped his gaze and she wondered whether he might actually be showing some remorse. His expression when he looked back at her, though, chilled her to the bone. 'That seems to be the general consensus,' he said. His tone was flat, his eyes so dark, they were almost black.

FIFTY-TWO

Naomi

I hadn't tried to stop Ben leaving. I simply didn't have the energy. I needed to preserve my strength to fight for my children – for Liam, in particular. I was growing certain now that he would need me to, and scared that, like his father, he was also 'different' enough to be singled out and bullied at school. That he might already be on the receiving end of bullying behaviour, which might account for his dark moods. Wouldn't any child be emotionally disturbed, though, with his world crumbling around him?

A cold hollowness spreading through me as I realised that the man I loved didn't exist, I went to the lounge window, wondering which direction he would take. Still, even after all that he'd done, the unforgivable lies he'd told, I worried that he might have a seizure while he was alone out there in the dark. Were those real? The thought struck me like a thunderbolt. Did he suffer from a stress-related disorder, or had he been using that as an excuse to get out of the house? Was anything he'd ever told me true? It felt as if everything – our marriage, the life we'd shared, the memories we'd made – was turning to dust.

Parting the curtains, I peered out of the window, and my stomach lurched as I realised he was talking to Sara. I couldn't make out her expression under the thin light of the streetlamps, but I could tell from her animated body language that they were arguing. Seeing her flail a hand towards our house, I guessed that the subject of their argument was me. Feeling cold inside, betrayed and unbearably lonely, I opened the window a fraction. Sara growled something as I did. I couldn't hear what. Ben didn't respond. Shaking his head, he studied her for a second and then walked around her.

Sara, though, clearly wasn't finished. 'Do you not have a shred of compassion, Adam Grant?' she shouted after him. 'Any conscience at all for what you've done? Is it your life's mission to destroy families? Destroy women? Is that what you get off on? Tell me, Adam. I'd be very interested to know. I'm bloody sure your wife would too!'

He stopped walking and turned slowly to face her, and I turned away. Sara was wrong; I didn't want to know. What had gone on between them, what might be going on between them – I didn't care anymore. Biting back the excruciating hurt, I went to the hall, took several slow breaths and attempted to compose myself. The children were awake – also arguing, I realised. I pressed a hand to my forehead, exhaustion seeping through me. I dearly wished I could climb into bed, crawl under the duvet and hide away. I craved dark, dreamless sleep, where this stark new reality couldn't reach me. I couldn't, though. To do that would be to give in. No matter how much I wanted to simply cease being, I had to keep functioning, to be the constant my children needed me to be.

Marshalling my reserves, I mounted the stairs. I was halfway up when a blood-freezing scream chilled me to the bone. '*Mummy!* Mummy, make him *stop!*' My little girl screamed again, a scream that pierced my very soul.

'Maya!' My heart racing, I charged the rest of the way up. Swinging around the newel at the top, I found my little girl weeping on the landing, her eyes wide and horrified, her hands balled into tight fists at her side.

'He's drowning her. He's drowning her!' She gulped back huge, hiccupping sobs.

My gaze shot to the bathroom beyond her, where I could hear the bath taps running full on. 'Stay there,' I warned her, trepidation tightening my stomach as I squeezed past.

Liam didn't move as I pushed the bathroom door open, didn't acknowledge me. It was as if he didn't even know I was there. Kneeling at the side of the filled bath, my nine-year-old boy was intent on his task. My daughter's reborn baby doll lay in the water, her long, soft hair fanned out around her face. She looked so lifelike my heart jarred. My boy was holding her down. His hand around her neck, he was holding her at the bottom of the bath.

'Liam!' I seized his shoulders, hauled him up and whirled him around to face me, roughly. Too roughly. 'What in God's name are you doing?'

He looked at me, his eyes unfocused for a second. Then, 'M-making her go away,' he stammered, confusion in his eyes as he searched mine.

I breathed sharply in, felt the foundations of my world rocking dangerously. 'Who, Liam?' I whispered, fear piercing my chest like an icicle. 'Who were you making go away?'

Liam dropped his gaze, burying his chin in his neck. He didn't answer.

Ben's mother. Recalling how distraught Liam had been

when she'd appeared, the anger that had emanated from him, the things he'd said – 'I hate this house and I hate *her*! I want her to go away' – my blood ran cold. Had he been projecting his anger, imagining that doll was her? Closing my eyes, I wrapped my arms around my son and pulled him tightly to me.

FIFTY-THREE

Naomi

With Maya tucked up in the main bedroom, where she'd said she felt safer – which was heartbreakingly telling – I went back to check that Liam had done as I'd asked him and changed his soaked pyjamas and got into bed.

'Okay?' I asked, studying him thoughtfully as I went into his room.

Liam nodded over the top of his duvet.

I walked across to him and sat down on the edge of his bed. 'You know what you did was wrong, don't you?' I tried to keep any condemnation from my voice. I would need to talk more with him about what had happened in the bathroom, but not tonight. He was exhausted, his complexion pale, his face etched with worry.

Liam nodded again, a subdued nod. 'Sorry,' he murmured.

I smoothed back his fringe. It was too long. I would have to book him a hair appointment, although not at Sara's salon, obviously. We needed routine, to get back to some normalcy. The thought that it might be a new normalcy, excluding their father, the man they both worshipped, both saddened and terrified me. I had to stay strong though, whatever the future might hold. I was my children's mainstay. We had to get through this, somehow, together. 'Did you brush your teeth properly?' I asked him.

'Uh-huh.' Liam looked up at me from under his eyelashes, his eyes, sharp hazelnut eyes that mirrored his father's, flecked with guilt. 'Sorry, Mum,' he mumbled again, and looked down.

'It's okay.' I leaned down to press a soft kiss to his head. It wasn't okay, though. We both knew it. 'We'll talk more tomorrow. You know you can always talk to me, don't you, Liam? About good and bad stuff? The way you're feeling?'

Liam answered with another small nod.

'Anger is allowed, you know?' I went on hesitantly. 'We just have to have a calm-down plan. When I feel overwhelmed, I count,' I said. 'In my head. And breathe, verrry slooowly.' I demonstrated, going cross-eyed as I did, which at least brought a tentative smile to his face.

'Come on, snuggle down.' Getting to my feet, I pulled his duvet up as he wriggled further down the bed. 'And don't lie there worrying. It rarely helps when you feel sad. Sleep definitely does.'

'I won't.' Liam looked up at me cautiously. 'Is Dad coming back?' he asked, his eyes filled with such uncertainty it tore a hole right through me.

'He will be.' I tried to reassure him, though I wasn't sure – about anything. 'He's just out walking. It's his way of dealing with his emotions.'

Another tiny nod from Liam, and then he closed his eyes – to reassure me, I guessed. 'Sleep tight,' I whispered.

After dimming his light, I headed to the door, collecting up his wet PJs from his chair as I went, along with the towel and clothes he'd taken off earlier. My step faltered as something dropped from the bundle to land on the floor at my feet. A chill of apprehension ran through me as I bent to pick the object up. Little Buttons. I stared at the raggedy teddy bear, disbelieving. My heart sank without trace as I registered that both his ears were missing.

'I found him in the garden,' Liam said, his voice a frightened whisper behind me.

FIFTY-FOUR

Sara

After negotiating twisting country lanes that took her deep into rural Worcestershire, Sara wondered if she'd written the postcode from Paul's driving licence down correctly. The property her satnav finally brought her to was a far cry from the rundown house in a deprived area she'd imagined he lived in. Situated in open countryside with scenic views all around it, the cottage she was staring at was beautiful.

He'd lied to her, blatantly. Why? To play on her sympathies in the hope of persuading her they should live together? But, assuming this was the correct address, why would he want to move into her house when this one was clearly worth much more? Had he been planning to sell this property to pay off some kind of horrendous debt she didn't know about?

Puzzled, she scanned the front of the property from her car. There were no lights on inside. Sara hoped to God that indicated that no one lived there – a whole other family he'd

neglected to mention. The idea of being party to his psycholog-
ical manipulation of some other poor woman made her stomach
roil. So what did she do now? She considered turning around
and going home. The night beyond the immediate perimeter of
the cottage was pitch black and she was beginning to feel
nervous out here, miles from anywhere and on her own. She
should just confront him, ask him outright what the hell he was
playing at. But then she would have to admit she'd gone through
his pockets and accessed his phone. A shudder shook through
her as an image of her ex crashed into her head, his vitriolic
reaction if ever she dared stand up to him. Recalling the flash of
fury she'd seen in Paul's eyes recently, his thunderous expression when she'd riled him about his attitude to Ben, she wasn't
sure she was brave enough to do that.

She could tell him it was over, to give back his key and go,
which would leave her with a thousand questions rattling
around in her head – most worryingly, whether he had sent that
letter to Naomi. If he had, based upon information someone
had fed him that she was having an affair with Ben – or Adam,
as she now knew him to be – then didn't that make him just as
much a jealous monster as her ex-husband had been? That
might all be nonsense, of course. It might be that he'd simply
taken a dislike to Ben, which Sara could understand. But there
was no escaping the fact that he'd lied to her, the evidence of
that was right in front of her eyes. And what about his daughter? Did she even exist? There was only one way to find out,
and that was to find some evidence that she did. And if she
didn't? Then Paul Mansell had an agenda and Sara needed to
find out what it was. The thought that she might have exposed
her children to someone who wasn't who he claimed to be made
it imperative that she learn the truth.

Gathering her courage, she shoved her car door open and
climbed determinedly out. An icy chill cutting through her as
she was suddenly exposed to the elements, she rubbed the

goosebumps on her arms and surveyed the property for possible means of access. There was a porch leading to the front door, a window either side of it and two windows above it. None of them appeared to be open.

Quietly cursing the gravel crunching under her feet, she walked to the front door, hesitated, then knocked and waited. Hearing no noise from inside, she stepped back, glanced quickly around, then went to check the two downstairs windows. Finding both were secure, she pulled out her phone, turned on the torch, and headed for the back of the property which, thankfully, wasn't fenced off.

After trying the back door, French windows and the kitchen window, she was heading back around the house on the opposite side when she spotted what appeared to be a downstairs toilet window. Shining her torch at it, her heart leapt as she realised it was open a fraction. Quickly, she stepped towards it, hooked her fingers underneath it and felt for the latch. 'Shit.' Sara cursed as a sharp splinter of wood forced its way under her fingernail. *Damn.* Extracting her hand, she sucked at a rich, red globule of blood, then steeled herself and tried again. Finally locating the latch, she nudged it upwards. It didn't budge. Cold sweat wetting her skin as she imagined police cars screeching up behind her, she had another go, and almost wilted with relief as it gave. Now all she had to do was get through the window, which might require Houdini-like skills. Also, something to stand on. She hurried back to the rear of the house, where she hoped she might find something.

Minutes later, she was balanced on top of an upturned mop bucket, from where, with some effort, she was able to swing her leg up and through the window. Manoeuvring herself until she was straddling the frame, she fed her other leg through and then wriggled around. Breathing a sigh of relief, she dropped to the floor, narrowly avoiding putting her foot down the loo as she did, then straightened up and reached quickly for the door. Her finger throbbed. She tried to ignore it, and with her heart thudding, she pulled the door open a fraction and listened. Hearing nothing but the loud ticking of a hall clock, she stepped tentatively out, stood perfectly still until she was sure she was alone, then hurried to check the downstairs rooms. By the light of her phone, everything took on a ghostly appearance, sending a shiver of apprehension the length of her spine. The furnishings weren't opulent, she noted: a basic farmhouse table and chairs in the dining room; standard three-seater sofa and armchairs in the living room; and a flat-screen TV. What struck her was that the place didn't feel lived in. Paul had been mostly at hers lately, so she supposed it wouldn't. It was more than that, though. It felt lonely. She was being fanciful, the ominous ticking of the clock feeding her imagination. She would be seeing actual ghosts soon.

Shaking herself, she ventured further into the living room and shone her torch around. Looking for photographs on the mantelpiece and finding none, she went to the TV cabinet and pulled the drawer open, thinking there would surely be DVDs indicating a child had once lived here, or at least visited. There was nothing there either, confirming what she didn't want to believe. She was heading back across the room when her eyes snagged on a newspaper on the coffee table. She bent to read the headline. It was old news, all about the Covid lockdowns. Sara shook off another icy shiver and headed quickly back to the hall – an old-fashioned space with wood-panelled walls and a dado rail, which added to the soullessness of the house.

She hurried upstairs. The first room she came across was the bathroom, which appeared clean and tidy but smelled damp and musty. The main bedroom had a similar unlived-in smell about it. Because Paul hadn't spent much time here, she reminded herself. Still, though, something felt off. She went to the wardrobe that ran the length of one wall and slid the doors open. One half of it housed men's clothes, the kind of jackets and shirts Paul wore. The single dress hanging in the other half had obviously been missed by his wife when she'd left. The fact that it was hanging half off the coat hanger, though, suggested she might have left in a hurry. The knot of apprehension tightening inside her, she closed the wardrobe doors and walked across to the dressing table. The make-up bag that lay there seemed odd. Sara never went anywhere without hers. Her gaze went to the coffee cup sitting next to it. Inside it, dregs of coffee and a thin film of green mould. It had obviously been there for ages – ever since she'd left, judging by the lipstick mark on the side of the cup. The place was stuck in a bloody time warp.

Unsure what she was looking for, Sara yanked the drawers of the dressing table open. There were a few items of lingerie in the top drawer, knickknacks and jewellery. She picked up an expensive-looking ring set with opal and sapphire. Would a woman really leave without that? Most tellingly, there was a packet of lorazepam, a drug Sara herself had once been prescribed for anxiety and sleep problems. This packet was over two years old, confirming her suspicion. The woman *had* left in a hurry, as if she were fleeing. And who would she be fleeing from if not Paul?

FIFTY-FIVE

Sara

The bedside tables gave her nothing: more women's bits and pieces in one; the kind of trinkets a man might keep in the other; a watch – one she was sure she'd seen Paul wearing; cufflinks; an old phone. No evidence of a daughter. Slamming the last drawer in frustration, Sara hurried to the next room. Seeing a desk against the far wall, she went across to it, pulled the drawers open and rummaged through them. Still she found no signs of the existence of a daughter. Her frustration mounting, she yanked the cupboard on the opposite side of the desk open so hard it almost came off its hinges. Kneeling down, she peered inside and discovered a shoebox. Inside it, photographs. There were albums too. Hoping at last that she would find what she wanted, she scooped the contents out and flicked through the loose photographs. There didn't appear to be any recent photos of a girl who might be his daughter, although there were many older photos of a young boy. Paul?

There was a familiarity about his features, but she couldn't be sure.

She captured his image with her phone and turned her attention to the albums. Picking up what appeared to be an old family album, she opened it carefully and scanned the various photographs inside. One in particular caused her to catch her breath: the same boy standing moodily on one side of an adult couple, with a younger boy and a little girl no more than a toddler standing the other. Alarmingly, the faces of those two children had been scratched out – as if with the sharp end of a pencil compass. Had this been Paul's family? He'd never once mentioned siblings, and he'd never talked about his parents – other than to say he'd lost them both in a car accident. Her heart had broken for him.

Trepidation twisting her stomach, she took another snap and pushed the photos back. Another album was full of wedding photos. Tentatively, she opened it and her heart jolted. The bride's face had been scratched out so viciously that the mount beneath was visible. Goosebumps rose over her skin as she studied the groom. Paul. Unmistakably. He was younger, obviously, and clearly in love. He was gazing adoringly at the woman. A woman whose face had now been obliterated. An icy chill washed over her, as if a cold draught had crept under the door, and she took a photo of that too, then closed the album and traced her fingers over the gold embossed inscription on the front: *You will forever be mine*. She hadn't been, though, had she? Is that what had angered him enough to scratch her out as if she didn't exist? Where was she? She'd never heard him speak to her when he'd supposedly been on the phone to his daughter – not once. There was no European number listed on his phone. Why had they left so suddenly? Questions tumbled over each other in her head. She still had no answers. Pushing the box and albums back into the cupboard, she stood and shoved the door to.

She was about to leave when she noticed some envelopes propped against a pen holder on top of the desk. She picked them up and turned them over – and her heart froze. There were none addressed to Paul Mansell. All were addressed to a Zachary Grant. Recognising the surname, her stomach tightened with fear. Naomi had been right. The realisation struck her like a sledgehammer. It was Paul who was the manipulative liar. How many lies had he told her? To what end?

Anger burning inside her, she photographed a letter, placed the envelopes back and hurried to the landing and on to the third bedroom. After thrusting the door open, she stopped and stared in surprise. She'd found no evidence of a child living in this house, but there clearly once had been. She studied the toy, which would have been a little girl's pride and joy, in confusion. This confirmed that his daughter did exist, but why all the secrecy and deceit? It didn't make any sense. She was studying the insignia on the framework when the shocking image of another little girl came starkly to mind. *Oh, dear God.* Her emotions colliding, she staggered back. What should she do? She might be wrong, but the nausea swirling coldly in the pit of her stomach told her she wasn't. Shakily, she pointed her phone to take another photo, then went to her texts, selected a recipient, attached all the photos and quickly pressed send. She was about to type a message when a voice behind her said, 'Find anything interesting?'

Sara froze, fear jolting through her. Before she had chance to open her mouth, he was on her. 'Why are you here, Sara, hmm?' His voice was curious, petrifyingly pleasant as he clamped his hand over her mouth.

Bile filled her throat, the sickly-sweet smell of his aftershave almost choking her as he locked his other arm around her chest and dragged her, struggling, to the landing.

'The important question, of course, is does anyone know you're here?' He paused, as if pondering. Her heart boomed, terror spiking inside her. What was he going to do? 'I think not,' he said, at length. 'Because you're breaking and entering, aren't you? Trespassing. Where you shouldn't fucking well be!'

'Mmmf.' Sara wriggled, trying in vain to free her hands.

'Big mistake, Sara.' His breath tickled her ear and repulsion squirmed through her body. 'If you had half the sense you were born with, you would have left well alone and kept out of everyone else's business.'

Panic rose like acid inside her and she kicked out. The heel of her foot thunked against his shin, but made little impact. He only tightened his grip.

'Silly bitch,' he hissed. Uselessly, she fought to find the floor with her feet as he hauled her along the landing. 'I can see now why your husband left you,' he went on, a hate-filled, one-sided conversation as he heaved her towards the stairs. 'You're all the same, aren't you? Never fucking satisfied, no matter how hard I try. Always suspicious, blaming and belittling me. Betraying me! Why do you do it?'

Stop! Please stop. Sara screamed inside, terror crackling through her like ice as he paused at the top of the stairs. Silence hung between them like the razor-sharp blade of a guillotine. 'We could have been good together, you and I, if only you hadn't insisted on meddling,' he whispered.

She teetered for an instant as he withdrew his hold on her. And then gravity pulled her, her body rolling and bouncing off every step, her forehead slamming into the stone tiles on the hall floor with a sickening crack as she landed.

His hand twisted cruelly through her hair, her head wrenched back, was the last thing she felt. 'You brought it on yourself,' the last thing she heard.

FIFTY-SIX

Naomi

Liam climbed out of bed as I stared down at Little Buttons in disbelief. I looked from the bear to him, then lowered myself to his level and took hold of his forearms. 'When did you find it?' I asked him, my gaze boring into his.

'I d-don't know,' Liam stammered, attempting to pull away from me. 'I can't remember.'

I held on to him, frustration building inside me. Sara had claimed that she'd found the missing cat and the bear in our shed. 'Whereabouts in the garden did you find it, Liam?' Cold foreboding gripped my stomach. 'Think carefully.'

He frowned guardedly. 'By the fence,' he murmured.

'Which fence?' I pressed him.

Liam's frown deepened. 'The fence between Sara's garden and ours. By the shed.'

So had Sara taken it to her house and then thrown it over, or had Paul? He'd disliked Ben from the second he saw him, for reasons that had become obvious. He knew about the affair. But it could equally have been Ben. My heart sank like a stone as I recalled him arriving home the very day the bear had gone missing with a new doll for Maya, almost as if he'd known.

'I didn't take him, Mum, honestly.' Liam's voice was tremulous. 'Am I in trouble?' His eyes were filled with nervous apprehension.

'No.' I gulped back a hard lump of emotion. I believed him. My boy's gaze hadn't faltered. He might be similar in nature to his father – clearly, he had issues I had to help him address – but he wasn't a liar. 'I'm sorry,' I whispered, hugging him to me. I didn't know who I could trust, but I had to be firmly on the side of my children. Their trust in me was absolute.

My thoughts went to Ben's mother. Had she been on his side, or tried to be? She'd lost one child. Had she lived in fear of losing another if her son were to be officially charged regarding the disappearance of his sister? Is that what had driven her to madness? I felt as if I was being driven mad by all that had happened in this house, all that I'd learned. I still didn't understand fully why he'd chosen to come back here. He'd said he'd had no choice, and with my pregnancy, I understood that, to a degree. There had been other options, though. We could have managed if we'd stayed where we were. I would have gone back to work. In doing what he had, he'd taken my choice away, and I couldn't help feeling that he'd played a part in the tragedy that had taken Elias from us.

Easing back, I looked into my boy's eyes, which were now flecked with confusion. 'You're not in trouble, Liam,' I told him firmly. 'And as long as you're always honest and try to be considerate of other people's feelings, you never will be. Okay?'

Liam answered with a small nod. 'I'll try. It's hard though, Mum, when I see people making you cry.' He glanced down, trying to hide his own tears, and I dearly wished I could hold him close and keep him safe forever.

'I'm fine, I promise.' I reached out to lift his chin. 'We've all been a bit sad, but now we have to stay strong and be there for each other. We're a team, aren't we?'

Another nod from Liam, but I could see there was a question in his eyes. He didn't ask it, and I was grateful. I needed time before I could even begin to try to explain what was happening with their father. 'If we're going to be strong, we'll need to get some sleep, though, won't we?' I gave him a firm look.

Once I'd led him back to bed, Liam climbed dutifully under his duvet. 'Can I read my book for a while?' he asked, glancing hopefully towards his Kindle.

'Ten minutes.' Knowing he was more likely to drop off while he was reading, I relented. 'I'll be coming up for a shower soon and I expect to see the lamp off. Okay?'

'Okay.' Liam grabbed his Kindle from his bedside table and settled down. There was still a troubled furrow in his brow, I noted, leaning down to kiss the top of his head. My heart wrenching for him, I left him be and went to peek in on Maya. She was sleeping, thank goodness. I resisted tiptoeing over to her and, squeezing back the tears I was determined to no longer cry in front my children, went wearily downstairs. The house seemed cold and empty. It had always been cold. By decorating I'd hoped to breathe some warmth into it. To banish my 'silly superstitions', as Ben had called them. He'd told me it was all in my mind. How could he have done that? Sara had been right. It was coercive behaviour.

Feeling chilled through to the core of me and so lonely, I placed my hands over my empty stomach. I missed my baby, the presence and promise of him. His kicks, at first like soft butterflies, and then vigorous, so full of life. An errant tear escaping my eye, I wrapped my arms tightly around myself. I had no idea where to go. The idea of sitting on my own in the soulless lounge made me want to sob my heart out.

Not even bothering to wonder where Ben was, because it simply felt pointless, I trailed to the kitchen to make myself a warm drink. Reaching the door, I stopped and turned back as my phone beeped from the hall table. I hesitated, knowing who it was before I looked. Was he trying to make this more hurtful, texting rather than calling? Steeling myself, I picked up the phone and checked the text.

I'm outside. Is it okay if I come in? Clearly, Ben could indeed find ways to make this more unbearable. Our marriage was broken. My world blown apart. Yet he was subtly shifting things so that it would be me who was responsible for the breakdown. Feeling another part of myself die inside, I swallowed hard and placed the phone down without texting back.

FIFTY-SEVEN

Naomi

Making a decision, I marched to the front door and yanked it open. He was standing away from the door, as if uncertain what reception he would get. He should be. For the sake of our children, I tried to quell the fury burning inside me. I wanted to hit him, physically lash out at him, and it shocked me. This wasn't who I was. And who was he, this stranger standing in front of me?

Wiping a hand over his face, he nodded – a small, defeated nod, as if understanding that he'd broken us, broken everything – then took a breath and walked cautiously towards me.

Despite my conviction to remain detached, as he neared me my heart jolted. Up close, he looked dreadful, dark shadows under his eyes, in his eyes. What jarred me most of all was the jagged cut to his cheek. 'What happened?' I asked, unable to help myself. I shouldn't care, but how could I just switch off my emotions?

Ben's hand went to his face. 'It's nothing,' he said, glancing down. 'Just a scratch.'

It was more than a scratch. It looked raw and painful. Was he really going to do this? Retreat into silence? Because if he was, what was he doing here?

Looking back at me, he clearly noted my despair. 'I got jumped,' he said, with an embarrassed shrug. 'Some kids chancing it at the reservoir.'

What? My heart turned over. 'You were out there in the dark?' I asked, surprised – and scared, for him. How could he be so matter of fact about it? He could have been badly injured. Killed. Though searching his face, seeing the bewildered anguish in his eyes, I knew he wasn't quite as laid-back as he appeared to be. He was being the Ben I knew – or thought I had known: a man who buried his emotions.

'I walk there sometimes,' he said, averting his gaze again. 'They didn't take anything. A dog walker came by, so...'

He made no move to come into the house, but despite how angry and crushed I felt, I knew I couldn't leave him out there. 'Are you coming inside, or are we talking on the doorstep?' I asked him, moving back to allow him in.

He hesitated, looked beyond me to the hall, and then, a mixture of relief and nervousness sweeping his features, he came in.

He was deathly pale, I noticed, feeling some of my anger dissipate. I'd been ready to scream at him, but it wouldn't achieve anything other than to upset the children. As I passed the stairs, I pressed a finger to my lips, reminding him they were in bed, then led the way to the kitchen.

'I was about to make coffee. Do you want one?' I asked, heading for the kettle. Quietly, I prayed this wasn't a manipulation, another attempt to play on my sympathies. He would hardly have injured himself, though, would he?

'I'd love one. Thanks.' He dropped tiredly to a chair at the table. 'Are the kids okay?' he asked.

'Not really,' I answered shortly.

'Should I go up and see them?'

'I don't think that's a good idea, do you?' Was he going to lie to them, too, I wanted to ask him, tell them everything was going to be fine when it was quite clear to Liam and Maya that things were far from fine?

'Right,' he said, and fell silent.

So there we were, an ocean apart. How had this happened? Hopelessness spreading through me, I bit my tears back and busied myself with the coffee-making. After switching the filter on, I grabbed some paper towelling, wet it under the tap and went across to him. He flinched as I reached out. Then, realising I only wanted to assess the damage, he relaxed a little.

The cut didn't look deep, but it definitely looked sore. My eyes flicked to his as I bathed it and then quickly away again. I couldn't bear the pain I saw there, which only served to heighten my own. 'It looks fairly clean, but you should put some antiseptic on it,' I said, moving away.

'Thanks.' He nodded. Then, 'Naomi...' He caught my hand. 'I'm sorry,' he said. His throat was hoarse, his eyes pleading. 'I know what I've done is unforgivable, but please believe I never set out to hurt you. You're the only good thing that's ever happened to me. I'll never forgive myself for not being honest with you.'

I fixed my gaze on the ceiling and blinked hard. I wanted to snatch my hand from his, to run away, but I couldn't. He knew I couldn't run away from *any* of this. 'What is there to forgive?' I rounded on him. I couldn't help it. 'What are you not being honest about? You need to talk to me, Ben. You need to tell me.'

He let go of my hand. 'I didn't hurt her.' His head bowed, he repeated what he'd already told me.

I watched as he kneaded his forehead hard with his thumb,

as if what he was about to reveal might be too awful to contemplate, and that thought terrified me. 'And?' I urged him.

He gulped back a breath. 'They took me back there,' he said eventually. 'My parents. Later that night. They thought I... I didn't hurt her.' He snapped his gaze back to me. 'I swear I left her by the water.'

Confusion and fear swirled inside me. What was he telling me? 'What happened?' I asked, my voice a strangled whisper. 'Ben, please, you have to talk to me.'

'There was someone else there,' he started haltingly. 'Someone I should have told you about when we—' He stopped, his gaze shooting to the hall as there was a loud knock on the front door. Shakily, he got to his feet, glancing cautiously at me as he did.

There was another knock, and the look now on Ben's face was one of tangible fear. Trepidation twisted inside me. I went quickly to the hall and, without pausing to think, pulled the front door open. I felt the blood drain from my body as I saw two police officers standing outside.

'Mrs Felton?' One of the officers smiled tightly.

'Yes,' I answered dazedly.

'Is Mr Felton home?' the officer asked, glancing at me questioningly, and then beyond me to the hall.

'Can I help you?' Ben said behind me.

A frown creasing his forehead, the officer looked him over as if measuring him up. 'DS Harrison.' He showed his identification. 'And this is PC Durrani,' he indicated the woman police officer to his side. 'We'd like a quick word, if we may?'

'About?' Ben's voice was strained. I turned to look at him. He looked petrified.

'A homeless woman,' the woman officer picked up. 'Locally known as Lily. We believe she may have been attacked at the reservoir this evening.'

FIFTY-EIGHT

Naomi

'Why are the police here, Mummy?' Maya asked tremulously from where she stood at the top of the stairs.

I hurried up to find Liam standing on the landing behind her. 'Because of Dad,' he muttered, his face an angry scowl.

'Liam...' I followed him as he stormed back to his bedroom, shepherding Maya along with me. 'They're here making enquiries about someone who got hurt at the reservoir,' I said, because there was nothing else I could say. 'I imagine they'll be knocking on everyone's door, not just ours.'

Liam turned warily back. 'Who got hurt?'

'I'm not sure,' I lied. 'Can you be a really good boy for me and look after Maya for a few minutes? I need to talk to them and I don't want to leave her upset. I'll come back up as soon as I can.'

Liam nodded reluctantly. I noted the troubled frown

creasing his forehead and made a promise to myself to talk to him. I couldn't have him internalising all of this.

'Can we wait in the big bed till you come back, Mummy?' Maya asked, looking between us.

'Of course you can.' I gave her an encouraging smile and nodded her towards her brother. 'I won't be long, I promise.'

'Come on. We'll play I-spy for a bit,' Liam offered, taking hold of her hand and leading her off to the main bedroom.

'Liam.' A turmoil of emotions churning inside me, full of both pride and concern for my boy, I stopped him. 'Thank you.'

He shrugged. 'No problem,' he said and trudged on.

Once they were inside with the door closed, I hurried back down to the kitchen, pausing at the door as I heard Ben's voice from inside. 'Why do you need to know my whereabouts?' he was asking, his tone one of discernible agitation. 'I told you, I was out walking. I often go there, sometimes running, sometimes to clear my head. I have no idea exactly where I was in the timeframe you mention.'

'But you were in the area?' PC Durrani suggested.

'Probably,' Ben answered vaguely. 'Why?'

There was a pause, then, 'We have an eyewitness report,' the woman supplied. 'A man fitting your description was seen attacking a woman at the location specified.'

Ben? I felt myself reel. Attacking his own mother? No. That was ludicrous. I'd never known Ben to be physically violent. Not ever. But I didn't know Ben, did I? He wasn't who he pretended to be.

The woman continued. 'We need to establish what your movements were in order to—'

'Whoa, wait,' Ben interrupted. 'Who? What witness?' His eyes met mine as I pushed the door open and walked in. He was desperate. I could see it.

DS Harrison glanced at me from where he was standing in

front of Ben, and then looked back to my husband. 'I'm afraid we're not at liberty to divulge who gave us the information, sir,' he said, professionally but curtly. 'You can appreciate why we would be obliged to follow the information up, though, particularly in light of the fact that the person concerned also supplied certain other information regarding your relationship with the woman.'

Ben's face drained of colour. 'I, er...' Swallowing hard, he closed his eyes. 'Do you mind if I get a glass of water?'

Harrison studied him hard, then nodded him towards the sink. PC Durrani stepped towards me – placing herself between Ben and the door, I guessed, my own throat running dry. 'The witness claims that the victim is your mother,' she said, her eyes narrowed as she studied Ben's back. 'That the two of you are estranged. Are you able to confirm that, Mr Felton?'

'We're trying to locate her,' Harrison continued, when Ben said nothing. 'Lily,' he added, and let it hang.

Still, Ben said nothing. As if playing for time, he picked up a glass from the rack and filled it, clinking it against the tap as he did. His hand shook as he lifted the glass to his mouth.

'We've looked for her in all her usual haunts,' Harrison went on. 'It appears she's nowhere to be found.'

'We did find her coat,' PC Durrani piped up. 'On the reservoir wall. It was bloodstained. We also found blood spatters. Enough on the wall and surrounding brickwork to cause us considerable concern for her safety.'

I snatched my gaze to Ben, my own blood pooling in my stomach. Why wasn't he answering? *Say something*, I willed him.

Ben spoke after an interminably long pause. 'I had a seizure,' he said reluctantly. 'Stress related. I was walking away from the reservoir, I think. I... I don't remember.'

The two officers exchanged wary glances. 'Have you had any contact with her recently, Mr Felton?' Harrison asked.

Ben placed his glass down, twirled it around, studied it intently. 'No,' he said.

Liar! Why was he doing this? Had he had a seizure? What did he not remember?

'Not as such,' Ben backtracked, his eyes pivoting to me. 'She came here once. It didn't go well. She left. I haven't seen her since.'

All of this was stated flatly, as if he didn't care that his mother might have been seriously hurt. Murdered? I couldn't believe that. My throat closed, tears now dangerously close to spilling over. I just couldn't.

DS Harrison glanced down, appearing to contemplate, then nodded slowly. 'And are you able to tell us whether your son has had any contact with your mother, Mr Felton?' he asked, looking pointedly back at him.

'Liam?' I choked out my son's name. 'No.' My heart banging with fear and bewilderment, I stepped forward. 'Absolutely not.'

Harrison gauged me carefully. 'And you're sure about that, are you?'

'Positive,' Ben answered categorically. 'He's never even spoken to her.'

'I see.' Harrison's gaze travelled between us. 'It's just that we have an eyewitness who places him at the reservoir around the same time as the last sighting of her.'

I stared at him, stunned. 'That's complete rubbish. He doesn't go to the reservoir on his own. I would *never* allow my children to go there on their own.' Anger unfurled inside me. 'He's nine years old. You're not seriously suggesting that he could have had anything to do with this?'

The man held up his hands, palms outward. 'I'm not suggesting anything, Mrs Felton. I'm merely trying to ascertain the facts.'

'Your facts are wrong,' I informed him, fighting to keep a

rein on my emotions. 'Whoever your witness is, they're mistaken.'

'Possibly,' the man conceded with another short nod. 'I think it might help clear a few things up, though, if Mr Felton accompanied us to the station. Completely voluntarily,' he added, glancing at Ben. 'At this stage.'

'Now?' Ben asked, palpable panic in his eyes.

'It would be useful to have your statement on file,' Harrison confirmed, his attention half on Ben and half on Durrani as her radio crackled.

'In the vicinity,' Durrani said into her radio. Then she turned to Harrison. 'Another shout, sir. The woman next door...' She glanced warily to Ben and back. 'A neighbour's reported her missing.'

FIFTY-NINE

Naomi

Please look at me. Ben either couldn't or wouldn't. Pressing his thumbs hard against his forehead, he bowed his head – and my emotions collided violently inside me. Where had he gone after the reservoir? Suspicion whispering insidiously in my head, I looked from him to the detective, whose gaze was locked hard on Ben. He made no attempt to hide the distaste in his eyes.

'How long has she been gone?' he asked, discernible agitation in his voice.

'Less than twenty-four hours,' Durrani provided, 'but—'

'For Christ's...' Harrison glanced in her direction. 'Isn't there another car in the area?'

'No one close.' She swept her gaze over Ben and then back to her colleague. 'It seems the risk assessment is high, though. She left her children with an elderly neighbour – took them across in their nightclothes and hasn't come back for them. She hasn't been in touch either. The neighbour says she has reason to believe she might be in danger.'

'And we've tried to contact her?'

Durrani nodded. 'Her phone signal was picked up in the vicinity of the reservoir.' Her gaze slid again to Ben. 'It went dead suddenly.'

'Right.' Harrison tugged in a terse breath. 'Can you get to the neighbour's house and establish what the facts are? And see if you can get an ETA on the nearest available unit while you're...' He stopped, his gaze shooting to the hall as there was another sharp knock on the front door.

Ben's gaze snapped up.

Harrison stepped in front of him as he moved to answer it. 'It might be better if Mrs Felton goes,' he suggested.

He thought Ben would run. He believed he had reason to. Confusion and nausea swirling inside me, my mind trying and failing to take in the incomprehensible news that Sara was missing, that my husband might have had something to do with it, I headed numbly to the hall. The knot in my throat grew more excruciatingly painful as I pictured Sara's children's bewildered faces. She must have left them with Joan, but why would she have taken them across to her in only their pyjamas? Where was she? Dread settled like ice in the pit of my stomach. Whatever my feelings for her, I felt certain she would never have gone off and left her children. That, if there was a problem, she wouldn't have contacted Joan. Why wouldn't she have? That thought landing like a stone in my chest, I pulled the front door open – and froze.

'Where is he?' Paul growled, his eyes thunderous as his gaze travelled past me to the hall.

I didn't have time to answer before he shoved past me. 'Where's Sara, you bastard?' he shouted, banging into the kitchen.

Whirling around, I flew after him to see him jabbing a

finger in Ben's direction. 'If you've hurt one single hair on her head, I'll break your neck, you fucking freak,' he spat. 'Where is she?'

'Hey!' PC Durrani skirted around him, placing herself between the two men. 'Cool it. Now! Or you're nicked.'

Paul's gaze was fixed on Ben. The air crackled between them for a split second, and then Paul moved, almost knocking Durrani off her feet as he launched himself at Ben.

Harrison was on him in an instant, locking his arms around his chest. 'Assaulting a police officer is not a smart move, mate,' he growled, as Durrani recovered herself, wrestled Paul's arms around his back and reached for her handcuffs.

'I am legally obliged to inform you that I am arresting you for assaulting a police officer in the execution of her duty,' she seethed, snapping the cuffs shut. 'You do not have to say anything, but—'

'What have you done with her?' Paul screamed. 'Did she tell you to get stuffed, damage your fragile ego? Is that it, Adam? You were always a moody little bastard, weren't you, even as a kid.'

What was he talking about? Petrified, I stared between them. Paul knew his real name. How? Had Joan told him? Why would he think that Ben had had anything to do with...? The letter. Recalling the contents, my head reeled. *Are you aware that he's having an affair? I think you may be in grave danger. Love can inspire, but it can also drive people to great acts of despair, madness or even murder.*

My mind ticked feverishly as I tried to make sense of what was happening. Paul had obviously known Sara and Ben were involved. Clearly, he thought they still were. Ben had argued with her – the thought cut through my chest like a knife. Ben and Sara had been arguing, right outside in the road. I recalled what Sara had yelled at him: 'Do you not have a shred of compassion, Adam Grant? Any conscience at all?' Nausea rose sourly inside me. What had he done?

'Did you lose it, Adam?' Paul went on, his eyes pure hatred, his voice full of vitriol. 'Did your temper get the better of you, is that it?'

'Back off!' Harrison warned him, as he and Durrani tried to manhandle him from the kitchen.

'Why don't you tell her what a caring bloke you really are, hey?' Straining to get back to Ben, Paul nodded towards me. 'How you lost it. With Holly. With the cat. You want to know how I knew he hated them, Naomi?' He glanced in my direction. 'Ask him, your loving fucking husband. What kind of bloke gets his kicks out of watching a cat drown, hey? You should ask yourself *that*.'

'He's lying. Inventing things,' Ben said, as my gaze shot towards him. His voice was shaky, his face ashen. 'Please don't—'

'Are you going to tell her about your sister?' Paul shouted as he was dragged into the hall. 'Or shall I?'

Stop. Please make him stop. My heart banging so hard I thought my chest might explode, I went after them. My children. They would be terrified. I had to get to them.

The back door slammed behind me as I stepped into the hall. I knew without turning around that my husband had run.

SIXTY

Naomi

Relief, on some level, had washed through me when Joan rang to say that Sara's children were safe with their grandmother, swiftly followed by a new kind of fear. She'd told me that, on finding the house empty and unable to contact Sara on her phone, Paul had gone across to her house. When Joan had told him she'd been so concerned about Sara's whereabouts when she couldn't contact her that she'd called the police, he'd been spitting with fury, swearing he would kill Ben. But why? What was the link between them that I was missing?

'How does he know him, Joan?' I'd asked her, desperately scrambling to fit the pieces together.

Joan had hesitated. 'I'm not sure,' she'd answered cautiously. 'I have my suspicions, but... The police are here. I'll call you back.'

She hadn't called yet, and I felt as if I was going out of my mind. I still couldn't believe that Ben was capable of violence, or that the police thought he was. I didn't think I could bear it. The most unbearable thing of all was that when I'd asked Liam whether he'd ever been to the reservoir on his own, whether he might have met Lily there, although he'd denied it, he wouldn't meet my gaze, and it struck fear right through me.

He and Maya had finally fallen asleep in my bed. I was grateful for that one small mercy. They needed to rest and I needed to sort through the clatter of thoughts in my head. Feeling jaded to my bones, I trailed to the kitchen. Listless with despair and exhaustion, I dropped into a chair, buried my face in my hands and tried desperately to quash the horrific images playing through my mind. My heart rate spiked as I pictured Holly, so like my little girl, and imagined the fear she must have felt while being held down in the freezing cold water. That's where she was, I was sure, lying cold and lonely at the bottom of the reservoir. But where was Lily? Where was Sara?

Clenching my arms around my ribs, as if I could somehow hold in the pain, I rocked silently to and fro. Everything was broken and distorted, and I had no way to fix it. I didn't recognise the man I was married to. I didn't recognise *me*. Even now, with everything pointing to the fact that he was guilty – the lies he'd told, the manipulations to make me believe those lies, the fact that he'd run – still I couldn't make myself believe it. How stupid did that make me?

The rumour mill would be turning. I'd seen neighbours gathering outside, gossiping. I couldn't blame them. With the police arriving and two women missing, they were bound to be. I had to deal with it. For my children's sakes, I had to stay strong and face whatever would happen next. Briefly, I wondered where Ben might be, and then, a jolt of visceral anger shooting through me, I swiped at my tears and pulled myself to my feet.

I was heading for the wine I badly wanted when my blood froze. There was someone at the front door – no knocking or hammering this time, more an odd swishing and rattling. Lily?

Hope rising in my chest, I rushed to the hall, stood stock-still for a second and listened. Hearing nothing, I reached to open the door. There was no one there. No one but the gathering crowd – some people I knew, some I didn't, all with hostile faces angled in my direction.

I was about to step back when I noticed something spattered on the path: rich red droplets, staining the slabs stark crimson.

Hearing again the strange rattling, I glanced towards the sound. The man standing on the pavement didn't try to hide what he was holding. He stared right at me for a blood-freezing moment, then rattled the spray can again, raised his arm and hurled it into my garden.

Hastily, I dropped my gaze, and recoiled in horror as I saw what was daubed across my front door. *MURDERER.* One single word, sprayed across the number 13.

SIXTY-ONE

Naomi

The two days that had passed had been the longest forty-eight hours of my life. I couldn't eat, couldn't sleep, didn't dare leave the house, not even to take my children to school. I didn't want them to be taunted, bullied and ridiculed. Children can be cruel. Adults crueller. I could feel the hatred seeping under the doors and through the walls. The people who stood and stared, nodded and pointed fingers, had good reason to hate me. I should have known. I should have listened to Sara. My heart stalled as the last words I'd spoken to her crashed into my head. *Was it because he took what was obviously on offer and then walked away? Did you get a kick out of it, Sara? Fucking my husband? Seeing me crumble?* Shame swept through me. Desperately, I wanted to take the words back, to reel my life back. But I couldn't, any more than I could bring Lily or Sara or little Holly back. I recalled my husband's look, his guilt and his shame as he'd spoken of what had happened to his sister. The tears on his cheeks as he'd insisted he hadn't hurt her. Why then was he running?

Reluctant to turn on the lights, even though the curtains were tightly drawn, I wiped away the useless tears on my cheeks as I negotiated my way down the stairs by the light of the streetlamp outside. The house was cast in shadows, hiding its secrets in dark corners. A shiver ran the length of my spine as I reached the hall. I'd had a sense of foreboding when I'd set eyes on the rocking chair, sitting upstairs like an ominous omen. When I'd found Little Buttons, once obviously loved and then abandoned here, I'd felt it. I should *never* have agreed to come here. But then, if my husband was guilty of the atrocities people seemed to think, wouldn't I have arrived at this place in my life anyway?

I was moving past the front door when a clatter outside froze me to the spot. My gaze went to the letter box. Someone had posted something unspeakably disgusting through it this morning. I'd felt devastated, angry and defeated. Did those people out there really think my children were guilty too? That they should be subjected to all of this?

Holding my breath, I waited, my adrenaline pumping as I wondered to what lengths they would go to punish anyone associated with a man they'd already judged. There followed another clatter and a scrape, causing my heart to leap in my chest. Relief flooded every vein in my body as I heard Joan's voice outside. 'Naomi,' she called. 'It's Joan. Are you all right in there?'

Wondering why she'd run the gauntlet of snap-happy journalists rather than phone, I went quickly to open the door while making sure to stay as far back as I could. 'I'm okay.' I smiled feebly. 'Do you want to come in?' I wasn't sure she would, for fear of being tarnished by association.

She looked me over hesitantly, then smiled. 'Thank you.'

Seeing the police car also parked indiscreetly outside, I

moved to help her with her walking frame and then closed the door fast.

'How are you?' she asked, scanning my eyes as I turned to her. 'Silly question,' she added, with a despairing shake of her head. 'I have some news,' she said. 'I would have phoned but I couldn't find my phone charger. Those mobiles are such newfangled things. I do wish I'd kept my landline.'

My stomach somersaulted. 'What news?'

Joan hesitated, her expression wary, and my blood ran cold. 'They're dredging the reservoir,' she announced.

Shock surged through me like a bolt of electricity, and I simply stared at her.

'I thought you would want to know.' Joan's look was now one of sympathy, and I wanted to break down in her arms and sob.

Parking her frame, Joan shuffled towards me. 'Come here,' she said, clearly sensing my bewilderment and wrapping me into a hug.

'I have to be there,' I whispered, though I wasn't sure my legs would carry me that far.

She squeezed me gently. 'Do you think that's wise?'

I nodded into her shoulder. 'I have to. I have to know.'

Easing back, Joan searched my face, her own uncertain. 'There's something else I have to tell you,' she said, reticence now in her eyes. 'I should have said something at the time, but I was so worried for Adam. For Lily, too.'

She dropped her gaze to the bag attached to her walking frame. My heart thundered as she delved inside it, then faltered as she withdrew a girl's patent red shoe.

Confused, I snapped my gaze from the shoe back to her face.

'It was Holly's,' she said. 'I remember her wearing them.'

'But...' I glanced down at it again. 'How...? Where...?'

'I found it in the gutter on the night Lily and Michael

forced Adam back to the reservoir.' Joan provided the answer to the question I couldn't squeeze out. 'I went across after they'd arrived home. I should have handed it in. I bitterly regret not doing so now. I debated whether to. The thing is, I don't know how it got there. I thought that perhaps Adam had picked it up while he was searching for her. I was scared for him. Scared that this might incriminate him. I didn't believe the things that were being said about him and...' She paused, her expression a mixture of wretchedness and guilt. 'I held on to it. When it was clear the police search was being scaled down, I... I thought it was better to leave well alone.'

I stared at her, utterly stunned.

'I know I shouldn't have,' she added quickly, clearly seeing my horror, 'but I honestly didn't think Adam was capable of such a thing. The other boy, though—'

'I have to go.' My heart pounding through my chest, I turned to grab my jacket from the hooks.

'I'll stay here with the children,' Joan offered, as I scrambled to the door.

A hard lump expanding in my throat, I nodded quickly, steeled myself and pulled the front door open. Then, careless of the faces angling towards me, the popping flashes and the tears that were half-blinding me, I ran.

SIXTY-TWO

Naomi

Tugging my flimsy jacket more tightly around me, I tried to ignore the hushed whispers of the clique of school mothers huddled just yards away. I'd once been invited into their circle. Now, standing outside it, I felt it acutely, the loneliness of being alone. Katie, the woman the others looked up to, was with them. In my peripheral vision, I caught her glancing furtively towards me. I kept my gaze fixed forward, concentrating on the activity beyond the police cordon, and tried to block out the speculation of those drawn by flashing blue lights and morbid curiosity.

'Any idea what they're looking for?' another woman who lived a few doors away from me asked fearfully.

'Body, I reckon,' a neighbour from the opposite side of the road surmised with a short 'tsk'. 'Has to be, doesn't it?' He nodded towards the police divers negotiating the curved wall of the dam to access the water where the reservoir was at its deepest. Other officers, dressed from top to toe in white suits, examined the brickwork, where blood spatters had been found. Under the harsh spotlights, the scene looked surreal, like something from a futuristic film set.

Truth, though, I'd come to realise, was far stranger than fiction. It hadn't been announced officially, but I'd heard the rumour rippling through the crowd. With Sara's phone signal having been picked up here, it was possible they were searching for two bodies: Lily's and Sara's. Would they find a third, I wondered, the little girl my husband's mother had searched endlessly for? How had her shoe come to be lying in the gutter? My mind a whirlpool of confusion, I swallowed back the dread mounting inside me as I watched and waited for my nightmare to unfold. Two officers had been tasked with keeping the public and hungry journalists straining at the cordon at bay, I noticed. I was grateful for that much. Once this hit the headlines, the whole world would know my husband was a suspect, that he was missing, probably running, and then there would be no escape from the hostility. I felt as if I had a physical thing pressing down on me. The smell, putrid, dank and earthy, filled my nostrils and I gulped back the nausea rising like bile in my throat. Rain, heavy and unrelenting, pitter-pattered on the surface of the water in time with the rapid thud, thud, thud of my heart. *It wasn't my husband.* I breathed in sharply He snapped once, with provocation, but he's not capable of these atrocities. He's *not!* The flash from a journalist's camera blinded me, and I wanted to run, go back to my house, bolt the doors and shut the world out, but I stayed where I was, dry-eyed with shock, my emotions frozen solid inside me.

Was my son capable of violence? Out of some desperate attempt to keep his world safe, might he have been the one who'd attacked a frail, defenceless woman? Fear crackled like ice through my veins as I tried to stop my mind replaying the scenario that petrified me: Maya weeping on the landing, Liam kneeling at the side of the filled bath, the reborn baby doll submerged under the water. I turned away from the reservoir as my little girl's horrified cries resonated through my head like some horrendous warning I'd failed to heed, stumbling and pushing my way through the throng swarming around me. *Ignore them.* I forced myself on, but I couldn't ignore them: the eyes that swivelled towards me, beams of hate burning into me; the whispers, too loud for me to ignore.

'That's her, his wife.'

'Do you think she knew?'

'Of course she bloody well knew. How can you live with someone who's obviously a complete psycho and *not* know?'

SIXTY-THREE

Naomi

I felt claustrophobic, as if the walls of the house were closing in on me, ready to swallow me up and make me part of its history, my children's voices echoing through it as surely as I could hear the haunting voice of the child who'd vanished from it twenty long years ago. Holly was singing softly, sweetly...

> *Teddy bear, teddy bear, turn out the light.*
> *Teddy bear, teddy bear, say, 'Good night.'*
> *Teddy bear, teddy bear, peekaboo.*
> *Teddy bear, teddy bear, I love you.*

'Stop!' *Please stop.* I pressed the heels of my hands hard to my ears, desperate to block out the noise in my head, the jarring noises around me: my phone ringing, the constant knocking on the door, the letter flap rattling, tabloid journalists shouting through it, wanting to 'give me an opportunity to tell my side of the story'.

Anger unfurling inside me as I heard another envelope being stuffed through the door, I flew to the hall, ready to yank the damned door open and fight back. My heart skidded to a stop as I found my boy standing there. His face was tight and pale, his body rigid as he tore the envelope in half and then tore it again. 'Go away,' he seethed, hot tears squeezing from his eyes, his chest heaving. 'Leave. Us. Alone!'

'Liam.' I approached him as he screwed the remnants into a tight ball. 'Liam!' Lunging forward, I caught hold of him as he moved towards the door.

He fought me. 'I need to tell them.' He choked back a strangled sob. 'Why won't they go away? I need to make them.'

'Stop.' Wrapping both arms around him, I gathered him hard to me, pressing my face into his hair and holding him tight. 'They'll get bored soon,' I whispered, as the flailing stopped and the fight left his body. 'They will go away eventually, Liam, I promise you.'

My boy looked up at me. 'Will Dad come back when they do?' he asked, his voice bewildered, such hope in his eyes I felt my heart fracture into a thousand pieces.

'I'm not sure, sweetheart.' Forcing my tears back, I squeezed him close. He was shaking, so frightened and disorientated by all of this, and I had no idea what to say to him. How could I tell him his Daddy would come home? How could I make false promises that would only rock his world further? I was about to tell him that whatever happened, his father loved him, when a loud crash followed by a shrill scream from the lounge froze my blood in my veins.

'Maya!' Instinct propelling me, I raced in that direction, ignoring the door that was being hammered behind me. Seeing the carnage in the lounge, the bay window caved in, shards of glass strewn across the carpet and my little girl standing petrified in the midst of it, my stomach lurched violently.

My heart bursting, I flew across to her and swept her up, encircling my arms around her and cradling her protectively to my shoulder. She was trembling, her whole body shaking, sobbing in terrified confusion. 'It's okay, baby. Mummy's got you.' A toxic mixture of rage and hatred burned inside me. 'I've got you, sweetheart,' I murmured. 'I'm here.'

Pressing my child close, I whirled around, heading back to the hall to shepherd my children upstairs, where they would be safer. Then I stopped short, my breath stalling as I came face to face with Paul. Stunned, I stepped back.

'Liam let me in.' He took a step towards me. 'I saw what happened. Are you all right?' he asked, his forehead creased with concern.

I didn't answer. 'Liam, come *here*.' He was still by the open front door and I beckoned him closer.

'It's okay.' Paul held up a hand in some attempt at reassurance. 'I only came to apologise – and to help, if I can. You don't deserve this. None of this is your fault. I can't believe what that bastard has put you through. As if cheating on you wasn't enough, Christ only knows what he's done to—'

'Enough!' Squeezing Maya closer, I stared at him, horrified and incredulous. Was he really oblivious to the fact that my children were right there, seeing and listening to everything?

Contrition flicked across his features. 'I'm sorry,' he said gruffly, glancing from me to Liam, who'd come to stand by my side. 'It's the truth, though, Naomi, and you know it.'

I shook my head in bewilderment. What was he doing here? The police had obviously released him, but why would he come here when he'd already caused so much upset?

'I know him, Naomi,' he went on forcefully. 'He's—'

'How?' I shouted over him. He clearly did know Ben, knew things about him I didn't, or claimed to, but... 'How could you know him? Why would neither of you have...?' The words died in my throat as someone else approached the front door.

A quizzical expression crossed Paul's face as he registered the shock on mine. Warily, he glanced over his shoulder, then, 'Shit,' he uttered, his face paling.

'Zachary, it is you,' Lily exclaimed.

My gaze swivelled from Paul to where Lily stood in the hall, her face bruised and her hair matted with blood. She looked shockingly frail. 'Zachary?' I repeated, my head reeling with confusion.

Lily's attention was fixed on Paul, her eyes full of trepidation. 'I knew it was him. I would recognise him anywhere. He has his father's eyes.'

My gaze snapped to Paul. A small tic spasmed in his cheek. He didn't speak. His expression was dark. Dangerous.

SIXTY-FOUR

Joan

Finding her charger in the kitchen drawer, Joan hurried to plug her mobile in. It was such a fiddly thing, not made with arthritic fingers in mind. Squinting and muttering impatiently as she tried to push the cable into the small socket, she stopped, pressed a hand under her nose and gulped back a sob. How had she missed the text Sara had sent? She needed to alert someone. The police were across the road. Someone had obviously called them about the mindless damage caused to poor Naomi's house, but it was DS Harrison she needed to speak to. He'd left her his personal number. She'd been searching for it when the damned battery had died. If only she could connect the wire she could... *At last.*

Joan's heart fluttered with panic as she waited for the phone to fire up. How could she have been so incompetent? She'd told herself she was going senile, wondering about this Paul character. The two of them living next door to each other, surely that wasn't possible? But it was. She should have warned Sara. Another wretched sob caught in her throat as she negotiated her way to her phone contacts. Finding the number, she pressed call and waited, every second that ticked by feeling like an eternity. 'Hello,' she said quickly, as soon as she heard DS Harrison's voice. 'It's Joan...' She trailed off, her heart dropping as she realised it was a recording asking her to leave a message. 'Please call me as soon as possible. It's terribly important,' she said wretchedly, then pushed the phone into her cardigan pocket and made her way to the hall. She would have to speak to one of the officers outside. She couldn't leave it. She cursed her clumsiness as she almost fell before she reached her frame by the front door. She was so slow, it was infuriating.

She pulled her door open and was searching for someone who looked likely to help when the phone rang. Extracting it from her pocket, she saw it was DS Harrison calling. Thank God. After she hurriedly explained to him about the text she'd missed, he promised he would be there soon.

True to his word, he arrived barely ten minutes later. Joan had stayed on her doorstep watching the commotion over the road. She couldn't see what was going on in Naomi's house, but at least the police had dispersed most of the crowd, bar the persistent media photographers. Some things never changed. It had been the same when poor Holly disappeared: journalists had camped on Lily's doorstep night and day. It was no wonder Michael had sunk into such a deep pit of depression, that Lily had eventually lost her mind, as well as her daughter. Joan shook her head in disgust and turned her attention to DS Harrison as he climbed out of his car and hurried towards her. 'Thank you for coming so promptly,' she said. 'I've been beside myself with worry.'

'No problem,' he assured her. 'I was on my way here anyway. Do you want to show me these photographs?' He nodded past her to her hall, no doubt seeking privacy away from the reporters, and then helped her back into the house.

'They're on my phone, attached to the text message. As I mentioned, there's no actual message, just the attachments, which, in itself, is extremely worrying.' Joan fetched the phone from her pocket and handed it to him. 'I feel absolutely awful about not seeing it. I don't use the phone unless I really need to. I don't think I'll ever forgive myself if the information could have helped find Sara sooner.'

She didn't think she would ever forgive herself for not giving the police that shoe all those years ago either. All of this was linked to little Holly. It had to be. She hadn't realised until recently, while watching the true crime shows, that the shoe could have had DNA evidence on it that might have helped establish what really happened. She wished dearly that she hadn't held on to it now.

'You did the right thing, calling me,' DS Harrison offered kindly. Trying to make her feel better, Joan guessed. She didn't. She felt inept and guilty, and so scared for Sara.

The detective arched an eyebrow as he thumbed her phone. 'You think the photographs might provide information as to where she might be?' he asked.

'The last one, most definitely.' Joan waited while he located it.

DS Harrison looked at it, then back to her, his brow furrowed curiously.

'It's a Girl Power Spice Girls bike,' Joan pointed out. 'They were very popular a while back, around the time Holly Grant vanished.'

The detective's frown deepened. Joan could almost see the wheels going round. Then, 'Christ,' he uttered. 'The bike that was never found.'

'Until now,' Joan said. 'The envelope's also significant,' she added, as he scrolled through the images. She waited while he fiddled with the phone and enlarged the photograph.

'Zachary Grant?' His gaze came quizzically back to her. 'Who the hell is he?'

'You might want to look at the other photographs,' Joan suggested. She watched as he studied them, praying that he could see what she clearly could in the wedding photograph. 'Lily's stepson,' she clarified, when he looked back at her in astonishment. 'Adam Grant's half-brother on his father's side, now going by the name Paul Mansell and also going out with Sara. I didn't see much of him, but I gathered from Lily that the boy was quite jealous of his father's new family – Adam in particular, believing he'd taken his place in his father's affections. Lily said that Zachary was often sullen and moody. A bully, by all accounts. I felt quite sorry for Adam. He was often tormented by the other children because he was a little bit different. Introverted, I suppose you'd call it. And Holly was no angel either. She would taunt him too, but I'm not sure that Adam would have—'

'We need to find him.' DS Harrison whirled around to the door, Joan's phone still in his hands. 'Sorry.' He glanced back at her. 'I'm sending these to my phone. Are you okay with that?'

'Absolutely,' Joan assured him, relief sweeping through her. She could feel in her bones that the address on the envelope was where they would find Sara – God willing, unharmed. She gathered DS Harrison felt it too.

He handed the phone back to her and raced on. 'What's happening over there?' he yelled at the female officer who was hurrying across the road from Naomi's house.

'Lily's turned up,' she shouted. 'Paul Mansell was also there, but apparently he's scarpered. You'll never guess what?' She stopped breathlessly at the foot of Joan's path.

'I think I probably can,' Harrison replied tersely. 'I need

units – any and all in the WR2 postcode area. And I need a squad car here. *Now.*'

Joan's hand fluttered to her chest as she heard him add, 'We'll need armed officers on standby.'

Making her way to the hall cupboard, she fetched the shoe. They might need that too. She would have to suffer the consequences for withholding evidence.

SIXTY-FIVE

Sara

'Shut the fuck up!' The door to the cellar shook as he smashed something against it. His fist? No, the sound was heavier, sharper. Like the handle of a shovel or, God help her, a hammer. What was he going to do? How insane was he? But she knew. He and his half-brother were both seriously deranged. It clearly ran in the family.

Gulping back her terrified sobs, she heaved again, retching bile as the stench of rotting flesh filled her nostrils. It permeated the air, seeping through the fabric of her clothes. She had no idea how long the woman had been down here, how long she herself had, what time of day it was, even what day it was. The pitch black was disorientating, pressing down on her like a dank, suffocating blanket. Her head was throbbing so badly. Gingerly she pressed her fingers to the wound on her forehead. It was gaping, her hair matted with sticky, drying blood.

He wasn't going to let her out. She was going to die down

here. Shuffling further into the corner, she drew her knees up and tried to make herself small. 'Why are you doing this? Did you never feel anything for me?' she croaked, her throat parched.

He didn't answer, and hopelessness washed through her.

'Please think of the children. Please let me go. *Please.*'

'Quiet!' He rapped again from where he still stood outside the door. Why was he just standing there? What was going through his fetid mind? Icy fear gripping her stomach, she stifled another sob, then retched again as the smell grew more pungent. She'd found her by accident. Fumbling around on her hands and knees, looking for something with which to defend herself, something that might help her find a way out of here, she'd recoiled in horror as the flat of her hand landed on something soft and wet. It had taken her a second to realise that what she was tracing with her trembling fingertips were the decaying contours of a face, eye sockets, cheekbones. Some of her flesh had come away with her hand. Her face had been scratched off, an attempt to obliterate her.

Jolting as she heard the metallic scrape of the bolt being drawn, she pulled her knees tighter to her chest and held her breath. The door didn't open. She waited. There was no movement. The door handle rattled, stark against the silence. Still, he didn't appear. It was as if he was toying with her, torturing her, trying to drive her out of her mind. It was a game to him. A game where he had all the power. Like a child pulling the legs from a spider and watching as it tried to get away, he was gaining some sick satisfaction from this. Anger, like thick bile, rose in her throat, and she reached to scrub the tears from her face. She had no weapon to fight him with, nothing but the torn and bloodied fingernails she'd scraped at the door with, but she would *not* make this easy for him. She would fight with every ounce of strength she still had left. She pictured her babies' faces, held on to that image and braced herself.

Finally, he opened the door, pulling it wide in one swift move. She winced, then blinked rapidly as her eyes struggled to adjust to the light. He didn't descend the stairs. His broad-shouldered frame filling the doorway, he stood stock-still at the top of them. Assessing the situation, Sara guessed. Wondering whether he'd terrorised her enough? Could he smell how terrified she was? Did the stench of her piss and her vomit along with rotting flesh satiate his perverse appetite? Or did he want more? Did he want her to beg, more than she already had, to whimper and grovel? Her anger turned to rage, white-hot inside her. She wouldn't give him that satisfaction. She didn't know how long she'd spent in this hell, but it was *he* who deserved to rot in it.

Her pulse quickened as he continued slowly down. She stayed where she was, biding her time until he was a few steps from the floor. Then, spitting and hissing like the animal he'd reduced her to, she unfurled herself and launched herself at him, her bodyweight hitting his shins full force.

She'd expected him to stop her. To kick out and swat her off like a fly. Instead, he went down, his face and chest hitting the stone-cold floor, the impact forcing the breath from his body and a vile curse from his mouth. Sara shuffled back on her haunches as he attempted to pull himself up. He was woozy, shaking his head – and she wasted no time. Her will to survive that of a trapped animal, she levered herself up and scrambled to the steps. She was halfway up them when he clamped a hand over her ankle.

No. She would not let him do this. If she was going to die, she would die fighting! With fire in her belly, she twisted herself round, her body at an impossible angle, the sharp edges of the steps digging spitefully into her ribs, and kicked out with her free leg. It had no effect. She could see the whites of his eyes, his pupils so large as to make his dark eyes almost black, the fevered determination within them as he crawled his way up her body.

He was looming over her, a slow smile curving his mouth, when she saw an opportunity. Hooking an arm around his neck, she yanked his face down, lifted her own, and sank her teeth hard into his cheek. Now it was him who was the animal, yelping like a wounded dog.

'Smile on the other side of your face, you bastard.' She brought her knee up sharply, twisted around as he flailed backwards and dragged herself up.

Once on her feet, she didn't get far. She hadn't expected to, but she hadn't made it easy for him either. She held on to that small part of her dignity as she sensed him behind her; refused to cry out as he grabbed her hair, threading it around his hand and twisting it so tight she felt sure he was going to rip the roots from her head.

'Such a shame. I quite enjoyed fucking you,' he snarled, his breath so close to her ear it caused her stomach to heave.

Please, God, help me. Please look after my babies, Sara begged silently. She could hear sirens, distant but growing louder. Too far away to save her. She squeezed her eyes closed as he clutched her throat, his fingers digging mercilessly into her flesh. Then she snatched them open as another male voice said quietly, 'Let her go, or I'll snap your neck like a twig.'

'Bullshit. You're full of it. You always—' His response was cut short by a sickening crack.

SIXTY-SIX

TWO DAYS LATER

Naomi

After a doctor's appointment, where I reluctantly asked for something to help me sleep, I made up my mind to go to the hospital to see Sara. I couldn't just leave it, not knowing how she was. Finding that she'd left the hospital, I drove straight back home. I wasn't sure she would want to see me, but I hoped she would. Ellie and James were still with Sara's mother in Cornwall, Joan had told me, and I couldn't bear the thought of Sara being alone. She would be so scared and lonely. Blaming herself, I suspected, when that was the last thing she should be doing. Zachary Grant had obviously had a Jekyll-and-Hyde personality, only showing her the side of himself he wanted her to see. As had Adam, I reminded myself, blinking away my tears as I thought of all that had been lost, all that my children had lost, the memories broken. Sara and I would both need help rebuilding our lives. My hope was that we could try to help each other.

Reaching Trowan Crescent, I stopped short of the house, staring at the activity ahead of me. I was shocked – not by the reporters, who seemed to have gravitated to the road in droves, blocking traffic and hounding residents in some headline seeking frenzy, but by the removal van parked outside Sara's house. Abandoning my car, I hurried towards Joan's house, dodging the microphones that were thrust rudely in my face and trying to ignore the cacophony of demanding voices around me.

'How do you feel about what your husband did, Mrs Felton?' one guy yelled.

I almost laughed. I didn't know how to feel. I was numb inside.

'Do you think history's repeating itself, Naomi?' yelled another. What the hell did that mean?

'How's Lily?' someone else shouted. I had no idea how Lily was, and that pained me. Or even where she was. I'd left her in the hall when I'd followed Paul – Zachary – out into the garden, where he'd vaulted the fence into Sara's garden and run. When I'd come back inside, she'd gone. The police had had a sighting of her, so I knew she was alive and well, and I'd promised myself I would find her, but then events had spiralled so horrifyingly and I'd done nothing about it.

I was severely pissed off by a woman who asked me how all of this was affecting my children. 'What?' I stopped to stare at her, confounded. 'Do you have children?' I asked her. She didn't answer, but I guessed by the flash of guilt that crossed her face that she did. 'Because if you do, you would know that it's all *this* that's upsetting them, wouldn't you?' I flailed a hand around. 'You're frightening them. Can you not just go away and leave us to pick up the pieces, for God's sake?'

She had the decency to back off, at least.

Joan opened her door a fraction when I finally managed to get to her house to actually check how my children were.

'They're fine.' She looked me over, concerned. 'We're playing Frustration. An old game of my son's. We have *Scooby Doo* lined up to watch afterwards. Are you all right?'

'Trying to be.' I dredged up a smile. Joan didn't look convinced. 'Would you mind having them a little longer? I hadn't realised Sara had been discharged. I wanted to pop in and see her, assuming she'll see me.'

'Not at all. I'm grateful for the distraction.' Joan shot an unimpressed gaze at the media. 'She discharged herself, apparently. She's going to Cornwall to stay with her mother,' she went on, quickly filling me in, her eyes clouding with sadness. 'I think she'll want to say goodbye to you.'

I hoped so. Prayed we could part amicably, even if not as the good friends I'd once thought we could be. If she didn't feel able to talk much now, there might come a point when she would need to. 'Give Liam and Maya a hug for me and tell them I'll be back soon.' I gestured Joan to close the door and, bracing myself, turned to push my way back through the fray.

After ringing her doorbell several times, calling through her letter flap and texting her, all to no avail, I was walking defeatedly back down her path when I heard Sara's door squeak open. The throng surged forward, and I whirled around and raced back as, peering apprehensively between the door and the frame, Sara beckoned me in.

Once I was in the hall, she slammed the door and turned to face me, and I felt my heart bleed for her. I hadn't been sure what I would find, but she was clearly utterly traumatised. Her hair, normally glossy and bouncy and rarely with a strand out of place, was scraped into an elastic band, and without a trace of make-up, her complexion was as white as snow. Gone were the leggings and figure-hugging top she would normally wear, and there was no sign of her blood-red rose tattoo. Instead, she was wearing an oversized top which swamped her and loose track-suit bottoms. She looked like a child. A small, frightened child.

'Oh, Sara...' My eyes strayed to the stitched wound on her head, the livid purple bruising on her throat, and my chest filled up. Instinctively, I reached for her.

But Sara drew back. 'It's not true,' she said, her eyes flecked with uncertainty as she searched mine.

I frowned, unsure what she was talking about.

'The things you said,' she clarified tearfully. 'What you thought about me – about Ben and me. It's not true. I don't sleep around, although it's my business if I choose to. God knows, enough men do,' she hurried on, the tears spilling down her face, the words tumbling out. 'But I've never... Would never.' She stopped, looked away and wrapped her arms tightly around herself. She was shaking. And in that moment, I hated myself.

'I know.' My voice catching, I moved towards her, hesitated, then encircled her with my arms. 'I'm sorry.'

Sara was as stiff as a board for a second, and then she relaxed into me. I was sure that if I hadn't been holding her, her legs would have failed her. 'Me too.' A sharp sob escaped her.

'You have nothing to be sorry for. *Nothing*, do you hear me? Never apologise for being you, Sara. You're caring, a good mother, and brave and beautiful into the bargain. Don't let that bastard damage your self-esteem.' I eased back to look firmly into her eyes. 'If you do, you're letting him win. We both are. Don't give him that.'

She squeezed her eyes closed, tugged in a breath and nodded.

I hugged her tight. 'I'm here for you, Sara. I promise you.' I'd never meant anything more in my life.

'Ditto,' she murmured into my shoulder.

'Can I ask you something?' I was hesitant, but things still didn't quite add up and I needed to know. 'About Ben?'

I felt her tense a little, but she looked up at me and nodded.

'Did you know him? Know something about him that made

you so...?' I trailed off, not knowing how to say 'antagonistic towards him' without it sounding like I was in fact laying blame.

She glanced down. 'I used to go to a survivors of abuse group,' she said, looking cautiously back at me. 'There was a woman there. It had taken her an amazing amount of courage to press charges against her partner. But Ben's photographic evidence was deemed insufficient and the guy walked.'

I processed. 'He told me,' I said. Now it made more sense.

Sara took a breath. 'I suppose that was honest of him.' It was said a little begrudgingly, but I understood why.

'It was.' I swallowed hard.

'What will you do now?' She looked me over worriedly.

'I'm not sure,' I answered honestly. I had no idea how I would get through even the next few days, but I had to. For my children. 'I have to talk to DS Harrison.' It was a meeting I was dreading. 'I'll call you once I know more.'

SIXTY-SEVEN

Naomi

Nerves churned my stomach as DS Harrison came through the security door into the police station reception area. 'Mrs Felton.' He smiled, extending his hand as he walked across to me.

'Naomi,' I said, offering my own. I wasn't Mrs Felton. I never had been. I had no idea who I was, who the man I'd married was, and I still didn't know what had happened to his sister. Now I was trying to take on board the fact that he'd killed his half-brother. Even though he'd done it to save Sara, that single act of violence made my blood run cold.

'Naomi.' DS Harrison nodded. 'What can I do for you?'

'What will happen to him now?' Despite everything, I still cared for him, the part of him I was sure I did know, the quiet, gentle person who was the father of my children. Someone I had never imagined would harm another living soul. But he had, hadn't he? My chest constricted painfully. 'Will he get bail?'

'That depends on the magistrates' court.' Harrison looked me over cautiously. 'Assuming his application is granted, he'll need to meet certain conditions, provide a permanent address, hand in his passport. If he doesn't stick to the conditions, he's likely to be arrested and stay in police custody until his court hearing.'

I nodded, understanding. He was asking whether Ben – Adam, though I still struggled to think of him by that name – would be living at Trowan Crescent. If he didn't have a permanent address, then he would be locked up on remand. How would he escape the stress he would undoubtedly be feeling then?

'What sentence is he likely to be given?' I asked, avoiding the subject until I was able to think things through more clearly.

DS Harrison rubbed his forehead thoughtfully with his thumb. 'That very much depends on the court. The charge of unlawful act manslaughter is a serious one,' he answered carefully. 'Factors indicating culpability, or otherwise, will be taken into consideration, such as that the unlawful act was in defence of another and that there appears to be no premeditation.'

I hesitated, then asked the question I wasn't sure I wanted to hear the answer to. 'How did he come to be there, at the house, when...?'

DS Harrison nodded, clearly understanding why I would wonder. 'He says he was on his way home, about to hand himself in. He claims to have followed the deceased, having seen him bolting from your house on the day of the damage to your window. I've no reason to believe differently. As yet, we have no evidence of Adam Grant having been in any other room at the property. He is of previous good character and as the woman held captive has corroborated his story...'

Sara. She would have died if not for Adam. Zachary Grant had been a monster. All that had happened – the cat being locked in our shed along with Little Buttons, the vile letter stuffed through my door – had been at his hands. I had no doubt he'd faked an account in the name of Nicole Jackson and had sent me that article, or that it was him who'd knocked Ben almost unconscious in the garden. He'd aimed to destroy Ben out of jealousy. He'd aimed to destroy me. The police had found traces of my blood on his van. I could only assume that, for whatever twisted reason, his half-brother had aimed to take everything away from him, the people he loved. It was still all so totally unbelievable.

'She is in no doubt that he saved her life,' Harrison went on, as I contemplated why Zachary Grant had so mercilessly manipulated Sara. He had gained access to the house next door to the house his step-family had lived in, the house his half-sister had vanished from. It was almost as if he'd been keeping watch over it.

'Judging by what we found in Zachary Grant's cellar, I don't doubt it either,' Harrison continued. 'Sentencing is ultimately for the court to decide, though,' he reiterated. 'The history of violence might have been a grey area, considering the circumstances around the disappearance of Holly Grant. We might never know what happened to her, but her bike being found to have been in the possession of Zachary Grant would seem to exonerate Adam Grant from any culpability.'

'Can I ask you about the shoe?' I ventured, praying that Joan wouldn't be charged with withholding evidence. 'Did it yield anything?'

Harrison shook his head. 'Nothing that would help. Your husband says he has no idea how it came to be where Joan claimed to have found it. He does remember his mother taking some things to the charity shop. That's a possible explanation, assuming that Joan is mistaken about the timing.'

Might she be? I frowned. She had appeared muddled – Sara had said she was – but was she likely to have got muddled about that?

'Our focus is on Zachary Grant,' Harrison continued. 'We gather from what Adam Grant says, and your neighbour's statement, that he was a nasty piece of work, even as a teenager. I suppose Adam Grant was an easy target, being two years younger. Also, a bit of a loner, by all accounts.'

I nodded, a cold shudder shaking through me as I considered the body they'd found in the cellar – Zachary's wife, murdered, indescribably cruelly. With the new developments, the dredging of the reservoir had stopped. They were going to dig the cellar floor up, thinking that Holly's small body might be found there. My heart bled for Lily as I imagined the endless torment she must have suffered, not knowing where her little girl was, never able to lay her child to rest and say a proper goodbye. Part of me hoped they would find her in the cellar. Another part of me prayed they wouldn't.

'Will he be returning to the family home?' Harrison asked, as I swallowed back the sadness clogging my throat. 'I ask because shortly after he was brought here he had a seizure. Stress-induced, according to the doctor. He needs to be with someone who is aware of his health problems.'

I knew then that I couldn't do it, couldn't leave my husband incarcerated when he didn't need to be, didn't deserve to be. Whatever his future – our future – held, to do that would be to allow Zachary Grant to win. I would not allow that.

SIXTY-EIGHT

Naomi

Zachary Grant had changed his identity – easily done, according to DS Harrison. As had Ben. I could understand Ben wanting to disassociate himself from his previous life, but Zachary's agenda, the police had assumed, was to keep watch on the house next door, hoping to make some claim on it. He'd changed his persona, his appearance, and wheedled his way into Sara's life, even inventing a daughter to gain her trust. I wondered, if he had had a child, whether that child would exist now. His wife had been about to leave him, but Zachary had made sure she never did. Her parents, who it turned out did live in Spain, hadn't missed her because they were estranged, their family fractured.

It was most likely madness on my part, but I hoped my family wouldn't be. Ben was my family, the only family I'd had for years. He was my children's father. I had to make the right decision for their sakes, but I couldn't do that until I had the whole story. What came out of Ben's mouth when he arrived home would define his future. My future. It would decide his children's. I hoped he was aware of that. There would be no more lies. I wouldn't allow him to manipulate me; I simply wasn't that person anymore. I could survive with my heart broken. I couldn't without my self-worth.

His car was still being searched forensically, but I'd decided against picking him up. I wanted to be standing face to face with him when we spoke. I needed to see into his eyes. Now, thanking God for Joan, who'd agreed to watch Maya and Liam while we talked, I waited, my heart thrashing like a frantic bird in my chest as I realised he was due any moment.

My stomach churned nervously as I watched a taxi approach. I backed away from the newly installed lounge window as it parked outside the house and he climbed out, reporters clamouring, microphone booms thrust towards him and cameras flashing in his face. I stepped swiftly back to the window as I heard Maya's unmistakable voice. 'Daddy!' she shouted gleefully. My insides turned over as I saw her charge down Joan's front path.

'Maya! Stay there!' Ben shouted, shoving reporters out of the way and setting off at a run towards her.

Maya. Dear God! My heart stalling, I flew to the front door, wrenching it open and stumbling out. I reached the pavement to see him sweeping her up as she reached the kerb and almost crumpled as the strength drained from my body.

Taking a shaky breath, I composed myself, determined not to give the media more fodder. My resolve in place, I pushed past the people around me, who at least had the good grace to pause in the face of what could have been another tragedy with media vehicles and sightseers driving up and down the road.

Ben was hugging Maya hard to him as I reached them. His hand on the back of her head, he nestled her gently into his shoulder. 'It's okay, sweetheart, Daddy's not angry,' he reassured her. 'But you have to promise to never, *ever* run towards a road without looking again. Okay?'

Maya lifted her head. 'I promise,' she said, her voice small. 'I missed you, Daddy.'

Closing his eyes, Ben exhaled shakily. 'I missed you, too, munchkin,' he said, his voice choked as he hugged her tightly back to him.

Hearing Joan call from her door, I snapped my gaze in her direction, then hurried towards where Liam was trying to help her out with her frame. 'I'm so sorry,' she said, appalled and clearly in shock. 'I had no idea she'd slipped out.'

'She pulled the chair in the hall across to climb up and open the door.' Liam looked guiltily up at me. 'Joan was in the kitchen. I should have been watching her. Sorry.'

'It's all right. It's not your fault. Your sister can be very headstrong sometimes.' I moved to give him a hug. 'I know. I'm her mum.'

There was a flicker of a smile on his face but his gaze was on his father, I noticed. 'Do you want to go and say hello?' I asked him. Until now, I'd tried to shield them from what was happening as best I could. From the media attention, though, they would have gathered it was something serious.

There was a shadow of uncertainty in Liam's eyes, but I could see he wanted to go to him. Giving him a reassuring smile, I moved aside, watching as he walked slowly towards his father.

Ben lowered Maya to the ground and encouraged her towards me, and then he waited, sensing that he needed to allow his son to come to him.

Liam paused, gauging him quietly. Then, seeming to make up his mind, he hurtled suddenly towards him.

Crouching quickly, Ben caught him, locked his arms around him and hugged him hard. 'Missed you, little guy,' he said throatily.

'Me too.' Liam's voice was muffled. I could see he was trying to hold back his tears.

Ben eased back after a second. 'Do you think you could be really grown up for me, Liam?' he asked.

Liam searched his face curiously.

'Your mum and I need to talk,' Ben explained. 'Do you mind staying with Joan for a little while longer and keeping an eye on your sister while we do?'

Liam considered for a second, then nodded. 'Okay.'

'Thanks, Liam.' Straightening up, Ben placed an arm around his shoulders and steered him towards Joan.

Liam stopped him. 'It's my fault, isn't it?' he blurted, looking up at him.

Ben frowned. 'What's your fault, Liam?'

'That you're in trouble.' Liam's gaze pivoted between Ben and me. 'I didn't mean it,' he went on tremulously. He was frightened, I realised with a jolt. I could see it in my boy's eyes.

I moved quickly towards him. 'What didn't you mean, Liam?' I asked, searching his face carefully.

Liam dropped his gaze and shrugged evasively. 'Whatever it was I did wrong,' he mumbled.

SIXTY-NINE

Naomi

Once the children were back at Joan's, with the door locked, Ben and I walked back to our house in complete silence. Needing a minute to gather myself, I went through the open front door and straight to the kitchen.

'Do you think the kids will be okay?' Ben asked, coming in behind me as I switched the kettle on, then switched it off and filled it.

I clanged the kettle back down, switched it on again. I didn't answer. I couldn't.

'At Joan's house, I mean, not...' He trailed off. Clearly, he couldn't bring himself to say, 'afterwards', when he was in prison and I was left trying to pick up the pieces of our children's world and glue it back together. 'Are you okay?' he asked.

A strangled laugh escaped me. Crashing down the cups I'd fished out of the sink – the dishwasher having not gone on, nothing having been done – I blinked hard at the ceiling, tried to hold on to my emotions.

'Stupid question.' I heard his sharp intake of breath. 'I just...'

'*Want* me to be?' My anger exploding, I whirled around to face him. 'I'm not okay, *Adam*.' I furiously enunciated this new name that was alien to me. 'The children are not okay. Do you think they're likely to be?'

His gaze hit the floor. He was ashamed. After all the lies, the conscious manipulation, he damn well should be. 'You have one opportunity to talk to me. One!' I told him. 'This is it.'

His gaze came back to me. He looked haggard, exhausted, so pale it was as if he had no blood in his body. I didn't care.

Except I did. God help me, I didn't know how not to. I felt as if I was hanging on to my sanity, my life, by a thread.

'If one lie spills from your mouth, if you're evasive about anything, then it's over,' I added, making sure it was crystal-clear that I wouldn't take any more. 'And just so you know, it will be over because *you* want it to be. That's what your lies will tell me, Ben – Adam – whoever the bloody hell you are.'

My heart thudding against my chest, I locked my gaze hard on his for a long, searching moment, then walked straight past him to the lounge.

After a moment, he followed, hesitating behind me as I stood with my arms folded and my back to him. 'Why didn't you tell me that he was your half-brother?' I asked.

'I should have done,' he answered gruffly. 'I wanted to. As soon as I realised he was here, I wanted to, but... I couldn't.'

Because his whole web of lies would have unravelled, I thought bitterly.

'I'm sorry,' he said.

'I've heard that before.' I wiped the tears from my face. 'Did you know the police are still digging at his house? They're looking for your sister's remains now. Were you aware of that?' I wasn't sure why I was asking him. Of course he would know. Perhaps I wanted him to know how much I knew. How much his children might one day have to know. The enormity and inconceivable horror of it all.

He didn't answer. I supposed he didn't know how to. Then, 'They won't find anything,' he said quietly, completely destabilising me.

I stayed where I was, motionless, as his words sank in. The implication behind those words. 'How do you know?' My blood pumping so hard I could hear it whooshing past my ears, I turned slowly to face him. 'How do you know they won't?'

He looked away, at the window, at the floor, anywhere but at me.

'Ben!' I shouted. 'Talk to me. Tell me!'

He kneaded his temples, glanced upwards. 'Can I sit down?' he asked, his gaze coming warily back to me.

I didn't reply. I stayed standing as he moved to the sofa and dropped heavily down onto it. 'He hated me,' he said, wiping his hands over his face. 'Zachary, he hated me. He hated Holly, too, but me more.'

I waited, watching as he pressed his forefingers hard to his temples, drew in a deep breath and blew it shakily out. 'He blamed me for taking his father – our father – away from him,' he went on, his voice hoarse. 'He blamed my mother, too.'

Lily. Had she been the 'other woman'?

'It was bullshit.' His voice was tinged with anger. 'As far as I know, his mother went off with some other bloke.'

My mind flew to Zachary's poor wife. How, to his broken mind, her attempt to leave him would have seemed like history repeating itself. Was that why he'd committed such a horrendous act?

'He was there the day Holly went missing. It was him who was taunting me. He made it his life's ambition to make mine a misery whenever he visited. When she...' He faltered, glanced down and squeezed the bridge of his nose hard.

I waited while he composed himself.

'When she cycled off, Zachary took off after her,' he continued throatily. 'I followed them. My back wheel was punctured, so I was on foot. I found her eventually, in the woodland bordering the reservoir. That's where I left her.' He stopped, making no attempt now to stem the tears. 'That's where my parents found her that night.'

My blood froze. Unsure I was hearing him right, I stared at him in shocked disbelief.

'She was so still, so cold, her lips tinged blue. I... I thought she would move. I thought she would breathe.' His voice cracked. 'But she didn't. She didn't. She was fucking well dead and I left her there.'

Fear crackled through me like ice as his tortured gaze strayed to the wall beyond me. The wall where the alcove should be.

SEVENTY

Naomi

They'd dropped the shoe. They'd dropped the shoe bringing her home!

'Naomi?' Yanking himself to his feet, Ben lunged for me as I raced to the lounge door.

'Get away from me!' Rage crashing ferociously through me, I veered away from him.

'Naomi where are you going?' He moved again towards me.

Twirling to face him, I splayed my hands out in front of me. 'Don't,' I warned him, as he took another step towards me. 'Just don't.'

Hurrying on, my emotions raw, I ran through the kitchen and out of the back door, stumbling blindly down the garden path until I reached the shed. The shed which sat in the shadow of the tree from which his father had hung himself. I'd imagined the pain that man had gone through, that Lily had gone through. I'd almost felt it. But it hadn't been grief that had driven him to take his own life. It had been guilt. Guilt that had driven Lily out of her mind. Guilt that had weighed Ben down, stifling his emotions. Shackling him. He was never able to break free of it.

Visceral anger burned inside me at what they'd done to that little girl. They hadn't spent years in agony, wondering what had happened to her. They knew. It had been her parents who hadn't afforded her a proper burial.

It didn't take me long to find what I was looking for. There was no lock on the shed door. Swiping the tears away, I reached for it, tested the weight of it in my hand. It was the right tool for the job. Dragging air past the hard stone in my chest, I turned back to the house, my step growing surer as I strode back up the path, through the kitchen and towards the lounge.

Ben was in the hall, his face ashen as he looked me over and then down to the heavy mallet in my hand. 'Naomi, don't,' he said shakily, staggering back as I pushed past him. 'Please stop.'

He came after me into the lounge. 'Don't do this, Naomi. We need to call someone.'

'Who?' I seethed, my voice pure contempt. 'The police? She needs someone to set her free, don't you see? Someone who cares about her!'

Pausing in front of the wall only to gather my strength, I lifted the mallet and swung it hard. Swung it again and again, purposefully, furiously, the crumbling plaster, broken bricks and cement all fuelling my determination.

'Stop.' Ben caught my arm as I aimed the mallet again. 'It's done,' he said quietly, nodding towards the wall.

I glanced at him, registering the torture in his eyes, then looked back to the wall. It was tiny, the little body swathed in polythene. My heart bled for sister and brother both as he lifted her gently out.

Holding my breath, I watched him lower her carefully to the floor. As he dropped to his knees, he pressed his hands to his face and sobbed. As he cried the tears that as a child he hadn't been allowed to, I went to him. I had to. I simply didn't know how not to.

SEVENTY-ONE

TWO WEEKS LATER

Naomi

Glancing at Ben as the curtains closed around his sister's small coffin, I saw the rise and fall of his throat as he swallowed, the tears spill down his cheeks. Unable to stop myself from offering him the comfort he clearly badly needed, I reached for his hand and gently squeezed it. He didn't react. It was as if he'd stopped breathing, but then, as 'Say You'll Be There' by the Spice Girls filled the crematorium, he dropped his gaze and gripped my hand hard.

I heard someone murmuring confusedly from the pew on the opposite side. Lily. She'd been allowed to attend the funeral, accompanied by a carer from the hospital unit in which she was being held, but Ben hadn't spoken to her. I could see the hesitancy in his eyes and I knew he was torn, but in the end he hadn't been able to bring himself to. He'd sworn it hadn't been him who'd attacked Lily that night at the reservoir. 'It wasn't me,' he'd said, his eyes agonised, when we'd finally sat down and talked. 'I hated her for what she did. I was scared when I saw her that day on the street after so many years – I knew then that this would all come out – but I swear I didn't hurt her.'

I believed him. I thought Zachary had been capable of attacking her to prevent the truth getting out, but Ben was not. I had been naive, but I'd been with this man for ten years. I knew he had problems. That he was an introvert who struggled to deal with certain situations. I'd been frightened for him, frightened when his emotions had fluctuated so dramatically, but I'd never felt under physical threat. For one guilt-filled, ludicrous moment, I'd considered it might have been Liam. And then dismissed it. The idea that a boy who would fix his sister's raggedy teddy bear would do such a thing was ridiculous.

The police were liaising with the Crown Prosecution Service regarding charges against Lily. DS Harrison's feelings were that the case was likely to be dismissed due to her extreme confusion and vulnerability. Still, I felt for her. I couldn't understand how a mother could have done what she had. Yet, part of me empathised. She hadn't wanted to let go of her daughter. To have lost her son as well would have broken her. Now, here she was, so broken she didn't really realise where she was.

Unable to ignore her, I left Ben once we were outside the church and went to have a brief word with her. 'I knew she was there,' she said as soon as I approached her. 'I heard her calling out to me. I can't think why Adam wouldn't let her come to me.' Her eyes, opaque and watery, were filled with bewilderment. She was referring to the time she'd appeared at our house. She had clearly thought Maya was Holly.

'He's such a good boy. I don't understand why he's so upset.' She glanced worriedly across to Ben, who was walking away to find our baby's grave. 'But then, he's always been sensitive. He was terribly upset the day he left Holly at the reservoir. We brought her home, but nothing would console him. I can't think how I came to lose her again.' She knitted her forehead and glanced down. 'Did Adam find her?' She looked back at me with an expectant look. I had no idea what to say.

'Come on, Lily,' her carer said kindly. 'It's time to get you back to the hospital for a nice cup of tea. There's cheesecake today too, if you fancy it.'

'Ooh, that would be lovely. I do like a bit of cheesecake.'

Smiling compassionately at me, the woman took her arm and guided her off. I couldn't help but wonder at what point her mind had started to recoil from the horror of what had happened. Or how Ben had managed to hold on to any scrap of his sanity in the more than two decades since. I didn't know whether we could survive. I felt I could find the strength and caring within me to try to be there for him, though. I'd pondered nature versus nurture, wondering what shaped people. Liam had inherited some of his father's traits, I believed that to be true. It was clear to me, though, that Ben's childhood trauma had shaped who he was, influenced some of his catastrophic decisions and made him feel unable to reach out. I hoped I was right, but I didn't feel he was fundamentally a bad person. He was my children's father. Little Ellie and James would have lost their mother if not for him. At his core, he was a good man, I was sure of it.

I found him at Elias's grave, his head bowed, his forefinger and thumb pressed hard to his forehead. 'Do you think your grandad will look after him?' he asked, glancing towards me as I approached. His pallor was chalk white, his eyes filled with torment and grief.

I nodded firmly. When I'd first set eyes on that rocking chair my thoughts had gone to my grandad and how superstitious he was. I felt now that, even from the grave, he'd been trying to warn me to be wary.

Ben smiled faintly, wiped an arm across his eyes and crouched down. 'Sleep tight, Elias,' he said, touching his fingers to his lips and then pressing them to the ground. 'Remember we love you.'

'Always and forever.' My throat tightening, I kneeled to join him. I had no idea what the future would bring, but in this moment, I felt there was hope.

EPILOGUE

Naomi

'Fancy a walk?' Ben asked, once he'd loaded the last of the dinner things into the dishwasher.

I glanced from the coffee I was making towards the lounge, where the children were glued to the movie *Turning Red*. Maya was tucked up with Little Buttons – complete with new ears – and Liam seemed more settled at last. 'I think there may be a revolt if I disturb them.' I smiled in Ben's direction. 'You go,' I suggested, guessing he would need his alone time now more than ever.

'I think I might.' He walked across to brush my cheek with a kiss. 'Clear my head.'

'Good idea. Make sure you're not too long, though.'

He nodded. 'I won't be,' he said with a small smile, and I felt awful reminding him about his curfew. He had to abide by it, though. We didn't know what direction our lives were going to take. Ben was trying not to show it – we were both trying for some kind of normalcy – but he was scared. If he was taken into custody now, so soon after Holly's funeral, I wasn't sure how he would cope. He was going to see Lily tomorrow, having decided he needed to in order to try to put his ghosts to rest. She'd apparently mentioned while talking to the police how keen her husband was on DIY, telling them how he'd altered and decorated the lounge. She hadn't liked it, she'd said, revealingly. I had no idea how Ben would handle talking to her face to face, albeit with an independent party in the room. It was bound to bring so much flooding back. But perhaps that was no bad thing. At least what had happened back then was no longer the dark debilitating secret he'd had to carry around for so long on his own.

Hearing the front door close, I went upstairs to make sure the children's clothes were ready for the morning. I still couldn't get used to the idea that Liam's room had once been Ben's room, which he'd shared with Zachary whenever he'd stayed. Judging by the relationship that had existed between them, it would definitely have been stressful. Ben's whole life had been stressful. It was no wonder he needed space to clear his head.

I was straightening Liam's bed – he'd obviously had another fitful night – when something bowed under one of my feet. A loose floorboard, I realised, bending to peel back the carpet and assess how dangerous it might be. With any luck it would still be attached to the joists. I pressed the heel of my hand to one end of it and the other shot up. I sighed, wondering at the soundness of the whole floor.

As I peered into the dusty space below, my heart missed a beat. There was a note. How long had it been there? Extracting it, I glanced at the child's handwriting and my blood froze. *I'm sorry, God. I never meant to hurt her.*

I felt as if the air had been sucked from my lungs. Who hadn't meant to hurt who? Were they talking about Holly? How long had this been there? The paper didn't look faded. But would it, being under the floorboards? Who'd written it? My breath coming in short, sharp gasps, I scanned it again, looking for similarities to Adam's handwriting. But it could equally have been Zachary's. My blood ran cold as the thought crashed into my head that this might be Liam's handwriting; that the person it referred to might be Lily.

My heart palpitating, I hurried to the landing and down the stairs. How could I ask him. I couldn't just thrust this at him and demand to know.

I found Maya on her own in the lounge, dancing Little Buttons on her lap while the film they were watching was paused. 'Where's Liam?' I asked, my throat tight.

'Kitchen,' Maya said, without looking up. 'He's getting us a drink.'

Leaving her to it, I went to the kitchen. 'How's the film?' I asked, pushing the door to behind me.

'Okay.' Liam shrugged, his attention on filling two tumblers with Diet Coke. 'Maya says she's going to poof into a giant red panda if I'm horrible to her,' he added with a smirk.

I walked across to him. 'I need to talk to you about something, Liam.'

Liam placed the bottle down. He didn't look at me, and something inside me knew that he knew what it was I was about to ask.

Crouching down to him, I took hold of his shoulders and steered him gently to face me. 'Did you go to the reservoir on you own? I need you to answer me honestly. Can you do that?'

Liam's cheeks were flushed, his eyes fixed down.

I breathed in hard. 'Did you go there, Liam? Did you see Lily there?' I urged him.

Liam's gaze came reluctantly to mine. 'I thought Dad was leaving us,' he answered, his voice small. 'I thought he might be walking there and I wanted to talk to him, but I didn't see him. She was there, though. I just wanted to tell her to go away,' he said, his eyes – sharp hazelnut eyes that mirrored his father's, begging me to believe him. 'She called me Adam. She said I was scaring her. But I wasn't. I was just standing there, honest. She ran away, and she fell, and... I didn't hurt her, Mum. I swear I didn't.'

A LETTER FROM SHERYL

Dear Reader,

Thank you so much for choosing to read *My Husband's House*. I really hope you enjoyed reading it as much as I enjoyed writing it. If you would like to keep up to date with my new releases, please do sign up at the link below where you can grab my FREE short story, 'The Ceremony'.

www.bookouture.com/sheryl-browne

Have you ever been lied to? I think many people are guilty of telling 'little white lies' – harmless lies told with good intention. Aren't Santa and the tooth fairy little white lies? Lies in a personal relationship, though, are not harmless. Lied to, you immediately feel disrespected, that you're not seen as worthy of the truth. Sometimes we are able to talk it through, to find forgiveness and move on. We all make mistakes, after all. We're human. Sometimes, though, deceit can irrevocably break a relationship. Loss of trust in the person you're with, in the relationship itself, can destroy it.

How big a lie can you forgive? Cheating isn't easily forgiven, but it is possible. But what if the lie is bigger? Much bigger. What if your husband, wife, or partner professes that the lie was told to protect you? What if this lie bred more lies? What if the truth behind these lies is devastating and seriously impacts on the people around you? On your children? On your perception of who the person is? Who you are?

If you feel with your every instinct that the person who lied is fundamentally good at their core and truly sorry, can you forgive, learn to trust again? To trust yourself? Him or her? Or are you being naive to even consider it? Thorny questions.

We leave our main character wondering. I'll leave you, the reader, to judge whether that person's love and trust was misplaced.

I would like to thank those people around me who are always there to offer support, those people who believed in me, even when I didn't quite believe in myself. To all of you, thank you.

If you have enjoyed the book, I would love it if you could share your thoughts and write a brief review. Reviews mean the world to an author and will help a book find its wings. I would also love to hear from you via social media or my website.

Happy reading all!

Sheryl x

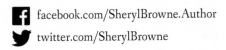

facebook.com/SherylBrowne.Author
twitter.com/SherylBrowne

ACKNOWLEDGEMENTS

Heartfelt thanks to the fabulous team at Bookouture, whose support of their authors is amazing. Special thanks to Helen Jenner and our wonderful editorial team, who work so hard to make my books shine. Huge thanks also to our fantastic publicity team. Thanks, guys – I think it's safe to say I could not do this without all of you. To the other authors at Bookouture, thank you for being such a super-supportive group of people.

I owe a huge debt of gratitude to all the fantastically hard-working bloggers and reviewers who have taken time to read and review my books and shout about them to the world. It is truly appreciated.

Final thanks to every single reader out there for buying and reading my books. Knowing you have enjoyed our stories and cared enough about our characters enough to want to share them with other readers is the best incentive ever to keep writing.